THE ORDER
OF THE
GOLDEN DAWN

The Fifth Essence Series

THE ORDER OF THE GOLDEN DAWN

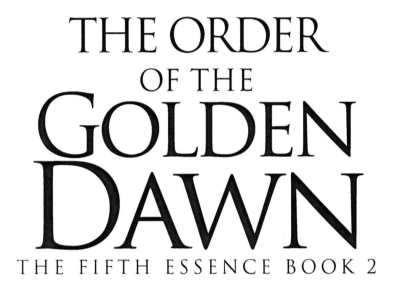

THE FIFTH ESSENCE BOOK 2

JANE WEST

TATE PUBLISHING
AND ENTERPRISES, LLC

Published by Tate Publishing & Enterprises, LLC
127 E. Trade Center Terrace | Mustang, Oklahoma 73064 USA
1.888.361.9473 | www.tatepublishing.com

Tate Publishing is committed to excellence in the publishing industry. The company reflects the philosophy established by the founders, based on Psalm 68:11,
"The Lord gave the word and great was the company of those who published it."

Published in the United States of America

ISBN: 978-1-68187-065-6
1. Fiction / Romance / Fantasy
2. Fiction / Romance / Action & Adventure
16.06.07

I delicate this book to Jackson. This one is for you, kiddo!

Jane West delivers once again scorching tension, unshakable danger and unparalleled loss. She never fails to keep the action tense and the risk high. This riveting tale brings a chilling touch to the reader making it impossible to put it down.

I'm not sure how West is able to keep doing it, but with each novel proves more exciting than the previous as she continues to raise the stakes in this spine-chilling tale leaving readers sitting on the edge of their seats.

The Order of the Golden Dawn is a masterstroke, sizzling romance, amiable characters and characters you love to hate and an unbending suspense makes this a read to be savored.]

Acknowledgements

M<small>Y LOVE FOR</small> my grandchildren are the inspirations that keeps me going. Thanks to my daughter who has been with me through thick and thin. Thanks to my fans and their wonderful reviews.

Give me a ladder and I will climb.

Contents

Asylum

SALLY MADE GOOD on her threat. The Supreme Court of Justice found me guilty for the murders of my mother and her two boyfriends. Headlines in the news nationwide read:

Crazed Daughter Snapped

*Teenage Girl, Stephanie Ray Collins, Turned Serial Killer
Leaving Trail of Murders!*

Somehow, the state had hard evidence against me. If you asked me, they pulled it out of a rabbit's ass. What a bunch of crap. From day one, my claim of innocence never wavered.

Anyway, it was an open-and-shut case. I pleaded no contest to the charges by the advice of my crappy attorney. The prosecution claimed luck was on my side. Under the circumstances, living with an insane parent who murdered my father, the judicial system deemed me as someone who snapped—a crime of passion, if you will.

The state charged me as a juvenile for the murder of Mom's boyfriend, Charles Dodson. Even still, the court finding a ten-year-old child capable of committing such a heinous crime, slicing a grown man's throat from ear to ear baffled me. Because why?

Charles stood a firm six foot four and weighed over two hundred pounds. The crime they charged against me was an impossibility. A child weighing less than a hundred pounds and less than half his height could not have carried out such a forceful assault. Dismissing all provability, the state somehow arrived at the conclusion that Charles died by a child—me.

The state's argument seemed fishy, after eight years, the evidence showed up out of nowhere. Supposedly, my fingerprints were smeared all over the butcher's knife. In addition, the police claimed to have found a bag of bloody clothes belonging to me, stuffed away in Mom's closet. Yet any imperative clue proving my innocence slipped past their dirty noses. My attorney, the state prosecution, and the judge ignored the fact that at the time of Charles' death, I was at school sitting in plain sight, first row.

Several folks were gunning for me. The hardest one of all to swallow was my mom, Sara. It didn't take a genius to figure out that she played a part in this atrocity. Money was the motivation. My stomach churned with bitterness just thinking about her betrayal.

For the murders of Francis Bonnel and Sara, I got off with an insanity plea. It could've been worse, knowing that little fact seemed to soothe the nightmares somewhat.

The federal judge sentenced me with no chance of parole to live the remainder of my life at Haven Hospital, located on the outskirts of Bayou L'Ourse, an insane asylum for the violent and criminally insane. I was the youngest in history labeled a serial killer, the second woman charged as such. The first woman received the gas chamber. I suppose luck had my back in a very screwed-up way.

On my twenty-first birthday, the US court of appeals, the fifth circuit, overturned my conviction. A release order was set in motion, granting my freedom. I had served my time. I knew better than anyone, it was a crock of shit, but; I'd take it to get out of this hellhole.

It was an early spring morning when the doors of the reformatory opened. A cool breeze tousled my tangled hair. The sun peeked just above the horizon. I haven't had a whiff of fresh air or a glimpse of the golden sun in three years. I made my way, one slow step at a time to the exit gate. Movement was difficult. Rarely, I was allowed outside my cell. Exercise at Haven was a myth, though, stiff muscles were the least of my problems.

The gentle sun felt soothing against my pale face as freedom caressed my dry, cracked lips. When my eyes focused on a tall, dark, lean figure by the gate, I first thought my mind was playing tricks. With all the drugs force-fed down my throat, I often suffered hallucinations. Majority of the time, I stayed in a state of confusion. Reality appeared as an illusion. Dr. Joy made sure I remained stoned.

Funny, how quick a federal ruling could go away by the flick of a Bic? Imagine that! For three years, the officials considered me a threat to society. They were so determined to keep me locked away forever, but suddenly, they changed their minds. The staff doctor reported that I'd shown great improvement through treatment. I no longer posed a danger to others or myself. It was uncanny how conveniently he arrived at his diagnosis this late in the game. It was a farce—a cover up. It always had been.

None of this seemed real. I never dreamed that I'd end up labeled a serial killer. It didn't take a rocket scientist to figure out how I'd gotten here. This was the work of the Order—the Illuminati.

Was any of this real? Did Aidan and his treacherous charms trick me into believing a lie—a genetically altered angel? I scoffed. Could I have imagined everything and like my mother be insane? It didn't matter now. The reality—I was a mere girl who fell in love with a demented con who played a very cruel joke.

As I approached the exit, I spotted a tall figure watching me. The glare of the sun blinded my sight. I could only make out a silhouette. It was not until I came into focus that my cloudy mind began to open like tiny drops of water to a dry flower. Slowly his face came into view.

Suddenly I froze. My knees nearly buckled under me. At first, I thought my mind was playing tricks. But no, he was real. I thought I had lost everyone.

"Chile, it is so good to see you!" Jeffery held out his caramel arms.

I stopped for a second, taking in the sweet vision. "Jeffery, is that really you?" It was all I could say.

"You damn straight it is!" He smiled brightly.

I dropped my small bag and shuffled into Jeffery's arms, melting against his warm chest. His arms squeezed tight around my shoulders, holding me close. Tears began to swell. "I can't believe you're here!" I feared since the charges, everyone had abandoned me. After all, I was a loose cannon.

"Aw, honey, I could never desert you. Are you all right?" Jeffery's forehead lined with worry.

"Yeah, I am now," I croaked through tears.

"You've gotten so skinny, gurrrl!" Jeffery held me out at arm's length, eyeballing me.

"Food was kinda sparing in there." I merely shrugged.

"To see you like this just breaks my heart, honey."

"I thought you"—my voice cracked—"forgotten." I tried to hold myself together.

"Honeychile, Dom and I have been trying to help you since the day they put you in this godforsaken place. We even hired the best attorney money can buy."

"Really! I had no idea." Shock washed over my face like ice water.

"It was a nightmare. Dom and I were denied visitations. In fact we were banned from the premises."

"Why?" I didn't understand.

"That's what we tried to find out. Our attorney couldn't even get anywhere with those rascals!"

I softened my voice. I didn't want any of the hospital's staff to overhear me. "They framed me. I didn't kill anyone, Jeff." Those words hadn't caressed my lips since that day they had taken me captive. It sounded strange even to me.

"Honey, I know youse innocent. And apparently, you must have a fairy mofo godmother because someone very powerful pulled some ironclad strings to get you released."

"What? They told me I was getting off for good behavior."

"Gurrrl, you'll believe anything. No insane murderer who's killed several mother-puck-n folks ever gets off for good behavior. Were you assigned a parole officer?"

"I don't think so."

"Of course you weren't! 'Cuz they know youse innocent." Jeffery's face crinkled into a wake-the-hell-up smile.

"I guess I'm a bit out of touch." My sluggish brain had trouble processing all this.

"It's okay, honey, youse coming home with Dom and me." Jeffery patted my back.

"Oh, I can't impose." I shook my head in protest. Although I was homeless, dropping my troubles on my friends was a liability I couldn't allow. If the Illuminati had enough power to incarcerate me for crimes I didn't commit, then they might go for round two? Which meant anyone I associated with could become a target as well. I couldn't let that happen to Jeffery and Dom.

"Gurrrl, did I not tell you, youse family?" Jeffery scolded me.

I scrunched my nose, "Jeff that might not be a good idea. Wherever I go evil follows."

Jeff rolled his eyes. "Now youse act-n crazy! No mo lip. Youse coming to live with Dom and me." Jeffery rested his hands on his hips with that divatude that only he could do, "I never say a damn thing I don't mean. So come on! Your home is our home. No, really. I ain't lie-n. It's yours. You paid for the house."

"What?" I didn't understand.

"Remember the key you gave me?"

I just stared blankly.

"Anyway, honey, youse a billionaire times a billion! Mr. Aidan made sure youse can own the world."

"I have money?" My words felt like an echo.

"Uh-huh, and that's an understatement! Now come on. We're going home. Dinner's waiting."

"Home! Where do we live?" I tried to push through the cobwebs shrouding my brain.

"Baby, New Orleans! Where else is there?" Jeffery grabbed my small bag, as I latched onto his arm.

Home Sweet Home

WHEN WE ROLLED up into the drive of our home in Jeffery's latest Lincoln, my eyes froze. Stammering over words, I coughed, "This—this can't be our house!"

"It sure is. We live in style. There's no better place than the Garden District here in New Orleans." Jeffery bubbled with pride. "I told you, les bons temps rouler!" (let the good times roll!)

"I hope so, Jeffery. I truly hope so." I endeavored to put on a happy face, but in the core of my spirit, my glee had taken absence. I didn't want to be a Debbie Downer. I wanted to believe better days were ahead. Nevertheless, despite my good intent, I had my doubts.

I blew out a raspy sigh as the memory of that day flashed in my mind. Sally's sick laughter still rang in my ears as much as the sting of Aidan's arms wrapped tightly around my ribs. To this day, my brain seemed riddled with holes. And because of that, the seeds of doubt were planted, giving me pause to Aidan's involvement. My captor's cowardly face remained obscured while his hand bared a diamond ring—the very same ring that haunted me in my dreams ever since I was a child.

Then everything went black, and my life came to a screeching halt. That was my last memory of that shattering day. When I'd awakened, shackled, I realized that my happiness had ended abruptly—forever.

Jeffery parked the car in the garage and cut the engine. He then turned to me with his bright, caramel face and said, "This is it!" Jeffery beamed with excitement.

"Huh, what?" I stared at Jeffery as though his voice sounded muffled like under water.

"Stevie, baby, are you sure you're okay?" Jeffery eyed me with deep-lined worry.

"I'm okay. I just need rest." The strength I once had seemed depleted. Perhaps when the drugs were out of my system, I'd feel better. Even still, I suspected, I'd never fully recover. That young girl, full of life and innocence that I once resembled died the day they stole her freedom.

Now I had to face the cold-hard facts. I trusted the wrong person, and I paid a heavy price for my faith. As a result, the only thing I understood was revenge—the air I breathed. Torment was the fuel that kept me going. Anger was my inspiration. Yet the force beneath my feet—was *rage*.

If I were smart, I'd move on. With the wealth that had been kindly bestowed upon me, I should make a new life for myself, leave the past in the past. Nevertheless, no amount of money could buy my way out of this baleful maze.

My gut kept telling me that Aidan's family wasn't finished with me. After all, I took their precious chance of world domination. I prayed my instinct was wrong. I wanted to be done with them, once and for all.

A gnawing memory kept tapping at my mind, a flash of visions I couldn't recognize. It felt as though I'd forgotten something, but what? Could it be another bad memory of that hospital locked away in my drug-hazed brain trying to dig its way out? If so, I preferred for it to remain buried, or even better—dead.

"Okay, let's get you in the house." Jeffery came to my side and opened the door. He gently slid his arm around my waist to help ease me out of the car. I guess I was weaker than I thought. Jeffery coaxed, "I'll have Dom fix you something good to eat. You do look a little pale, even for your white lily skin." He smiled sweetly, but by the bags under his eyes, I think he could've used some of his own advice. I worried that I was the source of his sleepless nights.

As we made our way to the house, I couldn't peel my eyes away. It was breath taking—a vision only in a magazine. Majestic and mystique, the century old mansion stood tall as if it was awaiting for our arrival. Merely painted white, with black plantation shutters embellished the narrow windows along the front porch. Ancient avenues of oaks lined the street, offering its cool shade as crepe myrtles colored the air with sweet perfume. The wonderful scent reminded me of my old neighborhood back in Tangi.

The house, in comparison to my previous home in Tangi, was no small fry. After all, it didn't get much better than the Garden District. Jeffery led me past the wrought iron fence, leading up a flight of brick steps that seemed eternal and just passed the steps, on the porch hung oversized ferns swaying gently to the light breeze.

The yard was small, yet its luscious green was inviting. Suddenly, I yearned to run my bare feet across its thick carpet. I couldn't remember the time last I'd felt the cool touch of grass. Tears began to sting, and I quickly wiped the moisture from my eyes. I wanted to hang on to my last shred of dignity until I was in private.

On the left side of the porch, I noticed a white-wicker swing with fluffy pillows of yellow and on the right side a wicker table with multi-colored chairs matching the flowers from the garden.

When we entered the house, the aroma of food floated in the air. Instantly, my nose kicked in from the delicious tang, taunting my growling stomach. Dom must be stirring up a big meal. I couldn't wait to eat—the perks living with a chef.

Then my attention shifted to the grand foyer. A sweetness scented the room of gardenias in a glass vase, centered on top of a round table, dark Mahoney, under the three-tier chandelier.

I stood there for a moment, gaping at the elegance. This was beyond my imagination. Stunned for words, I twirled around, slowly taking in the awe.

As Jeffery nudged forward, we entered into the sitting room. Sunlight filtered through the windows, bringing a wonderful warmth to the room. I spotted a grand piano sitting in the corner by the picture window. Soft accented chairs and a white stuffy couch nestled the cozy fireplace, in conjunction with bright Persian rugs adding color and elegance to the dark-wooded floors. Artistic paintings hung strategically on every wall, lending the home that good old Southern charm.

"Jeff, everything is so...so amazing." Tears began to fall regardless of my effort to hold them back.

"Come on, honey. Let's get you some food, then I'll show you your room upstairs. Dom and I fixed it up nicely for you." Jeffery smiled, trying not to show his unease.

"That sounds great." My smile tight, pinched. The old Stevie was gone and in her place came a broken woman left hollow.

Suddenly a faint meow appeared from underneath the piano. I glanced down and caught a glimpse of a large white puff of fur rubbing against the stool. My eyes went wide. "Is that?"

"It sure is! And you best be thank-n me too. That damn cat and I do not get along. He's noth-n but trouble." Jeffery grumbled.

Surprisingly, I laughed, and Jeffery's eyes glistened. It was nice to see his old spark back.

As soon as Snowball heard my voice, he came running to me. I grabbed my beloved cat into my arms and nestled him against my chest. His gentle purr felt soothing. I'd forgotten how much I loved that sound.

This time a flood of tears poured down my cheeks, not sad but joyous ones, the kind I hadn't had in such a very long time. I was home. I lifted my eyes. "Jeff, thanks!" I could barely speak above a whisper.

His deep-golden face beamed as he leaned in giving me a quick squeeze. "Come on before Dom decides to skin me alive. That cranky Frenchman has been waiting all day to see the likes of you. Besides, I'm hungry."

Unaware, for the first time in a long while, I felt numb. Numb was good.

Hence, regardless of how good everything seemed right now, I wasn't fully myself. It would take time to heal. My mind seemed to drift into nowhere-land, a vast desert of sand and tumbleweeds. I had no idea how long it might take to recover—if ever.

I possessed a stockpile of doubts, but one thing I could be certain—that being here in this lovely home with Jeffery and Dom was the right path in my recovery, or at least for now. I still needed to be mindful of their safety.

When we stepped into the kitchen, I was swoon by several mixtures of spices kicking up my grumbling stomach a notch. Even still, I paused. Just like most Southern homes, the kitchen was at the back of the house. The bright gallery came equipped with all the modern amenities, blended with that old world charm. The Wolf-stove seemed to be the focal point of the room, and the oversized stainless steel refrigerator promised a heavy stock of assorted foods. I especially liked the pictured windows, bringing in the outside to the indoors. The space had everything one would need—inviting and cheery as the rest of the house.

Dom, in his white stained apron, turned from the stove, and quickly his pencil-lined mustache stretched across his face into a bright smile. "Oh, how wonderful! The mistress of the house has returned." The chunky chef gathered me into his arms and hugged me tightly. He then held me at arm's length, eyeing me from head to toe like a father inspecting his soiled child from a day's play. "Look at you!" he tsked, making a clicking sound with his tongue. "You must eat. Come. Sit." He urged in his heavy French accent pointing to a round table directly in front of the far-left window. He pulled a chair out as I followed his lead and sat down. "I have made a feast for you, but I think perhaps you might eat something not so rich for the tummy, yes?"

Before I'd uttered a word of protest, Dom padded off, in short, returning with a bowl. He placed it on the table in front of me. "This is much better. Eat." he insisted, air swatting me.

I glimpsed down at the steamy curls drifting to my face and savored its salty aroma—*chicken soup*. Instantly, a smiled touched my lips as I looked up into Dom's gentle face. "It smells delicious. Thank you." I reached for my spoon.

Jeffery sat a glass of milk and a mug of Coca-Cola on the table beside me. He patted my shoulder, "baby, drink both of these," he advised. "Youse start-n to look a little pasty than normal," disquiet painted his face.

My hand instantly touched my face. "I am?"

Jeffery's nose crinkled. "I know youse naturally pale—but damn!" my good friend always knew how to flatter a girl.

I flashed him a black look.

Jeffery was right. My skin looked haggard. During my confinement at Haven hospital, the food provisions severely lacked. In fact, I couldn't recall eating, unless drugs were considered part of the same food group.

Only a unique type of employees worked at the Hospital. Monsters, I called them—not your typical Southern-hospitality kinda folks. Their behavior was pernicious. I assumed the Family employed them. I shivered. The abuse—a vision I wanted to forget.

I once feared the men in black. That changed the minute I entered Haven. The men in white were far worse—the orderlies. Even under my cloudy mind, I recalled how they got their rocks off by force-feeding drugs down my throat. I hated them and plotted their death. With a simple butter knife, I took some sick pleasure envisioning their murders. I never acted on it, but the desire persisted.

The orderlies often reported to the charge nurse, Betty, concerning my defiant behavior. Unfortunately, my reprisals fell upon unsympathetic ears. Nurse Betty favored her staff, condoning their misemployment.

After her precious boys kept coming back with busted-up lips and scratched-up faces, Nurse Betty took matters into her own hands. That was when she pulled out all the stops—shackles and a straitjacket.

Several months later, the doctor begrudgingly took a moment out of his busy schedule from snorting coke to examine my festering foot. The heavy shackles were too tight cutting off circulation. As a result, my foot needed amputating. From the lack of proper cleaning and nourishment, my foot became blue from infection. If I'd been anywhere else, I would've been hospitalized.

Dr. Joy and Haven feared imprisonment for their sadistic care, thanks to the doctor's paranoia, he ordered the nurse to remove the shackles, and I received the proper medical attention.

Betty and her minions didn't seem too pleased with the doctor's orders. They were determined to keep at least half of me constraint. Happily abiding by the orders of Nurse Betty, the orderlies kept me in a straitjacket.

Still I took some sick delight laughing in their faces when they had to remove the oppressing steel.

———◆❊◆———

I looked up with my spoon suspended. Two pairs of worried eyes were shadowing my every move. "Guys! Really, I'm fine." I attempted to convince them, but I didn't want to sound ungrateful either. After all, they could've left me at the gates of that appalling hospital. "I mean...I really, really appreciate all the trouble you both have gone through for me. So, stop worrying!" I forced a smile. To be honest, I might be trying to assure myself that as well.

Dom reached across the table patting my hand. "Why don't you let us do what we do best?" He smiled, stretching his pencil mustache even thinner.

"I'm sorry." I dropped my spoon into the bowl of soup and withdrew a faint sigh. "I don't want you guys to fuss over me." I couldn't be more grateful for their endeavor to nurse me back to health, but I had nothing to give back. I was empty and barren.

"We want to help." Dom smiled warmly.

I hesitated for half a second then I spoke up. "I have to ask. It's been on my mind for a while." I paused. I might be stepping off a cliff, but here I went anyway. "Have you heard from Aidan?" I blanched, fearing whether or not I really wanted to know.

Jeffery and Dom shared a strained glance. Jeff took the lead and answered. "Honey, we ain't seen Aidan."—He inhaled a sharp breath—"since that night you were kidnapped all sorts of spooky events have happened." Jeffery's taupe eyes bugged, full of fright.

"Like what?" Did I dare ask?

"For starters, that whole damn castle vanished, foundation and all. I'm tell-n you." Jeffery shivered.

I gawked in surprise.

Then Dom added, "We haven't heard from Aidan since the disappearance. His cell phone goes straight to voice mail. Everyone has disappeared, and we have no explanation why. Even his uncle Van and his son, Sam, have gone off the grid." The taunted wrinkles in Dom's forehead were stark.

Without warning, my stomach lurched. It was no secret, the two men were not my favorite. Sam was a psychopath, and his uncle wasn't any better. I couldn't vouch for the uncle's whereabouts. Although Sam, I knew exactly what happened to him. Aidan took his life. Though it was harsh, it was justified. Sam was going to rape me and leave me for dead. But, Aidan stopped him just in time. Consequently, not before Sam had beaten me to near death. Lucky for me, Aidan with his Druid magick, healed my wounds and saved my life.

Yet, when I thought about Sam, I felt I played a part in his abrupt death, not something I enjoyed dwelling on. I pushed the memory back and focused on the current issue. "Aidan is MIA?"

Jeffery chimed in. "That's an understatement! We have no mofo idea. We is still scratch-n our heads. I got a sneaky suspicion that his family used that voodoo shit and poof—castle and all those mofo-n jokers went bye, bye. Apart from Aidan, I hope none of them return."

Dom interjected, scolding his partner. "Jeff, you're too superstitious. There has to be a logical answer to their whereabouts."

"I beg your pardon!" Jeffery gaped. "Where the hell have youse been, mister?" Jeffery started waving his finger in Dom's face. "Explain to me how that damn castle vanished, Mr. I-Believe-In-No-Ghost? Even the rosebushes disappeared." Jeffery pursed his lips.

Dom kept his composure as he countered, "Clearly I don't have all the answers, but don't assume without facts, ma chère. Nothing around here is ever as it seems."

"Well, you need to stick to what you know best—cooking!" Jeffery fired back.

Suddenly I started to laugh—hysterical laughter. Both the men forgot about their tiff and shifted their wide eyes to me. At that moment, I'd lost my sense. I couldn't catch my breath. Soon Dom and Jeffery joined in, and the room filled with insane mirth.

It felt good to free this strange emotion inside me. The peculiar hilarity seemed odd to my ears, a sound that jumped ship since the asylum.

Nevertheless, with no warning, my mood changed like the wind. I started to sob, and the house became still. For a brief moment my two friends gaped in stunned silence.

I was a mess. The drugs were flushing out of my system faster than I'd expected and reality took its place. Looking down the barrow of a gun was hard to swallow. My life was a train wreck. I wasn't sure what was worse, dead inside or alive and despicable.

Time Lost

Aʟᴛᴇʀ I ʜᴀᴅ finished dinner, Jeffery found a perfect excuse to leave the dishes to Dom while he dragged me upstairs.

At the end of the hallway, we stopped at a door. "What's the hold up?" I questioned, reaching for the knob. Like a streak of lightening, Jeffery threw himself against the door, blocking my entrance. My brows furrowed, confused.

"Oh, no you don't, gurrrlfriend!" he waged his finger. "Not until you wear this." He pulled out a pink scarf out of his pocket, waving it in my face.

I snatched it out of his hand and grumbled, "All right, I'll put it on if you take that damn smirk off your face."

The tips of Jeffery's mouth stretched to the Grand Canyon. "Let me help. Turn around." He twirled his finger over my head. "No peeky-poo," he advised as my back was to him, "or else I'll slap your white-lily hands till they turn black." He cinched the knot as my head jerked backward. "You know, once you go black you never go back?"

I rolled my eyes as I rubbed my head. "Whatever!" I couldn't see it, but I felt my friend's smile of triumph.

With Jeffery's guiding hand, I stepped through the threshold, sightless by the scarf that was cutting off brain cells. It was *that* tight. If I even acted as though I might peek, Jeffery jumped on it like a fly on crap, swatting my hands. Sometimes Jeff could be one mofo.

"Okay, you can open them now." Jeffery beamed.

My breath stalled as my eyes raked over the spacious room. "Holy mother of god, this is my bedroom!" I turned to Jeff, astounded. "No way?"

"Way! Dom and I spruced it up ourselves. Do you like?"

I gulped. "Uh, yeah! It's sick!" I latched my arms around Jeffery's neck and squeezed.

"I suppose sick means you like it." Jeffery huffed.

I glimpsed up at my friend with a wide smile, "It means you rock! I adore it, Jeffery." I kissed him on the cheek.

"Okay, now youse get-n too grateful. Youse know how I hate that cuddly-kissy-kissy shit." Jeffery rubbed his cheek.

Funny, I found myself laughing, an actual laugh. "You haven't changed a bit."

"Oh, yes, I have!" Jeffery spat. "Now I belong to the snotty, rich-bitch society instead of wait-n on 'em." Jeffery waved his hand. "I got refined too. I can hold my little pinky out drinking nasty, hot tea, eating a stale, crumb cookie just like those gossip-n old biddies. I even got hats that can run circles around those old women, and I do mean literally."

I shook my head. Who's he fool-n? He hadn't changed one bit. I laughed to myself. I wouldn't have it any other way.

Wanting to pinch myself, it all seemed too good to be real. I focused back on my new surroundings. The bedroom was more than enough room, yet it was warm and inviting. Like all older Southern homes, it had a blazing fireplace to the far wall. Muted overstuffed chairs cozy-upped to the hearthstone for reading a good book by the warm fire. The room was adorned in gentle, soft creams with just the right touch of mint green and light lilac.

When my eyes fell upon the canopy bed, my breath stalled. Staring at the white netting took me back in time—Aidan's cottage. Memories, I didn't care to revisit, if ever. Maybe later Jeffery wouldn't mind if I removed it. I'd wait to ask him. I didn't want to spoil the moment.

Shaking off the willies of my past, I drew my attention back to the present as I padded over to the window hiding behind sheer curtains. I drew the drapes back and gasped. Below was a garden full of bright colored veggies. It was enchanting. Breathtaking cherry-blossom trees full of soft pink buds swaying in the breeze. I spotted an array of flowers that dotted the fence with every color imaginable.

For a second, my breath stalled until Jeffery tapped me on the shoulder. I quickly drew in a breath and glanced up at my friend. "Hey, there's more stuff to go bug-eyed over." Jeffery tugged at my sleeve.

"I'm coming." I tossed a gentle smile.

"I saved the best for last." Jeffery smiled and opened the double-door closet.

I gaped as though I was gazing into a wonderland. Mom's closet came to mind, but this closet was the mother of all. I turned to Jeffery. "You did this for me?"

"I sure did, honey. Of course I hope you'll let me borrow some of this divine fashion?" Jeffery teased, or I think he was teasing.

I entered the closet with my hand brushing along every delicate item. The closet seemed endless. To top it off, it smelled of brand-new clothing with the tags still attached. Moving on, the built-in shelves contained rows of designer shoes such as Louis Vuitton, Manolo, Gucci and Christian Louboutin. The chiffonier was stocked full with scarves, jewelry, accessories and even Victoria's Secrets apparel and PJs. Speechless, I didn't know what to say. Did I fit the role of royalty? I came from rags, and now I lived in a home fit for a queen. This all seemed too good to be true.

Spinning on my heels, I glanced up at my dear friend. "You must've spent a fortune!" I whistled. "Why spend your money on me?"

"Honey, it's not my money. Youse the billionaire, and you need to look like one. Those rags," Jeffery scrunched his nose, "are wretched. No offense." His face soured at my choice of ensemble—prison clothes.

I looked down at my clothing and turned to the full-length mirror in the corner. One quick glance and I staggered. The girl staring back appeared broken. "I'm pretty pathetic, aren't I?"

Jeffery's eyes moistened, "Aw, honey, just give it time. Dom will fatten you up, and those green eyes of yours will sparkle again. Real soon! Youse see." He wrapped his golden arms around me and I melted into his chest and sobbed.

I was the ghost of a person who once lived. I'd lost weight, my eyes were dull, and my hair lacked luster. I pulled from Jeffery's embrace, wiping the tears from my cheeks. Then anger nipped. Aidan and his family had stripped me of my spirit. Now I had to put the pieces back together. I wasn't sure I had the strength.

Jeffery spoke up, drawing me back to the present, which I gratefully appreciated. "You ain't got noth-n to fret about. Just think of me as your personal stylist." Jeffery twirled like a high dollar model, strutting down the catwalk.

Oh lord, personal stylist! Jeff's taste was, well, extreme. I had to admit he did a fabulous job picking out the new clothing, on the other hand, I had my reservations about him dressing me. "Huh! We'll see." One could say my taste teetered on the reserved side.

"What!" Jeffery shrieked as he placed his hands on his sassy hips. "Chile, I know my skills!"

"Yes—you do. It just might not be mine. I'm just saying." I shrugged.

"My style is definitely a step up from yours, honey." Jeffery eyed me like his bestie. "Gurrrlfriend—pffeaseeee! I'm gonna make you look good!" he snapped his fingers and twirled. "When I'm done, folks around here are gonna think youse royalty, as you rightfully are. Hash-tag that, sistah!"

Oh, brother! I thought inwardly.

Unwanted Guest

I GLANCED OVER at the alarm clock. Damn—two in the morning. My eyes wouldn't close. How ironic. For the past three years, I'd slept like a baby on cold metal. Sleep was easy then. Of course, I had a constant cocktail of drugs pumped into me, twenty-four-seven. But tonight, not even my Sealy mattress could subdue my spinning mind. I flipped my lamp on and sat up, drawing my knees to my chest. I spotted Snowball at the end of the bed, curled up, sleeping. WTF! Everyone, including the cat was sleeping but me. I felt antsy. My mom, Sara—I couldn't stop thinking about her. I'd had only a minute to process her death before I had been taken. Now accepting her gone didn't resonate with me. It didn't feel real. It was as if she'd merely moved to some tropical island, sitting on a white-sand beach drinking a Mai Tai. Any day, I'd hear from her. Yet logic said otherwise. My heart ached with regret.

Then I thought of Dad. The whole concept of Mom killing Dad shattered my core. Could I come to terms, knowing that Sara's selfishness cost my dad's life? Did I have any other choice? I had to accept the truth and find a way to move on. Yet how did I do that when my heart wrung with pain.

I had trouble deciding whether I hated Sara, or pitied her. Placing all the blame on her didn't seem fair. She had no control over her mental state. A human carrying a celestial fetus was a serious mistake. And her payment—Sara contracted a disease that altered her brain, turning her into a sociopath.

I blamed myself as if I'd committed the murder. I should've never been born.

The Order created me in an undisclosed medical lab. How exactly the scientist concocted an embryo between my dad's DNA and a celestial creature's DNA, blew my mind. What kind of creepy monster did they create? I shuddered over the thought. I had no clue to the kind of powers they bestowed upon me. I once heard I had powers of mass destruction. I prayed the rumor was a lie. It only made me feel more of a freak. Yet my creators called me a phenomenon—a genetically altered angel.

I thought superheroes were invincible. I certainly wasn't. Rather, a pathetic weakling fit my description more appropriately.

Powers? Where were my powers when they took me against my will? My captors in the name of their cockeyed justice knew they had the upper hand. I paid the price for their insidious sins.

It felt as though I'd stepped back into the medieval times. Their greediness spawned a witch trial, just short of a stake and a match. The courtroom was empty. Only my inebriated attorney, the state defense, and a black-cloaked judge banging his gavel attended my trial.

I'd scoffed at the empty jury seats—a bench trial, obviously. From that point on, my life was downhill. The attorney defending me cared more about his Jack Daniel's in his back pocket than clearing my charges. With a once-over look at him, I knew I was in trouble. His breath nearly knocked me over from the fumes of booze, and judging by his poorly pressed suit and the grime covering his once white shirt, he wasn't exactly in the condition to defend even a dog's case. In fact, he took dumpster diving to a whole new level.

As it went down, the Illuminati's thugs hauled me before a crooked judge who had a gut the size of Texas. My councilor stood by me in silence while the state argued their case. There were no objections made on my behalf. Rather instead, justice skipped out the door as the officer cuffed my hands behind my back, escorting me to my new home.

It didn't matter. Those in power had decided my misdeed before the indictment. It screamed loud and clear—the Illuminati had been the mastermind behind this set up. These members who stood before me were merely the puppets-on-a-string. As the story unfolded—Mr. Bodine, my attorney, lost my case.

That was when I came to stay at the lovely, Haven Hospital. After getting comfy, I accepted my lot in life. The drug-induced coma felt like a god send, anything to ease the misery. I was a dead person with a pulse stripped of any desire to live. I had no family. No friends to call. I was utterly alone, facing a life sentence for crimes I didn't commit.

The only thing that reminded me that I was alive was the deep-seeded tick that kept clawing at me. A memory lost? For the life of me, I couldn't remember what. I eased out a wry sigh.

I glanced about at my new surroundings. The beauty and riches seemed like a dream—but it was real. I was home, surrounded by people who loved me.

Then why wasn't I happy? Our material needs were more than plentiful. Yet not even an infinity of cash could fill the emptiness in my gut. Facing the fact that my mother had sold me into slavery nearly destroyed me, but the treachery that shattered my heart had been dealt by the man I gave my heart to—Aidan Bane De Pont.

I get why the Family and Sally turned on me or at least sorta. What I didn't get was what did Aidan have to gain? That night at the cottage, we entangled our spirits as one, infusing our magick forever. So by betraying me, didn't Aidan betray himself? Nothing added up.

Then that following morning, the bottom fell out. Sally and her anonymous co-conspirator abducted me. Although I never got a glimpse at my abductor, I sensed it was Aidan. His touch, his scent, I knew without having to see his face that it was him. Now I had my doubts.

I began to rub my temples, trying to ease an oncoming headache.

My troubles seemed to go much deeper. How did Aidan and the castle mysteriously disappear without a trace? How could an oversized house vanish in broad daylight? I shook my head, bewildered.

There was no rhyme or reason to this madness. Even the last words Aidan had spoken before he left my side that faint morning. I recalled his every word—*believe only half of what you see and none of which you don't.* His riddle played over and over in my mind like a forgotten tune. What did it mean?

The truth may never show its ugly face. Despite my gut instincts, one piece of fact I couldn't deny—Aidan had abandoned me.

I threw my legs over the edge of the bed, aggravated. I thought maybe I'd grab something to drink and visit the garden. Wearing only a white-cotton gown, I threw on a shawl over my shoulders and tiptoed down the stairs, careful not to wake the house. I went straight for the subzero fridge and grabbed my favorite drink, Coke, before heading out back.

A soft breeze gently tousled my hair as I stepped outside onto the patio. The aroma of pine and cherry blossoms delighted my senses. I kicked off my slippers and wandered out to the garden. The grass beneath my toes felt cool and invigorating. I spotted a swing nestled under an old oak tree in the far corner, apart from the garden. I glimpsed high above the leafs and whistled. "Wow! An old fashion swing. What a quaint little spot." A smile stretched across my face. It reminded me of my childhood. My father use to push me on a handmade swing he'd built from leftover wood. Gosh, I'd forgotten.

I slipped into the swing and pushed off. I felt like a child again, toes touching the starry sky. I didn't want to be anywhere but here. I was happy.

Suddenly I heard a rustle, obscured in the shadows. A chill snaked down my spine. I stopped as I searched among the trees—nothing. Then a shadow moved. I sighed. "Whew!" it was Snowball scurrying from under the hydrangeas. *Paranoid much?* I laughed as I watched my cat scamper off.

Then abruptly, I heard footsteps approaching fast. I leaped from the swing, scanning the garden and the thicket lining the fence.

Nothing.

Out of nowhere, echoes of footfalls pierced the air. I pulled the shawl tighter over my shoulders. My eyes raked over the stand of trees once more. Nil, no one. "I should go back in the house," I whispered out loud. I took three steps and halted dead in my feet. There under the moonlight, stepping from the shadows, an outline of a person in a crimson cloak, tall and very beautiful. My blood iced.

"Hello. Let me introduce myself." She slipped the hood down, though, not extending her hand. Without warning, the air became stiff. "I'm Aidan's sister, Helen. And my brother lost his life because of you." Arrogance resonated in the way she tilted her sharp chin. The mark of a true Illuminati.

But all that flew past me. I was stuck on, "Aidan's d-d-dead?" I gawked at his sister as a strong mistrust squeezed my lungs.

"Of course, how rude of me. You didn't know." Enmity coated her words with sweet honey. "You must forgive me, you were away." She gave pause. "I hope you enjoyed your stay." She smiled, but it wasn't your usual Southern-hospitality smile. There was wickedness behind those cherry lips—a flurry that I didn't want to tangle with.

"I didn't kill your brother."

"I'm sorry. I must have not made myself clear. I didn't say he died by your hands. I said you were the reason!" She hissed like a serpent ready to strike.

I narrowed my eyes, though, holding my tongue. I believed when opportunity knocked, you shut-up and listen. Helen loved hearing herself talk. Maybe through her need to brag, she might inadvertently shed some light. I interjected. "I dearly love chatting about family, but let's cut to the chase. How does an immortal die?"

"Why should I divulge any information to you?" she snorted.

If it involved a heart, I doubted she would've understood, but I tossed the dog a bone anyway. "I once loved your brother." I held eye contact—not letting this one out of sight for a second.

She sniffed haughtily. "Do you think my brother loved you?" The tall beauty snickered under her breath. "You *stupid* girl! That night at the party, he told me you were just someone to bed, like his many conquests before. He only intended to fulfill his duty—a promise to the Family. My brother couldn't wait to be rid of you."

Her words burned like acid, but I swallowed the angry vile down. I refused to show weakness. After all, that was what she wanted. So I replied with my own special brand of venom. "It doesn't matter now. He's gone. Another one bites the dust. Next." I shrugged, smugly.

The vixen blonde clenched her teeth. "My brother was clever. He captured you, didn't he?"

I wanted to stomp the smirk right off her elegant-but-wicked face. Rather instead, I threw a little shade with a smile on it as I jeered, "Apparently, he wasn't clever enough. He's dead."

"Shut up!" The blonde beauty roared, cornering me against the fence. "Say that again and I'll end your pathetic life right now!"

A smile tipped the corner of my lip. I'd struck a chord, all right. Mocking the dead was not in good taste, but with all the shade-throwing, I figured a little mudslinging at her hind-ass was well deserved.

Still there had to be more to her coming here than flaunting my past. "Why are you here, Helen?" I eyed her suspiciously.

The blonde assumed a posture of superiority. "Are you bothered by me?"

I laughed. "Bothered like a cockroach, but that's an easy fix." A deep, seedy grin played upon my face.

"Careful what you say, hybrid!"

Her idol threat didn't frighten me. She couldn't do anything to me that hadn't already been done. "So, are you here to announce Aidan's death? You're really starting to bore me." I feigned a yawn.

"Not exactly." Her eyes filled with dark portents.

"Why are you here at this ungodly hour, then? I have nothing else to give."

"You're right! Now that my brother's gone, our long-awaited goal is null and void. We made a mistake relying on a useless human."

I was done with this futile squabble. "Well, Helen, it's been lovely, but I'm leaving. I'm sure you can find your way back to the rock you crawled out from under."

"Stupid hybrid," she howled. "I didn't come to revel in your release from prison or your very generous cash flow, courtesy from my dead brother. I've been sent by the Family to give you a message."

I shook my head, exasperated. "There's nothing you or your family can say that interest me. Go home!" I demanded. I understood the Family's powerful reach better than anyone, and I knew when to pull out of a game that I was no match for.

"I'm more than happy to leave, but first, I have to deliver a word of warning."

"Go home!" I gushed, side stepping the blonde. I had one intent—leaving this bitch to wallow in her own spurious threats. I was done. "You have nothing to say that's worth my time." I threw over my shoulder as I headed straight for the house.

"They'll send someone far more dangerous than me!" The blonde called out. "I think for your sake you should listen."

I stopped dead in my tracks and slowly turned, facing Aidan's sister. I narrowed my eyes not caring if she saw my disdain. "Then get on with it," I snapped, "so I can be done with you and your damn family *forever*." I hated her and everything she stood for.

The blonde's face twisted as if she'd bitten into a rotten apple. "The Family sent me here to tell you," she paused. "Keep away. Don't go sticking your nose into things that you shouldn't. If you don't heed to our warning, your life," she hesitated, "and the life of the ones you care about will suffer. I hope we have an understanding?"

I stood there craving to snuff her lights out. Instead curiosity slammed into first place. It seemed suspicious all this much trouble for little old-hybrid me. I tossed an amused smile. "It sounds like your family is a little paranoid."

The blonde's lips curled in disgust. "Paranoia is not our forte. You should be mindful of where you step. I'm sure you wouldn't want to find yourself back at Haven." Without another word, the blonde beauty in the scarlet cloak disappeared from sight. My gut told me chances of becoming bosom buddies with Aidan's sister were slim. Suddenly a cold breeze swept through me. I quickly gathered my shawl tighter around my shoulders. It was time to head back inside —the sooner the better too.

See No Evil

WHEN MORNING ARRIVED, I needed a U-Haul to drag myself out of bed. After the encounter with blondezilla, my mind kept repeating questions like a bad rerun. Suddenly the sting of tears threatened. If only I knew how Aidan died. What if he'd fallen victim to his family as I did? I shook my head, feeling the weight of perplexity.

One truth I couldn't deny as I lay here alive—it proved that either Aidan or I could survive without the other. Contrary to his past claims. Still hearing of Aidan's death saddened me. I once thought he had been part of Sally's ploy. Now I wasn't so sure. And it ate at me. The only thing I had to go by was a life lost and a mystery that might never unfold. Frustration, pain, and rage smothered me. All I could do was lay my face into my palms and sob.

After a long good cry, I wiped the tears from my face and pulled myself together. I decided to go downstairs while the house remained quiet. Once I reached the kitchen, to my surprise, the aroma of piping hot coffee filled the air. Dom had set the coffee maker for 6:00 a.m. I wondered if he'd overheard my conversation with Aidan's sister. I worried I might be bringing mayhem to the house. I got a nagging feeling this wasn't the last I'd hear from the Family. Helen's threat rode on my shoulders like a heavy feed sack. I had to do something. I couldn't let her or that despicable Order harm my family. Yet the Illuminati had the strength of gods. They were everywhere—no escaping their clenches if they wanted you. Somehow I had to figure out a way to keep them afar. My family meant everything to me.

⁙

It was a nice morning regardless of my run-in earlier. I stepped out into the lawn. Right away, I spotted the vegetable garden roped off. I padded over to it as an admiring smile crept across my face. The leafy patch left me breathless. Everything was in a nice neat row. Assorted vines covered the soil in thick blooms. The garden diffidently had Dom's marvelous touch. There were onions, spinach, tomatoes, rosemary, and ginseng root. How odd, I thought. Ginseng was a magickal plant used in certain rituals. Ms. Noel kept a supply of it all the time. I learned of its use by watching her prepare it for her customers. I wondered if Dom knew of its magickal properties.

I made my way back to the tree swing. I refused to let a vile creature like Helen deny me the right to certain joys in my own home. Despite her opinion of how I obtained the house didn't matter. I earned it with my own blood. This home belonged to my family and me. I'd guard and defend this place like Daniel Boone fighting for the Alamo. We might go down in a blaze, but not without a good old-fashioned fight. Come to think about it, I should find a weapon. At this point, my so-called powers were useless. Having protection might not be a bad idea.

I slid into the swing and pushed off. As I climbed the great blue, higher and higher, the cool morning breeze caressed my face. The tension in my shoulders lightened. This very moment gave waking up a delightful purpose. I'd much rather do this all day than confront my pending troubles. Sooner or later, I had to come down and find a solution to hold the Illuminati at bay. The biggest question was how? What would be their kryptonite? If I discovered their weakness, I might have a chance in stopping the almighty beast. The world would be a safer place, and so would my family.

With no warning, footsteps approached, jarring me from my thoughts. At first I stiffened. Flashes of my recent encounter flooded my mind, but when I spotted the on comer, I quickly relaxed by exhaling a Down-At-The-Heel sigh. "Oh good god! You surprised me." I gasped in relief.

"Stevie, I'm sorry. I didn't mean to startle you. I wanted to bring you this." Dom handed my shawl to me. "You will catch your death of cold out here." He scolded me.

"Thank you." I reached for the soft, fuzzy cloth and wrapped it around my shoulders. It was the only thing I had left of my mother's. Though, he didn't have to bring it to me. A little guilt pinched. I glimpsed up at Dom, "You don't have to fuss over me. Really! You're not my employee."

"Perhaps, but it is what I do best." He stalled for a second, peering over at the roped-off garden. He nodded at me, "You like my vegetables?" He smiled, that kind of smile of contentment, but I sensed there was something else troubling him.

"Yeah, the garden is sprouting." I slowed the swing as I dug my heel into the soil.

"Oui, I overheard your conversation early this morning," he stared out into the garden. "That intrusive creature needed tossing out on her sweet derrière." Obviously Dom disliked Aidan's sister.

"You know Helen?" my brow arched.

"Knowing, non! It is not necessary. The girl is disarranged. It is like a poisonous viper. You may not know the species of the reptile, but you know not to get near it. She is nothing like her brother. Aidan, through all his faults, had a heart. This girl is as wicked as her black magick." It seemed Dom knew more about the Family's inherited practices than I'd given him credit for. Obviously, Jeffery and I underestimated him.

"What do you mean, Dom?" My inquisitiveness tickled the hairs on my back.

"My beautiful child, I may play the role of naïveté, but I am far from ignorant."

"Wait! You know about their—umm—special talents?"

"I've seen plenty of strange, unexplained things around that family to know they are not in the same gene pool of—let's just say, normal." Dom's French accent seemed more profound than usual.

"But I heard you argue with Jeffery."

"Oui! I prefer to leave that little tidbit apart from Jeffery." His mustache tipped upward. "You know how he can get with certain subjects. Protecting him is for his best interest and our peace of mind. Yes?" Dom winked as his thin mustache stretched across his face.

A faint smile caressed my lips. "Oui on that one!" I paused with a more serious note. "Dom, just how much do you know about Aidan's family?"

"I've been waiting for you to ask." He nodded toward the house. "Why don't we go inside and discuss this over breakfast? You look like you can use another cup of coffee and something nourishing to eat. Yes?" Dom tossed a warm smile.

"Sure, lead the way." I returned his smile. Whatever Dom knew excited me and frightened me at the same time. I might as well brace myself for the worst.

Until I stepped inside, I didn't realize how nippy the early morning was. The warmth rushed across my face, and the smell of bacon aroused my appetite.

Jeffery had already joined the table, holding his fork erect. I supposed skinny folk get cranky when hunger struck. I laughed to myself.

Dom had gone all out preparing breakfast with a fine table spread of maple, walnut, and blueberry syrups to go with the huge mountain of waffles drenched in butter along with scrambled eggs and crisp bacon.

Aside from the delicious eatables, the best part about this wonderful feast had nothing to do with the food. My glance bounced around the table at two faces. It touched my heart to be sharing this beautiful morning with my two best friends in the whole wide world, and for that, I felt honored. They truly were my family. I think my father would've approved.

For a short while, we ate in silence, then Dom and Jeffery shared a strained glance. Dom went to clear his throat. A discussion was about to commence. I dreaded it too. I withdrew a deep sigh and laid my fork down, waiting for Dom to start.

"Oh, for God's sake!" Jeffery huffed. "Just say it. We're gonna become petrified before you get around to it!"

I stifled a laugh.

"Jeffery! Where is your patience? We can't just blurt it out. This poor girl has been through enough. We don't need to pour salt on an open wound." Dom argued.

"Well, it's better to throw the whole cup of salt on the wound all at once than to drag the misery out little-by-little sprinkle on a festering sore!" Jeffery folded his arms, pursing his lips.

"I'm getting to that part if you'll settle down." Dom gave his long time but annoying partner a disconcerting glare before focusing back to me. "My sweet, Jeffery and I are very concern for you. You have awakened some very powerful enemies once again. We are fearful for your safety."

Jeffery squirmed in his chair. Apparently he was full of nervous energy.

I could relate. My teeth were on edge too. It was certain that my dealings with the Illuminati hadn't ended. "Yeah, after the visit from Aidan's sister, I've been thinking about getting a weapon." A tight smile snagged the corners of my mouth.

Dom whetted a gentle smile in return. "Let me first say, nothing happens by accident. The Family is quite crafty. Throughout history any catastrophic event that has transpired, the Family has been the masterminds behind it. Wars and famine are not by chance. It is the Order's ploy to bring mankind down to his knees. Even the death of your father was no accident. His deflection cost him his life by the hands of someone he trusted—your mother."

All of a sudden, I felt regret squeezing my lungs. "Where is my mom's grave?"

There was a hint of sadness behind Dom's eyes. "The Family took your mother's body before Jeffery and I had discovered what happened."

"Was she given a proper burial?" My stomach began to roil as my appetite dwindled into a sharp pain.

"I am sorry," Dom paused. "Your mother's body was cremated."

"No! I didn't even get to say my last good-byes to..." My words stalled. I could feel a rush of tears coming.

"We inquired of Sara's ashes, though, we were too late. The Family had disposed of her remains."

"I appreciate your efforts." I shrugged. "I don't expect Aidan's family to show me any kind favors." I glanced at the garden to compose myself.

"Jeffery and I apologize for not..." Dom trailed off.

Jeff interrupted. "We did everything we possibly could." He reached over and grasped my hand.

I flashed a short smile. "I know. You both have been a huge blessing. Thank you both for everything." My eyes glided between two sets of troubled eyes. "I have so many questions spinning in my head. Where do I begin?"

Dom cleared his throat. "Hopefully, I can assist you with some of your dilemmas."

"Anything that can help, I'm grateful for it." I leaned in closer. Dom had my full attention.

"You see for the first time since the beginning of man, there is something the Order of the Golden Dawn fears."

"Don't you mean the Quest?"

"Non. This entity of the Illuminati is much older than the Quest. These are the originals. They are the firstborn."

"Did Aidan come from this clan?"

"This line is through his ancestors. As history foretells, they are the ones who created the secret society. Let me explain." Dom moistened his lips. "This sector was the first scientist who began experimenting with genetics. They were the ones who created Frankenstein, if you will."

My eyes orbed. "Freaking no way?"

"Not as we know in the movies, but yes, they loved playing God."

"That's creepy." Chills shimmied down my spine.

"Oui! They are very dangerous. Although, they are not the most feared. Any power they cannot mimic or possess terrifies them. That one is," Dom slipped Jeffery a furtive glance, then back to me "the Fifth Essence. That is you, mon chéri." Dom extended a gentle smile.

I crinkled my nose. "Wait! You know?"

"Oui. Jeffery and I figured it out. The Order would not have gone through great lengths to capture you if you were a mere human. They would've simply taken your life."

Shock pulsed through me as I sat there unable to speak.

"It's quite all right if you wish to take a rest. I know this is so much to absorb." Dom's brown eyes were soft and understanding.

The churning in my stomach deepened. "I appreciate your candor." I hesitated. "There's something else." I dragged in a piercing breath. "Aidan is dead." I spat it out as if it was poison. "His sister shared this with me early this morning." Considering everything, I had a gut feeling that Aidan's death and the disappearing castle was linked. It definitely had strange and eerie stamped on it. When I lifted my eyes, I saw Dom's and Jeffery's stunned faces. It pained me to see the starkness in their eyes. "She refused to go into any details." My shoulders slumped. I felt drained from this unrelenting nightmare.

"Lord, have mercy on my soul! Jesus, take me home, NOW!" Jeffery began fanning himself like he was about to faint.

Dom quietly torpedoed a calm-down scorn at Jeffery before he commented. "I'm not sure I can believe everything this woman says."

"Yeah, me either, but you haven't seen Aidan since his castle vanished. It certainly appears as if…" I couldn't finish saying the words—*Aidan's gone.* I feared if I said it out loud, then I'd have to believe it. I wasn't ready to completely accept his death.

"Yes, it all seems incredulous. The last time we saw Aidan, it was that night when the two of you were together in the pool house." Dom cleared his throat. "I went looking for you to make sure you were safe. When I saw you with Aidan, I assumed everything was fine."

"I sure as hell wasn't okay." Jeffery pursed his lips. "I got tied up and locked in a mofo closet by that rascal, Aidan's cousin, Sam. I hate dark places, and I hate that boy even more." Jeffery crossed his arms in a stew. "That nasty booger was hiding around the corner, waiting for you to leave before he jumped me."

I clutched my chest, gaping. "That explains how Sam knew where to find me." Shock trickled down my spine as my eyes dropped to the floor. I half murmured to myself. "He must've heard our conversation." My eyes slid over to Dom. "That night when you came to check on me, it wasn't Aidan you saw. It was Sam. He had the ability to mimic anyone."

"Oh dear lord! We had no idea." Dom inhaled an alarming breath. "I am so, so sorry! When I saw you in his arms, Jeffery and I assumed you were safe. If we had only known…"

"Don't blame yourself. How could you've known? The real Aidan found me, but I was nearly dead." I paused. "He killed Sam for hurting me." My eyes slid to Jeff. "You don't have to worry about Sam ever again." I tossed a pinched smile.

"Lord have mercy!" Jeffery chimed. "I swear good thang too! Never in my life have I wished a fella dead… but that sadistic creature, I'd happily sweeten his tea with rat poison and be smile-n in his face while he's down-n it and ask-n for more. Huh-hmm,

I sure as hell would!" By the firm glint in Jeffery's taupe eyes, his intent screamed loud and clear.

I reached over to Jeffery. "He's gone, so maybe you should save that poison for the real rats." I smiled, but it was strained, and right away I went to the next question. "Did Aidan ever catch up with you two the next day? He left me at the cottage to find you both."

Jeffery and Dom looked at each other with confused faces. "No. He never showed up," Dom said. "We tried finding out what happened to the two of you, but the Order had stepped in and brushed everything underneath the rug. Coupled with Aidan's disappearance, Jeffery and I didn't have a clue to your whereabouts. It was not until we saw your face broad-cast over the news did we realize that you were in deep trouble." Dom shook his head, baffled.

I wrapped my arms around my waist, trying to hold off a panic attack. "I'm very sorry for what I've put you two through these past three years."

"Don't worry yourself," Dom smiled. "It wasn't your fault."

"Still the same, it hasn't been easy on you guys either." I tossed a bitter smile. "You both can rest assure that I won't be stirring up any hornet's nest. Whatever his sister is protecting, she doesn't have to worry. I plan to keep my distance from her and that vile family, forever." I tried to ease the guys' worries. Nonetheless, I couldn't forget Helen's threat. A person filled with raw fear was unpredictable and highly dangerous. If I were Helen, I'd watch my step. No way in hell would I let her or the Order hurt my family or take me back to that sadistic hospital.

"Yes," Dom continued. "Regardless of your noninvolvement, it appears that the Illuminati is feeling uneasy having you free. Not too many people can rattle the Order as you have, my dear."

"They fear me?" I found that hard to digest. The Family thought of themselves as the almighty. "Those coldhearted bastards framed me for murder and made sure I stayed locked away in hell, stone-faced with drugs for three solid years. I'm the one who fears them!"

"Contraire, my child, you are a force to be reckoned with. And because of this very fact, I am certain that Helen's visit has a hidden agenda. What we must do is find out *what*."

"I think it's clear. They want me out of their way, dead or alive." I speculated.

Then all at once Jeffery erupted. "If they could've taken your life, you'd be stiff as a board rotting in some unmarked grave right now. Lucky for you those evil-white-ugly mother-puckers are terrified of you. Why do you think that hospital kept you shackled and comatose? After all, youse the most badass mofo out there—*The Fifth Essence!*" Jeffery snapped his fingers, full of swag.

"I rarely ever say this about Jeff, but he's right. Yes?" Dom admitted.

"It is hard for me accepting my strange abilities. I don't feel supernatural. Rather, I feel helpless, which is very human."

"You must embrace your destiny, mon ange." Dom advised. "Right now you are vulnerable. For this reason, we need to take measures reassuring your safety. A trainer can help you learn self-defense. As for tapping into your angelic skills, along with your Druid gifts, we can't be much of assistance there. However, it is not an impossible feat. We will find away."

"Druid?" Surprise, shock, and stun, all rolled in one, attacked my brain. "I'm not Druid!" I shook my head. "No way!"

"Can you be certain of that?" Dom's brow shot up. "You are your father's daughter."

"My father?"

"Oui! Your father comes from the Druid bloodline.

My brain felt paralyzed. "I had no idea!"

"Why do you think the family arranged for you and Aidan to join in union?" Dom asked.

"Aidan explained part of this to me. Clearly he left out a few details."

"Oui. The Family knew that with your magickal abilities and Aidan's Druid bloodline, your children will be immortal. Sickness and death will be a thing of the past. Some refer to you as the new-age Eve."

"Eve! That's the first I've heard that." I squirmed. "There's no way I'm having a million kids!"

"Yes, that does seem extreme." Dom cuffed his mouth, hiding a laugh.

"Call me yellow, but I don't want any part of her! That's just icky!" I shuddered.

"I know this is daunting." Dom's eyes softened.

I averted my eyes to the large window, wishing I had never left the comfort of my swing. I straightened my shoulders and slid my eyes back to Dom. "I guess now that Aidan is no longer with us, the Family doesn't have much hope for a perfect race and a one-world government." My stomach fluttered like butterflies as I thought about the past and an imposing future I once faced. Still nothing was matching up.

"Oui. It does seem their future is at a disadvantage now." Dom rubbed his mustache, thinking.

"What about the infusion between Aidan and me? Shouldn't I be dead too? If Aidan was truly dead, then that theory was a fallacy."

"Nothing is certain, chère. Aidan's theory could've been misconstrued."

I shook my head, "Aidan didn't make mistakes. He was too careful."

"True. However, the Family was treading on unknown waters. You were the first trial to succeed. Perhaps, this was another lie." Dom questioned.

"I don't know." Now I was really confused.

Dom went on. "There were other trials. Different. Although, sadly, the mothers died during birth. The children who successfully survived had a blended mix of fey DNA, like Sam."

Jeffery blew out a sharp sigh. "That explains why Sambo was so mean!"

"Yeah, Sam." I raked my fingers through my hair.

"Honey, don't you fret any over that no-good count. He was plum evil." Jeffery spewed his feelings as he wiggled in his chair.

I shrugged. "Anyway, how did the fey become involved with the Illuminati?"

"Well," Dom continued. "You've heard of the Nephilim giants?"

"Yes, my dad read the Bible story to me when I was a child."

"Then you know the Nephilim were the offspring of the angels and the daughters of man?" Dom asked.

"Yes, I remember."

"Did you know that the giants were the gateway for the fey race?"

"Really! How so?"

Dom began, "as the story foretells, the giants are evil in every sense—"

I interrupted, "Are you saying the giants still exist?"

"Not the ones from the ancient world."

"Was there another world?"

"No, the same earth, just another dimension. It was called the Time of Ole, the biblical era...the world before the flood. " Dom clarified.

"Oh, yeah, before the flood."

"Oui! During the Time of Ole, angels walked among man. Some were friends with Noah. Of course, their relationship took a drastic turn when the angels took the young daughters of man. This angered the humans and enraged the angels' creator. Angels and humans having intercourse were forbidden in the ancient world. Angels were not meant to have human desires and create offspring—half-angel children. In the eyes of their creator, it was apostasy, an unforgivable act. As for the aftereffect, the angels were punished for their lust."

"What sort of punishment?" The hairs on my neck stood straight up.

"Since the celestial beings were perfect creatures with eternal life, they faced eternal destruction for the act of treason. However, first, their creator had to set an example for the heavenly body to see the consequences for disobedience. Until their allotted time, the rebellious angels were marked as an outcast and bound to the earth, no longer permitted to enter the heavens." Dom's shoulders tensed.

"I'm confused. How does this have anything to do with me?" I glimpsed over at Jeffery, who was starting to go pale. I slid my Coke over to him. Without delay, he snatched it up and down it like it was a shot of whiskey.

"I'm getting to that. Please allow me to explain."

I nodded, silently.

Dom exhaled sharply and continued. "The Nephilim reached adulthood very quickly. Soon the giants followed in the footsteps of their angelic fathers and mated with other humans and every other creature as well. Subsequently, the children of the Nephilim created a new race—fey. They're referred to as seelie." Dom paused, giving me a moment to let it sink in.

"So the fey have survived all these centuries?"

"Funny you should ask. The Nephilim offspring received protection by the Illuminati."

"I thought the first Illuminati formed a secret society in the early seventeen hundreds as the Knights Templar?"

"My dear child, they emerged much later under the Order of Solomon. The Illuminati have been in existence since the beginning of time. Actually, Cain was the catalyst for the Family's true beginnings. Cain became the true founder of the Order of the Golden Dawn."

"This just seems uncanny all wrapped up with a pretty pink bow on top." I cringed from the visions encircling mind.

"Yes. Now that you are part of the world of extraordinaire, you can see it has many faces. It's something you mustn't ever reveal to anyone nor forget."

I called to mind a secret Aidan once revealed to me. Through the craft of a very powerful and dark spell, he conjured immortality for himself. A lot of good it did him. I shuddered. "Don't worry. I will take this to my grave." I just found a whole new freak-out. I squeezed my waist trying to hold it together.

Dom smiled, but it didn't touch his eyes. "The Illuminati had always been interested in science. The Order realized they had something exclusive, so they agreed to provide shelter to the young fey if they agreed to abide by the sealed contract."

"What is it with this damn family and contracts?" I scoffed. "So the children of the Nephilim survived the flood?"

"That is correct," Dom said.

"What happened to the original giants and their mothers?"

"The giants didn't have as much luck as their children. Even the Illuminati knew they couldn't coexist with the Nephilim. However, they did extract DNA from the adult Nephilim, but that was all."

I wrinkled my nose, unclear. "Dom, how did the Illuminati know about DNA back then?"

An impish glint hid behind Dom's eyes. "The angels, of course. They assisted in mankind's creation."

"I guess that makes sense." I shrugged, picking at my cold food.

"It does seem incredible for man to have such advanced abilities that early in time. However, before mankind was even a thought, the knowhow of science was always there among the angels." Dom took a sip of his coffee.

"So, you were saying about the giants?" I propped my elbow on the table, still playing with my food.

"Yes. As I was explaining… no one succeeded in reigning the mighty giants into submission. For this reason, the Family left them and their birth mothers behind, sealing their fate once and for all. The deluge took their lives."

"What happened to the angels?"

"They took their true spirit form."

"How did the Illuminati and the offspring of the Nephilim survive?"

"The fallen angels assisted in carrying the old ones to the highest peak, sealing them off in a cave were the water couldn't penetrate. When the water receded and land resurfaced, they came out, though, weak and thin. They survived by feasting on others who didn't have as high of a position. The lesser ones were much more expendable."

I fought back the vile that tried to crawl up my throat. Then a question popped into my head. "Dom, how did you come across this information? This isn't in the Bible accounts."

"You are correct. The Illuminati have kept historical records from the beginning of time."

"I remember Aidan saying something about how they kept meticulous documentation of my father's death, but I had no idea their accounting went back to the beginning of man's existence."

"Man's existence began long before Adam and Eve." Dom flashed an erudite grin. "But that story will have to be told another time. How I came across the accounts, well, when you have worked for someone for as long as I have, a trust is established. Many of their secret meetings, I prepared their meals, and I was permitted to be amidst the red robes. Eventually, they trusted me with a key. At night, when the house was quiet, I'd sneak down to the hidden chamber and snoop through their records."

"Aidan explained the books were protected by black magic. How were you able to get past that?"

"Yes, they are very protective of their scrolls. It is their bible."

"Then how were you able to go unnoticed?"

Suddenly a roguish grin hid under his mustache. "I had the key to unlock the protective spell. Like I said, they trusted me."

I gawked at Dom as if he was the cat that ate the canary. "If you had been caught, they would have..."

"True, but I managed to stay under their notice."

"I should be taking lessons from you." I smiled with a newfound respect.

"I do have a few tricks up my sleeves." He smiled back, then he took a long-winded breath. "What I've discovered...is astounding and quite disturbing."

"Do tell!" I held my breath.

Dom furthered his story. "After the deluge, another race of fey began. This time the new fey became the offspring of the angels and the adult children of the Nephilim, creating a much more distorted fey, the unseelie."

"Wait! Are you saying, the new fey mated with grandpa?" Right away my stomach roiled.

"Oui. To humans this act is disgusting, but angels are supernatural beings as well as fey. The problem lies with the celestial sovereignty. Creatures of this nature are forbidden to mate. As the punishment for their treason, any offspring will be cursed with darkness."

"Holy crap! I'm part of the curse." All of a sudden, sheer black fright swept through me.

"Non, non!" Dom echoed. "You are not of their sort."

"What makes you so sure? Aren't I the product of the same?"

"Oui! But you were created in a lab. The angel's DNA you share did not have intercourse with a human. You are much different—a genetically altered angel." Dom assured.

A moment of silence settled between us as I gulped down air, trying to settle my pounding heart. Then I asked. "Okay, I'll take your word for it. Though, I don't understand why the history lesson?"

"I think it's important for you to know the Family's past, present and future. It may save your life someday." Dom confessed.

"Okay, I'll listen." Yet, I really wanted to retire to my room and check out forever.

Dom cleared his throat as he finished the rest of the story. "There are several panels of divine adjudicators. The Illuminati is one."

"Crap! Those sons of bitches are everywhere." I didn't know why this surprised me.

"This is a fact, my dear. Since the beginning of time, the Golden Dawn has had their hands in the cookie jar one way or another." Dom shrugged.

"How can they get by with these hideous acts?"

"Some deeds are better left in the shadows, my dear." Dom's face appeared sober. "I have a feeling their grand scheme of things is much larger than ridding the world of sickness." Dom withdrew a tattered sigh. "I'm afraid they are creating an army."

I glanced again over at Jeffery, and his expression had changed from bulging eyes to tongue hanging. Shit! Was he going into shock? Still, Jeffery better not drool on me. "Oh my god! Fey on steroids," I whispered.

"Oui! A mass production of super-strength fey."

"So if they are creating an army of fey, why didn't they contain Sam? He was like the hulk when he morphed into a gigantic monster." I shuddered from the flashes of that horrendous night.

"I think they decided to use him as a decoy.

"Dom, what do you mean?" I asked, baffled.

"Sam had mastered the skill of trickery. Unfortunately for Sam and everyone that he came into contact with suffered. As Sam became progressively worse, no one could control him. Simply, Sam needed to be handled." Dom's last word clung to my mind—*handled.*

The hairs on my neck began to prickle. I knew that term too well. "The Family handled my father." I felt sick.

"I gather the Family terminated Sam."

"Yes! However, his death had a double-edged sword. They appointed Aidan as the eliminator. When Sam found out, he became enraged. He fell into the Family's hands, as they had hoped." Dom pushed aside his cold coffee.

I interjected. "I think I know where this is leading." I clasped my hands under the table to hide the trembling.

Dom nodded in silence.

"Sam sought out revenge against Aidan by coming after me." It was all too clear. "Aidan played along, convincing me he'd saved my life, confessing his dying love for me as we rode off into the blazing sunset." I took a moment, letting this sink in. "The Family orchestrated that attack. It was a ploy to get me to trust Aidan. But why? What did the Family want from me?" I shook my head, mystified. "Every event that transpired since I stepped foot on Louisiana's soil had everything to do with a master plan to catch me at my weakest moment and snag me..." I was speechless. I'd been a fool. "I played right into their hands!" I murmured mostly to myself. Stunned, I placed my hands over my face, feeling the impact of the veracity. Just when I thought I had washed my hands of that family, I found myself still in the same deadly whirlwind. I thought it was over. Rather, I'd just begun. I raised my head, and my glint caught Dom. "I never was in any real danger of losing my essence or my life was I? It was all a stinking lie! What have they to gain from this vicious ploy?"

"Whatever reason they have, it is enough for them to have locked you away. I find it quite suspicious to drop your charges and set you free." Dom's brow arched, speculatively.

I sat there numbfucked. Dom reached over with his untouched glass of Coke, pushing it directly in front of me. I grabbed the drink and gulped it down quickly, wishing it had a kick to it.

Then it hit me like a head on collision with a freight train. I slammed my glass down with force. I looked straight into Dom's eyes with solid awareness. "They wanted me pregnant. Oh dear god! I have a child!" It wasn't a question, it was a statement. I shot to my feet in a whirlwind of panic. The chair flew backward, crashing to the floor. I could barely ask the heartening question. "Do you think my child is still alive?" My heart felt like it was going to break in two.

Dom hesitated, his eyes dancing, thinking. "Yes, the child has to be! Why else would Helen warn you to stay away? They must be hiding the baby."

Sweat beaded across my forehead. "I have a child!" I barely whispered. Those monsters had my baby. What if they are hurting her? With my eyes wild with worry, I glanced over at Jeffery, rocking and hugging himself. I desperately wanted to join him. "That's why Helen was trying to frighten me. They're hiding my child. Those conniving, devil-dealing, bastards!" I cursed. A knife twisting in my gut would've hurt less.

"What did Helen say?" Dom asked, disquiet colored his face.

"She warned me to stay away or else." I cringed as my mind rushed over her baleful words.

"Or else what?" Dom stared at me with numb horror.

My face grew ashen. "She threatened my life and both you and Jeffery too."

"Oh my! Aidan's sister is quite a catty one." Dom tapped his finger on his chin, thinking. "We need to take precautions—an alarm system, perhaps."

"Or I can move. If I'm gone, they'll leave you and Jeffery alone. Besides, no high tech alarm system is going to keep this girl out. She's gifted." I picked my chair up off the floor and sat it upright. Though I wasn't in the mood for sitting—too antsy. I began to pace.

"No. We won't let her run your life or ours' either. This is your home. We will deal with this as a family."

"Dom!" I stopped in midstream pacing. "I don't care about my life, but I can't have " Suddenly Jeffery snapped out of his coma and sprung from his chair.

"I say hell to the no! That white-no-count-high-priced-ho ain't kick-n you out of our home. Besides youse got the checkbook."

"Jeffery!" Dom gaped.

"I was just say-n." Jeffery shrugged.

Dom flashed Jeffery a I'll-Deal-With-You-Later glance. Then his eyes slid to me. "Stevie, I know your heart must be breaking."

"My heart has already been shattered a long time ago. This"—I clenched my teeth— "this has me enraged!"

"If this helps any, I believe Aidan cared for you." Dom's face softened.

I threw up my hands in disgusted resignation. "There's no excuse that can cover his treachery. I lost three years of my life, framed for crimes I didn't commit. I lost my mother, my father. I lost my innocence. I lost my will to live. And the biggest loss ever—losing my child, who may or may not be alive." I took a deep breath, calming my rapid heartbeats. Then remorse struck. I shouldn't have taken my anger out on my friend.

"Dom, I'm sorry." I peered outside the window, easing my breath, slowly. The breeze was blowing lazily as the trees swayed gently back and forth. I wanted to find my way back to the swing and forget the woes that beseeched my spirit, but my mind kept jumping around like a rock skipping over water. Then I knew what I had to ask next. The answer beckoned me, and I could no longer deny its thirst. I held my gaze on the trees, eschewing eye-contact with Dom. "Do I have the DNA of a fallen angel?" I boldly dared.

Dom gave a startle gasp. "I think you are better off not knowing."

"I disagree." My heart lurched.

"I can't be certain. However, I do have my méfiance (suspicions)."

"Do you think this angel was an accessory to stealing my child?"

"It's possible." By the distortion in Dom's face, it was plain to see that he was warring with himself over whether or not he should reveal the truth.

With no warning, Jeffery slammed his white-knuckled fist onto the table, bringing both Dom and me to his full attention.

"Dom, if you don't tell her, I will." He threatened. "She needs to know the whole truth!" Before Dom could gather a full sentence, impatient Jeffery bellowed like he was a one-man choir. His eyes latched onto mine. "Yes! You have mofo-bad-angel-blood inside you, gurrrl." Then Jeffery used his indoor voice. "But that doesn't mean you're a bad person. Just a little spicy is all."

Dom threw Jeffery a lemon-lime glare.

"Holy mother of god!" My knees buckled. Quickly, I grabbed the table for support.

"Chile, don't go and break your neck. Let me help you." Jeffery glided me back into my seat. "I'll get you a refill." He snatched up my glass and shuffled off.

Then I focused back to Dom, "I'd like to know his name." It suddenly became crucial for me to know the other side of my bloodline.

"A name, yes. I haven't met this creature, only stories, and I pray I never meet him."

"Is there a way to call upon him?"

"No, I refuse to help you there! Stevie, you are treading on very deadly ground." Dom spoke in a stern tone. It had taken me back. "You must leave him alone," deep-seeded lines etched across Dom's forehead. "Do you understand me?"

"I need to know his name! I want to prevent myself from becoming like him." Tears welled up.

Then Dom gathered himself from the table, and before he retreated upstairs, he turned to me and announced, "If you insist—*Mustafa*."

Looking for Evil in All the Wrong Places

After the past few weeks, I'd grown tired of lying in bed, feeling sorry for myself. Sooner or later I had to leave the sanctuary of my bedroom and face the world. I'd decided to take Jeffery's advice and paint the town red. Nothing better than a little music and a whole lotta liquor to lift the spirits. I didn't make a habit of drinking. My mother had problems with the juice. I refused to follow the same path. But sometimes, it didn't hurt to let loose. As it stands, my mind needed a break. Constant worry that I might have a child wandering god-knows-where was worse than me cutting out my own bleeding heart. A break was in order.

After a pampered bath, I threw on an oversized towel and went to my own personal department store called, the Closet. I had no idea what to pick out—too many choices. I looked through garment after designer garment until I came to one outfit. I held the dress up, examining its threads. "Hmm." Jeffery might actually be a fashionista after all. The mini dress shimmered in black sequins, cut to hug my hips. The front dipped down revealing far more than I liked. It was the little black dress that could, and, of course, hooker heels—black pumps lined in gold spikes. "Crap!" I held up the shoes. "I hope I don't break my neck in these puppies!"

I made my way to the cosmetics area and seated myself in front of the lit mirror. I glared at my unruly hair. As I held the brush in my hand, staring at the young girl before me—a stranger at best. The gentleness in her eyes had vanished, but something else took its place—grit, perhaps. Who was this girl, a shadow of the person she once was? The sparkle in her green-eyes had returned, but behind that shine laid a deep-rooted sadness. I wondered if she would ever find happiness?

Focusing on the present, I gaped at my hair with a snit. At least that part of me hadn't changed. The mess on top of my head was still unruly and defiant. I decided to make the best of it. I took the blow-dryer and ran it through my hair every which way. Messy was what I wanted, and messy was what I got. I did some teasing to give more fullness and height. Bed-head hair seemed to fit my outfit just perfect. Wild woman in spiked heels. Quite appropriate, I thought.

I blinked, empty, examining at the final results. She looked nothing like the real me. No amount of makeup, hairdo, and name-brand clothing could hide my despair. So much had happened in the last three years to fill a century.

I may have a child out there. I didn't know why, but I sensed a girl, no more than a toddler. I wondered who she favored—Aidan's blue eyes and black curls, or my freckles? Tears began to build and I pushed back the lump. One thing I knew—I couldn't sit on my thumbs any longer. I had to find her.

I remembered that morning at Aidan's cottage like it was yesterday. Sally's intrusive knock at the door, listening to her cruel accusations of crimes I didn't commit. Yet, the most disturbing—threatening to take my unborn child. Back then, I didn't believe her. Now, I wished I had. Perhaps I could've stopped her madness. Though, I didn't have a chance. I was out numbered. Sally didn't execute my capture alone. Whoever assisted her was quite clever.

I once suspected Aidan as her accomplice. Now my heart filled with doubts.

A frosty shudder shot through me like a heavy blizzard. I rubbed my arms, trying to knock the chill off. During my lovely stay at

Haven Hospital, sometimes I dreamt of Aidan's beautiful face whispering sweet nothings into my ear. I could taste his salty kisses on my dry lips, but it was only a dream. A dream that only fools dreamt. Despite everything, my heart still ached for him. I'd turned into a sniffling fool. How could I love a man whose heart was black? I looked forward to the day my heart stopped beating. The pain—gone. Until then, I would remain a prisoner. I wiped a fallen tear.

There were far more important things to worry over than the loss of a Janus-faced man—my voice of reasoning would say. I planned to start snooping around. If I have a child, I'd find her. The best place to start would be Haven.

———❧❈☙———

Jeffery met me downstairs. He knew some of the hottest bars on Bourbon street. After all, he'd lived here in New Orleans most of his life.

After arguing over what use of transportation, Jeffery and I both agreed driving would be a buzz-kill. Neither one of us wanted to be the designated driver. We'd planned on doing some heavy drinking. We considered taking the streetcar, but the ride would've taken too long. So we chose to take a cab.

Soon the two of us in our wild attire and sparkling ensemble made our way to the infamous Bourbon Street.

The late-spring evening was as sultry as a midsummer night, and it didn't take long for my clothes to start sticking to me. The worse part, Jeffery didn't know the streets as well as he'd bragged about. Go figure!

"Jeffery," I huffed from walking. "I'm not taking another step. I have permanent blisters after tonight."

"Come on, my favorite bar is down one more block." He tugged on my arm.

I jerked back. "That's what you've been saying for the last five blocks! Pounding the pavement isn't my idea of a good time in the sweltering heat."

"Don't get your panties in a bunch, Ms. Swing-n Dixie." Jeffery swatted at me.

"Hey," I jabbed myself, "I'm not the one with a Dixie."

"Oh, you think your cute don't you? That's just tacky." Jeffery pursed his lips.

"I tell you what, let's trade shoes. My heels for your flats." I arched a brow, challenging him.

"Are you cray-cray? I ain't wear-n them suicide heels."

"You insisted I wear these pumps!" I shrieked.

"Yes, I did cuz I wasn't gonna wear 'em on my fabulous feet. Them thangs will give me bunions."

It took everything I had not to smack him upside the head with one of my bunion-making-heels. Instead, I glared at him with my arms folded.

"Look, com'on. There's a bar across the street. See the neon sign." Jeffery pointed. "We go-n there!" He pulled on my sleeve.

"If you chicken out, I'm hailing a cab and calling it a night."

"Shut your pie hole. You said pick one. Did I not do that?"

I just rolled my eyes. What was the point in arguing?

There we were standing directly under the bold neon sign that read, *Mephistz*. I flashed a sidelong glance at Jeffery and asked, "You come here?" disbelief coated my voice.

Jeffery scoffed. "I come here all the time. Now quit your bitch-n. We found a bar." He gave me a little shove through the entrance door.

Once inside, a rush of smoke and careless chatter bathed my senses. The lighting was dearth, only the soft glow of candles dotted the darkness. It was nothing special. Although, the bar held a good-size crowd.

Unexpectedly, odd music began to tickle the hairs on my neck. Summoned by its strange peculiarity, I followed its sound as if I'd been enchanted by the pied piper, himself. I spotted the live-band straight back on a small dusty stage. Directly in front of the platform, couples and singles filled the floor, dancing seductively as though they were alone in their own private quarters. Not of my own volition, I had to join the floor. My feet, my desires took control.

"Hey, Jeff! Order me a drink." I tossed over my shoulder, half dazed as I pushed past him. Before he could stop me, I'd disappeared, swallowed up by the smoke and sea of people.

Breathless, I entered amongst the dancers. I paused closing my eyes, letting the melody weave its magick into the pores of my spirit. I tossed my hair back, surrendering myself to its temptation.

Bewitched by its touch, my hips swayed back and forth as though I was making love to a long lost lover. Taken against my own will, I was no longer in control of myself; yet it felt good and—familiar. The spellbound music carried me to a place far away, and I surrendered as it ravished every inch of my body.

Without warning the music stopped and the enchantment had been broken. My eyes popped opened, and there standing before me was the most intense gold eyes I'd ever seen. A man. He was perfect. Long, velvety blonde hair to his shoulders, tall and broad. He wore a T-shirt, white, showing off his bronze tan, and a pair of faded jeans on the tattered side. Gorgeous didn't seem to justify his beauty. However, his glare told another story. He seemed angry with me for some odd reason.

With my brain still hazy, I didn't hear Jeffery walk up behind me. I only realized it when he snatched my arm and whispered in my ear. "Honey, I think we gots to go. *Now!*" He insisted, tugging at me.

"Why do we need to go? I like it here." I held my glare equably at the stranger.

"I think your friend knows best." The stranger barged in. "You're not welcome here!"

All of a sudden, I felt like a spectacle—every eye in the room had fixed on me. My cheeks flushed, and at that moment I wanted to be invisible. I knew I could do either one of two things, A: duck my tail and run, or B: stand my ground and go out with a blaze of glory. I chose B. "Last time I checked, this is a public bar." I straightened my shoulders back and held my gaze.

The stranger's eyebrow perked. "I see." A slight smiled tugged at the corner of his lip. "You're a brave girl or just stupid." He mocked.

"What is your problem?" I narrowed my eyes. This dude needed to go back to the bar and take up where he left off—playing with himself.

The irate stranger took a step closer, our noses nearly touching. His breath played upon my cheeks. "Little angel!" He hissed. "Leave while you still can." The glint in his eyes appeared predatory. And Jeffery and I were invading his turf.

Suddenly the atmosphere was stifling, and I couldn't breathe. I latched hold of Jeffery, "let's go." I scoffed at the stranger with a scornful retort. "Sorry for trespassing, your hind-ass." Amusement danced in his eyes, yet, he remained silent and hostile.

<hr />

Several blocks later and added blisters to my feet that we finally found a resting spot where we felt safe enough to stop. We spotted a bench and both of us flopped down taking a load off, heaving for air. Hence from the pouring sweat and my aching feet, I refused to take another step. I snatched the heels off and began rubbing my raw feet, wincing over the pain. At that point, I swore off heels. Barefoot was the new trend for me. I'd take my chances stepping on glass any day opposed to wearing those torturous heels ever again. *Despicable heels much!*

"Gurrrl!" Jeffery jarred me from my aching feet. "What just happened back there?" Jeffery's breath came in short puffs.

"I have no idea. I don't know what came over me. The music had some sort of hold on me." I shook my head in confusion.

"Music? I didn't hear any music." Jeff gawked in disbelief.

"You didn't hear the strange tunes?" I stared at Jeff, unbelieving my ears.

"Nope. It really looked funny too! All those strange people dancing to air. I started to wonder if I was deaf, but I could hear the chatter."

"Holy crap! For real?" Shock veiled my face.

"For real!

"That's really weird."

"Gurrrl, I didn't have to hear it anyway. You were a seductress, front and center stage. You sure as hell surprised me. I didn't know you had those kinda moves. I thought for a minute you were gonna bring down the house."

"Jeff, hush! I was just dancing." I tried to brush my humiliation under the proverbial rug.

"Don't be embarrassed. All that yummy testosterone in that bar was make-n me woozy too!" Jeffery started fanning himself. "They all had their eyes on you, girlfriend! Including that angry-hot-as-hell-hunk of man."

I rolled my eyes. "I didn't notice. I was too busy staring down the grudge of Christmas. Did you see his angry eyes?"

"Um-hmm! I sure did, and some other parts too!"

An unwelcome blush crept into my cheeks. "Jeffery, have you ever heard the phrase too much information?"

"Maybe! But that don't mean I'm gonna stop say-n what's on my mind."

"Give it a rest. This night has been bad enough." I couldn't help but feel a little rattled, and that music seemed to have drained my energy.

"Not all was lost tonight. Something good came out of this excursion. Well, two things actually." Jeffery corrected himself.

"And what, pray tell, could that be?" I held my breath. With Jeffery, it was like Cracker Jack's. You never knew what you were getting.

"Okay, Miss Smarty-panties. First, we got out alive, and second, that guy is h-o-t. Delicious with a hot-fudge sundae and a huge, juicy cherry on top of a mountain of—"

"I get it! I get it! He's *fine*." I covered my ears. "I learned a long time ago looks weren't everything. You didn't see his behavior toward me? He acted like a real asshole."

"Well, if I recall correctly, Miss High and Almighty, you were a bit snippy yourself."

"*ME!* He was rude, *first*." I shrieked. "All up in my grill, trying to intimidate me. I should've coldcocked him."

"Maybe that's true, but he saved our lives. Did you not see all the dark stares?"

I nearly bit my tongue over the irony. "He threatened us!"

"Well, now that you put it like that, you do have a point. But that mofo was *fine*."

"Then, Jeff, you date him. I'll go back and get his number for you." I turned in my bare feet to head back, but abruptly, Jeffery grasped my arm.

"No, no! That's fine." He threw his hands up in protest. "I can admire that lovely man from a distance, a very far distance." Jeffery confirmed with a pout following. I stifled a laugh.

"Come on!" I nodded toward a different direction. "Let's not make this night a total bust. I don't know about you, but I could eat a beignet right now."

"Girlfriend, you must've read my mind. Besides, it wouldn't hurt you to put on a little weight. As for me, I'm black and fabulous. I can eat anything I want and never gain a pound."

I rolled my eyes as I started my way down the sidewalk to Café Du Monde. They made the best beignets in New Orleans.

Strange and Eerie

I T WAS 4:00 a.m. I had awaken with a start. A tree limb kept scratching at the window pane, making me jumpy. Even my cat, Snowball, seemed edgy. I finally gave up on sleep and went down to the kitchen to fix a cup of hot cocoa. Maybe it'd take the jitters away, and I could finally get some shut-eye. Moments later with my piping-hot cocoa in my favorite heart mug, I went outside to the back garden. A light breeze blew against my face, tossing my hair about. The air smelled of crepe myrtle as I drew in a deep breath. I loved this garden. It gave me a sense of serenity and peace. I'd never get enough of this luscious patch if I lived to be a hundred.

I sat at the small table and sipped on my cocoa. My eyes washed over my mug. When I was a young child, my dad bought me a mug much like this one. To me, it meant more than a ceramic mug. It was a little part of him, a memory I cherished. My mother, on the eve of her death, out of jealously, shattered the original mug into pieces. It was the only thing I had left of my father. Mom wanted to punish me. She faulted me for the death of her boyfriend, Francis.

Sara cruel words continued to haunt me. She hated me as much as she hated Dad. Sadly, those were the last words she'd said to me before her demise. She blamed me for all her woes. A part of me agreed. Her human body wasn't equipped to carry an alien fetus. Hence, it damaged her mind.

Enough of the past—too much pain. I exhaled. I finished my last drop of cocoa, then I thought about the swing.

A little fear hit me, yet I dug my heels into the soil and made my way to my favorite spot. Screw Helen and the Family! If they really wanted me, they'd find me, regardless. No point in letting them stop me from enjoying the comforts of my home. I jumped into the swing like I had so many times as a young girl and pushed off as the cool wind caressed my face. I closed my eyes, gliding to and fro. The crickets were singing and the tall oaks rustled through the gentle breeze. I heard a mockingbird chirping in the distance. A smile crept across my face. I could spend the rest of my life right here in this spot, content. A long sigh followed. It was only wishful thinking; too many demons to slay and not enough time in the day to slay them all.

I trembled over what the future held. With mistrust bouncing off my shoulders, it was time to set my plan in motion. I needed to find a way inside Haven and to their files. It was going to be tricky. No doubt the Family had me under surveillance— watching me from afar. I suspected any record of my childbirth wasn't going to be in plain sight. Neither here or there, I wasn't going to let that little detail discourage me from trying. There was a chance that someone might have left a paper trail.

My worst fear was whether Aidan had followed through with his promise to the mystical beast, Crius. If so, my chances of finding her would be nada. She'd be lost to me forever. God help them if so.

Something else had my mind baffled. Why hadn't they killed me? Whenever the Family finished with their lowliest subjects, they guilefully eliminated the nuisance. They exposed of my mom. So why would they keep me alive?

Considering Dom's theory, I seriously doubted they feared me. They were too powerful and imperious to be intimidated, even by their own creation, me, a genetically altered angel.

Last but not least, another mystery to throw into the brewing pot—the angel, Mustafa, who I shared DNA with, if he truly was evil did the apple fall far from the tree? Should I take Dom's advice and stay clear of this angel? On a more positive note, could this creature be an allied and help me find my daughter? On the other hand, if Dom was right about this angel's stance, did I want to take the risk? I shuddered over that concept. I was beginning to feel as if my life was heading for a collision.

Then that bar, Mephistz came to mind. Everything about that place screamed Déjà Vu—the music, its seductive lure, like an intoxicating drug. Yet strangely, Jeffery didn't hear a note. And that golden-eyed beauty, why the hostility? Maybe he recognized me. After all, I was a known felon. Though, I sensed my reputation had no bearing on his aversion toward me. Nonetheless, it didn't matter. I had no plans going back to that bar.

I bit the bottom of my lip, thinking. I thought later this morning, I'd take a trip down memory lane to Tangi. I'd like to check out the empty field where Aidan's castle once existed. I suppose dropping by Ms. Noel's was in order too. I hadn't seen my elderly friend since the trial. Maybe she could help. Ms. Noel had an uncanny way of knowing things which may lead me to my child.

⟶⠶✳⠶⟵

By eight o'clock that morning, I had dressed in a white tank top and jeans, slipped on my sneakers, and threw my backpack over my shoulder before heading downstairs. Even though my trip was no more than a couple of hours away, I made sure I had everything I needed: a few snacks, water and a GPS system on my cell. Last but not least—my trusty dagger, tucked in its sheath, strapped to my inner thigh. I never left home without it. I zipped downstairs to find Jeffery. I needed a favor, and I was sure he'd help me.

"I say *HELL* to the *NO!*" Jeff screeched.

"You mean to tell me you don't trust me to drive your Lincoln?"

"That's right! I don't let anyone drive my baby."

"Have you forgotten...I bought that damn car!" Hitting below the belt often didn't happen; however, sometimes a girl's gotta do what a girl's gotta do.

"Oh, now that's just tacky!" My unyielding friend slapped his hands on his hips, staring me down. "The only way youse gonna get my car is if I'm driving it. No further discussion." Jeffery displayed a full-blown prissy stance.

Hey, why am I fighting over his car? I thought. *I'd forgotten, I had money!* "Fine! Can you take me to the nearest car dealer? I'd like to buy my own stinking car."

Jeff rolled his eyes. "Miss Thang, do you even have a valid driver's license?" *Damn! Now Jeff's trying to be my father.*

"Well, Mister, Fancy Pants...I don't know!" I admitted. Then the fight halted, and we both burst into laughter.

After I renewed my license, Jeffery and I went directly to the nearest Ford dealership. With cash in hand, I paid the ear-to-ear-grinning salesman one fine price for one very special Mustang. This little sweet sports car fit me perfectly. I really didn't care for those obscene luxury cars, and somehow, me driving one didn't seem right, so I thought a cherry-red, rag-top Mustang would be the perfect middle ground.

Reluctantly, Jeffery didn't want me trailing off by myself and getting into trouble. Of course, he knew how to drive a good point into the ground. In fact, his words would ring in my ears forever.

"You got to be outta your ever love-n mind, bitch! You rubbing your nose where it doesn't belong at that haunted, vanishing-into-thin-air castle is plum stupid and insane!" Jeffery rambled in a fiery.

"I can handle it. I have to do this, and no, you can't go! I have to do this alone," I said with determination strapped to my hip.

"Fine! I don't care much for driving your brand-new Mustang any ole how!" My friend pouted like a five-year-old.

"Wait! You won't let me drive your oversize, slow-moving-heavy-priced-heap, Lincoln, but you expect me to let you drive my Mustang?"

"That's beside the point." Jeffery crossed his arms, refusing to see the correlation.

"It is the point! You're not driving my car with the top down in your hideous satin bold-pink suit, black bowtie, waving at all your high-society stuck-up friends."

"Now that's below the belt. I'll tell you like I tell Dom...youse just ain't got the flair for fashion like I do." Oh, Jeffery had flair, all right. I just wasn't sure about the fashion part.

"Jeff, my dear friend...no one can do flair like you!" I smiled with an impish grin.

"You know, that's right! Now may I take my friend for a test drive?"

Off I went down the wide open road with the top down, my hair to the wind, and the soothing sounds of the roaring engine purring beneath me. It felt as sweet as milk to a suckling baby. The taste of freedom on the highway couldn't have been more invigorating. Skipping out and finding adventure away from all my troubles seemed perfect for my ailment.

Nevertheless, I didn't have the luxury of leaving for long. There were too many loose ends in my life. Sooner than later, I had to confront them. Time wasn't on my side. I needed to investigate my imminent uncertainties.

I withdrew a pensive sigh, staring at the long stretch of highway. How did I wrap my head around all this? I felt so disconnected to a world I hardly believed to exist. And worse, I was a stranger to my own child. I wish I knew at least her name. It might make it more tangible. I blew out a frayed breath. I must be crazy, wanting to dive in blindfolded over a child's existence that hasn't been confirmed. This could be a wild goose chase. By the same token, I had to seek my undying hunch. I'd never forgive myself if I didn't try to find her. I couldn't move on until I found the truth. I had no choice.

This wasn't going to be easy. The Family wouldn't like me digging into their affairs. After all, they took great measure, sending Helen to deliver a message, hoping to convince me to back off. The Great Oz had spoken. I laughed to myself. Since when did I ever listen to any advice?

Where do I start? Vital records, maybe. Most birth records were public. My gut told me that mine had been destroyed. So where did I start looking? If my calculations served me right, I had the baby nine months later from the date that I first arrived at that hospital. I must have given birth during heavy sedation.

Whatever drugs they used, it had to have been very potent to have kept me oblivious to my growing belly. Any memories of a pregnancy or giving birth, I drew a blank. Nothing. How could a woman not know she'd given birth to her own baby? Anger began to brew.

That family, through their entire existence, has brought nothing but death—millions in their wake, and yet they continued to survive like a cockroach.

If they took my child, they will pay dearly. I would rein havoc on their miserable souls. I suppose that was the dark angel inside me.

———◆═❖═◆———

Pulling up to the main gate of the castle, my mouth fell open. This couldn't possibly be the right place. What once reminded me of a mighty fortress now lay before my eyes weathered—only a gate swinging half off its hinges, creaking back and forth. It was as if it had been adrift for years. Even the paved drive had eroded with potholes and cracks. How could something so magnanimous turn to ruin so fast? It had aged far past its time. This couldn't be natural. This had to be the work of dark magick. It reeked in the atmosphere.

As I inhaled the breath of caution, I drove past the entrance and followed the well-trodden path. When I reached the end of the driveway, I stopped abruptly. The most unnerving part of what lay before me was what I couldn't see. Nothing but a field of weeds—no evidence of the castle nor its foundation.

"This isn't possible!" I mumbled as I eased out of my car, combing the area for any unwanted visitors. The Family might not take too kindly to trespassers. I reached down to check my trusty dagger. Protection had become a necessary evil. I patted my dagger for reassurance.

I made my way over to the center of the vacant field where the castle once stood in its imposing glory. Golden broom-sedge and marigold flowers had grown amok up to my knees. No sign of life besides a squirrel or two stirring among the trees. I stood in the middle of a field of weeds, slowly twirling as in slow motion, taking in the whole panorama. I couldn't believe my eyes. "Talk about pulling up root." I grumbled.

I gasped as an icy breeze blew through my hair. This whole place reeked of eeriness. There was one more place I wanted to look at before I got the hell out of here. I waded through the high weeds trying to find the marked spot only by a few paces from the ancient oak tree that once shaded the rear of the castle. I kicked around hoping to stumble onto the same meddle knob, the door leading to the encrypted chamber. Surely it hadn't vanished too. I got down on my knees yanking up thorny vines in the spot that I swore where it was last seen. Nothing. I sat back on my heels as my eyes raked over the soil. It was gone like everything else. I gathered myself to my feet, peering the stand of trees. I wrapped my arms around my waist and got this terrible feeling of someone watching. Though no signs of anyone or anything stirring amid the brush, only a crow perched on a low branch of the oak, cackling. He seemed in distress as though my presence disturbed him. Oddly, I saw no other birds. A rush of chill bumps covered my arms.

Then it came to mind how terrified Sara became over the sight of a black raven. Looking back, there may have been some logic to her hysteria.

I couldn't get out of there fast enough—kicking up the dust as my tires sped away. Leaving that godforsaken place in my rearview mirror eased the tension in my lungs. I never wanted to look back ever again, but I couldn't cast it aside just yet. I had a child somewhere out there. Until then, I was stuck in this world of peculiarity.

Next, I was headed for Ms. Noel's place. I worried she might not be very welcoming. The last time we spoke, I'd stormed out of her house, leaving on not the best terms. And now I had a shady past. Folks were funny about people like me, especially violent felons. Even though I was innocent, in the eyes of many, I was a hardened criminal.

Despite my past, it would be nice to see her pleasant smile again. Setting aside my visit, uneasiness clenched my gut. The small house I once lived in only two doors down from Ms. Noel's was a sore spot for me. Too many bad memories beseeched my mind. It was the last place I'd seen Mom alive. Confronting my feelings over my mother's death wasn't something I wanted to face now. I felt responsible for her death. If I hadn't asked Aidan to give her that stupid dust, she might be alive today. A tear escaped, and I quickly wiped it away.

There were so many questions unanswered. Did Dom have the straight truth about Aidan's involvement in the Family's master plan? Should I have ever trusted Aidan? If he could leave out the crucial part about his longtime marriage to Sally, what else was he hiding? If the dead could talk what would Aidan say? Did I ever think Aidan truly loved me? I did. I saw it in his eyes. He revealed so much through those deep blues. At times it was like gazing into a crystal ball. Now the answer to that question would never come to light. Only he could clarify his true feelings. In the meantime, I had no other choice but to assume the worse. The worse being for the sake of his family, he turned his back on me. So what good was a love like that?

I questioned why he died a needless death. He was loyal to his family. Why would they dispose of him? Besides, the man knew how to take care of himself very well. He was an immortal. I was inclined to believe he'd walked this earth for many years, more than several lifetimes. I was sure that throughout his long life, he had encountered a few life-threatening altercations. He was quite skilled in surviving. So then, what caused his death? Good question. With any luck, the answer might lead me to our child, or whether the toddler existed.

Then I thought back to that morning at the cottage, Aidan's last words to me were like a riddle: "Believe only half of what you see and nothing of which you don't." What did it mean? I drew in a harsh breath. All these mysteries were bringing on a pounding headache. My brain lately did nothing but swim in a whirlwind of confusion.

Funny, the one good thing that came from all this—I no longer had those nightmares. When my freedom had been taken, the dreams stopped. Strange, I thought.

To be honest with myself, all these fairytales seemed nothing more than a twisted castle in the sky. Regardless, I had to keep my mind wide open. If I wanted to remain alive, I had to accept that there were dark forces surrounding me.

Therefore, if I was going to hold on to the last shred of sanity, I had to push aside my disconcerted feelings for Aidan, bury them so deep within that they could never resurface. I needed all my focus on finding my child. Aidan was gone forever. Things were different now. The old Stevie died with him. The new Stevie was less fragile, a change for the better. For the sake of our child, I had to keep my mind on the target. That meant steering clear of any distractions, including a moment down memory lane.

One fact I'd take to my death was that falling in love brought trouble. The heart was too treacherous. After all, it nearly got me killed.

Did I think I'd ever trust another man enough to let him close to me? Could destiny have someone else in store for me? I hoped not. Aidan shattered my heart.

———— ❧✳❧ ————

Soon I turned the corner onto St. Anne Street, a place I called home before Haven. I paused as my eyes fixed on my old house. It had aged so much. Vacant and withered, it appeared abandoned. The grass was overgrown and the paint had cracked and peeled over more than half the house. I slowly pulled up into the drive. I sat there with the car idling, biting my bottom lip. I had to go inside. I turned the car off, slipped the keys out of the ignition and flew the door open. If I hesitated one second, I feared I'd coward. My stomach churned as I approached the house. The steps were in need of repair. A couple of the boards had rotted in two. I eased around, stepping lightly until I reached the porch. I stood before the door. My hand paused barely touching the knob. Then I turned it. To my surprise, the door creaked opened. My heart hammered as I forced my feet to move past the threshold into the empty living-room. I glimpsed at the interior stairs. I swallowed hard. Before I realized it, I'd made my way up, to my mother's bedroom. I froze at the door. I raked over the room, barren, curtains torn half-way hanging from its rod. Between the cobwebs and dust, it appeared that no one had lived in the house for some time. All the furniture was gone. Perhaps the landlord died. Whatever happened, the charm and warmth had gone. Suddenly I felt stifled. I couldn't get out of there fast enough. I ran down the stairs and out the door as quick as my legs could carry me. I leaped in my car and put the car in reverse and floored it.

Not but two doors down, I stopped in front of Ms. Noel's house. I waited a moment as I clinched the stirring wheel, trying to pull myself together. I should've left well enough alone. I scoffed. That never was my forte. I eased out a long sigh.

I placed my hand over my eyes, squelching through the sun's glare, and there Ms. Noel stood, waiting for me. Some things never changed. When I reached the top steps, she instantly grabbed me up, like I was the prodigal child returning home. For the first time since my release, I let myself have a good cry. I suppose it was past-due. A flood of tears came as I lay in my old friend's embrace. I wept like a baby. Finally, after what seemed like forever, we both pulled ourselves together and went inside.

Once my eyes adjusted to the dim lighting, I became startled. I knew the house had aged, but *condemned* hadn't crossed my mind until now. As my eyes swept over the living space, it desperately needed renovations. I feared at any moment the house would come crumbling down right on top of us. When my eyes landed on Ms. Noel, she attempted to brush off my worries. "Oh, honey," she waved her hand. "Don't mind this old place. It's just like me. Some things are more droopy these days is all." She flashed a toothless smile. I didn't expect anything other than her upbeat attitude. Nothing seemed to rattle her constant smile.

From the lack of care for my dear friend and her deficient living conditions, I knew she couldn't stay here any longer. "Ms. Noel, pack your things. You're coming home with me," I announced.

"Oh, that's nonsense, Chile. I'm staying right here. I can't leave my home. My momma gave birth to me in this old house, and I'll die in it too." My elderly friend patted my arm. Hence, she stayed firm to her reasoning.

No way in hell that I could leave her in this shack. "Okay, I'll tell you what I'll do. How about you come with me for a little vacation while I make arrangements to repair your house?" I smiled brightly.

"Nah! That's too much trouble. Don't be frett-n over me. I'm just fine, baby."

"Ms. Noel, I can't leave you here. This house is unsafe. I can't believe the city hasn't condemned your house."

"Don't worry, Chile. I threw away that old yellow paper that some uniformed man posted on my front door. Stop your fret-n I have magick protecting my home. No city feller is gonna come and remove me."

Right at that moment, I spotted a bright-yellow sign kicked halfway under the couch. I picked it up and quickly scanned over the letter. I was right about my suspicions. The Board of Health had declared this house condemned.

"Ms. Noel, the city is demanding for you to leave your house in less than two weeks. If you don't come with me, you'll end up homeless. I can't let that happen."

"Baby, I can't turn my back on my home. This old house has watched over me since childbirth, and all my belongings I can't leave behind my crafts. Why some of my spirit books are traced all the way back to my ancestor, Marie." Ms. Noel appeared distraught.

"Don't worry. I'll hire someone to pack up all your possessions and move it all to my house."

Suddenly, Ms. Noel's shoulders slumped as she gave in to a defeated sigh. "I reckon I don't have a choice."

I felt terrible. Even worse, I feared this house collapsing on top of her. "Don't worry. I have more than enough room for you, and besides your favorite nephew lives with me too!" I squeezed her hand gently. Ms. Noel just nodded her head. "Let me call a moving company and get things rolling. Then I'm going to take you out to eat." I smiled, trying to hide my worries. "Are you eating, Ms. Noel?"

"I eats when I feel like it, but lately I haven't been feel-n much like cook-n. This house gets too hot, and I'm just ailing too much lately." Ms. Noel appeared in pretty bad shape. I suspected her meals were infrequent. She appeared a bit pale. I feared her health had waned a great bit since last I saw her. When we return to New Orleans, I planned to get her in to a doctor, the sooner the better. Since money wasn't an issue, I'd see to it she got the best medical care possible. It'd be nice to put this money to good use.

<hr />

When we returned home, there were swarms of family members, young and old, waiting for Ms. Noel's arrival. When Jeffery laid eyes on his great aunt, tears streamed down his cheeks. He had no idea how bad her living conditions had become. Supposedly, a local family member promised Jeffery to look after his aunt and swore she had things under control by frequently stopping by to check on Ms. Noel and running errands to the grocery store, even cooking for her as well. Come to find out, the money Jeffery had been sending only got as far as the kinfolk's pocket. Not one penny went to Ms. Noel. Upon discovering this, Jeff nearly spit nails, and I was right with him.

Evidently when I'd called home to let the guys know that Ms. Noel would be staying with us for a bit. Jeffery and Dom contacted a few of the family members. Then those folks called other family members, and before we knew it, our yard and home swarmed with people from all over the state, an overdue family reunion.

Dom and Jeffery went all-out with decorated tables set outside in the lovely garden, filled with platefuls of every delicious dish. Many brought gifts and their own special dishes as well. There were at least ten different sides of Southern fried chicken from various family members. Plus, there were hot-water cornbread, collard greens, potato salad, mustard greens, macaroni and cheese, corn on the cob, barbecued ribs dripping in spicy sauce, mudbugs, catfish, shrimp gumbo, and desserts out of this world—a feast for a queen, indeed. But the best part of all was watching Ms. Noel's face gleam with pure happiness.

It was *her* special day. Dom seated her at the head of the main table as the queen she deserved to be, and everyone gathered around her with hugs and kisses, welcoming her home. I stood back, quiet to myself as I witnessed the love and devotion everyone expressed for this wonderful lady. I'd never seen so many smiles and tears all in one place at the same time. There wasn't a dry eye in the house, including mine too. I felt blessed to be part of this happy event.

Even with all this wonderful joy, a part of me felt sorrow. A sense of loss tugged at my heart—the loss of my parents, a lost love, and even a child I'd never cradled. A yearning began to stir within me. I found myself craving the soft touch of my baby, a child stolen, taken against my will. My eyes brimmed with tears, and I pushed them back. "No!" I said to myself. "I won't do this today." Today belonged to Ms. Noel and her family. My day would come, just not today.

In the morning, I planned to call around and see about getting Ms. Noel in to see a physician. With a doctor's care and Dom putting her on a healthy diet, she'd be as good as new in no time at all. Another thing I should add to the list was Jeffery's fashion designer. I imagine his aunt could use some new garments as well. I wanted to roll out the red carpet for this sweet lady, give her the best of everything.

<hr />

That late evening, after everyone had gone, Ms. Noel finally said her good nights to everyone and went to bed in one of the guest rooms downstairs that we had planned on making a permanent bedroom for her.

After I had washed the last dish, Jeffery caught me off guard. In one swift sweep, he'd grabbed me up and hugged me so tight he nearly knocked the wind out of me. As he held me, he spoke through choked tears. "Thank you so much for bringing my aunt home." He sniffled. "You don't know how long I've been trying to get her to come live with me. No matter what you say, once my aunt gets a notion in her head, you can't talk her into noth-n!" The genuine gratitude in Jeffery's tearful eyes touched me.

"Don't beat yourself up, Jeff. She's here now. I'm going to get her in to see a doctor tomorrow. She's going to get the best care money can buy. With Dom's cooking, your aunt will be as good as new." I gave my friend a tight squeeze.

"Stevie, thank you."

"For what?"

"If it hadn't been for you, I wouldn't have this sweet life I have now. It's because of your generosity that I don't have to worry about my aunt's care. I appreciate everything, and I love you, and gurrrlfriend I never say noth-n I don't mean. Just like I won't hold it against you that you're not fabulous and black like me, of course." Jeffery teased as he did his twirl just like a high-dollar model.

I rolled my eyes and laughed. That's my Jeffery. "Of course." I smiled brightly. "To be honest, I'm not the one you should be thanking." I hesitated. "It's Aidan who is responsible for all this extravagance." I shrugged my shoulder, feeling a little sad. "I suppose that's one good deed he did for us."

"I miss him, you know." Jeffery paused. "Do you?"

I withdrew a long sigh and ran my fingers through my hair. "The Aidan before the betrayal, I do." I glanced down at my feet, trying to collect my raw emotions. "There are times I want to smack him hard for deceiving me. Then there are times I wish I could feel the comfort of his arms once more. He had a way of making me feel safe and secure." I felt a knot in my throat surfacing. "Still, even that was a lie," I said in a solemn voice.

"I believe he loved you as much as he possibly could love anyone. With that said, even when a person loves you, it doesn't mean they is good for you. With Mr. Aidan, raised in that no-count family, they screwed up his mofo mind." Jeffery shook his head.

"What happened to him?"

"Gurrrl, you don't know?" Jeffery's eyes rounded to saucers.

"Know what?"

"One could say he finally flew over the coo-coo's nest."

"Why do you say that?" instantly, I felt the sensation of a spider crawling up my back.

He killed his parents, child!"

I think my heart needed a jump-start. "W-w-what?"

"Gurrrl, his parents were monsters—torturing kittens sorta shit. He snapped."

"I had no idea!" I stood as if shot and waiting to fall.

"Yeah, he was only twelve years old. That's some fucked-up shit." Jeffery shook his head.

"No shit!" I just froze. I knew my mom had her own demons, but damn.

"Anyway, I believe the Family brushed it under the rug, and his uncle took over raising Aidan and his sister."

"I'm not sure that's any better," I said.

"I know that's right! That uncle of his is full of all kinds of black juju." Jeffery crossed his arms.

"When did you find this out?" I leaned against the counter.

"I didn't knows about it until that Halloween night. It was earlier that evening when I overheard Aidan and his uncle in a heated argument. I think his uncle was holding the double murder of his parents over his head, maybe blackmailing him."

"Wow!" I looked away, disgusted by the infamy of that family. Then a thought hit me like a baseball bat across the back of my head. I glanced back at Jeffery. "Do you think their fight might have a correlation to my getting framed and Aidan's death?"

Jeffery shrugged. "With that family honeychile, anything is possible."

"Don't I know that!" I shivered over all the possibilities.

"Gurrrl it's nonsense to try to figure those mofo folks out. Forget them! It's the past, and Aidan's gone. There's love out there for youse. Now you needs to get out there and find it!"

"I don't know. I just don't believe it's for me." I shrugged.

"Don't be stupid! You're young and beautiful. You have this really huge heart, and I think youse deserve to have true love, the sort of love that wiggles your toes. Your one true love who will lay his mofo-n life down for you. That's the love I'm talk-n about," Jeffery said with attitude, snapping his finger.

"When you find that kind of love, let me know." I grimaced. "I don't put much stock in that soul mate stuff. Look at my parents. My father's love for my mother cost him his life. If that's love, then I say no, thank you. And look what love has cost me. Three years in a mental institution for murders I didn't commit. And that's not the worse part. Love may have caused me the loss of my child. I have no clue whether she's alive or dead." I stopped. I had to put a cork in my brewing emotions. It was wearing me down something fierce. I felt her spirit pulling at me every waking minute. I thought my heart was going to rip in two. My face felt heated. I took a deep breath, slowing my heart rate down along with my temper. "Jeffery... love for a man has too high of a price for me to risk. I don't have anything else to give!" I sternly announced.

"Chile, I feel your pain"—Jeffery shook his finger—"but one of these days, you're going to want to get back on that horse. I promise you, and this time, it's going to be the real mofo-n deal." Jeffery's eyes twinkled.

The Promise

Exhausted from the day, when my head hit the pillow, sleep came in only minutes. It wasn't until 2:00 a.m. I'd awaken from a stir at the end of my bed. My heavy eyes slowly opened as I spotted Ms. Noel sitting down at my feet. Startled, I sat up, gasping. I rushed, asking, "What's wrong?" alarm flooded my hazy mind.

"Oh, baby, I couldn't be better. I want to thank you for today. It was very kind of you to bring me to my family."

"Ms. Noel, it's not necessary to thank me. Let me help you back to your room. You need your rest."

"Nah! Catin, (pretty girl) you don't worry your pretty little head about me. I'm gonna be just fine. In a minute I'm going home, but before I leave, I want to tell you something."

A sudden spurt of panic jolted me. What did she mean she was going home? She must be delirious, I thought. I strained my eyes from the faint moonlight wafting through the window. I could see only a thin outline of Ms. Noel in her nightgown, "remember, your home is with us now," I said, getting this eerie dread.

"No, I don't mean this home, baby. I'm talk-n about my home upstairs."

Upstairs? Now I knew something was off. "Ms. Noel, we are upstairs. You climbed the stairs to my room." I started to reach for the light, but something stopped me.

"Now you need to listen to me because I don't have long before they come for me," she whispered in a low voice. My brows puckered, baffled. "There's a young man with gold eyes."

"What?" I stared at her, wondering if I might be dreaming.

"Hush, baby, listen," Ms. Noel scolded me.

Okay. I'll hear her out, and then I am calling 911.

"The gold-eyed man came to me in a dream. He wants me to tell you to seek him out. He can help you find your baby, honey."

My throat went dry. How did she know about my child? Then again, Ms. Noel had an uncanny ability of knowing a person's deepest secrets. "Wait! How do— " Ms. Noel didn't let me finish as she continued.

"He saved your life that night at that gin joint with the strange name. Jeffery and you had stepped into a world that only few have witnessed. The gold-eyed man stepped in to protect you both. Stay close to him. He will guide you through your journey."

"I don't understand?" my eyes blinked with incredulity.

"Baby, I have to go now. They're calling me. Take care of that nephew of mine. Give him my love. I love you too, baby."

"Wait! Ms. Noel. Let me help you to bed." I slipped from the covers and slid out of bed. When I turned back, I realized I was alone. The end of my bed was empty. "Ms. Noel!" I called out, mystified. Quickly, I flipped my bedside lamp on. The light shed its glow around the room, but I saw no sign of a living soul. Chills tickled my neck. I flopped back down on my bed, releasing a nervous giggle. Could I have been dreaming?

With no warning, an icy breeze fluttered through my hair. I wrapped my arms around my waist as I rushed to close the window, yet to my surprise, I found it was shut close.

Before I had a chance to digest what had happened, I heard bloodcurdling screams coming from downstairs. It was Jeffery! I panicked. With no time to consider, I fled downstairs, taking two steps at a time, following the distressed cries. As I reached the guest room, I stopped. There stood Dom at the bedside of Ms. Noel, consoling Jeffery as he lay over his aunt's limp body. She had died in her sleep. Right away I went to Dom's side to help with Jeffery. At this point, we couldn't do anything for her. Ms. Noel was gone.

Just seeing the pain in Jeffery's eyes broke my heart, and I felt the sting of tears myself, but I held mine back. Right now Jeffery needed our strength, and breaking down wouldn't do anyone any good. Even still, I felt stun. The death of Ms. Noel didn't feel real. Only moments ago, she had been talking to me.

The coroner announced Ms. Noel's death at 1:55 a.m. How could that be possible? She had awakened me at 2:00 a.m. Had I been speaking to Ms. Noel's ghost? I shivered. Maybe I should keep this to myself. I might've been dreaming. A very vivid dream, if so.

Since the passing of Ms. Noel, Jeffery wasn't handling it very well. His relentless weeping kept Dom busy. Her death had heartbroken all of us, but it hit Jeffery the hardest. I took it upon myself to handle the funeral arrangements. For Jeffery and the family, I wanted nothing but the best, and the best meant the traditional New Orleans—jazz funeral.

Down here, folks did things in a large way. I'd never seen a procession where the grieving family danced to a lively band parading down the streets of the city. Some attending came dressed in bright colors of gold and purple with feathered hats. Men in top hats marched alongside a glitzy horse and buggy, carrying the coffin.

Jeffery and Dom were at the head of the march as the line of family members and friends went back as far as a mile. Many came from all over the state, from people Ms. Noel treated with her special herbs to folks she'd greeted in passing.

Watching Jeffery fall apart had tugged heavily on my heart. I knew he blamed himself for his aunt's death. I wanted to comfort my dear friend and reassure him it was her time to go. Maybe after things settle, I should tell him about my visit with Ms. Noel. I think it might help Jeffery deal with his loss. After all, she did give me a message for him. I should honor her last wishes.

The funeral had been quite emotional, not a dry-eye throughout the day. Poor Jeffery was a broken mess. It took several of us peeling him off his aunt's coffin before they dropped her into the ground. Jeffery's deep belly cries nearly ripped my heart out. I'd never seen him so distraught. Dom had the patience of an angel. He never left his partner's side.

After the procession, folks came to the house. A few family members while eating some of Dom's famous deserts told stories about Ms. Noel. I gathered by the pleasant tales, she was a well-loved woman by everyone. It had been a sad day and yet, a day of celebration.

⚬⟶⟶❈⟵⟵⚬

It was twelve o'clock midnight, and only a few folks were stirring about on Bourbon Street. Strange, I thought. The city that never slept must be taking a nap.

I stood in front of the neon sign that read, *Mephistz.* The very same bar Jeffery and I were abruptly asked to leave. I must've lost my mind because here I stood once more, glutton for punishment. Stupid, I knew. I was about to make the same dimwitted mistake, only this time I had a completely different purpose. Tonight had nothing to do with partying. Rather, I came to follow through with a promise I'd made to a dying friend or, should I say, dead. I shivered. But that wasn't my only reason. If this stranger with the gold-eyes had any information leading me to my child, I had to take my chances.

I looked down at my hands. They were trembling. Quickly I hid them behind my back. With these tight satin leggings and a clingy blouse I poured my body into, I didn't have any hiding spots. Aside from my uneasiness about this bar, I sensed something different about this golden-green-eyed man. In my short life, I'd been in the face of some dark-hearted sons of bitches, but this one had me quite intrigued.

"Okay," I said to myself. "On the count of three."

When I entered the bar, it hadn't changed any since Jeffery and my last visit. Nothing out of the ordinary. Even though the joint was empty of patrons, a thick cloud of smoke like fog wafted in the air, coupled with a pungent scent of sweat and liquor. Typical dive, I reasoned.

I made my way over to the bar. An older man bartending came over to me. "What's your poison, little lady?" He flashed a smile. I returned the kind greeting with a curt smile. I tried to mask my jitters, though I got the feeling this guy saw through my charade. "Just Coke tonight. Thanks," I shouted over the music. He tossed another lopsided grin.

"You were here the other night? Where's your friend?" He spoke with a whistle, indicating he wore dentures.

"He's home. I came alone."

"Oh, I see." The bartender seemed suspicious as he lazily popped the cap and handed the Coke to me, still in the bottle.

"What? A girl can't go to a bar alone?" I squirmed a bit.

The server smiled back with a glint in his eyes. "Depends," he said with an impish grin.

"Depends on what?" I challenged, trying to keep my cool.

"Depends on what you're looking for." To me, his eyes seemed too intense for a man his age. "I say you're here on business by that Coke you're drinking." The bartender picked up another glass, wiping it spotless with a white cloth.

"You are a smart man. I do have business. In fact, I'm looking for a man about six foot five, blonde hair to his shoulders, late twenties, golden eyes, nice looking. Uh...you know." I surprised myself on how I popped off details about the dude's appearance.

"He was here that night." I took a quick swig of my Coke, trying to play it cool.

"And what would a nice lady like you want with this gentleman?" The server continued wiping the glass.

"Isn't it obvious?" I threw the question back at him. I didn't feel like explaining myself, so I tried to pull it off like I had the hots for the guy.

He laid his glass down, flipped the towel over his shoulder, and looked me straight in the eye. "Nah, that ain't it." Then the corner of his mouth tipped slightly upward. "Not that he wouldn't be flattered by your offer." He shot a knowing wink.

This guy knew how to get a rise. "What's wrong? Is your friend afraid of a little old girl?" Unpredictably, the bartender's dull eyes narrowed. Abruptly, I felt the heat of his glint, I dropped my gaze. Though when I raised my eyes to meet his, my breath lodged in my throat. It was as though a veil had lifted and—poof— the golden-eyed dude stood in the bartender's place. My brows shot up with astonishment. "Do you make a habit of disguising yourself, or is the old gizzard really you?"

Please say no! Please say no! Okay, I was having a weak moment. I had to admit the golden-green-eyed guy had some serious eye candy going on and way too hot to be a dirty old fart.

"Beautiful, for you, any time." He flashed his pearly whites. A tingle washed over me. I had to stay focused. As stately as he might be, I refused to become ensnared again by a man, so I ignored my weakness. "Someone sent me here, saying you could help."

"Really. Like what sort of help?" He leaned over the bar, inching closer to me. I pulled my shoulders back, distancing myself.

"I need to find someone."

"Look, Freckles that sounds like a job for the police." He rose back up and began wiping the same glass with a snarl of irritation across his face.

"The police won't help."

He suddenly stopped rubbing the damn glass as our eyes locked. "Why is that?" His voice was as grave as his eyes were piercing.

"Because I need to infiltrate the Illuminati," I dropped in his lap.

He leaned in again, only closer, dropping both the glass and towel. "What could that family have of yours that you're willing to lose your life over?" All the flirting went out the door, and an icy stillness seized the air.

At this point, no need to beat around the bush; either he was willing to help or not, so I blurted it out. "My child." I stared back at him as a faint glint of shock took hold of the stranger.

He stood frozen. Then suddenly he hurled a glass across the room, shattering it against the wall. Shards flew from the explosion. I flinched from his sudden reaction. Coming here might've been a mistake.

"Who fucking sent you?" He demanded.

I thought for sure he'd be hurling me next. "Ms. Noel, my friend." I swallowed hard.

Although agitated, he seemed to simmer down some. "Did she? How is Ms. Noel?" He asked as he ran his hand through his thick hair.

"She died. We buried her only a few days ago," I replied, not taking my eyes off him.

"I'm sorry to hear that. She was a good woman." He went back to wiping a glass, only more vigorously. "However, she was wrong." He still continued polishing the glass.

"Wrong about what?" I said.

He looked up at me with exasperation strong in his eyes. "There's nothing you can do. The child is dead."

His cruel words cut me down to the bone. I narrowed my eyes. "Sorry to have bothered you, whatever your name is." I was wasting my breath. I turned to leave.

"Val," he said to my back. "Short for Valor. And you are?"

I faced him and said, "Stevie."

"Stevie, where is the father?"

"Dead," I said flatly.

"How did he die?"

"I don't know." I stood tense.

"Did the Illuminati kill him?"

"Perhaps."

"Were you married to him, or was he just a boyfriend?" Strange that he'd ask such a personal question. Why would he care?

"You want the truth?"

"Yeah, I do." He appeared more than curious.

"The father was neither."

His brow arched. "Neither? You don't look the type for a one-night stand."

I huffed. "Look, mister, either you'll help me or not. I don't see where it's your business about my love life."

"Does your deceased lover have a name?"

"Yes."

He glared at me, waiting for me to say.

I rolled my eyes. "Aidan Bane De Pont."

The golden-eyed man smirked. "I've heard of him. He's part of the Illuminati family."

"Yes."

"And this child of yours is Illuminati?"

Now my temper started to surface. "No! The child is mine. I gave birth to her, not that goddamn family!" I fired back in my defense.

"Okay, okay! I get it." He stuck his palms up in defense. "You're a mom, and you want your child back."

"Are you going to help me or not?" I held my breath.

"Hmm...let me think about it." He paused as though he was running it through his head. "Yeah, about that...no way in hell! There's nothing in this universe that can penetrate the forces of that forsaken occult. The child is as good as dead, and the sooner you face that fact, as harsh as it seems, the better off you are and everyone around you."

Talk about blunt! "Listen! I didn't come here to get a lecture, you jackass! No one knows what that family is capable of doing better than me. Whether you help me or not, I'm getting my child back! Got it!" I had my fist white knuckled to my side, ready to start swinging, but instead, the ground started shaking underneath our feet, and our argument halted. When our eyes exchanged, there was a mirrored shock. Abruptly losing control of my footing, my feet flew out from under me. It happened so fast I had no time to catch my balance. Expecting a sharp pain shooting up my backside from the hard concrete floor; instead, I found myself nicely tucked against the gold-eyed man's chest as he held me steady. The rumbling ceased, but my heart picked up where the vibrating floor had stopped. For a moment, I felt flustered. When our eyes locked, he had a curious gleam in his unusual eyes. "That was you!" He whispered. "What the fuck are you?"

Then I remembered his little masquerading trick and his swift speed rescuing me from the fall. "I could ask you the same thing?" I threw back at him. The speckles in his golden eyes shimmered, stealing my breath away. I was putty in his grasp. Crap! *Weak much?*

Men! You Can't Beat Them Up, or Can You?

WHAT A FREAKING jerk! I spilled my heart out to him, practically begging for his help, and all he could say was "'Get out!" No explanation. Nothing! And he couldn't just ask me politely. Compared to last time, he'd been as sweet as a porcupine, which was a step up to this. To make matters worse, he had the nerve to carry me out and drop me dead center on my ass on the sidewalk. And his last words, "Go home, Freckles. I told you not to come back." He then hailed a cab and left me there as he disappeared back into his damn bar. I didn't understand why Ms. Noel sent me to him? She was wrong about this jackass. There was nothing nice about him. If you called egotistically self-absorbed and arrogant nice, then I'd pass on this one. Forget him! I didn't need his lousy help anyhow.

⟶⟶✳⟵⟵

That following week, we did our best to get back to our usual routine. Of course, the whole house continued to mourn over the loss of Ms. Noel.

As the next week passed, Dom kept us fed and did everything he could to comfort his longtime partner of twenty-plus years. It touched me seeing how Dom lovingly cared for Jeffery in his time of grievance. Family support played a huge part in getting over the hurdle of a deceased loved one. In time, the pain of loss would ease for Jeff. Ms. Noel would've wanted it that way too.

In the meantime, I decided to do some of my own detective work. Of course, I kept it on the lowdown. If Dom and Jeffery caught wind of my plans, they'd lock me up in the wine cellar and throw the key away or, even worse, insist on coming with me? Sweet, but not smart. I had to do this all by myself.

Haven Hospital, I figured, would be my best place to begin. Like most hospitals, a filing system was a given. I assumed Haven attained records of their patients as well, and with any luck, they had a file stashed away of my child's birth. It may be a mission impossible, but it was my only shot.

I gave in to a bleak feeling. Would the Family be careless enough to trust Haven with valuable files? Chances were slim. There might be a clue—anything that could lead me to the whereabouts of my child.

Breaking into Haven was a cinch. The hospital never kept up with modern times by upgrading to computers. They stored everything in a hard copy. That meant any old sap with a little motivation could get easy access to their archive.

I had a solid plan on how to get my hands on that file too. Well, sorta solid. At least when I played it out in my head, it seemed rational.

<hr />

When 1:00 a.m. rolled around, I headed down to a popular spot. A speakeasy, New Orleanians' slang for bar, located in the Upper Ninth Ward district. A dive, I wouldn't take even the infamous, Jack the Ripper. No worry though. I could handle myself. If I could survive the iniquity of the Illuminati, anything else was a piece of cake.

I discovered this place during my stay at Haven. Back then, it didn't mean anything to me, but now, it might just be what the doctor ordered. I overheard a couple of orderlies talking about a bar they hung out at down at the Bywater area, south of the Mississippi River. After listening to the orderlies' lewd chats,

I figured it must be a sleazy dive. Judging by their character, I couldn't imagine anything else.

I overheard one particular fat cat bragging about being a regular. Seeing that it was a Saturday night, with any luck, the bastard might be getting his jollies off at this dive tonight. Since he worked at the hospital, he'd have easy access to the office, meaning he could steal my file. I thought if I sweetened the deal with a generous incentive, it might motivate him. I heard he had a gambling problem and was hard up for cash. It sounded insane, but dangling the rabbit in front of this fat son of a bitch just might be my ticket. It was a long shot. Those employed at Haven were sadistic and twisted just like their prototype, the Illuminati, but if I could appeal to the orderly's greed, he might be inclined to help. After all, money was the root of all evil. This creep was greedy and evil. He should play right into my hands.

When I saw the weathered sign hanging from a rusty chain, the words were barely legible. It read: The Devil's Den. I thought, how fitting. There were dives and then there were *dives*. For safety reasons, I didn't want to become conspicuous. To hide the fact that I was a girl, I found an old cap and a sweatshirt that should've been thrown out long before now. I even went as far as tying down my boobs, making me appear flat-chested and less curvy. Since I was sweating like a pig under all this clothing on the hottest night of the year, my stench should repel any admirers.

I strolled in like I owned the place, yet, vile was rising up in my throat as I nodded tostrangers—no one knew the better. The joint spilled over with crowded bodies—shoulder to shoulder with all sorts of creepy. Personal space at this dive didn't exist. Stepping into New Orleans nightlife had its risk, but this rat-infested bar took front and center. My eyes raked over the place. Talk about strange bedfellows. The smell was different here than at Gold-Eyes' bar. The stench of liquor, sweat, and something else—sex—filled my senses. Yuck! I thought.

There were tables centered around a lit stage and a silver pole right in the middle of it with a nude girl spread-eagled, begging for tips. On the other side, there were more intimate settings behind sheer curtains, providing obscurity. I was right. It was a strip joint. I noticed that all the eyes were glued to the nude women, which meant less attention on me. Now all I had to do was find my guy.

I cleared my throat, hoping my voice didn't sound too high-pitched. With caution, I approached the guy behind the bar. I figured if anyone knew this cat, the bartender would. I leaned over the counter, standing on my tippy-toes, waving down the server. I didn't want to shout out the name. I preferred the element of surprise. "Hey do you know Joe Harrell?" I asked.

"What's it to you?" he smacked his gum, eyeing me suspiciously. Why did all bartenders ask the same questions? Did they learn this at Bartending School?

"It's worth a little something, something." I flashed an impish grin, slipping him a crisp hundred-dollar bill. The bartender eyed the cash, then he looked me straight in the eyes. The man wasn't much to look at, but by his husky size, I summed him up as someone not to piss off.

He took the money and nodded toward the back at the last curtain in the far corner. "Joe's over there. One of our girls is with him. You're welcome to join him." The bartender grinned, showing his rotten teeth. My lips curled in disgust. I didn't even bother with a reply.

I craned my neck to spot the back of the lounge. The lighting, like every other bar, was dim and smoky. Pulling myself off the bar, I etched my way through the sordid crowd. With each step, I kept running ideas through my brain of other options than this one. Hence, I coming up empty-handed. Looked like I had no other choice. I drew in a biting sigh.

When I reached the last cubby, I jerked the curtains open. Sure enough, there he lay, half-naked with a young girl that could've been my younger sister—a minor, I thought. My guess, the kid had to have been no more then sixteen.

It was obvious that I'd interrupted something by the glower on his face. "Hello, Joe! Remember me?" I sneered, oozing sarcasm. The orderly pulled himself up into a sitting position, grunting like a stuffed pig.

He glimpsed up at the half-naked girl as she gathered what little clothing she possessed, covering her body. "Honey, why don't you go get me a cold one?" he croaked in a deep throaty voice as he reached over and slapped her ass. I took one look at the scared girl, and right then, I wanted to castrate the dirty perv.

"Hey! I know you!" His beady eyes slithered over me from head to toe. Creepy bumps whittled up my spine. "Fancy see-n you here. You must've missed Old Joe. You and me had some good times." He winked. "Doubt you remember. You were fucked-up." He grinned, flashing his nasty teeth.

Then it hit me. The bastard had his way with me during my drug-induced stay at Haven. A sudden spurt of rage coursed through my veins. Instinct took over as I flew into that disgusting animal with murderous eyes. His sick laughter echoed in my ears. It reminded me of a pig's gurgling after a throat slashing. Without thinking, I struck him hard with my fist, pounding his face over and over. I got a few good licks in before he bounced me off of him like a rubber ball, slamming me into the brick wall.

He snarled, leaning to the side, spitting out blood. "You need some stroking?"

At that moment, I wanted nothing more than to cut his testicles off and cram them down his throat. I needed to stop this fiend from hurting anymore girls. Without hesitation, I lunged for his throat with my dagger in my hand. The pig acted faster than I'd expected. Quickly he dodged my deadly swing as he yapped, "You stupid bitch!" His face had gone blood-red. "I tell you what!" the pig gritted his teeth. "I'll give you a little reminder of the fun we had back at your old home, Haven."

Without delay, he grabbed me, thrusting me down on the dirty floor, my dagger went flying out of my hand as his body fell on top of me crushing my lungs. If I didn't get this cow off me, I'd suffocate. That wasn't the worse; every raucous part of his body pressed against me. I wanted to vomit but I feared I'd aspirate. Shit!

Suddenly I felt a stinging blow to my jaw. It felt like he'd dislocated my chin. Dammit, that hurt! As the blows kept coming, blood spread over my face. My mind started to become fuzzy with each iron-clad blow.

Then he changed his position, and in one strong jerk, he started ripping my clothes off! I screamed, yet no one came to my aid. I cursed him as hard as I fought back. I took some sick pleasure knowing that this time I wasn't easy pickings.

In a last-ditch effort, I took my thumbs and pressed hard into his eye sockets. I tried slamming them back into his pea-sized brain. His face became contorted in agony as he howled a string of curses. Abruptly, he jerked back off me for a brief second and that was all I needed. Swiftly I scrambled for my dagger, only a few inches from my reach. I clasped my fingers around the hilt and dove for his jugular.

Unexpectedly, the orderly had fallen backward. Not wasting a moment, I flew to my feet, lunging for that animal's throat once more. Until that pig bled out onto the floor, I had no intention of stopping.

Without warning, my body was propelled off my feet. Someone had hold of my pants, dangling me in midair. "What the fu—!" My eyes fell upon the last person I'd expected to see—Gold-Eyes?

"Put me down!" I ordered. I could hear in the background that filthy pig screaming his lies.

"I didn't touch her! That crazy bitch tried to kill me!" He shouted into the crowd that had gathered around, but the one voice who caught my attention was the one holding me back.

"Put me down! That pathetic swine deserves to die." I growled.

"Not until you simmer down, girl." Gold-Eyes spoke with authority.

"Simmer down?" I raged. "That disgusting worm tried to rape me! You freaking simmer down!" I screamed at him while he continued holding me captive. With an exasperating exhale, my captor, in one clean sweep, disarmed me, taking my knife away, and as if I was a feed sack, he threw me over his stalwart shoulder. I pounded his back and kicked, cursing him all the while, but he made no attempt to free me. "I swear you're next if you don't let me at that fat brute!" I cursed through gritted teeth. He ignored my threats as my defiance didn't faze him. His silence infuriated me.

It was not until I reached some unknown apartment on the top floor above the dude's bar did he release me. "Sit down over there on the couch." He barked at me as he sat me down in the middle of what I assumed was his pad. By then I didn't have any more strength to fight, so I flopped down on his leather couch. It felt cool to my back, which seemed to calm me.

He disappeared to the back, returning a few minutes later with an ice pack and other more interesting items. My eyes went straight for the shot glass and the Jack Daniel's in his other hand. Without a word, he filled the small glass to the brim and handed it to me. I gladly accepted the gold liquid. I downed the whole thing in one gulp. It burned like hell going down, but the warmth soon spread to my toes. I laid the glass down with a bang on his coffee table.

Apart from my raw throat, I uttered, "More!" I wiped the liquor off my mouth with my arm sleeve. Without a word, he grabbed the empty glass and poured another full shot and handed it back to me. "Thanks," I choked out, giving him a quick glimpse. Gold-Eyes grabbed a kitchen chair, dropping in front of the coffee table, directly facing me. In one stride, he swung his long leg over the chair and sat backward. He crossed his arms over the back of the chair and focused his attention on me. It was then he'd broken his silence. "What happened back there?" He asked in a placid voice.

I leaned back, placing the ice pack on my face. I winced from the sting. Then I shot the stranger a dark smoldering look and said. "Why do you care?" I still felt a tinge of anger.

Apparently, my comeback struck a nerve. "Look, you little hellcat! You nearly got yourself killed. That place is bad news."

"I can handle myself," I snapped, battened down with woebegone shame.

"I see that." He paused. "What's a nice schoolgirl like you going out to a roadhouse full of depraved creatures, who'd rather eat you, than look at you?" His eyes seemed haunted by some inner anxiety.

"Look! This is my problem. Besides, the last time I asked for your help, you dropped my ass on the sidewalk and walked away. Why concern yourself now?" I tossed him a bold glare.

"Freckles, you're not as tough as you think." He didn't hold back the ire in his tone.

I didn't have time for any lectures. I jumped to my feet too quickly and stumbled to my feet. The liquor rushed to my head, causing the room to spin. Crap! I'd forgotten that I'd not eaten today. My nervous stomach had been churning something fierce all day. Suddenly I needed to leave. I raised the back of my hand to my forehead, feeling sick. "It's late. I'm going home." I slurred my words as I staggered to the door. Gold-Eyes gently grabbed my arm, pulling me back in before I reached the door, or did he catch me before I fell? My mind was a bit muffled.

"It's nearly two in the morning," he said. "Sleep in my bed. I'll take the couch." He smiled but it didn't touch his eyes.

That morning I'd awakened to a throbbing headache and stiff muscles. I couldn't tell which hurt the most, my face or my head. Right away I picked up the aroma of bacon. I could hear the sizzling. I thought, how strange. When was the last that I'd heard

Dom cooking from downstairs? Then my memories slammed into my brain. Oh crap! I was at that bartender's apartment and in his bed half-naked. Startled, I jumped up, landing on my feet, yet wobbly. The liquor from last night still lingered. Talk about a cheap drunk. I never was much for holding my liquor, not that I'd had many nights boozing it up. Obviously, I'd passed out. I noticed my change of clothing, or lack of. The Band-Aid wrap had been removed along with my torn sweatshirt and jeans. Now draped over my body was a jersey shirt that definitely wasn't mine. It hung on me like a curtain, and it had some sports team across the front with a number on the back. Yuck! I hated sports.

I peered through the glass doors and spotted a blanket and a pillow lying on the couch. The dude must've slept there last night. Whew! I took a breath. That made me feel a little better, although I wasn't too sure how I felt about him undressing me.

I opened the French doors and entered into the small living room. The apartment was smaller than my bedroom. It screamed "man cave," but it had its charm.

I heard a cheerful voice from the kitchen. "Good morning!" I followed his voice and met his stunning smile around the corner in a very small kitchen. It seemed he had prepared breakfast for the two of us. My eyebrow arched in question. Why the fuss? Neither one of us even liked each other.

"Did you sleep well?" He flashed a lopsided smile, pulling me away from my thoughts. A scowl crossed my face. I wished he wouldn't do that. I hated dimpled smiles, and his teeth were too straight. Shouldn't he be doing this for his girlfriend?

"I need to get home. Where's your phone? I need to call a cab." I sounded aloof. What was the point with the nicey nice?

"I'll take you home, but first you need to eat."

I made a sour face.

"Come on! I cooked all this food. The least you can do is try to eat." His brows creased like I'd hurt his feelings. Damn! Why did he have to be so sweet?

"Okay," I begrudgingly agreed. "I'm not big on breakfast. Got anymore Jack Daniel's? Got a bad hangover." I tipped my shoulder upward in a shrug. Geez! He didn't have to stand there gaping. WTF?

⎯⎯⎯⎯•⊱✳⊰•⎯⎯⎯⎯

When we sat down at the small kitchen table, it felt too intimate. The breakfast table only seated two places, and our knees kept brushing against one another.

I suppose he was trying to be a courteous host. He even went as far as setting two aspirins by my plate and a glass of OJ. Apparently, his guest didn't get alcohol for breakfast. Bummer!

Halfway through the eggs and bacon came the annoying questions. "So, how did you know Ms. Noel?" He asked, making light conversation.

"She was my neighbor back in Tangi," I said, still looking at my plate, playing more with my food than eating it. I tried to avoid eye contact. His eyes were too penetrating, which only made my headache worse. Besides, I didn't want to get chummy. Keeping my guard up meant no mess.

"I'm sorry to hear about her passing." He appeared genuine.

"Yeah, it sucks." I continued staring at my plate. This polite chit-chat wasn't necessary.

"So, why did you go to *The Devil's Den* last night?" he cut to the chase.

"It's personal." I curtly replied. Then I heard his deep sigh and a fork falling onto the plate with a hard ding. What was it with this dude breaking dishes?

"Look! I'm sorry I put you out on the street," he admitted with irritation.

Now he had my attention. I looked up from my plate. "Are you apologizing for both times?" I glared at him with a raised brow.

"Yeah, I guess I am." Those eyes of his were too penetrating. It felt as though he saw right through me.

"Why did you throw Jeffery and me out of your club that first night?" I stuffed a forkful of eggs in my month.

"I know your kind."

I blinked with surprise. I remained silent as he continued.

"The music. It affects you in the same way it affects others of your kind—our kind."

"I have no idea what you're talking about," I denied.

"You don't lie very well, do you?" He smirked, not expecting a reply. "Humans can't hear the music. It's on a different frequency."

"Frequency? Like a dog whistle?" I mused, but inside I was freaking out.

"No. More like celestial." Gold-Eyes lent a tight smile.

"Celestial?" This had to be some fluke. How else would he have known?

"Yeah. The music appeals to our spirit. It's like catnip to a feline."

"The music?" This time I dropped my fork and gave him my full attention.

"Yes, the music." There was something hidden in his smile.

"And you're like me?"

"Well, not exactly." He paused. "My beginning came from divine creation, not man-made."

"Divine creation?" I tried staying cool. Rather instead, alarm swallowed me whole.

"That's correct."

"Created by God?" Was he insane?

"Yes, we are a race of angels. Our kind are called *Zophasemin*. Zop for short."

"Zop? That's a funny word." I forced a smile.

He paused, fixed on my face. "Don't be flippant with me. I know who you are. The streets are full of information about you."

"Sure! And my mother and father are fairies."

"Actually, your mother was your host. You were not conceived naturally." He leaned back in his chair, with a cocky stare.

I reeled with astonishment. "I haven't a clue to what you're meaning."

His brow shot up. "Are you going to skirt around the truth all morning?" The speckles in his eyes stood out more than usual.

I glimpsed down at my half eaten food trying to decide how to proceed. Was I crazy for wanting to know more about my origin? I raised my eyes. "Tell me more?" Would letting my secret out of the bag be so bad?

"Like myself, you are celestial. You could say you're ninety-nine percent celestial. You do have a small portion of human DNA and something else that I can't put my finger on."

"How can you tell?" I wasn't sure if he was insane, but I wanted to hear what he had to say.

It looked like he held back a laugh. "Like myself and my race, we can see human aura. With you, not only do you have an aura, you carry effusion, which is the outflow of celestials."

"Effusion? I've never heard of that."

He raised an eyebrow. "It's like a translucent mist or essence, for a better word."

"Do I have that—?" damn I sounded too eager.

"Yes, along with your aura as well."

"What does my aura look like?" My heart pounded against my chest. This dude better not be jerking my leg.

"With every human, it's different. Your aura is a rose, but when you get angry, it turns a deep purple. Effusion is more of a sense rather than a color."

"That's interesting." I didn't see colors or sense any effusion.

"Your aura is very soft, but your effusion is much stronger, more like one of us."

I might as well put down my shield. I had to know. "Why don't I see this myself?"

"The only thing I can conclude is that you haven't tapped into your senses in your brain. It should come naturally." He shrugged. "It's possible that your human side is blocking the outflow of your effusion, kind of like a cold with a stuffed-up nose. I wouldn't worry. It will come in time. After all, you are strong." He reassured me.

"If I'm mostly like you, then why did you throw me out of your bar?"

"The others would've sensed you were mixed—part human." His face was solemn.

"That doesn't explain why you kicked me out of your bar."

Suddenly his lips thinned like a razor. He cleared his throat nervously. "Most Zop look upon mixed as the Nephilim giants—impures or inbreeds."

"So what if I'm not exactly like them? Nothing's wrong with diversity." The insult pierced like a dagger rammed through my heart. "My father's blood was pure and good!" Anger began to rise. It all didn't seem fair. At last, I'd found a race like myself, and yet, I was revered as an outcast.

"I'm sure your father was an exceptional man. As it may be, to the imperial, it is irrelevant. A pure-blooded Zop, looks upon the spawn of angels and humans as an abomination."

"I'm not an offspring." I pointed to myself.

"I know it's hard to understand our ways, but regardless of how you were brought into this world, the fact is, you are not created in the divine light. For the Zop, they perceive you tainted."

"Do *you* think as they do?" My eyes tightened. I didn't know why I suddenly cared about his opinion.

"Well...let me see. I broke up a fight that you were about to get your pretty little head sliced off and could have damn well gotten myself killed, and I'm sitting here with you in my gracious home, and I never allow anyone in my humble abode, not even a woman I'm bedding." I felt my cheeks flush over that vision, not that I cared.

He continued, "I gave you my bed, which I missed dearly last night, and last but not least, I cooked you breakfast. I never cook, not even for a woman who has shown me great affection." His gold eyes sparkled. "Did I answer your question?" He seemed amused while he waited for my reply.

By his starkness, a tingle spread over me—it bothered me. I wanted to run rather than yield to a long forgotten emotion this stranger had aroused within me. A sensibility, I'd preferred to steer clear of. Then a thought crossed my mind. If he wasn't interested in bedding me, then what did he want from the disgusting, impure? "So," I asked. "Let's stop with all this chitchat and just say what you really want."

"I want nothing," Gold-Eyes said, revealing only a stone face.

"Then why waste your time on telling me all this? Why didn't you let the pure Zop have their way with the girl on the wrong side of the heavens?"

He paused. I couldn't read his thoughts. "I don't know. I felt responsible for you." He shrugged.

"Responsible? Yeah right!" I scoffed. "So, why did you set me out on the sidewalk when I came to you for help?"

He ran his fingers through his somewhat messy hair and let out a deep sigh. "I know the Family probably better than you. We go back a long ways, too much history. Don't care much for 'em either. I know how they work and how they think. Your friend is right, sending you to me." He paused. "However, my days of fighting the Family are over. I keep to myself these days. Like I said, too much history." His jaw twitched. It was obvious he felt the backlash of the Illuminati as much as I had.

Unanticipated, a spark of hope glimmered. Perhaps if I offered him an incentive, he might be inclined to help me. The inspiration for most was money. And by the meager furnishings of his apartment, he probably could use a few bucks. "Name your price." I blurted out. "I can pay you for your help." I dangled the bait. Everyone had a price.

Quickly, his face twisted into anger. "You think I'm doing all this for money?"

I shrugged without answering.

"I don't need your money!" He snarled, jumping to his feet. "I think you've worn out your welcome! Don't ever step foot in my bar again. I won't protect you if you do." Gold-Eyes reached over, grabbing me up in one sweep, carting me out the door and down the stairwell, halting at the sidewalk. Once again, he deposited my ass on the sidewalk. Then he put two fingers in his mouth and whistled at a taxi that was approaching.

The cabbie had no more stopped and rolled his window down when Gold-Eyes shouted, "Take this girl home, and don't bring her back." He then placed a wad of money in the man's hand. The driver nodded, "Yes, sir!"

My face was beet red from shock. Okay, getting put out twice on the sidewalk was starting to become a habit. Yet this dude didn't know me very well. I was worse than a pesky gnat. The word no to me only meant a challenge. I'd be back. *I ain't afraid of him or his kind.*

Defeat I Will Not Accept

I T WAS NOT until Jeffery's eyes nearly popped out of his sockets did I realize I'd returned home that morning in only a football jersey. I was sure a few questions were raised between Jeff and Dom concerning my lack of attire.

Escaping their queries only lasted until that evening. The interrogation commenced when I came down for dinner. Only seconds had passed before Jeffery started a flood of questions as we seated ourselves at the table. "What did you do last night? I dare say it must've been...hmmm, interesting," Jeff inquired, sweetly. Dom remained quiet, only rolling his eyes now and then.

"Oh, out and about," I answered lightheartedly.

"Well, I might not know the out part, but I sure can guess the *about* part." Jeffery eyed me suspiciously. Dom just cleared his throat, glaring at his partner.

"Yeah, and what might that be?" I didn't want to tell the guys what I'd gotten myself into last night.

"I sure do like your jersey. Been watching any football lately?" Jeffery asked nonchalantly.

I scoffed. "Nope, not one."

Then ole Jeff let it rip. "Gurrrl, if you don't spit out what mess youse got yourself into last night, I'm gonna turn youse over my knee and whoop yo' ass until the damn cows fly! Forget the mofo-n pigs! Youse had Dom and me up all night worry-n over youse! For all we knows, youse could've been ly-n in a ditch dead."

A bit shocked, I knew Jeffery would've made good on his threat. And worse, I deserved it. "Guys, I'm sorry. I was looking into a hunch of mine, and it backfired."

Jeffery eyed me suspiciously with one brow raised. "Well... from what I can tell, it looked like thangs went pretty damn good. Who's jersey you wear-n this morning, missy?"

My cheeks felt like fire. "It's not what you think."

"What am I think-n then?" Jeffery challenged.

"Hmm, you know." I rolled my eyes. "A friend loaned me his shirt. I sort of had a little scuffle last night, and my clothes had gotten a bit torn, that's all." I shrugged my shoulders and took a bite of my pizza, feeling the heat of four eyes on me.

Jeffery and Dom shared a cheerless glance. Dom spoke up. "That's some scuffle. I see your bruised face. Yes?"

Damn! The makeup didn't work. "Well, about that...I sort of fell into a...hmm door."

Jeffery chimed in. "Uh-hmm, and that damn door just jumped right out in front of you too." Jeff's voice was full of cynicism.

Dom, with his wise patience, intervened. "Stevie, Jeffery and I care about you and your safety. When you stay out all night and come home the next morning...pardon for my bluntness... looking like a tom cat with your hair a mess and barely dressed, we fear you may be behaving recklessly. We are only worried. You can understand? Yes?" Dom's voice of reason never failed to set me straight.

A deepening hue of shame struck me tenfold and I let out a defeated sigh. "You won't like what I have to tell you. First, it's not what you think. I don't have a lover." Talk about embarrassment.

"A lover is our least worries. We fear far darker things, my sweet." Trepidation spilled over into Dom's voice.

"I don't mean to trouble you. It's just I can't go through life not knowing if I have a child. I owe that to myself and especially to her—even if I die in the process."

"Her? Do you know for certain you have a daughter?" Dom asked.

"No. It's just a gut feeling."

"What can we do to help you?" Jeffery asked with genuine concern.

"Oh no!" My eyes widened in alarm. "I don't want either one of you in the middle of this. I can't have any more bloodshed at my expense. I love you both too much to let you get involved with my problems."

"But my sweet," Dom interjected. "We are already involved, simply by association. We are in this together."

"Maybe so, but I'm still not going to ask for your aid. I can't ask that of you. I think as long as you both stay neutral, the Family will leave you alone." I tossed a tight smile.

"The friend who loaned you the shirt is he or she helping you?" Dom asked.

"Not yet, but he will." I had a mischievous glint in my eyes.

Jeffery went pop-eyed. "Oh my god! You've been keeping company with that drop-dead gorgeous guy from that bar. Gurrrl, you can't deny it! I see it written all over your face."

"It's not like that!" My cheeks blushed.

"Uh-hmm... Chile, I knows when you're ly-n. You like him, and I knows it!"

"Trust me when I say there is no love there. I mean nada!"

Jeffery rolled his eyes, bobbing his head in a rhythmic motion, full of attitude. "Uh-hmm... If youse say so." Jeffery's mouth tightened into a stubborn line.

I bit my lip, doubting if I should ask this, so I just blurted it out. "Jeffery, I need your advice on something."

"Sure, honey. And what might that be?" My friend sipped his hot cup of java.

"How to seduce a man?" Without warning, Jeffery showered us with his coffee, and Dom's face paled. For folks who were not parents, they sure did act as so.

That night before I left the house, Jeffery and Dom both gave me strong instructions, or more like rules. Jeffery wanted to go with me to make sure I didn't do anything stupid. I had to do some fast talking. I assured him my plans were mildly risky, and if I was going to get a man's attention, I didn't need my good friend tagging along. He might throw a wrench in the plans.

One thing I felt for certain, celestial or human, they both understood sex. So I was going back to that bar this time with my guns loaded. If I could catch Gold-Eyes' attention, he might be more persuaded to help me find my daughter. I had to try.

When I stepped out of the cab at the bar, I heard wolf whistles by a couple of dudes passing by on foot. I instantly tugged on my short dress, questioning Jeffery's choice of attire for tonight. He swore this would do the trick. So far, by the looks I got from those two strangers, Jeffery might be right. The dress was a bit too bold for my taste. It clung to my curves like second skin. Normally I'd never wear a garment as such, leaving so little to one's imagination. The color, a bold red, with a plunging neckline screamed s-e-x. I thought any minute my boobs would flop out. I worried the dress might slide up and reveal my tiny thong, which rode up my ass. For the life of me, I couldn't see why any woman in her right mind would wear such uncomfortable garb. WTF! The spike boots that came to my knees reminded me of hooker heels, which equally matched my wild hair and cherry-red lips that made me look like I'd been stung by a bee. I fit the perfect description of a lioness on the prowl. I guess in a way I was on the prowl but for another kind of hunger.

I stalled before going inside and took a long breath. I tucked my boobs in for reassurance and entered the bar. A daunting thought crossed my mind—what if this didn't work?

I ducked in a shadowy corner and watched as customers mingled about, just like any other night. The bar was humming with chatter. Maybe I should try this another night when it wasn't as crowded. On second thought, if I backed out now, I may never get the courage again. So I lifted my chin in defiance and straightened my tight dress and made my way through the smoke-filled nightery. "Damn, if this doesn't work, I'm going to look ridiculous." I mumbled to myself.

As expected, it was dark, and the stench of strong perfume and whiskey wafted in the air. My nerves seemed to have gotten the best of me. My hands shook like an alcoholic having dry heaves.

Then a bitter thought appeared. I was among my own kind, yet I had never felt more as an odd man out, or in my case, a woman. I had to pull myself together. An enchantress didn't tremble like a coward.

My eyes combed the dim place, trying to spot my target. If he were the kind of male I sized him up to be, he should fall for my bait. I listened to Jeffery's instructions on how to walk seductively. I hope I got the swag down, even still, Jeffery put me to shame.

That mood-altering music began playing. The tunes were different, yet it had the same effect. I tried tuning it out. Regardless, its lure was stronger than my will. The song beckoned my sensuality. How could I refuse something that seemed as natural as breathing. "Screw it!" I said to myself.

As I edged my way through the crowd, I spotted Gold-Eyes behind the bar, in the amidst of a conversation with a couple of very beautiful women, but once his eyes landed on me, the women were cast aside as his hunted gaze quickly fixed on me. A moment of triumph wheeled my heart. For some unsung reason, the notion of him with another woman struck a chord with me.

I tossed an enticing glance his way, knowing he would take the bait. I seductively swayed my hips as I slowly raised my arms up into my hair, toying with it as I walked onto the dance floor. While the music infused my spirit, I discarded my inhibitions and became a seductress. When I glanced up at my target, our eyes locked. The corner of my cheery lips tugged into a smug. I began to let the music possess my mind and body as I summoned my lover. My hips began moving back and forth, letting the music make love to me. Hypnotically, I gave myself over to the music as it reeled me in. Like an enchantress, I taunted every eye who so dared looked upon me.

When my eyes opened, there he stood, a spark in his eyes that was much different than last time. Desire, perhaps? My breath caught. I'd forgotten how beautiful he was. He reminded me of a king, awaiting his mistress. His golden eyes ravished over me from head to toe. I teased him back with a titillating smile. Then I reached for him, and he took my hand, gathering me into his strong arms, up close and very personal. The warmth and comfort of his firm body against mine gave me a tingling sensation and his scent—sweat and, oddly, a field of wild flowers, nearly set me off into a lustful tailspin. His hand pressed against the small of my back, drawing me tighter. As his sweet breath taunted my bare neck, my heart pounded against my chest. Then he whispered in my ear, "Do you have any idea what you're doing to me?" His voice was thick and breathless.

"Why don't you tell me?" I softly teased, throwing my long locks of hair over my shoulders. My hands began to comb his firm chest as my eyes eagerly washed over him. Swiftly, he lifted me up onto his hip, and we began to dance. It was hot and dirty as our bodies pressed against one another. I surrendered myself, letting him carry me away into the spellbound music. His sensual touch sent chills over my body and I found myself yearning for something that had taken absence since that night with Aidan. Before I knew what was happening, he leaned in and kissed me, devouring my lips like a man, hungry and rough. I thought he was going to take me right there on the dance floor, yet, the most frightening part of all—I wanted him too.

All of a sudden, he withdrew. I opened my eyes, still under the enchantment, confused, murmuring, "What's wrong?" Then I gasped by his thin lined frown. Before I could gather my senses, he'd swept me up, ushering me out the front door. It happened so fast that I conscientiously couldn't make heads or tails of what had transpired between us, until he'd deposited me on my ass at the sidewalk, and I was gulping down the city's air. Then I realized my fate. The spell had vanished. I knew my attempt had failed by his unyielding jaw. Crap!

"What the hell just happened in there?" He pointed to his bar as he towered over me with his face low enough that I'd felt the ire of his breath.

I knew this wasn't going as I'd hoped. The passion in his eyes had elapsed, and in its place came hostility.

I tried to play up to him. "I don't know what you mean. Can't a girl take a shine to you?" I puckered out my cherry lips. Apparently, luck wasn't on my side. It seemed my scanty attempt of flirting only inflamed Gold-Eyes temper.

"Do you have any idea what this"—he waved his hands over my curvy body without touching me—"does to someone like me?" His jaw flinched.

"You don't like my dress?" I fluttered my eyelashes, awkwardly. I think I hit an all-time low of making a fool of myself.

His brows creased with ire. "It doesn't matter what I like. This isn't you!" his tone came off as if he was parenting a child.

Despite his inflection, he was right. Nonetheless, I didn't want to hear it. "Don't talk to me like I'm a kid!"

"You are a child!" his curt voice lashed at me.

"Like hell if I am!"

He gave a deep throaty laugh. "Yeah? Just how old are you? And don't lie. I'll know if you're not being truthful." He warned.

I got in his face and declared, "old enough to fuc—!" Before I could finish my smartass-adult comment, he jerked me up and in one sweep, opened a taxi door and threw me in the back seat. I was certain he'd gotten a good view of my lacy red thong as my short dress rode up my ass. Then he tossed the driver, the same one from last time, a wad of cash, and gave him strict orders.

"Take this half-clothed little girl home. Directly home. If she even looks as though she's coming back here, I want you to report back to me immediately." He commanded with authority to the driver. The cabbie simply nodded.

Then Gold-Eyes turned his angry blaze back to me. His face twisted with annoyance. "Little girl, you've got a lot of nerve coming up in my bar, trying to seduce me. Keep your ass at home! Go to school and behave yourself. Your parents need to put you under lock and key." He then slammed the door shut.

He was sending me home, and I had to get his attention. So I screamed. "Wait!" Frustrated, tears streaming down my face, "I need your help. I can't do this alone. You're the only one I know who has a chance in finding my child. Ms. Noel said you could help me!"

"What does a feeble old woman know?" He clenched his teeth. "Go home! You're too young to be playing these games."

But I wasn't giving up that easily. He didn't know me that well. "You think I'm a child. I'll tell you what I am." I hung my head out the window, trying to jar his attention. "I'm a mother determined to find her lost child!" I yelled through choked tears. "Even if that means sleeping with you!"

Disconcerted, Gold-Eyes kicked the tire and ran his fingers through his blonde hair. Clearly his hesitance exacerbated his dilemma only worse. I could see his struggle, but then he drew back. His face became stoic. "Freckles, I wish I could help you, but I can't." With that said, he nodded to the driver, and before I could say anything else, the taxi rolled away.

I watched from the rearview window the growing distance as we both stared back at each other. For a second, I thought I'd caught a glint of regret, though I must've been wrong. He stood frozen, watching my departure, with no attempt in recanting his decision.

After we had turned the corner, I faced back around, feeling the full effects of defeat. Every hope I had was left back there standing at the curb. I should've known using my sexuality wouldn't have changed his mind. What a fool I'd become. He didn't have to worry about me any longer. I finally got the message. I was going to have to do this on my own.

I put on my determined face. I couldn't allow this little bump in the road stop me. But for tonight, I just wanted to wallow in my pity.

Help

L AST NIGHT I managed to get past Dom's and Jeffery's notice and scurry to my bedroom before they were the wiser. It was not until the next day after lunch when Jeffery sought me out. I assumed they had figured out that last night didn't turnout the way I'd hoped by my hibernating all morning.

I was still in bed, lying low under the covers, when a soft tap came at my door. I bit my lip, reluctant to answer. I knew stalling would only delay the inevitable. Giving in to a recalcitrant sigh, I groaned, "Come in." I didn't really feel much for talking. Setting aside my foul mood, I suppose I needed to reassure them I was still alive and fine as one could expect under the circumstances. The door opened slightly, and Jeffery's head peeked inside.

"Is it safe for me to come in?" He merely whispered.

"Yes," I replied, tugging the coverlet over my head.

Jeffery stepped in and sauntered over to my bed and flopped himself down on the edge. "I take it things didn't go as planned." Jeffery patted my foot, followed with a consoling smile.

I peeked over the blanket. "You could say that." I let out a shameful sigh.

"Gurrrl, I know a little voodoo that can take care of this jerk! It works too! I've used it a time or two." Jeffery's chin lifted with pride.

I giggled shaking my head. "That's not necessary. Besides, I doubt it will work on his stubborn ass." I sat up, drawing my legs to my chest. "He wouldn't even hear me out." My heart sunk like an anchor at sea.

"The dress didn't get him stirred up?"

I scoffed. "That's an understatement. At one point, I thought he was going to take me right there in front of everyone."

"Girlfriend, I can't imagine any straight man refusing you!"

"I don't know what to make of him. We were kissing, and then suddenly he was dragging me outside to the curb. He hurled me in a cab, ordering the driver to take me home, never to return to his courtly bar, ever again." I shook my head in disbelief. "I was mortified. How could I ever show my face again after that fiasco?" I took an exasperated breath. "I only asked of his assistance in finding my child. Yet I squashed that chance." I swallowed back the tears that threatened.

"Oh, honey, I don't think it's as bad as you think."

I squeezed my knees to my chest, regretting the stupid charade I tried to pull off last night. What was I thinking? I should've known listening to Jeff's advice might've not been exactly the smartest approach. Though, I couldn't blame him. After all, it was my stupid idea. Stupid as in being that the man saw right through my desperate attempt. I frowned to myself as I shrugged in reply.

"Now listen!" Jeffery wagged his finger at me. "I know things didn't go quite as planned for you, but don't give up just yet. It sounds to me this guy cares about you more than you think. It's obvious, he stopped himself before he ruined your virtuous reputation."

"My virtuous reputation?" I scoffed. "Oh, the dude cared all right! He dumped my ass on the sidewalk!"

"Was that before or after he kissed the hell out of you?" Jeffery's lips pursed.

"It was after."

"Did he approach you, or did you approach him?"

"He came to me," I moaned.

"Where at the time did this encounter take place?"

I blushed, hiding under my lashes. "On the dance floor."

"And were you dancing like that night we were together?"

"Uh...yeah." My cheeks blistered with embarrassment.

"Uh-hmm! Gurrrl you hooked that man line and sinker. He's into you, but, it sounds like you might've frightened him."

"That's not it. I don't believe Gold-Eyes is easily intimated."

"Wait! What did you just call him?"

"Gold-Eyes," I said, confused.

"Honey, did you ever find out what his actual name is?"

"Yeah. Briefly, we exchanged names."

"So, has the man ever called you by your first name?"

I rolled my eyes. "No, not that I recall." I didn't see Jeff's point.

"What does he call you?"

"Hmm Freckles," I confessed.

Jeffery burst into laughter. He laughed so hard I thought he was going to break a rib. I *on* the other hand, didn't see the humor. I sat there silent, waiting for him to let me in on the joke. "Girlfriend!" he wiped the tears of laughter from the corners of his eyes. "That man may not know it yet, but he has fallen for you! He gave you a pet name. It's called an endearment." Jeffery's self-assured grin stretched from ear to ear. "Men aren't that creative. They don't waste time on mushy stuff unless they really like youse. If he's calling youse a name such as Freckles, youse have cha-cha on that man's heart, gurrrl!"

"You once claimed I'd done the same thing to Aidan." I tried to smile, rather instead, I grimace.

"Yes, and I still do. Nowhere is it written youse can have only one true love. Although sometimes with love comes heartache. It ain't always pretty with a pink bow, my friend." Jeffery smiled. "But this one is different. Youse see." He winked.

"You didn't see his beet-red face and hear the asperity in his tone." I shook my head with incredulity. "If he had any interest in me, he'd be more obliged helping me find my child." I waved my hand, dismissing my crushed faith. "It doesn't matter now. Finding my child is more imperative than winning favors from a man I hardly know. I can't allow any more distractions."

"It isn't always that simple, boo." Jeffery disputed.

"Either way, he's not knocking at my door offering his gallant hand." I turned over on my side and pulled the cover over me. I didn't have the patience or the energy to discuss this any longer.

Jeffery patted me on the leg. "I think he'll change his mind. Some folks have to let the idea settle a bit before they make a firm commitment. Let's not forget the Family's position has less than ethical practices. They are complicated as they are ugly with bad juju. Just be patient, he'll come around. Mark my word!" With that said, Jeffery left my room, shutting the door quietly behind him.

The next day, I decided to get down and dirty, close to Mother Nature. My mind was tight with thought of how to proceed with my next plan. At Haven, the nurses' shifts changed at twelve midnight. They were usually busy scurrying about with their routine for the night. I thought if I went disguised as a nurse, I could slip in the office where they keep the files, find my case and slip out before anyone realized what happened. It was a weak plan. Though, it was all I had. I wished I had Aidan's ability to pop in and out of thin air. It certainly would make my mission easier. Unfortunately for me, I guess that was one talent I didn't inherent. A big disappointing bummer, if you asked me.

Today I promised Dom I'd help out with the garden. There was a good bit of work that needed to be done and he needed an extra hand. I didn't mind. It felt good working the cool soil. I sensed a connection to the earth's richness, getting my hands dirty and grit under my nails. I started with sowing a small patch for the fall vegetables. The rolls I dug out weren't perfectly straight, but Dom said the plants didn't care about precision. As long as they had plenty of dirt and water, they'd grow. I decided gardening was my new passion. Dom seemed to appreciate my unskilled aid too.

Jeffery didn't like getting his manicured hands ruined or for that matter, doing anything that meant menial work. I often wondered how he managed the trade of a butler. I suspected Aidan didn't expect Jeffery to carry out the traditional role. Though, Jeffery was very loyal. I sensed there was a kindred spirit between Aidan and Jeff by my conversations with both men. For Dom and Jeffery, my heart went out to them that neither one had a chance for closure with Aidan's death. Although Dom or Jeffery never discussed much at the dinner table, I sensed the lost took its toll on them more than they revealed. It certainly had affected me, even knowing of Aidan's betrayal.

Any who, apart from unpleasant memories, it was a wonderful autumn day, great for planting. A shift in the weather stirred the trees, bringing in a brisk coolness as the sun caressed my face with its consoling warmth. I felt enlivened. After being confined at Haven for three long years, not allowed a simple glimpse of the sun's golden rays made this day a wondrous treat that I'd cherish for the rest of my life.

It was great working in the garden, but my time with Dom was especially endearing. I'd discovered he was quite well-read of the medicinal use of plants. He reminded me of Ms. Noel in that way. I'd obtained quite a bit of knowledge from watching her prepare common herbs such as jimson weed for asthma. It was in high demand during the flu season.

Near twilight and many rows of new seeds planted, leaves raked into piles and burned, my face had become beaten by the sun's kisses. Dirt and mud had spread from my bare feet to my hair, I was a frightful mess. The hopes of ever becoming clean again would take several washings, yet I didn't care.

Dom had finished for the day and left me to myself as he went inside to prepare dinner. I wasn't ready to give the day up and decided to finish up a few more spots. I had my heart set on planting a few more flowers such as periwinkle, lantana and marigold along the side of the house. I thought I'd touch up the veggie garden with a little more tilling. It was important for the plants' roots to have room to flourish.

I think I enjoyed the garden even more than Dom. There was something special about this patch. My troubles seemed to dissipate while digging my fingers into the soothing dirt. It was the best medicine for a heavy heart.

I found myself humming to a favorite tune while hunched on my knees in the middle of the flower bed, digging with a handy trowel. I thought I'd plant the lantanas against the house first since they would grow the tallest, then the periwinkle and set the bright gold and orange marigold last to line the flower bed. With my small garden fork, I worked the moist soil until it loosened. I prepared small holes for each flower and then dumped each plant one by one out of its little plastic cup as I dropped the flower and its roots into the individual hole. Then I packed the dirt around each stem so the rain wouldn't wash it away.

Out of the blue, I heard Jeffery's throat clear. I thought, *Oh dear, what does that man want now?* All day he'd been bugging me about everything underneath the sun. I didn't even bother to look up at him standing behind me.

"Jeffery, not now! I'm busy," I snapped, irritated. Whatever he wanted could wait. I wasn't going to the store for him looking like a mud wrestler. Then I heard his throat clear again. *Aw hell!* I thought. I twisted around, not giving a thought to my state of appearance. Rattled, I realized it wasn't Jeffery as I held my hand over my eyes trying to block out the sun's glare. The sun shadowed my view of the tall stranger, blocking his face. I froze unsure who stood before me. After my visit with Helen, I wasn't too fond of unannounced visitors. Then he smiled. I swallowed down shock. Not even the sun could hide that lopsided grin. I gawped, unsure.

"Gold-Eyes?" I called, doubting myself. He gave way to a snort as he sidestepped, blocking the sun's rays, coming into full view as he mused, "I hear mud is a great skin product." His eyes glistened, raking over me from a mud streak face to my soiled feet.

Startled, I leaped to my feet, losing my balance. Gold-Eyes reached out, but not fast enough before I'd fallen onto his chest. I hadn't notice his white shirt until my hands had landed on his chest. I instantly jumped back, stammering over my words. "I-I-I'm s-s-so sorry!" instinctively as though my brain had stopped, I quickly started rubbing the mud off the front of his shirt, only making it worse. Under the muse of his golden eyes, I had no doubt he thought of me as a blundering idiot.

He grinned wide, wiping the dirt off his chest with no avail. He chuckled, "It's fine." Then he paused as our eyes hitched for a silent moment. Right then, I realized how much I loved his speckled eyes. Whenever he smiled, the gold glistened. "You... um...wear dirt well." He commented as he let out a soft laugh, something I'd never heard him do.

I was quite thankful for the shroud of mud, hiding my blushing cheeks. I composed myself as best I could under the circumstances and asked, mystified, "Why are you here?"

He pulled his eyes away for a second and then looked back into my perplexed face and relented, "I'd like to reconsider helping you."

My eyes orbed. "You're serious?"

"Yeah...I guess I am." His full lips gave a half-tug smile. Without a second thought, I leaped into his arms, mud and all, and something magical happened. He began kissing me. It was not demanding or possessive but sweet and tender. A kiss of endearment? When it ended, it was as though time had stood still. A quiet understanding came between us. His eyes had filled with a gentleness. It touched me and I giggled. "Umm, your shirt!"

He glanced down at his once-nice, clean shirt, and slipped me a sideways glance. "Yeah...I guess I'm staying for dinner. Since you got my shirt dirty, I think it is only fair you wash it." He grinned, impishly.

I bit my bottom lip. "Yeah, you're right." I paused, "Jeffery can wash it." I smiled brightly.

———— ❈ ————

I had left the men downstairs to their discussion over sports and boy stuff. I hurried with my shower. After the hot water had run its course and a ton of dirt followed the trail of water down the drain, I jumped out grabbing a clean towel wrapping it around my dripping body. I quickly brushed my teeth and attempted running a brush through my defiant hair. My face was a bit red from the sun, so I didn't bother with makeup. Tonight, I decided to be me, barefoot and bare face. No glitz or glamour.

When I came downstairs, I had on my old tattered blue jean cutoffs and Gold-Eyes' jersey—perfect for a relaxing evening with a new dinner guest.

Jeffery had loaned our guest one of his T-shirts. I think he had a sneaky reason behind his generosity. The shirt had to have been two sizes too small. It hugged every defined ripple in Gold-Eyes' washboard stomach, along with the short sleeves hugging his biceps. I had to admit, it was quite distracting. I found myself kicking Jeffery several times under the table. Gawking at the dinner guest displayed a lack of manners and sparked a deep embarrassment that I'd preferred to keep to myself. Nonetheless, I had to thank Jeff later for the T-shirt. Nice thinking, I thought.

After the wonderful meal Dom prepared, a true Louisiana meal of mudbugs, fresh corn on the cob, and boiled potatoes, we settled down in the sitting room for a beer. I hated the stuff and preferred sweet tea. Jeffery decided to entertain us with his recent piano lessons. I smiled, clenching my teeth through the torture of "Bridge over Troubled Water." Never once in tune, I discovered that the screeching of chalk across a blackboard was much more enjoyable than Jeffery butchering a perfectly good song.

On the other hand, our guest, Gold-Eyes, was gracious enough to keep himself together and managed a kind smile.

Once Jeffery finished, he stood and took a bow as if he had played a profound performance equal to Mozart's or Beethoven's. Needless to say, I felt a yearning to have my foot up Jeffery's backside.

"Bravo, bravo!" We all cheered. Despite the encore, I think we all secretly hoped he wouldn't insist on a repeat. Setting apart from Jeffery's enthusiasm over his new found hobby, I thought about cutting the strings in the piano. There was only so much one could bear.

Before long, Jeffery lost his interest in the piano and moved on to the paintings on the wall. He loved his taste in art and loved showing off his modest knowledge of the artists as well. Dom allowed Jeffery the floor. He sat back passively and joined in the conversation whenever Jeffery stopped for a breath. Dom didn't seem to mind. I think he appreciated Jeffery's flair for life. When we got into the mid part of the evening, I interjected by nudging our guest. "May I have a moment with you in private?" I asked, half whispering.

Gold-Eyes' smile dwindled down into a slight tug at the corner. "Certainly. I'm all yours." I couldn't help feeling a little nervous. I gave him a tight smile and took his hand. As we rose to our feet, I announced to the guys, "Hey, fellas. I need to have a moment with Gold—" I stopped in midsentence. It occurred to me that I'd forgotten his name. I glanced up at my guest, and there appeared a little grin taunting at the corner of his mouth.

Jeffery saved me from total humiliation by butting in and doing the honor of officially introducing us. He cleared his throat. "Let me have the pleasure. Stevie, I would like for you to meet Valour Cross." Jeffery very gallantly pointed to our guest. "Val for short. And Val," Jeffery glanced at me—"I'd like for you to meet the one and only Stephanie Ray Collins. It's Stevie for short." Jeffery's taupe eyes sparkled with mirth.

My cheeks were blazing under the humorous gaze of Val's eyes. I hid behind my lashes as I mumbled. "Nice to be on first-name basis."

"Likewise, Freckles." His voice was deeply rich, yet playful. Goose bumps covered my arms. The good ones.

Dom and Jeffery didn't help the matter any when they both snorted laughter. Some things never change.

Jeffery thought it'd be more private for our guest and me to sit outside on the front porch. We were far away enough from anyone's earshot.

The full moon caressed us with its silver light and a nice evening breeze rustled through the trees. Mockingbirds were chirping among one another, a sound I never grew tired of hearing.

I didn't want to sit in the swing. It brought back too many memories of a time that I didn't care to revisit. I suppose there may be some residual feelings still lingering over Aidan. Why else did I still get a tug at my heart whenever something reminded me of him? Perhaps in time, the pain would ease.

So I went and sat down on the top step, and Gold-Eyes followed, sitting down next to me, stretching out his long legs. If he questioned why I chose the steps and not the swing, he didn't ask. I was grateful.

The house sat on a hill where we could see all the way down to the end of the street. The Garden District was breathtaking— tree-lined sidewalks with rows of stunning Victorian homes standing in their glory—a delightful sight I once thought only existed in magazines. Sometimes I had to pinch myself to make sure this was my life. Despite the remarkable life that had been bestowed upon me, if given the choice, I'd give up all of this to have my child back.

Gold-Eyes or I should say, Val, cleared his throat and brought me back to our pending discussion. I glanced up, but not before I could veil my sorrow. His speckled eyes softened, and I knew he had caught a glimpse of my sadness. I quickly looked away, but it didn't matter. He saw my heavy heart. Even though, his eyes filled with a gentle ardor, he didn't ask why the sad face. Instead, he wrapped his arms around me and hugged me tenderly. We shared a moment of silence. Then with a deep sigh, he began probing me about my plans.

"Do you have any idea where you want to start looking for your daughter?" His tone was serious and direct, stirring the air with nobility.

"Yes, I have it all planned out. I want you to break into Haven Hospital and steal my file," I confessed, straight up. I figured no point in beating around the bush. Val gulped the last bit of beer down and crushed the can with his bare hand. "Uh...you don't ask for much, do you?" He spoke in his deep baritone voice.

"Well...unless you have another idea, it's the best I've got." I didn't look him in the eyes. Rather, I kept my eyes focused straight ahead. "I figured Haven hospital will have my medical documents. Just maybe the birth might be in the same files."

"Wait! The guy at *The Devil's Den*, he worked at that hospital. You had planned on bribing him—"

I didn't know if he was asking a question or stating a fact. "Yeah. Unfortunately, I didn't get that far." I picked up a pebble and threw it at the mailbox down at the iron gate *Ting*. It bounced off the box. Then a curious question hit me. "How did you know I was there?"

Val shifted, hesitating before he answered. "Mac, the bartender recognized you, so, he called me. My friend knew you were in over your head. That place is not exactly a spot for the weak at heart."

"You think I'm weak?" I snapped my head up, glaring at him.

Val paused briefly as he searched into my eyes. "No. I don't. But I do think you jump before you think." He smiled. "It took some gumption to do what you did. Still, stupid." His eyes gleamed with what appeared as admiration.

"Yeah, it's starting to become a bad habit of mine." I smiled to myself.

"You gotta be careful tracing off to those back alley joints. You're asking for a whole set of problems."

He didn't have to tell me. I knew far too well about creatures lurking in the shadows. Then it dawned on me. "How did your friend know me?" I stared into his face. Something I just realized—I liked his chiseled chin and his strong jaw. He was handsome, though, different than Aidan. Aidan had swagger and the arrogance to match. Val seemed more grounded, yet a leader with dignity.

"To be honest, it wasn't much of a secret. Mac saw you that night I threw you out of my place. Our little encounter sorta developed into a hot topic among the regulars." He paused, tinkering with his keys. "I'd sent a warning to the locals to ban you." Val tossed a short smile. It was disturbing enough that our tiff ended up as gossip. The banning part, I didn't care about. Yet there was more than what he was telling.

"What's the other reason?" Our eyes locked. The gold specks in his deep green eyes glimmered under the moonlight.

"My friend knew I had a fondness for you."

"Oh!" I said, surprised. I didn't know what to say. "Uh... thanks," I said awkwardly.

He took a sharp sigh and got back to the subject. "So you need me to break into this hospital?"

"Not exactly." I tucked a loose a hair strand behind my ears "I think with your ability to copycat other people, you can masquerade as one of the orderlies. All you have to do is find the file, grab it, and get out."

"Do you know the layout of the hospital?"

"No." My face squinted like I'd eaten a bug. I was hoping he wouldn't have asked me that. Clearly, I wasn't prepared. "But that orderly at *The Devil's Den* knows."

"You think that fat bastard will help you after you tried gutting him?" Val snickered to himself.

"No, but I think he'd do it for a hefty price," I argued with confidence.

"How much?"

"Whatever it takes." An impish grin grazed my lips.

"You're that rich?"

"Yep," I replied.

For a brief moment, our eyes hasped. A hush rendered. With a long sigh, he exclaimed, "That guy, the father, he must have hurt you pretty bad." It wasn't a question. It was an observation. I didn't answer. I didn't have it in me. I looked away, peering off down the street.

"Okay, I'll get the layout. And you, my friend, will stay put. Safe out of harm's way."

"Oh no! I'm going with you. I didn't say I wanted you to do this alone." Sitting on the sidelines was out of the question. I was in this 'till death.

"We're going to do this my way, or else I'm walking," He sternly threatened.

My teeth set, ready to lock horns. "Oh, no! I'm in this with you, all the way."

"Sorry." He smiled. "My way or the highway, Freckles." He stared back at me with an inflexibility set in his jaw.

I paused a moment to collect my cool. I needed his help, and I didn't have many options. In fact, he was it. I had to take it or leave it. "Okay," I withdrew a defeated breath, "agreed, but one more thing?"

His shoulders stiffened. I knew he was dreading my next request. "Will you teach me how to fight? You know, street fighting?" Like I said, why beat around the bush? My friend shook his head and grinned.

Then he looked me straight in the eyes. "You never cease to amaze me. I'll teach you. Be at my place bright and early tomorrow morning." Then he hesitated. "If I train you...don't expect me to powder puff it. I'm going to treat you like a man." Val leaned in with his lopsided grin. "I hope we have an understanding?" his eyes danced.

"I wouldn't expect anything less."

"And oh...don't wear those damn cutoff shorts. They're too distracting. Wear sweats, and pull your hair up too."

Talk about blunt, I thought. "All right, I will if you stop calling me Freckles." I bargained.

Val snorted a laugh and shook his head. "There are no deals in war, sugar," he stated, handing the crushed beer can to me. "Gotta go." He rose to his feet, pausing as I stood up on the top step, our gaze even. I thought he was going to kiss me. I saw he wanted to in the gold speckles of his warm eyes, but he pulled away. Instead, he softly slugged me in the arm, like a little sister. We were just buddies, nothing more. I guess that was best.

I watched as he trailed down the long steps. Once he reached the iron gate, he turned back to me and called out. "I like you better with no makeup. Your freckles stand out." He tossed me a sideways glance, dangling his keys in his hand. Without another word, he rode off on his Harley. My eyes followed him until he was out of sight.

Funny he should say that I thought. Tonight, I *was* me. No fancy clothes or hairdo—just me.

No Pain
and Tell Me Again...
What's the Gain?

I COULDN'T FALL asleep that night. Worry kept clouding my mind. As much as I needed Val's help, I found myself concerned over the target I might be putting on his back. After all, he had nothing to do with this fight. He knew the Family. Even more, he possessed knowledge of their operations. So it wasn't like he was going in blindfolded. Surely he could take care of himself. Still I was asking a lot.

Odd how he changed his mind when he was dead-set against getting involved. I wondered if the money had persuaded him, though, he didn't mention his price. If money was his motivation that was fine. I preferred to keep our relationship business. Personal might become a hindrance. I had to keep focused on finding my daughter.

That early morning, I sat in front of the mirror at my makeup station. Staring at my disheveled hair, I thought change was past-due. A new look with a new attitude was just what the doctor ordered. Quickly, before I changed my mind, I reached in the drawer and pulled out a pair of scissors. In only a few clean swipes, the lustrous locks fell to the floor in a heap. Once finished, I looked at myself in the mirror. What was left caressed my heart-shaped face. Quite fitting for the present Stevie, I thought. Now

Val couldn't complain about my hair getting in his onerous ass' way.

After I'd showered, I went to *The Closet*. I shook my head. Only Jeffery would think to name a closet, but I had to admit, it was impressive. I looked through each piece of clothing, and nothing came even close to what Val instructed. "Nothing sexy." I tapped my finger on my lip. I snatched a pair of black leggings and Val's jersey. The leggings were tight fitting, but the T-shirt, three sizes too large, covered all the sexy parts—my boobs and butt. What else could there be?

Time was running out, and I didn't want to be late on my first day. If he thought I didn't take this seriously, he might change his mind. So once I finished dressing, I took the stairs two at a time. No time for breakfast, so I grabbed a piece of toast and headed out the door. Both the guys were still asleep. I'd apologize to Dom later for missing his morning feast.

———⟢✳⟣———

When I arrived at the bar, I took the back stairwell to his apartment directly above his establishment. For some strange reason, my heart began pounding at my chest. I drew in several deep breaths to calm my pulse. I started to knock, but as I raised my hand, the door flew open, and there he stood dressed in a white T-shirt hugging his beautiful six-pack and exposing his well-formed biceps. A little thrill shot through me, though, the excitement was short lived. By the starkness in his eyes, I sensed agitation. "You're late!" He barked.

"I am not!" I bellowed. "You told me early. I'm up before the damn rooster's crow! Besides, the sun's not even up, yet." I retorted while I stormed past him. I brushed against his arm without budging his footing.

"I told you to wear sweats. What's this?" He tugged on his jersey that I brazenly had worn. I jerked it out of his hand and snapped back. "It's fine. No skin showing. What's your problem?"

The playfulness in Val's face from last night had vanished and a mean-eyed green monster had taken camp inside the dude's body. "That shirt defines every curve. And the pants? What were you thinking?" His hard eyes raked over me from my flip-flops to my boobs.

"I thought it might be a smart move to use my best features to throw off my opponent." I stood with my hands on my hips, challenging his comeback.

Val's eyes flashed with humor for a second until his attention drew to my hair. "What is this?" He snatched a short curl.

I swatted his hand away, feeling annoyed at his faultfinding. "I'm just trying to be one of the boys."

"I think that's impossible, Freckles." His eyes sparkled, flirting.

"Whatever!" I shot back, trying to hide my rosy cheeks. "Are we going to get down to business?"

Val's eyes combed over my body with a lopsided grin followed by a deep breath, "Come on." He opened the door waving at me to exit first as he followed behind. The whole way downstairs, I felt the lustful heat of his eyes glued to my ass. It was obvious to me by his slow-moving feet taking deliberate care in each step down; his footing echoed in the spillway. Thankfully, my back was to him. My face blistered with embarrassment.

We finally stopped in front of a metal door that read, Private. My nerves were getting the best of me. I'd been in plenty of fights during school, but I had no concept of how a Zop fought. I eased a fretful sigh.

Val jiggled his keys as he stepped in front of me, unlocking the door. Holding it open, he spoke for the first time since the top floor. "Ladies first." He mused. I assumed his good mood stemmed from his gawking at my ass while descending three damn flights of stairs. I think shopping later is in order for an over-size pair of sweats. I rolled my eyes at him as I entered.

Once we were inside, he flipped on the lights. It took a moment for me to take in the whole place. "Wow! Talk about souped-up!"

I whistled. "This has to be at least ten thousand square feet?" My eyes orbed.

"Yep, actually a little more." A proud smile stretched his lips. Obviously this place had a vital purpose for him. Then my face twisted with curiosity and confusion. "What does one man do with such a huge place?" I inquired.

Val's brow shot up. "Oh, there are many things one can do in a facility such as this," he replied with a hidden undertone. I wasn't sure I wanted to know the entailment.

The dwelling reminded me of something out of the dark ages. It was rustic and smelled of men, sweat and a rust scent like blood. The vast room was dimly lit and appeared built solid with large wood beams from the ceiling to the floor like a centuries-old warehouse. The word gym didn't quite explain it. As my eyes raked over the spacious place, it left me cold. I remembered my studies of European history, how the Middle Ages were known of torture techniques that were less than humane. The devices used in that barbaric period were inconceivable, and even harder to believe there were people who enjoyed conjuring the most gruesome devices. If my memory served me well from my studies, I recognized one device that was called a Judas Cradle. It looked like a wooden stool, only the seat was shaped into a sharp cone, not flat and certainly not meant to be used for casual sitting. They would strip the person down to bare skin, then hoist the prisoner up and drop him on the sharp spear ripping his rectum. The picture in my mind was quite disconcerting. I noticed another device called the Rack. It was believed to be the mother of all torture devices. It consisted of a wooden frame with two ropes fixed to the bottom and another two tied to a handle in the top. I remembered reading—the torturer turned the handle, the ropes would pull the victim's arms, dislocating bones with a loud crack. If the torturer kept turning the handles the limbs were torn right off the body.

I flew into Val, appalled. "What the hell kind of place is this?" I spun on my heels, leaving.

Val grabbed my arm, halting me. A lopsided grin flipped up as he exclaimed, "In my world, sometimes we have to resort to drastic measures."

My stomach roiled. "You mean to tell me that after all these centuries, you, a Zop have to resort to such barbaric methods out of the dark ages?"

"I know this is hard for you to understand, but the world of extraordinary is cruel and savage. If you want to stay alive, it would be best for you not to forget that."

How could I come back with an argument to that? I knew as long as there were people in control like the Illuminati, no one was safe. I hated to admit it, but Val was right.

My eyes drifted to the far wall where a long line of weaponry stood erect in glass cases. Before I realized it, I was standing in front of the glass, eyeballing the items with curiosity. In my history lessons, I'd never read anything about swords. Each one had an unique design. Some of the etching was worn and faded.

My eyes fell upon another device encased by its self that reminded me of a skewer. Strange how it hummed as if it was singing my name. As I examined the odd spear, I assumed by its weathered condition, it either had been ill-treated or it was very old.

I turned to call for Val, but he had been standing behind me. His step was light as a thief. It reminded me of Aidan, and a slight prick tugged at my heart. Without hesitance, I pushed my memory away. I forced my focus back to my more recent interest. "What is this?" I touched the glass, peering at the object, curious of] its strange effect it held on me.

"It's very ancient. According to legend, it's cursed. It's deadly to anyone who uses it."

"Cursed?" I whispered without taking my eyes off the box.

Val rubbed his chin, hesitating. "Have you ever heard of the Spear of Destiny?"

I gave him a sideways glance. "No. I haven't." My interest spiked.

"The name was given by a Roman soldier after piercing the heart of Jesus of Nazareth."

My eyes bounced back and forth between Val and the spear. "You're kidding?"

"I only wish. The relic has mystical powers. Powers to wield the world to his or her will."

"Holy mother of god! And you keep it here?" My mind reeled with astonishment.

"Yep! It's not going anywhere. I made sure of it."

"What if someone steals it?" I had to ask.

Val released a wired sigh. "They're a fool if they do."

"Why do you say that?"

"Simple. Anyone who uses the spear dies once it leaves their possession. The spear has left a trail of kings and dictators dead in its wake. They say that's what happened to Hitler." He shrugged. "That's why I keep it in the box. It's held captive by a protection spell."

"Holy cow! If this fell into the hands of the Illuminati it would kill them. Like the black plague, it'd wipe every one of those sons of bitches right off the face of the earth."

Val's face soured. "The curse doesn't affect the Order. They are immune."

"How is that possible?" I gawked with disbelief.

A lopsided grin stretched the tips of Val's mouth. "If you are as evil as the curse, the curse is useless. It's like a vaccination. Once you've been exposed to the virus, you become immune."

"Oh my god! The Order can never get their hands on this spear!" I felt sick, suddenly.

"Precisely!" he grimaced, staring at the spear. "I plan on keeping it out of their reach." He placed his hand on my shoulder. "Let's get back to why we're here." He stretched his arm out, pointing to the opposite side.

I lagged for a moment still hanging to the glass, unable to peel my eyes from the spear. Whatever enchantment adhered to it, I sensed it was insidious and very powerful. It was as though the spear was screaming my name. Unexpectedly, I shivered.

I pulled myself away and trailed after Val to the center of the room where floor-mats lay, spread out on the floor.

As we halted in the middle of the blue mats, Val extended his hand out to me and said, "Give it up." He demanded in his deep voice.

My brows knitted, baffled. Without thinking, I blurted out, "Like hell I will," — He cut me off, rolling his eyes.

"No, not that." He grinned, mischievously. "Your knife, please." The gold speckles in his eyes sparkled.

"How did you know?" Surprise covered my face.

He grinned like a young boy discovering hidden treasure. "Hmmm...in your walk."

"Smart-ass!" I retorted. Val remained staring at me with his open palm.

"Sorry, but my knife stays on me," there was no compromising when it came to my blade.

"I've seen how swift you are with that thing, and I value my neck and a few other precious parts too well to trust you with that damn blade. Hand it over"— he knitted his brows daringly— "unless you want me to take it?" he tossed a lopsided grin.

I entertained the thought, tempting fate, but I relented. I didn't want to wound him before I got my first lesson. I took a deep breath and blew it out. "Okay, but turn around. You've seen enough of my ass for the day. Must I give you bare skin as well?"

He flashed that mischievous crooked smile of his and teased, "Why be shy now? I saw exposed skin that night you wore that red dress...nice lacy thong."

I felt a rush of heat to my face. "I thought you said I was getting the same treatment as the boys?"

Val laughed. "Fair enough." He groaned, turning his back.

Keeping one eye on him, I slipped down my leggings to my ankles. Good thing I didn't have to give him a peep show. I wasn't wearing any panties. After I'd unstrapped my trusty blade in its sheath and clothed myself, I cleared my throat. "Okay, you can look now."

When Val twirled on his heels, facing me, I slapped the loaded sheath into his opened hand. A glint of victory glittered in his eyes as he tossed it over on a table in the corner. I folded my arms, feeling the bunt end of irritation.

If he saw my discomfort, he didn't let on. "Now let's get down to business." He eyed me carefully as if I was a horse for sale. "What are your abilities?"

I blinked, taken off my feet. "Excuse me?"

"Zophasemin have special gifts." He shrugged. "You know, supernatural abilities. What can you do?"

"I...I don't know," I stammered. It had never occurred to me that I might have a gift.

Val's brow arched. "Wait! You haven't developed your powers?" He said that like I had a contagious disease.

"What part of no do you not get?"

His brow flipped up. "Where were your parents while you were growing up? Did they not teach you anything?" Val's comment really grinded against my last nerve. I decided to sandblast his ass with my whole life's story. I didn't know why, but I felt I needed to explain.

"I had parents! Unlike yours', mine were human." I furthered with my story, "Like you once said, my beginnings started in a lab. My mother—or should I say my handler who posed as my mom for eighteen years—never revealed my true identity."

Val listened quietly.

"As I understand, my parents couldn't conceive. Finally with my mother's coaching, my father went to see the Family's renowned specialist, Dr. Astor. Soon my parents leaped with joy that their long journey had finally ended with great promise. The doctor reassured them that he could help Sara with her infertility problem. The Family and Dr. Astor guaranteed their medical breakthrough would work. Only before they started the treatments, my parents were required to sign a blood contract before the treatment commenced."

Val remained intent, listening.

"As conning as the Family was behind my father's back, they sweetened the deal by offering my mother a ton of money if she'd permit additional experimenting to the fetus outside the original agreement. Without any details to what the scientist planned on doing, Sara didn't bother asking. The money seemed to be her primary concern."

As I kept spilling my horrible story, Val's face became more drawn.

"All parties agreed that once I reached the age of eighteen, I would be handed over to the Family."

I noticed Val's jaw twitched, though, he remained still.

"Behind closed doors, Sara and the Family signed a secret B-contract with further details promising her great wealth."

I could see the more I spoke, the more his eyes appeared wry.

"When I was eight years old, my father started having second thoughts. He privately went to the doctor asking if the B-contract could be stopped. My father, Jon, once a family member of the Illuminati, didn't know anything about the side deal my mother made in secret. The Family didn't want him in on the deal. They knew my father wouldn't have agreed, so they kept him in the dark. His values were impeccable, directly the opposite of his family, the Illuminati."

Val cracked his knuckles as the tension in his face grew.

"Unknowingly, my father became a liability by threatening my mother's chance of becoming a millionaire. Once my mom received word of my father's cease and desist order, she approached the Family asking for help. The Family had invested a great deal in me. According to them, I was their true fountain of everlasting life. They considered me as their savior."

I kept on spilling my truth. "According to the Family, my DNA had been genetically altered, infused with celestial and human nucleotides, creating an unique genetic code. How they managed to conjure that up goes beyond my understanding. Then as an embryo, I was implanted into a vessel—Sara. I knew nothing of my true nature or that damn Family until I became the ripe old age of eighteen. It was not until then when I discovered my destiny, and my life changed forever. My "loving" mother agreed to hand me over to those monsters once I reached adulthood. She made good on her promise. She delivered me into the hands of the Illuminati for a huge sum of money."

"Freckles," Val interrupted, "I had no idea." His eyes softened.

"Yeah, it gets better." I went on to say. "Next, I was sealed to be mated with a chosen member of the Family. His name was Aidan." I paused. "Unknowingly, I fell in love with this man. I knew he was dark and very secretive, but he pursued me until I could no longer deny my heart. He convinced me that he loved me. He assured me he didn't share in his family's antics. I believed him." I tried to hide my pain. "Certain members of the Family, or some refer to them as the Order of the Quest, set out to steal my Essence. In order to save myself and the man I loved, Aidan, I believed if I gave myself to him our powers would lock together. I once thought this act would prevent anyone from taking our lives, that we would be safe from the Illuminati."

Val stood there with his arms crossed. I couldn't read his stoic face now, still, I continued.

"But I was wrong. I was set up. The morning after I'd given myself to Aidan, he and his wife, Sally kidnapped me, framing me for murdering my mother, and her two previous boyfriends. Proof of my innocence never mattered. The Family was gunning for me. I was sentenced to a life time in an institution for the criminally insane. Three long years I stayed in a small cell drugged with no hope of ever seeing daylight. Every day they forced me to lie in a pool of my vomit and feces."

I paused, questioning why I was telling this stranger my whole life. Come what may, my hesitation didn't stop me. "It wasn't much of a party staying at Haven Hospital. The first year I was contained in solemn confinement. The hospital claimed I had violent tendencies. Placing me into the mainstream would've been too risky." I sneered at my next words as I spit them out, hoping for some relief. "I believe their real reason had to do with concealing my pregnancy. The Family wanted it to remain a secret. So they kept me pumped with drugs through the whole duration of my pregnancy." I didn't wait for Val's reply. "If they couldn't extract my abilities, then they'd take the next best thing—my child." I looked away. "That's my theory." I shrugged. I stood there reeling. I'd hoped that he might somehow gain an understanding of how damaged I'd become, but at that point, I couldn't go any further.

As expected, my human side snapped. I started shaking. Tears began streaming down my cheeks. Every nerve in my body felt on fire. I collapsed to the floor, covering my face with my hands, weeping hysterically. I think at that moment, I'd lost my mind. My whole body shuddered.

In the next breath, I felt the comfort of two stalwart arms drawing me into a blanket of consoling warmth. Val held me silently in his arms as I shook from the flooding tears, which wouldn't cease. I heard his soft voice in between my sobbing, easing my open wound. For the first time in a very long time, I felt safe which I thought would be an impossibility after Aidan's betrayal.

It was a good while before the tears dried, and all the while, he kissed my head and cooed with soft words—of love?

⬥⫷❋⫸⬥

It was much later when I woke up to find myself alone in Val's bed. Even through the dimness, I recognized his room. I must've dosed off most of the morning. I yawned into the pillow, and I suddenly picked up his scent. A long-forgotten stir began to rise. The reality of being alone pained me, and I couldn't stand the feeling. I wanted him. I called his name, "Val?" I whispered with a sleepy voice.

"Yeah, coming!" He called back to me. He entered the room, bringing me carryout soup. "Hey. Sleeping Beauty is awake!" He smiled brightly.

"What time is it?" I asked, rubbing my eyes and yawning.

"I don't know. About eleven."

"In the morning?"

"No, night, Freckles." Val laid the soup on the nightstand. "I thought you might like something to eat." He started pulling the lid off the soup.

"Don't," I asked.

He glanced over at me. "Don't what?" His eyes implied confusion.

I reached over and tugged on his T-shirt, pulling him into the bed with me. All I wanted was to feel his arms around me once more. I craved his touch, his scent. I yearned to taste his sweet lips. It didn't take much of a tug either. He hungrily followed my request. The soothing pressure of his weight on top of me felt wonderful. It didn't take long before I had found myself lost in his kisses. They were much different than before, more possessive.

His hands drifted to my bare skin underneath the jersey, and soon the shirt found its way to the floor. Shortly after, his T-shirt followed, showing exactly what I'd expected, a beautiful six-pack against his tawny skin. His hands were devouring, and I began to thirst for more. After he unsnapped my bra, he gently slipped off my leggings, leaving me totally bare. His pants were unzipped, showing a trail of hair underneath. Soon off they joined the pile of clothes on the floor. Before long, we both delighted in each other's climbing desire.

My hands trailed over his firm body, and his hands began to sizzle over my hot skin. I couldn't remember if making love to Aidan felt as exciting. The Zop was definitely growing on me, and here I was in the heat of passion, yearning for him to quench the fire that grew deep inside me. He was hot! Obviously I wasn't his first. His hands and kisses were too skillful.

As he worked his magical hands over my body from my breast to the lower region, I moaned for more, arching my back. I guessed by his sultry eyes, I think he wanted me as much as I wanted him. It was freeing—lovemaking with no expectations, no commitment, just uninhibited passion. I ravished in this new awakening.

Then it happened. Val lifted his head as our eyes hitched. In his husky voice, he whispered, "I could get used to this sharing my bed, sharing my life with you." Unexpectedly, he broke the rules. Briefly, he paused. "I'm falling for you, Freckles." I pulled away, searching into his gentle eyes as why he'd gone soft on me.

My brows knitted as I rose up on my elbows. Val didn't move, still hovering over me. "Come on! Let's not do this!" I nearly grimaced.

Disappointment twisted his face as he exclaimed, "I tell you I'm crazy about you, and that's all you can say?" I could see the hurt and disappointment in his eyes. Better to let him down now than to string him along.

"You don't have to make this into a mountain. Relax. I'm not looking for any sort of commitment with you. We're friends and business partners with occasional benefits. Isn't that what you guys dream about? Sex with no chains?" I got a little sarcastic. Yet the instant it left my lips, I regretted it. I was really starting to act like a bitch just a tad too much these days.

Val pulled himself off me and turned his back to me, sitting on the edge of the bed. I lay there, feeling a bit exposed and confused. Trying to make sense of this, I asked, "Why are you upset at me?" I reached out to him and gently nudged his back.

His head tilted to the side, looking over his shoulder. "You can't even call me by my name. My name is Val. Say it!" He demanded.

I didn't get why he was acting this way but okay, whatever. "Val! Val! Val! Happy?" I sang out, glowering at him as he faced me. Countenance covered his face silently.

Then he broke the quiet tension by saying, "I can't do this." He ran his fingers through his luscious hair. "I refuse to share my bed with you as long as you have feelings for him."

Wow where did that come from? I thought. "What difference does it make? Aidan's dead!" My comeback felt harsh and too cold. Even still, I didn't get why he had a problem with my past lover.

"It matters to me! I won't have you like this."

"Like what? Naked in your bed?" My voice spewed with aggravation.

"No! I mean I won't make love to you until you're over Aidan—free and clear!" His golden eyes burned through my heart. Hence, an uncomfortable quiet fell between us. Then he gathered his clothing and, with strain, he snapped, "Get dressed. I'll take you home."

Oh no, he just didn't! Irritation combed through me. "That's okay! I wouldn't want to trouble you." My voice dripped with ire. "I can catch my own cab. Hey! Maybe it'll be that same driver you've often thrown cash at, ordering him to get rid of me." I laughed with scorn. "I'm not good enough to hang in your bar, and I suppose that goes for your bed as well. That's just rich!" I hissed. As I angrily snatched up my clothing, the bravery of nudity disappeared along with our passion expiring. Suddenly, I rushed to cover my body from humiliation.

Val's eyes softened as his voice filled with sadness like he'd lost something precious to his heart. "That's not it, and you know it!"

"Then tell me your reason. Why?"

"Sometimes there's more between a man and a woman than just sex."

A pain of guilt struck me. At the same token, it made me even angrier. I couldn't help how I felt. "Don't judge me! I know all about letting go and trusting. I did that, and look where it got me! Prison!" I screamed. "I never want to give another man that much power over me ever again!" I took in a barbed breath. "If you want more, then you need to look elsewhere." I stared coldly into his longing eyes, but my words of endearment wouldn't come. So I did what I knew best. "Fine! I'll call my own cab!" I grabbed my cell.

As I gathered my things, I kept my back to the marred guy in the room, but then it quickly came to me why I was here in the first place. I knew I had to swallow a little pride. Losing my chance at finding my daughter wasn't an option. Whether I wanted to admit it or not, I needed him. I suppressed my angry feelings in order for me to talk to him calmly. I cleared my throat, "I still require your help. I'm willing to pay you handsomely for your trouble." I held my breath, waiting for his response.

Quiet settled for a brief moment. Only his splintering sigh drifted in the dim room. "I don't want your money." His words sounded hurt, yet deliberate. "I keep my word. If I say I will do something, I do it, regardless. Give it to charity." Val replied crassly. I felt the blaze of his words. It wasn't what he said, but the tone. Shame flushed my cheeks. I couldn't look at him. I felt bad enough. He continued. "Be here in the morning, early." And he disappeared, leaving me alone to my loathsome self.

⤞⋆⋆⋆⤝

Riding in the cab, home, an ache deep within my gut knotted. I hated what had happened. He wanted more. It was apparent in his wounded eyes. The past Stevie would've fallen head-over-heels in love with him. He had all the right ingredients to make a perfect boyfriend—easy on the eyes, strong and protective, and far too considerate to waste on me. Not trying to beat myself up, but I knew the we-part wouldn't work.

I should've not let my guard down. Yet I'd wanted him, plain and simple. I wiped a tear away. Despite my selfish desires, if I allowed myself the luxury of caring, Val would be getting the short end of the stick. I was only a fragment of a woman—defective. As long as my past continued to emerge with my present, I'd never be whole. I might as well face it. Until I found peace within myself, I was not my own. I withdrew a glumly sigh. The only thing that mattered right now was finding my daughter. Anything outside of that was pointless.

Miasma

WHEN I ARRIVED home, Jeffery had been waiting up for me. I suppose both Jeffery and Dom had been concerned for me after I'd missed all three meals today. A guilty feeling hit the pit of my stomach. I'd forgotten to call. I withdrew a deep sigh. After years of having very little to eat, missing meals didn't seem that big of a deal to me. I assumed since I was only a smudge of human and more celestial, my body didn't require a lot of nourishment. Growing up with my mom, my lack of need to eat turned out to be a blessing. We didn't have much more than the shirts on our backs, even more so with food.

I followed the light to the kitchen where a renowned foot was tapping vigorously against the hardwood flooring. I rolled my eyes and murmured, "Good grief!" I didn't have to guess who had been waiting up for me.

Jeffery's voice echoed from the kitchen, "Gurrrl, get your butt in 'ere!" he called out sternly. My breath caught in my throat. "Oh mother of god! Is he pissed at me too?" I mumbled.

Once I seated myself across the table from Jeff, he placed in front of me a steaming bowl of soup. It was my favorite, chicken and dumplings coupled with Dom's famous Dee-Dee rolls. The bread was so moist every bite melted in my mouth. It was the modern-day manna. It was that divine. I didn't waste any time digging in.

"Thanks, Jeff! What's up?" I asked, peeking over the curls of steam while I blew into my spoon. I noticed the worried lines on Jeff's strained face.

"Dom's been sick today with worry. I sent him to bed with one of my sleeping pills. Well, actually, the pills are his. I just borrowed them any hoot. I hope your evening went well?"

All at once I felt like a kid again under fire. There was a pinch of sarcasm in Jeffery's tone. "I'd had better." I shrugged, drowning my memories of the day in my dumplings.

"We had a visitor today." Jeffery kept tapping his foot, and soon his fingers joined in.

I knew right away this couldn't be good. "Who?" My breath steeled.

"Oh, it ain't that horrid clan." Jeffery chirped as if he'd read my mind. "Someone you will never guess in a million years."

"Just end my misery and cough it up already!" I grumbled as I dropped my spoon into the soup, making it splatter onto the table. I reached for a napkin and started dabbing.

Jeffery's face soured as though he'd smelled something poignant. "Honeychile, youse need to stop be-n so snippy!" he lectured, full of attitude.

"Sorry. It's been a rough day." I squirmed in my seat.

"I'd love to hear about it, but you have a visitor!" Jeffery sounded agitated.

"Jeff, I love you, but can it wait until morning? I'm just not feeling it."

"No, ma'am! It sure as hell can't." Jeffery's lips pursed. I knew whenever my friend made that tart face, he meant business. I might as well grin and bear it. My only hope was that whatever it was that he needed off his chest didn't last into the wee morning hour. "Shoot!" I conceded.

"Okay, Miss Stevie, smarty-pants, close your eyes. It's a surprise!"

Without a clue, I heard soft footfalls coming behind me, not heavy like Dom or loud like Jeffery but light and quick like an athlete. Like a shot I felt cool hands over my eyes and a soft voice following. "Guess who!"

Immediately I knew. I swirled around in my chair, and there stood my good friend, Jen Li. I hadn't seen her since that terrible day.

Jumping to my feet, I embraced my welcomed friend. We shared in mirth and tears of joy. "I can't believe it's you!" I stood back, gazing at Jen, still in disbelief.

In life you only have a few true friends, and that described Jen in a nutshell. "Yeah! Your friend, Jeffery, looked me up." She nodded to the oddly quiet man, tapping his foot, feverously. "I had no idea you were living here in New Orleans. I'm going to UNO here. I got a scholarship in volley-ball, so here I am, a college student." She smiled, flashing her bright white teeth against her brown skin.

That's funny. I could've sworn Jen played basket-ball. I chewed on the inside of my lip, thinking. If my memory served me well, she preferred the more aggressive sports. Suddenly Jeffery caught the corner of my eye. His cheeks had bloated as if he was holding back vomit, and his eyes were glazed. I'd be the first to admit that Jeffery had his weird moments, but this was really strange even for him.

Suspicion began to stir.

"How did you end up here?" Jen broke my train of thought.

"Well, I came to stay with Jeffery and Dom." I smiled, trying to put on a good face.

"Jeff told me about your mom's death. I had no clue!" Jen reached out, placing her hand on my shoulder. "I'm sorry I wasn't there for you. I had no idea where you had disappeared to. Even Sam was struck with bewilderment." Jen's face seemed genuine, but Sam died before I'd disappeared. Perhaps she had the days mixed. I keep forgetting it had happen over three years ago. To me, it seemed like yesterday.

"Yeah—uh—a lot of things have changed. When did you last see Sam?" I kept my gaze even.

"Let's see?" Jen gave pause. "It was the next day at school."

Unearthly chills slithered down my spine. Why was she lying? "Are you sure you have the right day?" I tried to be inconspicuous.

Jen's face etched with incertitude. "No, wait! It was that night after the Halloween party. He took me home. I had a little too much to drink. You know me! Partee-hardee!"

That was peculiar. The Jen I use to know didn't drink. On the contrary, she was a health nut. "How late did you stay?" I held my breath. I remembered Sam telling me that Jen had stayed home. Aidan later that night exclaimed that the party had been canceled. Now Jen was telling me Sam had taken her home. I wasn't sure who to believe, so I went with my gut.

"Oh! We shut the party down!" she bragged. "I don't know maybe three in the morning." She tossed an impish grin. Creepy bumps popped up over my arms.

"That's really odd."

"Why do you say that?"

I wasn't sure who this person was standing in front of me, but I knew who she wasn't. I smiled kindly, "it's just strange that you would say Sam carried you home. The party had been canceled." I watched her body go rigid.

"Wow!" she swallowed. "You know I was pretty drunk. Maybe I have it confused with a later party."

I arched a brow. "You might have gone to another party, but it wasn't with Sam."

Her eyes grew like marbles. "What do you mean? Of course I was with Sam. We were dating."

If I had any doubts before, I certainly didn't have them now. "Jen, you weren't dating Sam. Gina was his girlfriend."

"That two timer! He was dating her too?" there was a hint of pretension in her feigned shock. "I'd love to give him a piece of my mind."

I shuffled my feet nervously. "That's going to be hard to do. Sam is dead." I swallowed a pinch of guilt. Casting logic aside, I couldn't help feeling somewhat responsible for Sam's death.

"He died?"

I glanced down at my feet, then back at her shocked face. "Uh—actually he died on Halloween night, three years ago." There tension in my jaw ached. "You see it would be an impossibility for Sam to have taken you home that night or any other night following."

"Damn! I'm really confused." She giggled as she scratched her head. Then her eyes latched onto mine. "How?"

Shit! I didn't want to tell her the truth. "A car accident." I flinched, lying.

"A two car accident?"

I shook my head, greenly. "No. No other driver. He came around a curve too fast and lost control. His car crashed into a tree." I lied again.

"Man-oh-man, that blows!" Jen made a whistle.

"Yeah, life's been surreal," I confessed, feeling the mockery in my voice.

Then unexpectedly Jen switched the kernel as though Sam's death hadn't registered with her. "Are you still dating Aidan?" It was no secret that she didn't like the dude, but her lack of feelings seemed off the charts.

"No, I haven't seen him since high school." The topic for discussion with this girl was getting more bizarre. Now she was team-Aidan!

"Aw, sorry to hear that. I'd hoped you two would've gotten engaged." Everything was off with this conversation, including Jen's unexpected visit. I slipped a sideways peek at Jeffery. His face had drawn pale, and he was unusually still. If I were a betting woman, I'd make a wager that this visit had the mark of the Family. If Jen was under a spell, we needed to help her.

"Do you remember that day when Sam and you met up with me at Ms. Noel's?" I searched deep into her brown eyes to see if there was a small glimmer of recollection, though, I saw nothing supporting my suspicion. If Sam had put her under an enchantment, why hasn't it expired after three years?

Jen wrinkled her nose, then she asked in an off-beat voice. "Ms. Noel?" she tapped her finger on her chin. "Wasn't she the owner of the diner?"

I remained calm. "Yeah, her! Fairly young, had a bunch of kids. We'd babysit for her from time to time. Remember?"

"Oh, I sure do! Those kids were brats too." Jen affirmed, staring vacantly at me.

I turned my attention to Jeff. Even he was off tonight. His face appeared aloof—trance like. So I shook his shoulder, hard. After a moment Jeff blinked. It was as if he'd come back to life. "Lord have mercy! Was I sleep walk-n again?" He shrugged his shoulders, trying to wake-up.

"Wake-up, boo. I got a question for you." I insisted in an unruffled voice.

"Hurry-up! I'm tired." Jeffery growled. "I just can't stay up like I use to."

"Jeff!" I rested my hand on his shoulder. "Tell me again how you got in touch with Jen?"

"Oh Lord have mercy!" Jeffery exasperated. "Why would I say I looked her up? The gurrrl found us. She came knock-n on our door this even-n all prissy-in-pink, insist-n to see youse. I couldn't chase the bitch off with a broomstick. She wouldn't leave."

"Where's Dom?" I snapped.

"He's upstairs, sick," Jeffery tossed his hand toward the stairs, seeming unfazed. A cold stir crept over me, nothing was adding up.

Immediately I faced my questionable guest. My eyes blazed with mistrust. "Who the hell are you?" I felt for my knife. Damn! I'd forgotten. I'd left my steel at Val's. Without being too obvious, I scanned the room for anything I could use as a weapon.

The only way I could best describe the passage before my eyes was as if I was in another person's dream, and I was a mere by-stander watching. In a flash Jen's body began to seize, thrashing violently, face distorted. Next, her body imploded, shattering fragments of something like glass in every direction. Quick on my feet, I lunged across Jeffery with my back to the flying shards, shielding us both as we toppled to the floor. My whole backside was bathed with an unknown substance that felt wet and cold. Blood, came to mind. Instantly I touched my neck and drew back the moisture on my fingertips. I glimpsed at my fingers, gawking. It was only water. WTF? When my eyes lifted, I gasped. There were hundreds of tiny molecules floating aimlessly in the air and evaporating into vapor.

Then in a quick blink, the murky mist vanished, leaving no proof of existence. All evidence of Jen was gone.

"What the hell!" Jeffery leaped to his feet.

Alarmed, I rushed, "Go check Dom!" a bone-chilling expression colored Jeffery's face as he sprinted up the stairs.

In the meantime, I scoped the kitchen-cabinetry for an easy weapon. I went through several drawers before I found Dom's goodies. My eyes nearly went bug-eyed as I gazed down at the Shun knives, high-quality made from Japan. I realized then that I wasn't the only one in the house with a knife fixation. I admired the glimmering collection, smiling. Quick with ease, I locked my fingers around the hilt of a thinner blade. Itching to test it out, I tossed the chef's knife in my palm, getting a feel for the steel. It was perfect, nicely balanced with a little heft.

Without warning, screams emerged from upstairs. Thrust from my thoughts, I dashed in the direction of the bellows. When I reached the threshold of Dom's bedroom, my breath lodged in my throat. Jeffery was leaning over Dom's body, screaming blood-curdling cries. Shear panic slammed into my chest. Then my lungs expanded once my eyes landed on the lump on the floor. Dom had been bound by rope, gagged with duct-tape. He was alive! "Thank goodness," I breathed, grateful for the wall holding me up as I filled my lungs with air.

Hysterical, Jeffery sobbed. "I'm sorry! I don't know what came over me!" Jeff's shaky hands weren't much use loosening the tight rope. I fell beside him offering my aid. "Hey boo, let me do this. Your hands are trembling." Jeff nodded still weeping as he sat back and let me take over the task.

My hands weren't much better. Thank the stars that I had Dom's razor, sharp knife to do most of the work. Willing my hands steady, I began sawing the rope in two. "The Family did this!" I hissed through clenched teeth, fiercely working the blade back and forth.

Once I freed a very shaken chef, Jeffery assisted Dom to the lounge chair by the large window. Tears welled as I watched poor Dom rub his wrist. I sat back on my heels, releasing a winded breath. "Are you okay, Dom?"

Dom nodded, his face pale and drained. "Oui! I will live." He gave a wry smile. Apparently, he was in a little pain, the rope had made thin-lined cuts. I think in a day or so, the cuts would be a faint mark, but the memory of tonight, I feared may linger for life.

"I can't believe I did this to you!" Jeffery cried. "I swear I don't remember tying you up."

"Jeff, I'm fine." Dom broke in, breathing a bit heavy. "You were under a spell." He soothed his distraught partner. Then Dom's eyes shifted to me. Determination was irrefutable in his jaw. "It is imperative that we take measures protecting ourselves. This can't wait, I fear."

Guilt began to abrade my gut as though I had an ulcer. "Guys," my voice quavered. "I am so sorry!" I ran my fingers through my short curls. "As long as I live here I'm endangering your lives. I should find another place."

"Nonsense!" Dom barked. "You're staying here, and that's final."

"If I stay, we need to hire big, beefy guards that know how to use an arsenal of weaponry!" I countered.

"I second dat!" Jeff conferred as we broke down and started laughing over Jeffery's remark and the eldritch night.

Apart from the short moment of humor, I knew my next move was unavoidable contact the one person who understood the Family's darkness probably better than me—Val. I pulled out my cell phone from my bra and speed-dialed. My heart pounded as I counted the rings. Finally, he picked up.

"Hello." A little chill washed over me as I heard his drowsy voice.

I blurted out, not worrying if I sounded desperate. "I know you're mad at me. You have a right to be, but something bad has happened. It's got the boys and me scared. Can you please come over?" Dead silence fell for what seemed like an eternity. Then I heard something familiar—a sigh.

"Yeah, let me get dressed, and I'll be right there." *Click.*

I dropped my phone back in my bra and looked up at the guys to find two sets of eyes targeting me.

Jeffery decided to chime in. "You just amaze me. You treat that poor boy like dirt, then you call him in the wee morning hour, asking him to get out of his nice, warm bed to help you out, and with no questions asked, he comes to your rescue. Gurrrl, you better start treat-n that man better!" Jeffery scolded me, wagging his finger in a heat of fiery.

I popped off, "how do you know his bed's warm?" By the curl of Jeffery's lips, I surely thought he was going to chase me down with the same broomstick, he threatened Jen with.

Less than half an hour later, we heard the doorbell. Even though we were expecting Val, the chime sent us jumping out of our skin. After making sure the guys were settled, I scurried downstairs to the front-door. I saw through the glass Val standing patiently with his hands in his jean pockets, rocking on his heels. A little spurt of excitement struck as I realized how cute he looked with his disheveled hair. He had that "just rolled out of bed" look. It was a good look for him. Chills etched down to my toes. The good kind. I swung the door open, and before

I could contain myself, with no given thought, I threw myself into his arms. He held me back for only a split second before his comforting arms tightly wrapped around me. As I began to melt into his consoling warmth, my body started trembling and tears began to streak my face. Geez, this was not how I pictured this. I wanted to betray strength rather than a display of some sniffling milksop. Val seemed to bring out the sappy side of me.

I choked through the words. "I think the Family is trying to hurt us." My voice filled with unhinged fright.

Val craned his neck, combing the area of the house to see if he spotted a glimpse of any suspecting shadow lurking around the skirt of the house. Then speedily, he ushered me inside and closed the door behind us, locking the bolt. "What happened?" His gold eyes filled with worry.

I wiped the tears off my face with the back of my hand and began telling him the accounts of the night. By the time I finished, Jeffery walked-up behind me and interjected. "Uh-hmm! It was like Jasper the friendly ghost. I tell you! The girl just turned pale-white, and her body went poof! It was like out of a horror movie!" Jeff spoke in his high-pitched drawl. I was glad he decided to come downstairs and join us. After all, he spent more time with Jen than I. He may recall something that could be helpful. Yet on second thought, whatever that creature was, it had Jeffery under some hex.

Val stood there in silence, taking in our tale of the night. I turned to Jeff and asked, "Is Dom okay?" concern saturated my voice.

"He's still shaken, but this time, I really did give him a sleeping pill. He should rest good with that pill!" Jeffery explained.

"How about you, boo?" I rubbed his upper arm, consoling him. "Are you okay?" I smiled. My heart went out to him. I knew far too well how he must feel. Though, Jeffery might find it hard to accept his innocence, he was blameless for his actions. We were all puppets on a string when it came to the Family's mastery.

Tonight wasn't any fault of Jeffery's. He had been under some sort of mind-control, not of his own.

"I think I'm done trip-n." He drew out of his pocket a crisp-white napkin and dabbed the sweat off his forehead. "I sure ain't drink-n no mo cool-aid."

I glimpsed at Val hiding a suspicious smile behind his fake cough. I wanted to laugh too, but I didn't dare. I didn't want the wrath of Jeffery's broomstick on my tail. Just the same, I had to give it to old Jeff. He could make any fright into comedy. That was what was so special about him.

"Fellas," I suddenly felt a rush of chill. "I think we have been cursed." My eyes bounced between both men.

"Now let's not jump to the gun just yet," Val advised. "What purpose would someone have to hurt Jeffery?"

"I'm guessing it was a trap for me, but the plan back-fired." I answered.

"Good hunch, Stevie, but why not just tie up both men and surprise you with an ambush?" Then his steady gaze slid to Jeff. "No offense, my man."

"None taken, but you did give me a good idea...uh, never mind." Jeffery quickly masked a funny expression on his face, then he focused back to the conversation, "Come on! Let's get some food. We can talk in the kitchen."

Jeffery laid out a batch of Dom's homemade chocolate-chip cookies and made a strong brew of coffee. After seating ourselves at the table, sipping the coffee and sinking our teeth into the fabulous, gooey cookies, Val broke the gleeful silence reminding us why we were here in the first place. "Okay," his gold-eyes were directed at me, "now tell me why you think this had anything to do with the Family and dark magick?" By the hard lines in Val's face, I was certain this strike was larger than I'd initially envisioned. I was frightened too.

"Who else would stoop to such a low?" I reasoned.

"Have you two ever heard of a *miasma?*" Val asked.

Jeffery and I shared a glance, and in the same breath, we both bellowed, "Nooo!"

"Well,"—Val took a deep breath. "I think what you all experienced was the work of an evil mist known as miasma."

"That name has spooky stamped all over it." I quavered.

Jeffery broke in, "forget the mofo spooky! Whatever that girl was, it stunk worse than any skunk I'd ever come across." He pinched his nose, twisting his lips into a scowl.

"Come to think about it, I noticed a smell too. I kept thinking the stove had a gas leak. Weird!" I grimaced. "I don't know why I didn't mention it."

Val interjected. "Stevie, you may have been under the enchantment like Jeffery."

"I think your right. I wasn't myself, now that I think about it." I wrapped my arms around my waist, trying to ease my nerves.

Val continued, "My friends, what you have encountered is a rare type of incantation." He rubbed his bristled chin, thinking. "What is strange to me is that the cast is seldom used to harm anyone. However, its foul odor can clear a herd of elephants."

"A spell that stinks! That's just rich!" Jeffery groaned.

"It's a very powerful incantation." Val went on explaining. "Whoever worked the spell is a craftmaster. Not just anyone can conjure a miasma."

"What did you call it?" it sounded like a childhood disease, I thought.

"It's pronounced as mē'azmə." Val emphasized the sounding.

"I still don't understand. Let me see if I understand you, correctly. What we saw tonight was not my friend. It was a miasma." Suddenly I felt as if I was sinking into a black hole.

"That's correct." Val confirmed. "Your friend might've appeared real, but in truth, you were merely seeing a projection."

"Do you think this mysterious craftmaster is trying to harm us?" I knew for the sanction of my family, I needed to open my ears and take heed. Yet I alone may not be enough to protect them.

"It's possible." Val sipped his now lukewarm coffee. "Though I can't be certain." He set his cup down and sighed. "By the same token, I do suspect that the miasma was sent to spy."

My brows furrowed. "Spy! How?" I felt the hairs on my back stiffen.

"A miasma," Val furthered, "is similar to astral projecting. Rather than a flesh and blood human materializing before your eyes, the craftmaster remains anonymous, hiding behind the miasma."

"Talk about hiding in the closet." Jeffery rolled his eyes.

"Talk about a coward, if you ask me." At that point, I wanted to smash something, I was so mad.

"A dangerous coward, if you will." Val ran his fingers through his hair. "I think I might better stay until sunup. Don't bother finding me a bed." Val rose from the table and I followed. "If you and Jeffery will excuse me." He nodded. "I'll be busy ridding the house of bad energy and working protection spells." Val turned to Jeffery who remained seated, crunching on a cookie. "You got any sea salt and sage? White candles and purified water, I'll need as well."

"I have sea salt and sage. And if you consider my finger in the water purifying it, then I got that too!" Jeffery joked, or at least I assumed.

I was ready to get this project started. We couldn't rid this house of bad juju fast enough.

"Oh!" Val turned a serious eye on me. "It's time you meet our kind."

My breath stalled. "I thought you said the Zophasemin hated my kind. Remember, I'm impure?"

"True. Don't worry. I have it handled. This is my gang. They follow me and will do whatever I ask."

"So you're a gangbanger?"

"No, sweetheart. I'm the leader of the Zop. No one messes with me unless he has a death wish and that includes following my orders."

And there it was—Val the great leader, assuming a posture of superiority by that lopsided grin of his. I didn't see that coming. Then it hit me. "Val, did you order your gang to leave me alone?"

Jeffery watched in silence, still nibbling on the same cookie.

"Oh, the lady calls me by my name. There's a first!" Acid coated his baritone voice.

"There's no need to be so sensitive."

He snorted a curt laugh. "Sensitivity is what sets the Zop apart from the rest."

"Oh, and you kicking me out of your bed was a tradition?"

"Now who's the sensitive one? I just chose not to make a whore out of you. I like to think of myself as a gentleman." Val's soft eyes abruptly hardened.

I hated fights, but I never backed down from one, and I wasn't going to change that tradition now. "For your information, your hind-ass, that's my decision. I think a woman should have the same freedom as a man, sleeping with whomever without being pegged as a fille-de-joie." I glared angrily at the towering demigod—a giant, six-five, against my small frame of five-five. "Furthermore, for your information, I don't go jumping from bed to bed. I've only had one partner in my life, and that was a onetime deal, so watch what you call me!" I glared at the mighty man.

A strange noise disrupted our heated argument. Both Val and I halted turning in the direction of the galling sound. It was Jeffery chomping on popcorn, now sitting frozen and bug-eyed. We had forgotten we were in mixed company.

Unfortunately Jeffery didn't' get to see the ending of the show. Once he saw the blaze of Val's face, he quickly scattered upstairs. I on the other hand had to finish the heated discussion with one irate Zop.

I twirled on my heels with fire in my glint. "Do we have to continue this pointless argument?"

"Stop avoiding the inevitable. I get that you're afraid to admit that you have feelings for me." Val charged.

"Don't be ridiculous!"

"Really! Is this how it's going to be?"

"I have no idea what you're referring to." WTF! I wished I'd escaped with Jeffery upstairs.

"Stop being coy with me. Admit it! You don't call me by my first name because you're scared of letting that tender heart extend pass your nose.

"Actually, I never call my employees by their first name." There went my smart mouth.

When I saw the anger in his eyes ignite, it took me back a step or two. My once-gentle Ben didn't seem so gentle any longer. He paused while never lifting his scowl at me. Next he lowered his voice to a mere whisper. "He really hurt you didn't he? I know deep down this isn't who you are." His words tortured me softly, "I didn't want to just have sex with you. I wanted to make love to you. You are deserving of nothing less."

I stood there frozen unable to speak. How stupid could I have been to overlook this? I think at that point, I'd hit my lowest low. I had been too wrapped up in my own selfish desires that I'd forgotten to consider Val's feelings. What a fool I had become.

I started to reach out to touch his face, but by then his face glossed over, closing himself off to any further conversations in relation to our intimacy issues. I knew any attempt on my part would be futile. I dropped my hand to my side and stood there staring back at him in silence.

As if our discussion had never come into play, he went on to say, "You might want to make another pot of coffee. It's going to be a long day." He hesitated. "I'll be outside if you need me." I stood frozen, watching him exit the house.

Obviously he felt hurt. I didn't know what exactly he wanted from me. If he wished for my heart, I'd gladly give it, but he was asking the impossible. My heart stopped beating a long time ago.

Discovery

T HE GOLDEN DAWN was just peeking over the horizon when Val stepped back into the house. He'd finished smudging the exterior with sage. By his drained face, and damp hair from the cold dew, I began to grasp that this ritual was an intricate venture. The rite demanded hours, and considering that he'd had little sleep, the tall order had taken a toll on him.

Ms. Noel once explained to me the importance of a protection spell the cleansing could only be performed by the craft maker someone with a particular kind of magick. Any other caster standing in the energy-field might disturb the sacred ground, contaminating the incantation.

Keeping that in mind and the huge argument between Val and me, I thought it might be wise to steer clear. Besides, right now, I hated myself. Val was right. My mind seemed to linger in the past. I wasn't sure if Aidan had anything to do with it, but I was certain my child did. If he couldn't understand my plight—I didn't see our relationship blossoming into anything significant.

———◆⤜✳⤛◆———

Val didn't waste any time getting to the interior. Since the same rule applied, I stayed in the foyer, sinking into a comfy chair, keeping out of the way. Quietly I listened to his gentle footfalls as he moved willowy throughout the mansion, chanting an ancient language.

After a short time, my eyelids could no longer hold its own, and sleep followed. Hours had past when a soft tap on my knee awakened me. I opened my droopy eyes and there bigger than life, kneeling before me was Val. His face appeared weary and his beautiful golden eyes were blood-shot, but a sweetness had replaced his angry glint. I instantly smiled, and a thrill shot through me. I was happy to see he wasn't mad at me any longer.

An aroma of breakfast drifted through the house. I knew right away Dom was back to his old self, preparing breakfast for everyone. My French friend loved early mornings. He had us all beat with age, yet, he often worked the longest and hardest. Jeffery, I'd decided, was an immutable fixture collecting dust.

"Are you hungry?" Val asked.

"Yeah. I could eat." I stretched and yawned.

Val flashed a crooked grin, extending his hand. I smiled back, taking him up on his kind gesture. As he hoisted me onto my feet, I lost my balance, falling into his arms. Whether it was an accident or Val's intention, I'd never know; but when our eyes met, we froze, as if time stood still, lost in each other's captivating breath. His hands rested on my hips, a slight caress of his thumb brushed against my bare-skin right above the waist band of my pants, spreading goose bumps over my body. Visions of the past night in his bed came rushing. My breath hitched as I watched Val slowly begin to lean in for a kiss. Only a fraction away, right before Val made contact, Jeffery peeked his head around the corner, clearing his throat, loudly. Val and I both jerked back, startled as Jeffery barked. "Food is get-n cold!"

With disappointment riding skirt-tail, our trance faltered, and the enchantment broke. I withdrew from Val's arms and followed Jeffery.

⬥━━━━❖━━━━⬥

At the table, everyone seemed quiet and into their private reflections of the night before. Dom cleared his pallet and addressed Val. "Thank you for your help. We are very grateful."

The left corner of Val's lips quirked into a brief smile. "Don't mention it. I'm glad to help." He paused, switching to a more serious note. "It is crucial for us to find out why this unknown presence is targeting you good folks." Val advised.

Dom joined in saying out loud what I was already thinking. "I think we won't have to look very far to find this ur—iscélérat (scoundrel)."

"I suspect everyone at this table assumes that the Family is responsible." Val disclosed, "however, this miasma isn't their style."

I jumped on the wagon this time. "If it's not the Family, then who is it?"

"Right now I can't put a face with the name, however, I believe it's a sole entity haunting you for its own personal reasons." Funny, I thought. I just realized that I'd never seen Val in his own element—strong and confident. I felt...enamored.

"Oui!" Dom agreed. "Do you have any idea why we are being targeted?"

"No. Not yet." Val went on to explain. "That's why we need to get to the bottom of this black magick. I think if we find the motive, we'll find the person behind all this hex-spying."

Jeffery butted in with a shriek. "Hold the hell on!" he raised his hand in the air like he was about to give the sermon on the mount. "Can those evil mofo spies see us in the bathroom?"

Dom rolled his eyes, Val and I shared glances but quickly diverted our eyes off in another direction to avoid an explosion of uncontained laughter. Val cleared his throat, pushing down the mirth, "Bro, just make sure you're covered-up when you do any extra curriculum."

I couldn't hold it any longer as I spewed over the brim of roaring laughter.

Val and Dom somehow kept their composure.

"That's just fine, missy!" Jeffery fumed at me. "I have a broomstick with your name on it." He pursed his lips.

I'm sorry, boo." I snickered, nearly breaking a rib. I wiped the moisture from my eyes. "I couldn't help it." I snickered again.

Jeffery folded his arms, his face blistered from ireful silence.

Dom took the table and asked, "Do you have any suggestions of how we can find this mysterious malefactor?

Then I intervened, straightening my shoulders back, taking a much more serious tone. "There is someone I suspect who might be behind this ploy. She's well trained in the arts of magick. I saw her vanish with my own two eyes, and she detests me."

"What's the girl's name? I can get my peeps to check her out," Val asked, sipping his coffee.

"Helen De Pont," I revealed.

Val's sip suddenly spewed forth, shooting poor Jeffery in the face. Jeff shrieked, springing from the table and running for his bathroom, leaving a trail of curses in his wake.

Dom followed after Jeffery, and I snatched a napkin for Val. When I handed him the towel, I arched a suspicious brow, asking. "Do you know this bitch?"

Val's voice was raspy, burning from swallowing the coffee down the wrong pipe. "In passing," he coughed out.

"Uh-hmm. Sure there's not more to it?" My voice laced with *"you're lying!"*

"Hmm...I know of her." Val dabbed the dark liquid off his once white T-shirt. By then, Jeffery and Dom had returned. Val quickly moved on to the next subject, his voice still hoarse. "I have made arrangements for one of my fighters to help. He's going to stand guard. No one leaves this house without him. Everyone sticks together, even if it's the market or the bathroom."

Jeffery flinched, holding his hand up, waiting for permission to speak.

Val nodded his head, acknowledging Jeff.

"Does your guard have to stand over us in the bathroom? I mean," Jeffery shifted in his feet, "I like company, but even for me, that's just a bit TMI."

"Affirmative, bro!" Val gibed. "I will personally see to it that my fighter never leaves your sight." Val slipped me a sideways glance and winked.

I held back the laughter that begged for release. Dom as usual, shook his head, keeping silent.

"You are one cruel mofo!" Jeffery huffed. He pivoted on his feet, stomping up the stairs as curses wafted throughout the mansion.

The doorbell rang, and we all jumped. Val assured us it was one of his fighters that he'd requested for duty. He went to the door and brought his sidekick to the kitchen, where we all waited. The Zop-fighter wasn't quite as tall as Val. He was shorter and boxier, more compact. His features were dark hair and deep-brown eyes, nice looking, yet he paled in comparison to his leader. Val stood at least a head taller and was leaner. Although, they both could've passed for giants. "Hey...everyone, this is Razz. He'll be watching over you until we correct the problem."

Razz nodded his head without speaking a word. His expression was stern but with ease until his eyes landed on me. He quickly stiffened, eyeing me with caution. As you know me, I never back down. I eyed him back just as equally cautious. The young Zop appeared a few years younger than his commander. By his stance, he reminded me of an English bulldog.

Then a bizarre incident happened. They began to exchange conversation in their native tongue, a strange, foreign language. I gasped when I realized I understood the words. Before I could contain my excitement, both Zop's eyes switched to me. I quickly pulled myself together, confessing, "silly me. I bit my tongue. Ouch! It hurts. I'm gonna go check it out." I lent a tight smile. Talk about awkward.

As my back turned, I couldn't help the fat grin that spread across my face. I understood their alien language. WTF! Yet I didn't care much for what I was hearing from the shorter Zop and his opinions of me.

Val didn't waste any time assigning me to my new regime. I had to learn how to as Val called it, stretch my abilities. First, I had to do a stupid breathing exercise similar to learning how to push within your gut, like a singer. Best part of the training—the Commander in Chief, Val, allowed me the privilege of practicing in the garden.

The assignment was tedious, mundane and uninspiring. I kept checking the time as it dragged by. After a while of uneventful stretching, I decided to take a break. I went straight for the swing.

Time elapsed. I didn't' care. I was happy, swinging back and forth with my toes reaching for the white-puffy clouds in the sky. I leaned back, eyes closed, enjoying the crisp cool breeze brushing across my face.

Then my little bit of happiness abruptly halted in midair. Stunned, my eyes flew open. I'd found myself locked in an iron embrace, facing two very angry gold eyes.

"What do you think you're doing?" Val's voice had a healthy dose of exasperation slapped between two slices of bread with me in the middle.

"I'm taking a break!" I snapped. "I'd been out here since the crack of dawn." I tried squirming out from under his grip, but my attempts were futile. He was much stronger.

His brows knitted. "Do you think my exercise is too tough for your tender behind?"

Oh, no he didn't! Thems fight-n words! As we say in the south.

"That tender *be*-hind you're referring to," I spat as I struggled to free myself from his iron-clad hold, "is as tough as you and any of your gang!" My eyes blazed at my captor. Then abruptly he dropped me, causing me to land on my ass with a thud. "Ouch!" I mumbled.

I scrambled to my feet, fist loaded, ready to fight. Obviously Val sensed my irritation. He'd not bothered hiding the smirk athwart his face. I first wanted to smack him. On second thought, what was the point? He'd just dodge my blow, and my luck, I'd end up over his lap with my ass exposed to the palm of his hand. He had turned into a brute. I wanted my gentle Ben back. This tower looming over me with the fragrance of acerbity was not my sweet Val.

"No breaks! You are Zophasemin. It's time you start acting like one."

There was something almost predatory in his tone. I didn't like it one damn bit either. "My weak humanity is what drives me. I am proud to claim my human side. After all, I am my father's daughter. Don't you ever forget that!" I hissed, shoving my hands into his chest. Though, he might as well have been a rock. He didn't even waver against my thrust.

Without warning, the grand warrior, Val, burst into a roar of laughter. Unaware, I heard another source of chuckles on the back of my neck. I twirled on my heels to find the Zop fighter, Razz, shooting a barbed-wire grin down at me, leaning against my favorite tree. That was all it took—I simply snapped. "What's so damn funny, Zop?" Before I had realized what I was doing, I'd thrust my knife straight at him, missing his head only by half an inch. The blade notched the tree, making a metal chime. My eyes flashed fire, that same burst of flames like Aidan's as I revealed my secret. *"I understood every word you said last night, Razz. I'd tread lightly if I were you."* I spoke with clarity and confidence. Apparently, the Zop had a problem with my Druid blood. He'd made it clear if it weren't for his Commodore, he would've enjoyed killing me with his bare hands. He looked upon me with disgust—a fifty impure. He even went as far as to insult my father, and for that, I *hated* him.

Both Zops stood frozen in stunned silence. *Good,* I thought. "I'm hungry." I announced. "I'll be in the kitchen if you care to find me." Without another word, I left them there to their gaping faces.

I heard Val bark orders at Razz to stand watch. I high-tailed it to the house. I needed distance between those two lugs and their stupid Zop pride.

When I stepped into the kitchen, Dom and Jeffery had disappeared, leaving the table set with a delicious spread of cold cuts, various sorts of cheese, pickles, lettuce, and chips. It wasn't fancy, but I liked it this way—simple.

I'd already taken a seat at the table with my sandwich in hand when Val strutted in from outside. After washing his hands, Val sat down in the chair next to me. It appeared that his eyes were filled with wonder. I held my breath, trying to hide my snarky grin. Nonetheless, my pride didn't lesson the effects of my piqued feelings. Val should've never brought that creep into my home.

Finally, he broke the unbending quiet. "How long have you been speaking Zophasemin?" Catching a sideways glance, I noticed that Val had a glint in his eyes like he'd caught my hand in the cookie jar.

I first swallowed my bite, then I answered, eyeing my food. "I haven't a clue to what you mean. I can't speak Zophasemin. I only understand the language. And it was not until I overheard the two of you babbling in your native tongue did I realize I could interpret it." I refused to face him as I took another bite of my sandwich.

"Then explain to me," he pushed, "how you were speaking my native tongue just moments ago?"

The corner of my lip tipped into a sneer. "I so was not speaking your stupid language." I vehemently denied, still keeping my gaze to myself.

"Stevie, you spoke our language better than any Zop."

I snatched up a chip and popped it in my mouth as if I was unfazed. "Maybe you need to clean the wax out of your ears, Commodore. I only understand Zop."

Val blew out a harsh sigh, "Be as it may, I think the only right thing for you to do is apologize to Razz. You nearly ended his life with that damn knife of yours." He bit down into his sandwich, taking almost half. It seemed his bite was bigger than his bark.

"What the hell!" I snapped my head up, facing the golden beauty, clenching my teeth, sparks flying mad. "I can't believe you!" I screeched. "First of all, how can you bring that jerk into my home when he wishes nothing more than to rip my heart from my chest? You're not protecting me. You are putting me in harm's way with that beast who walks the grounds aimlessly."

"You're wrong. Razz won't go against an order. Forget what he thinks!" Val tried to blow this off like I was having a P.M.S. moment.

"It will be a cold day in hell before I ever apologize!" I avowed. "You made a bad judgement call, Commodore."

Val lowered his head for a second and took a jagged breath. "I'm sorry. I didn't have much of a choice."

"You have a choice. Don't invite him!"

"Look! You might as well get used to not being the most popular among our kind." I got the impression that Val was out of his element. How could he truly understand my stance? After all, he was the perfect Zop.

"For your information, I'm good with unpopularity. I've had that all my life. It's the Wanting-My-Head-On-A-Silver-Platter part that I'm having an adjustment problem with."

"I'm sorry, Freckles. I did warn you. It's our way. I can't change tradition." Val's jaw tensed, but his eyes were elsewhere. I suppose he had other situations more pressing than my little ole life.

"Our way?" I stormed. "Excusez-moi! Not mine! I'll never hate someone merely because of their origin."

"I understand you haven't been raised in our culture. We are a proud race. We wish our kind to stay whole and pure."

"Oh my god! That's the real reason you pushed me out of your bed." I stormed. "It has nothing to do with my heart belonging to another!" My green eyes threw shards at him.

"Don't be ridiculous," he scoffed. "Now you're acting like a woman."

"Ridiculous! Is that anything like a Zop female?" I struck back.

"This conversation is over!" Val demanded as anger rolled off his body.

"I'm sorry, but I'm not one of your soldiers. Answer my question!" I ordered fiercely.

"Which question? You ask so many, it's hard to keep up." Val met my heated stare.

"Did you not want me in your bed because I'm part human?" I repeated under clenched teeth.

Val blew out a wind of frustration. "The human part wasn't an issue at the time. I wanted you to myself. I didn't want to share you with another—even if he was dead. I meant what I said." He halted his words briefly. I saw the struggle in his face. "However, after considering this connection you and I share, I believe we are better off as friends. My culture and customs are very important to me. This is who I am. If I gave you my name in marriage, I would bring shame to my kind. And worse, our children would be an outcast as well as you and I. I don't want to do that to you or my unborn children. So you see, there's no future for us. And I think you would be better with a human or a Druid."

I sat there dumbfounded, staring at him. What was it with these guys and their freak-n family ties? I didn't know why his words stung so much, but they did. Why would he say that to me? I never planned a future with him. I didn't dare. In fact, I never gave him any indication that I expected us to become a couple. Now that he'd admitted openly that we had no future, assuming that I'd expected more, set my teeth on edge. "I guess this means I won't be getting a ring?" Sarcasm sugar coated my words.

It didn't help matters any when he smirked at my reply. "Guess not!" he relented stiffly.

Then I let him have it. "You know...I never asked for any commitment from you. As far as I was concerned, you were a mere entertainment. So don't get all worked over with worry that you're going to crush me. I never thought of you as a permanent fixture anyhow." I pushed from the table and charged outside. I needed a distraction, anything to get my mind off the burn of Val's words.

I made my way to the tree where I'd left my embedded knife, deep in the bole of the oak. In one angry jerk, I ripped it from the grasp of the oak.

Suddenly my attention shifted to footsteps behind me. I twirled around with my trusty knife in my hand, ready for whatever came next.

"You're pretty good with that knife," Razz addressed me in his tongue.

To my surprise, I replied back in his native language as if I'd been speaking it my entire life. "My throw was off. I was aiming between your eyes." I eyed him cautiously.

"I heard you're a spit-fire." His hunted eyes raked over me sending eerie chills over my body. "I suppose if I were in your skin, I'd be a bit angry too." The Zop stepped closer into my personal space. "Our ways may seem unfair, however, it has worked for our race—centuries, in fact. It's nothing personal."

"None taken. I know my place, but you need to know yours as well. Don't get me wrong, I do appreciate your assistance. However...this is my home and my family. You will respect my position as long as you are here. I hope we have an understanding." I held my proud chin high.

"Fair enough, impure." His dark glint made me want to coil, but I refused to coward under his condemnatory eyes. "Know this as well, if I ever catch you out and free of my leader's protection, you are fair game."

My brows knitted in confusion. "I don't get how you can hate another only because he or she is different."

"It is not another. It is impures we detest."

"Why do you hate us so much?"

"Mixing our kind with yours is forbidden."

"Who instills this idiocy in your head?"

"Our creator, naturally."

"A creator who is prejudice?" I couldn't wrap my head around his barbaric belief.

" My creator is *righteous.* Your kind wasn't meant to exist. We are pure. Our kind does not destroy each other in war. Rather, we stand together as brothers, whether we like each other or not. Humans are wasteful and selfish. War is used for greed. Zophasemin are selfless. We would lay our life down for our brothers. Tell me—would your humans do the same for you?"

"For the most part, you are right. Humans at times can be very self-absorbed, yet not everyone. Unlike your kind, mankind was given a choice—a freedom to decide for themselves. There is nothing far greater than the gift of freedom, to choose your own destiny. So my answer to your question is, I'd lay my life down in a second for anyone I love. And those two humans inside my house who's been gracious enough to feed you would return the favor to me at any given moment. It's called humanity." I ended the conversation by walking away. I'd had it with politics and self-righteous pricks. The human part in me was really starting to make me proud. Screw these prideful Zops. They should watch themselves. They were on my turf.

Hidden Treasure

A LL WEEK IT had been miserable. By all the bruises and body aches, one might wonder if I was the redheaded stepchild. Val was beginning to think my human side affected my Zop abilities. He tried everything in his powers to awaken my dormant abilities, but instead, he got the human side of me cussing at him.

I did have some gifts. I was quick on my feet and swift with a knife. I'd gotten very good with my aim. I hit my target nearly every time. At least I had that going for me, even still if I ever came up against a supernatural, my chances of winning were slim.

I decided I needed a human break. I didn't feel I was getting any closer to reaching my goals or finding my daughter. I wanted to decompress. So I headed for Bourbon Street—plenty of action there. It was a Friday night, and it was certain the streets would be hustling and bustling with folks.

A little guilt pricked my conscious as I had snuck out like a grounded teenager. Val gave Razz strict orders not to let anyone leave the house, and that order especially was directed at me. But if the truth-be-told, the Zop soldier didn't give a rat's ass if I choked on a carrot stick. In fact, if it were left up to him, I'd be dead by his doings.

Funny though, why did Val seem different? He was full-blooded Zop. He didn't appear to be offended by my anomaly. Rather, he protected me. I couldn't figure him out. He hated my kind, yet he came to my rescue every time. There have been a handful of times I could've lost my life if it had not been for him. So why the big deal about my birth? Should I be punished for something I had no control over? I had no say in my birth no more than the color of my skin. Why couldn't the Zop nation abandon their prejudiced ways? Perhaps pride made them blind?

And no argument, Val was prideful, arrogant, too confident, kind, gentle, sweet...I shook myself hard. No niceties! I warned myself inwardly. It made me weak. I had to remember he was nothing more than a device for helping me find my daughter. I shouldn't forget the Zop leader stood with the enemy. His *kind*. It seemed my list of adversaries kept getting longer, and my friends kept dwindling down.

Still I didn't understand what came over me the other day at lunch. Val denying any future between us really stung. It felt like a stab through my heart. I didn't see us as a couple, so why did I get all irked?

Soon my cab stopped, and I reached over the seat and handed the driver his fare. I slid out and shut the door behind.

Stepping up on the sidewalk, I breathed in the surroundings. I adorned downtown, the Spanish architecture bold yellows and various shades of orange, the jaunty music and neon lights. It was my little piece of king cake.

The tourist were starting to stir. Chatter was growing as the crowd thickened. The spirit of good times hung in the air. The whole street seemed on fire tonight. Jazz music flowed onto the street. People were merrymaking, hopping from bar to bar, boozing up for that splendid hangover the following morning.

Certain hot spots here weren't exactly for the fainthearted. Unfortunately, it didn't matter how tough of a stomach a person had, most didn't have a clue to what lurked in the dark shadows.

Speaking of which, I planned to steer clear of Val's bar. First, I didn't want word to get back to him that I was hanging around in the French Quarter, and two, I didn't want to run into one of his Zop comrades. Losing my head tonight wasn't an option.

Wanting to be left alone, I wasn't in the mood to attract any interest, so I wore a tank top and my cutoff jeans. I didn't bother with makeup. To hide my face, I wore a cowboy hat I'd had for years. It was pretty beat-up and tattered. I figured it'd help me to blend in with the crowd.

In case there was some trouble, I came prepared. Hiding under my shorts, I strapped my dagger to my thigh an easy reach for the unexpected.

It was not until I reached about halfway down the street that I came upon an new-age bookstore. It read, *Magie Noire.* I knew what that meant—Black Magic.

It continued to read, *Tarot Readings, Spells, and Herbal Magic.* "*Open,*" the neon sign read.

The small bookstore reminded me of the one in Tangi, so I decided to explore it. I had a few bucks on me. No telling what I might find.

I pushed the door open, and the bell jingled as I entered. Once the door closed behind me, a strong whiff of incense, sandal wood, hit my nostrils. The scent carried me back to a simpler time— memories of Ms. Noel. I paused a moment, trying to adjust to the dim lighting. I missed my elderly friend. Looking back, I knew I wasn't very opened to Ms. Noel's beliefs. I think now I'd take it quite differently. After my world had crashed three years ago, I learned the hard way that with age comes great wisdom. I wished she were still alive so I could tell her that too.

Jarring me from my thoughts, strings of beads rattled, alerting me to the clerk returning from the back. A dark-skinned lady came out and greeted me with a warm smile.

"Welcome, my friend! Feel free to look around. If you need my assistance, just call." She spoke with a deep Jamaican accent.

I smiled back, replying. "Thank-you. I'm just looking." I couldn't help but admire her attire. It was quite impressive. The material appeared to be cotton, but it was far from ordinary. The garment wrapped around her whole body in bold blue, purple, and bright orange. To match, she wore some sort of cloth wrapped around her head. It was as lovely as the dress. I loved her gold loop earrings too. It seemed to go with her style very well. My eyes trail down to her feet, and oddly, she was barefooted. *That's the way to be,* I thought. I hated wearing shoes too.

I began thumbing the books. I think the store carried every book of witchcraft, voodoo, and spells that ever existed. The shelves scaled all the way to the ceiling. Next, I browsed the candle section, tarot cards, and magickal herbs.

When I came to a display, my eyes rested on one item that stood out from the other trinkets. I'd seen this root before. The plant had been carved into an ugly doll. I was so drawn to the weird thing that I couldn't stop myself from picking it up. I brushed my hand across it, noticing the rough texture of the strange bauble. The color wasn't any better, it reminded me of tobacco spit.

I knew I must've appeared totally out of my element when the storekeeper interrupted. "Dat tis a poppet." The lady spoke in a heavy accent.

I jumped, startled. I didn't hear her approach me from behind. "Some call it Obeah doll much like voodoo. In the hands of the wrong person, it can do great damage." She pointed to the strange carving. "You mustn't touch the doll." She eyed me with caution. I didn't take the lady as confrontational, rather instead, she seemed direct.

"Oh! I didn't mean any harm." I quickly laid the doll back on the shelf. "It's just so…unusual." I clasped my hands behind my back. I felt a little uncomfortable, like a child getting scolded.

"I am certain you did not mean to bring ill, but before you handle any-*ting*, you must know its origin. You must handle a poppet very carefully. One wouldn't want to spread bad juju onto another." She paused for a moment, gazing deeply into my eyes as if she could see every dirty secret I'd ever possessed. I began to shift a bit, feeling the unease. "You are different. Not fully human, no?" She asked as if it was a common question.

I blinked with surprise, "I'm sorry?" This stranger couldn't possibly know me. Although, she seemed harmless enough.

She softly giggled. "Child! You heard me. No worry, mon. You will come to me when the time is right."

"You remind me of a friend I once knew." I tossed an uneasy smile.

The lady paused, then her forehead creased with curiosity. "What does a young girl as yourself need with such a powerful tool like *tis?*" Her accent was as strong as her deep-brown eyes were penetrating.

I snorted a short laugh. "You wouldn't believe me if I told you. I don't want the doll, actually. It reminded me of my friend. She once used these dolls, and..." I stopped in the middle of my sentence.

"Your friend...she is gone?"

"Yes, she passed away a few months ago. She is greatly missed."

"I am sorry for your loss. You have lost much for someone so young."

The lady seemed to have read me well. It was almost eerie. "Yes, I have," I replied curtly.

The lady paused, eyeing me like I was a tea-leaf reading. I started to shuffle my uneasy feet from the presage she seemed to hold over me. "I have a gift for you. I've been waiting for you." The lady turned and made her way to the back, past the string of beads, disappearing from sight. I began tapping my foot nervously listening to the string of beads clattering. I thought about making a clean get-away as my eyes bounced back and forth from the string of beads to the door, but my curiosity rendered me. I waited holding my breath.

Soon she reappeared with a small white box in her hand. "I've been saving this for you. This, my child, belongs to you." She smiled and opened the plain box. Inside laid a necklace with a stone. It was beautiful, like flickers of fire with glimmering gold. It reminded me of Val. There was something else, I touched it—a humming in the stone. I gasped as I glanced up at the lady. "Yes." She spoke softly. "It is called Angel Fire."

"It is beautiful," I nearly choked with amazement.

"There is more to it than its beauty. It calls to your true name." The lady smiled as though she possessed a secret about my life.

My brows knitted. "What do you mean?" A bit taken aback; I questioned her motive.

"Oh, don't be afraid." She laughed. "I'd recognize you anywhere, my child." She extended her hand and introduced herself. "I am Mardea."

I took her hand and shook it, but I sensed an uneasy stir. I pulled my hand away and responded cautiously. "Glad to meet you. I'm Stev—"

The dark-skinned woman interrupted. "I know who you are."

Thrown off my guard, she clarified her intent. "No worry, mon. It is not I whom you should fear, Essence. I am on your side, and lately, I hear you could use a little support." She smiled kindly at me. "'Tis necklace is a talisman. It will help you tap into your magick. There is a blockage deep within you. It is a binding spell, coupled with several others to mask over it. Someone doesn't want your powers to emerge.

My eyes orbed. "Who would do such a thing?"

"I don't know. Though, I can tell you dat they wish to fool you into *tinking* you have no abilities. Don't let them trick you! You are very powerful, so you must wear this stone at all times. Never take it off, my child." The lady fastened the necklace around my neck as I stood there uneasy holding my hair up.

My fingers gasped the stone. "I don't understand. How do you know me?" My mind swooned with trepidation.

"Someone close to you asked me to keep this necklace until you came. He's a loyal believer of the old ways, and he wishes to protect you from your powerful enemies. Wear tis. Never take it off or the spells will return."

"I'm confused. Who left this for me?"

"I'm sorry. This person wished to remain anonymous."

I shook my head in bewilderment. "How do you know you have the right person?"

"I saw you in a vision." The dark-skinned woman smiled.

"Did this person give a name?" I asked with urgency.

"My child, you already have the answer." She seemed surprised by my asking.

I had to take a stabbing breath. "What did this admirer look like?" I asked as chills skated across my skin.

"He was very well dressed. It was obvious he had money. His features were tall and dark, very handsome, but his most outstanding feature were his blue eyes." The woman watched my reaction closely. "He referred to you as Princess."

Right then my breath caught in my throat. My hands started trembling. This couldn't be possible! "When did he give this to you?"

"Hmm...only weeks ago."

Holy shit! Aidan?

"Please tell me what all you know. I must have every detail!" My urgent voice submerged in panic.

"He did give me a message to give to you." The lady's dark eyes held a secret that I had to know.

"Please, what did he say?"

She hesitated, unsure she wanted to reveal her mysterious messenger. "He said it was not he who betrayed you...and one more." The lady gave pause.

"What else?" I pressed, impatiently.

"Dat your daughter is alive."

I staggered over her last words. How could I believe this stranger? I tightened my eyes with disquiet. "This must be someone's idea of a joke!" Now I was pissed. "Lady, what game are you playing?" Doubt colored my fear.

She smiled to herself as if she recalled a private joke. "He told me you would accuse me of lying, so he gave me something only you would know." The lady went back behind the counter and reached underneath and brought out a glass jar with holes punched in the lid. "Here." She slid the Mason jar across the counter to me. "He said this should be proof enough." I gasped. I couldn't believe my own eyes. Inside the jar took me back to a time I once wanted to forget—a firefly fluttering about.

Then I fainted, collapsing to the floor.

Feathers Ruffled

"WHAT THE HELL were you thinking, Stevie!" Val screamed, his face beet red.

I'd never seen him this angry before. I felt every inch of his wrath striking me, flinching each time. Damn, damn, damn! I would've gotten by with it if I hadn't passed out. Just my luck! "Calm down! I'm fine." I rested my hands on my hips. I was cloudy on the details of how Val found me. When I had awakened, I was back home in my bed. It was not until later when I'd joined everyone in the garden that I'd been struck by the big goon's temper. From one corner of my eye, I saw Dom and Jeffery cringing. From the other corner of my eye, I saw Razz gloating. I hated that *Zop*.

"You were not only putting yourself in danger but everyone else in this house as well. The very folks you vowed to give your life for!" Val's words hit me hard like closed fist to the face. He was right about that part. I turned to Dom and Jeff. "I'm sorry, guys. What I did was selfish. I won't do it again. I promise." My eyes glistened with tears.

Jeffery spoke up. "It's okay, honey, but I hope you got lucky, b'cuz I don't understand what possessed you to be so stupid." Jeffery tossed a little shade at me. I couldn't help but laugh. Jeffery always had a way of making light of the worst situations.

"Oh, I got lucky, but it's not what you think." I smiled through my tears.

"Lardy sakes! This I gotta hear." Jeffery rolled his eyes. He was such a drama queen. Dom tossed me a short smile, and Val glared at me. Razz's eyes tensed with suspicion which I'd just about blew a gasket when my eyes stopped at him. Honest to God's truth, if I had to look at one more scowl at that piece of shit, Razz, I was gonna snap.

"Look, Zop!" My heated eyes turned on him. "I've about had it with your goddamn glares on my back. You got something to say, then say it!" The soldier needed an attitude adjustment, and I swore one more smirk from that son of a Zop, and I was going to give him an adjustment.

The Zop soldier began to speak in his tongue. "I have plenty to say, whore! I think my leader has gone soft. It is forbidden for any Zop to mix with such company as yours. We waste our time and energy standing watch, protecting a spoiled brat who doesn't care for anyone but herself." Razz spat at my feet. "Go back from the rock you crawled from, fallen angel. No Zop will ever accept you. You are foolish if you think my leader will ever claim you. The only use you offer is on your back. Our leader would be wise to remember his place." Razz's eyes simmered with hatred. I glanced at Val. His jaw was set in stone as his whole body exuded the force of authority.

"You are insubordinate, soldier." Val stepped between us. "Stand down, or I'll show you how soft I truly am!" He gravely threatened.

Then the Zop turned his inimical position on his commander. "Why should I when the inbred has challenged me?" His eyes bore repulsion, aiming at me.

I had enough of the Zop's bellyaching. I stepped up. "Let's see what the asshole's got!" I challenged, standing with my shoulders straight. "I'll fight him!" Even through the rush of anger, my internal voice screamed, *Crazy bitch, you're gonna get killed!*

Val turned to me. "Do you think you're ready for combat?" His eyes were tight. Clearly, he feared for my safety.

"I'm ready as I'll ever be," I said as I glared at the hostile Zop.

"You remember everything I've taught you?" It seemed as though Val's eyes were searching for a way out.

The way I saw it, I had no choice. Fair or not, I had to confront my enemy. Like it was second nature, I honed in on my very large opponent.

"All right then, let the fights begin." Val met Razz's heated stance. "I give you permission to engage in this duel only with your fist. There will be no weapons, nor will anyone lose their life today. Do I make myself clear, soldier?"

"What's the fun in a few bruises and a busted nose?" There was a deep-seeded edge of hatred in Razz's voice.

"You'd do well to follow an order. If you break it, I'll kill you myself. Do we have an understanding?" Val's eyes glistened with malice.

"I give you my word." Razz promised, gritting his teeth from antagonistic regret.

Then Val turned to me and reached his hand out. "Hand 'em over." He curtly ordered. I grimaced as I pulled the knife from my boot and slapped it into his hand. Still it didn't satisfy him as he stood there with his hand still extended and his brow raised. *Geez!* I rolled my eyes. I really needed to get a new hiding spot. Reluctantly, I unbuckled my other knife that had been tucked under my shorts and tossed it to him.

"Now you can fight," Val announced.

I sucked in a healthy dose of oxygen and released it slowly. In my combat training with Val, he taught that breathing in a fight was vital for stamina. If you become winded, you lose your concentration and strength—two very important tools if you were to survive. I rushed through my mind over all the techniques that I'd learned as Razz and I crouched down circling one another.

We swapped insult after insult. I think what made him lunge first was a cheap jab about his momma forgetting to teach him manners while she had an overactive hobby of lying on her backside. I didn't know why, but comments about a dude's mom got a rise every time. I scoffed in his virulent face, watching his face blaze with violent intent.

Oddly, I guess, the bigger the Zop, the slower the responses. When he lurched for me, it seemed as though he moved in slow motion. With little effort, I dodged him by side stepping. It was funny when he slammed his face down onto the gravel. My laughter was like a sonic boom breaking the sound barrier, seeing his butt sticking up in the air as his face lay flat into the sharp rocks. Nonetheless, my mockery only made him more enraged as he took me by surprise. This time, I wasn't as quick. As a consequence, I paid for it when he thwacked me down to the ground. My head hit first, throwing me into a burst of pain while he threw himself on top of me, pinning me underneath him.

The Zop's weight was crushing my lunges. He had to weigh a good hundred pounds more than me. We were unmatched, to say the least. By his smirk, it was obvious that he knew he had the advantage. I knew if I didn't get out from under his iron grip, he was going to pound my face until I was dead. I refused to give him that satisfaction.

Before I had a chance to brace myself, I felt a sharp jab to my left jaw, then my right, and then my left again. His blows were so forceful I felt my jaw snap out of socket and pop back in as he continued to cold-cock me with his massive fist. I had to stop him soon, or else there wouldn't be much left of me to beat.

Suddenly the blows stopped, following a sharp pain at the nape of my wet, sticky head. He'd grabbed my hair and nearly jerked it out by its roots. I gritted my teeth to keep from screaming out from the pain. The Zop leaned in with his foul breath and whispered in my ear, "I bet you like it rough. Maybe I should take you, like my friend at the hospital when you were too drugged to scream. Unlike him, I like my humans screaming. And with you, I'd make you do more than holler." His depraved voice sickened me. I forced myself to look directly into his twisted face. Yet my training hadn't prepared me for this. I drew in a sharp breath, startled by his oil-like eyes, no white, no pupil, only a fiendish black.

Then the sudden rush of memories of that hospital jarred me back to my pending danger, and I used the anger to unfurl my powers. I released the beast that resided within me. What happened next, I couldn't say. I may have blacked out. The best way that I could describe the way things went down was that my Essence had awakened. As the consuming force grew, it devoured my entire being. Stevie vanished, and a monster had taken her place. It was similar to that experience with Aidan in the girl's restroom, but this—this felt like the Granddaddy Mac of Hiroshima.

It all happened so fast. A sudden burst jolted me like lightening, pushing its way out, then it came to me. In one easy sweep, I freed my arms. I felt this searing heat surge forth through my hands. It was like fire, only it didn't burn. Streams of light forged as I shoved my hands against Razz's chest, blasting him onto the hard ground like a rocket missile.

Blood and sweat streamed down my face, but I didn't let a little thing as such stop me. I jumped on that bastard, and I began beating his face, returning the favor. After his face started looking more like raw hamburger, I top my next blow with my knee violently thrusting between his legs. As he doubled over, squealing like the pig he betrayed, I laughed in his face. I regretted I couldn't castrate him, by the same token, I did take delight knowing he'd be out of pocket in the lovemaking department.

Suddenly the party halted. Before I had a chance to make my next move, Val snatched me up and held me back. "Enough! You proved your point," he ordered.

"Like hell I have!" I shrieked, fighting to get loose. "That son of a bitch threatened to rape me. He was in with that pig, Joe from Haven! He deserves to die!" I hissed through clenched teeth.

"Are you sure?" Val stood tall, in control as his one arm held me tight.

"Yes! He just admitted to it in my ear." I spat.

"Enough fighting for one day! You proved your worthiness." He clasped his hand on my shoulder. "Go get cleaned up." Val stood firm. He turned to Jeffery and Dom. They were quiet spectators with faces that had gone pale.

I felt awful that they witnessed my fight. I realized from this event today that even though we shared a house together, our worlds were very different. They were not accustomed to violence as I had become accustomed to. I think in the future, I should be more mindful.

Val addressed Dom and Jeffery. "Take her in and see to her wounds. I'll be in shortly. I have some business first." He grimaced.

I had a feeling he wasn't too happy about Razz's threat. True, we were in a full-blown brawl, but rape was *rape*. I suspected that this act was forbidden in his culture as in the human's world. I didn't care what Val decided to do with that disgusting jerk as long as I never had to lay eyes on him again, or else I might do all the innocent girls out there a favor and kill him myself—the racist bastard.

Gifts from the Dead

"HOLD STILL!" JEFFERY ordered. "Girlfriend, he worked your face good!" Jeffery gently swabbed my face with alcohol. I tried not to flinch, but that stuff burned like a mofo.

"Ouch! Can't you be easy?" I leaned away grimacing.

"Gurrrl, you amaze me. You fight a man who is more than double your size, and youse bitch-n over a little alcohol on a little old scratch? Chile, go on!"

I took in a deep breath. "I know, but he had it coming," I said in my defense.

"Gurrrl, you could have waited until he dozed off and got 'em with the cast-iron skillet? That's how my momma used to get my daddy. And let me tell you, it worked too! Daddy learned to sleep with one eye open and never stray again. He liked to roam a bit too much. You know, 'Water always runs to the river,' that's what my momma would say." Jeffery dabbed the cotton ball with more alcohol.

I stiffened from the burn, then I exhaled, feeling very human. "I'm sorry that Dom and you had to see..." I couldn't get my sentence out from the sudden wincing.

"Dom and I were terrified for you. We had no idea how you were going to fight off that big old ugly mofo. We're mad as hell at Val too. He should've never allowed that beast to touch you—Zop's tradition or not! I don't care. That fight should've never happened."

Jeffery seemed adamant about his standing. He seldom wavered in his opinions. Something I wished I could instill in myself.

"I never wanted him here." I flinched again from the alcohol.

"Well...I think I've done as much as I can." He tossed the bloody cotton ball in the trash can. "You're lucky that these wounds are superficial. That animal could've killed you!"

"I know. It's me and my big fat mouth." I agreed.

"No, bitch! It's your big fat temper!" Then Jeffery snorted a laugh. "But you sure did surprise Dom and me. You whooped that Zop's a-s-s!" Jeffery emphasized as he high-fived me. "Lardy have mercy! What was that glowing stream that shot from your damn hands? Dom and I thought you were gonna set the place on fire! Youse one bad angel!"

I shook my head, still stunned. "It just felt like a herd of wild mustangs needing to be set free. It was the most awe-inspiring thing and the most frightening experience I've ever known." I shrugged my shoulders as I reached for my angel-fire necklace, still latched to my neck.

Dom entered my room with some hot, soothing tea and some chicken soup. Leave it to Dom to think of the perfect remedy. Tea, food and sleep were exactly what I needed, though I was too stoked. I suppose the effects of the fight wore heavily on me. Every time I thought about Razz's threat, I got pissed-off all over again.

"This will make you feel better. Oui?" Dom placed the tray over my lap as I leaned back in bed. I didn't know what the big fuss was about. I only had gotten a few scrapes and bruises. No broken bones, not even a busted nose. Then I remembered the beating of my life from Sam. If Aidan hadn't reached me when he had, I would've died. I shivered over the memories, memories of Aidan and the feelings he stirred within me.

I smiled, hiding my spike of sadness. "Thanks, Dom, but I'm fine. Really! It's the other guy you should worry about." I winced.

"I don't think so. I hope he suffers très!" (greatly) Dom spoke with apparent anger in his voice. "Your friend should've had Razz removed from our home long before now."

Dealing with the ominous presence from the Family hadn't been easy for the guys. A sudden stab of guilt struck. "I'm sorry, Dom. I didn't mean to put you two in the middle of this toil." I grimaced.

"No!" he said with vigilance. "It is not for you to apologize. You did nothing wrong. That creature had abhorrence for you the moment he set eyes on you. Constantly making anti-Semitic comments at you in your own home is unacceptable. You, no worry! End of discussion. Sleep now! Yes?" Dom smiled and patted me on my foot.

"I love you, guys, you know." Getting a bit misty-eyed, I pushed through the biting pain and smiled.

———— ✤ ————

Dom and Jeffery had left me to rest, but before I dozed off, I overheard a conversation outside my door. Jeffery had pulled Val to the side. It sounded like Jeffery was giving him the what-for talk.

"You should never have let that beast come to this house to begin with. He nearly killed Stevie. But I'm sure glad she showed him! That mofo deserved a good wallop-n!"

"I'm truly sorry for Razz's behavior. I give you my word, I will handle him accordingly."

"Good, cuz if y'all come up into my house again, threatening my girl, I'll take a buckshot to your lovely ass!" Jeffery warned. "You need to protect her from trash like that. She's a good person, and she deserves nothing but love and devotion. You understand me?" I pictured Jeffery waging his finger in Val's face. I almost giggled.

I heard Val's voice. "Yes sir! I will lay my life down for her. That's how committed I am to your girl."

"You make sure. Any-oh-how, I doubt your soldier will have the balls to come back here. My gurrrl neutered that Zop!" I heard Jeffery snapping his fingers.

Then Val gave way to a short laugh. "Yes, sir. Indeed! That little woman is as fiery as her hair."

That was the last I heard before I drifted off to sleep.

———— ⋗❊⋖ ————

When my eyes finally opened, the house was still. I glanced at my alarm clock, and it was two in the morning. The lights were out except for the night light I kept on my dresser. I glanced around, and my eyes landed on Val sitting in the accent chair next to my bed. I smiled to myself, listening to his gentle snores and the rise and fall of his chest as he slept, but from the way he was hanging out of the chair, he looked miserable. The chair didn't accommodate his size very well. Most of his long body hung over the chair. I took a deep breath, watching. There was a sense of peace watching him sleep. Without thinking, I reached over and nudged him. His droopy eyes opened slowly, and he glanced over at me.

"Hey. Come lie down with me. I promise to behave." I smiled even though it hurt like hell. My face took a good beating from Razz.

Val stretched and yawned, then he turned to look at me. Our eyes locked for what seemed like forever, then with a deep sigh, he whispered, "I think I can help your injuries." He slid over to the bed and pulled me into his warm arms. I welcomed him as his citrus scent engulfed me. He leaned in without putting his weight on me, and he mumbled something in my ear as he brushed his hand gently over my body.

Immediately a sensation of warmth came over me, penetrating throughout my body. When he finished, a calm settled over me, and the aches and pain completely vanished. After he murmured sweet nothings in my ear, my eyelids became heavy, and soon I drifted off to sleep, nestled in his caressing arms. The last thing called to mind was a gentle kiss right before my thoughts slipped into a peaceful slumber. I remembered thinking how easy it was being with Val.

Mardea

EARLY THAT MORNING, I began to arouse from a dead sleep. As the haze of yesterday came to mind, my eyes slid over to Val. Obviously he'd been waiting for me to wake up. He sat relaxed in the chair by my window, sipping a fresh brew of coffee. With the sound of my sheets stirring, his eyes slid over to me. A cheery smile stretched across his face as he spoke. "Good morning, Rocky!"

"Good morning," I mumbled as I rose up on my elbows, spying his coffee. "Is there any coffee for me?" I almost salivated for his cup.

"Yep, a potful."

"Well, where is it?" I said, a bit muddled.

"Oh! You meant do I have a cup for you?" Val attempted to play innocent as his eyes rounded. I glared at him, puzzled.

"I guess. I have to go get my own?" I said, feeling a bit pestered.

"I suppose." He sipped, acting as though he was disinterested.

I stared at him as a tinge of annoyance began to grow. I pondered a moment, trying to access his peculiar mood. Then I blurted it out. "What the hell has crawled up your ass this grand morning?" My eyes narrowed.

"Oh, you caught that, huh?" His eyes met mine as equally.

"I guess I did." I bit back.

"Shall you go first, or shall I squeeze it out of you?" Val's eyes hardened.

WTF! "Don't I at least get a cup of coffee before you start in on me?"

"What possible reason would I have to start on you?" His mouth had set in stone.

I'd had it with this guessing game. "How about you just spit out what's on your mind? I haven't developed mind-reading, *yet*. Just fill me in on the blanks already!"

"Hmm...where shall I start?" His eyes nearly bore a hole through me. "What were you thinking, going to that bookstore?"

"Are we back on that subject?"

Val just stared at me in silence.

I rolled my eyes. "Because I could. It called to me. I don't see what's the big deal."

Val snorted a laugh. "The necklace you're wearing, it reeks of powerful magick. Black magick."

"It does not!" I barked. I couldn't fathom that this little stone came from a dark place. "The lady at the bookstore gave this to me." I relented, nonchalant.

"Who gave the necklace to you?" his brow arched.

"I told you, the clerk!" I skirted around the truth. I wasn't ready to reveal my source. Strange though, I felt like I'd cheated on Val with another man.

"That's all? Just that ugly necklace?" Val watched me skeptically.

"No. There was a message for me." I bit my bottom lip.

"Which was?"

"My daughter is *alive*." I couldn't stop myself from smiling.

"And this unknown person confirmed this?"

"Yes!" I threw my legs off the bed, sitting up, excited. "We can't keep wasting time. We have to get into that hospital and find my records. I know—"

Val cut me off with a wave of his hand.

"Whoa! Hold on!" He leaned forward, bracing his elbows on his knees. "We are going to do this when I say so. I'm not going in there half-cocked with no backup. It all has to be well planned."

"What's there to plan? You can change your face. Go in there looking like one of the guards, ingress—egress. It's that simple." I pointed out with irritation in my voice.

"It's not that simple. What if the real person I'm mimicking is there? Also, I need to know where they keep their files. I doubt they keep their records in plain sight. They're too crooked to be that stupid. Remember, I have to leave with the file without getting noticed."

"When will you have the plan in order?" My heart felt like it was going to leap out of my chest.

"An anonymous allied is getting it for me. I'm meeting with my informant tonight."

"Sweet! Where are we meeting this person?"

"Hell no!" Val bounced in his chair, his face red again. "We aren't going. I'm doing this alone."

"You can drop me off at the corner. I'll stay out of sight."

"Absolutely not! Do you want to scare off the only lead we have?"

"No, of course not."

Val sat there with an odd expression, staring, as if he was trying to blueprint my mind. "I have to know who gave you that necklace. This time I want the whole truth, or you can find someone else to help you."

I rolled my eyes, tugging the covers off me. "What's the big deal? It's a *necklace*."

"Did the stone come from *him?*"

My eyes orbed. How the hell did he know? "That's impossible! He's dead." I closed my eyes. I couldn't hide anything from Val. He seemed to hold some truth serum over me. Not that he deserved to know about Aidan. He had no claim on me. Still I felt it was only fair to come clean.

"Okay! Yes," I blurted out, betraying myself. "I think it might've come from Aidan. But I can only go by a stranger's word." I looked away, feeling the sting of guilt.

"I'm guessing that Mardea's been keeping in touch with your ex-lover hasn't she?"

"Wait! How did you know her name?" *I didn't recall the storekeeper ever introducing herself.*

Amusement danced in Val's golden eyes. "I told you once, I have spies everywhere."

I glared at him in shock. What was the point of hiding the details of my little discovery? "She didn't know his name, but she gave me proof." I squirmed, feeling a bit uneasy.

"And?" It was only a solitary word, but I could feel Val's agitation loud and clear.

"Fireflies—a nest of fireflies. It was our special hideaway in the forest." I tossed a shameful shrug.

"I see." His jaw twitched.

I sat there in silence. I didn't understand why he seemed bothered.

"Why are you acting mad?" I asked straight out, even if I didn't want to hear his reason.

"Oh! You think I'm jealous of *him?* A man who is dead." His eyes sharpened. "Do you want to know why I wouldn't make love to you?"

"Yes," I whispered.

"I sat watching you sleep. I don't know why, but I have this strong need to shield you." His face took on a look of deep regret that puzzled me. "Anyway, I heard you cry in your sleep...and it was *his* name you called out."

"I'm sorry. I don't have control over my sleep talking." I sat there, lost for words. How was this my fault?

"True, but it can be a window to what's really in your heart."

"When are you going to understand that Aidan is my past?"

"That's the problem. As long as you still love this man, you will never be open to another. That's the reason I couldn't sleep with you." Val paused. "If I can't have your heart, then I don't want any other part of you. Freckles, it's all or nothing for me." He looked dead serious.

I shook my head. He was starting to wear my nerves thin. "Bullshit!" I attacked. "It's not my past that keeps us apart. In fact, Aidan has nothing to do with the reason we are not together. How can we be together when your kind despises me? Did you not say to me we couldn't be together because I'm defective? Remember? I'm a dirty impure!" I threw myself off the bed and stood in front of him white fisted and half-naked with only a T-shirt barely covering my ass. I didn't care. I wasn't in the mood for shyness today. Val's eyes combed over me, painfully slow. He stopped as our combative eyes met.

"We seem to have some obstacles to hurdle." His mocking lip tugged at the corner of his mouth.

"Look! I can't erase Aidan, and I wouldn't want to if I had a choice. If it were not for him, I wouldn't be who I am today. But...he's my past, meaning, my feelings are buried along with his death. He's gone! And you're here. All I know is when I'm awake, it's you I think about, *not* Aidan. It's your arms I crave. It's your kisses I long for. It's your touch I yearn to feel. I only want to share my bed with you—only you." The pain behind my eyes was clear. "For now that's all I have to give, Val." I whispered his name. I'd been trying to avoid saying his name. I felt if I let his name escape my lips, I'd lose myself, forever. Regardless of my insecurities, it was time I stopped letting my past dictate my future. I had to face it. Spite our differences, I had feelings for Val.

Val eased out of the chair, making only one stride to reach me. He was so close I could feel his warm breath on my face. Gently with his thumb, Val began caressing my cheek. My breath stalled just when I thought he was going to kiss me, instead, he murmured. "Sorry, that's not enough for me, Freckles. Like I said...it's all or nothing." And with that said, he pushed past me and left my room, shutting the door behind him.

In a fit of rage, I picked up his coffee cup off the nightstand and hurled it at the door. It shattered into a million pieces, splattering coffee all over the door. "Gold-Eyes, you're an insufferable ass!" I screeched watching brown liquid slowly drip down the white door.

Blueprints to My Heart

S INCE THAT MORNING, I hadn't heard or seen Val in over a week, not even as much as a phone call. If I didn't know any better, I'd think he was avoiding me. I threw my phone down on the table, annoyed. I flopped down at the kitchen table, shoulders slumped. Giving way to a defeated sigh, I felt abandoned.

Though we'd parted on a bad note, I understood his frustration. In the same breath, I didn't know what he expected from me. I couldn't undo my past with Aidan any more than Val could change his heritage.

This yearning inside me felt worse than blisters on my heels. Regardless of my heart's desire, I had to face the reality that whether or not Aidan was included in the equation, the fact remained that Val and I didn't have a future together. I had to keep Val's best interest at heart. I couldn't stand back and watch him become ostracized by his race on my account. It would be too selfish for me to put him in that position.

To be fair, even if I wanted to, I couldn't make a decision of where my heart stood. My stomach knotted. When I'd walked into Mardea's bookstore that evening, little did I know my life was going to change course—meaning, the already-sticky triangle just became more complicated.

As it stands, if the storekeeper, Mardea, was telling the truth, then Aidan was alive and he had our child in his safety. That certainly changes everything. Perhaps all my pending questions would come to a light.

Considering all things, I couldn't exclude the Family. It hasn't left my notice that they could be behind this travesty. Either way, if Mardea was telling the truth or lying, I needed to watch my back. An act of haste could get me killed and worse—losing my child forever.

Before I could proceed forward in my life, I needed to find my child. My next move...finding out if Val had stumbled across any helpful information. If I were a betting girl, I'd bet that the Zop leader took it upon himself to seek this storekeeper, Mardea out and confront her. Val made it very clear that he didn't trust her, nor did he care for the necklace either.

Despite Val's cooling off, I had to see him. If he didn't want to come to me, then I'd go to him. I couldn't sit around the house any longer.

━━━━⟡❈⟡●━━━

One hour later, I stood in front of Val's bar, trying to settle my nerves. I wasn't sure if my uneasiness came from running into Razz or confronting Val.

I'd rushed getting here. I threw on the first pair of holey jeans I could find, a light tank top, my scuffed-up cowboy boots, and my western hat. Makeup took too much time, so I dashed some water on my face and brushed my teeth. I figured I looked perfect to hang out with the scumbags who frequent the bar. Obviously, the Zop clan was not my fav. I had a problem with prejudice pigs.

Keeping that in mind, I brought back-up—my trusty dagger. I never left the house without the steel. I'd gotten pretty handy at throwing. I could hit a snake, thirty feet. It'd be nothing to thrust a blade between one of these jokesters' eyes.

Shortly after, I entered the bar like I owned the joint. Wasting time wasn't my forte, so I directly went straight to the bar. A young man behind the bar approached me. The glint in his eyes told me he knew my kind—an impure. "What will it be?" his disdain was apparent.

"I'll take a beer, dark draft, and Val, if he's around?" I flashed a sugary smile.

The guy scoffed, nodding. "He's over there."

I pivoted on my heels, immediately dropping my beer. "That son of a bitch!" I hissed through clenched teeth. Gawking incredulously, I stood there, beer spattered over my clothes. "What is *she* doing here?"

Then I heard the bartender snort behind me. "It's one of those on-again-off-again affairs."

"She's not a Zop. So you approve?" derision spilled forth from my tone.

"My approval doesn't matter. Just glad his girlfriend doesn't stink like an impure."

I scoffed over my shoulders at the bartender's dig. I wasn't going to dignify that comment with an answer.

It wasn't hard spotting Val. His blonde locks stood out among the crowd. He was in the center of the dance floor, dancing with his partner. Suddenly a sinking sensation washed over me, like I was falling into a black hole. I couldn't rip my eyes away as I watched.

A lopsided smile seemed glued to Val's face, though, I knew that look. He once looked at me that way, along with something else I'd not seen before—a man in love. Apparently, the whole world knew, including the hired help but me. By the way their bodies pressed together, swaying to the music, there was no question, they'd shared more than just friendship. All this time, he never mentioned a girlfriend, but one thing I couldn't deny—I had to confront this bitch once and for all. Before I gave it another thought, my dagger left my hand. End over end, it sailed through the air past the crowd, right on target, the dagger nicked his lover's ear.

It all went down so fast. In one instant, she yapped, grasping her bloody ear. The room fell silent, following only a second later an echoing thud, piercing the wall clear on the other side of the bar. I smiled to myself. I got the results I wanted—Val's attention and that bitch's hands off him.

Seeing the girlfriend's starkness, only sweetened my endeavor until I realized that every eye in the joint had my back for a target. Despite the potential of getting mobbed, the only pair of eyes that I'd concerned myself with was the livid gold ones blaring at me. One glimpse of his steel jaw and I knew I'd crossed the line. At this point, a fight was inevitable, but his anger didn't seem so important. I wanted to know what he was doing with *her*.

I kept my feet planted to the ground and teeth gritted, staring back as Val charged straight for me.

Now in my face, he towered over me with a six-foot-five fierceness—consuming and threatening. My heart hammered against my chest.

I raked in my fear. I couldn't let a little thing as death stop me from confronting him. I stiffened, bracing myself for the storm.

"Just what the hell do you think you're doing?" Val wailed through clenched teeth.

"Oh...just playing with my little old knife." I flashed a mischievous smile.

Then *her* hand snaked around Val seductively, trailing the line of his chest. Obviously, she knew his body very well. It took everything I had not to beat that despicable woman with my bare fist.

As I expected, the bitch interjected with a sultry coo. The sound that would prompt me into having my memory wiped in order to forget. "Fancy meeting you here, Steve." She purred of acid.

"You must be on break." I snarled "Rumor has it that the corner's a bit slow these days. I hear they pay whores well, but only if they have all their teeth. You might want to offer a discount." I taunted as if the devil sat on my shoulder.

She snorted a tight smile. "What the hell are you talking about? I have all my teeth."

The blonde had no clue. "Yeah! Not for long." I spat her name as if it carbonized my tongue, "Helen!"

I etched my hand to my second knife hidden in the back of my pants. Helen had the speed of a cheetah and claws to match. I wasn't about to let my guard down.

Val stepped between us, blocking me from anychance of taking down the blonde. "Helen," he ordered, sternly. "Stay put! Let me get rid of this nuisance. I'll be back shortly." He winked at her. Then Val turned a cold eye on me, swooping me over his shoulder, carting me outside to the goddamn sidewalk *again*. It was starting to become an annoying habit. Once more, I seemed to have found myself left on the curb like an empty milk-jug.

When we were out of earshot, he set me down roughly. Shaken off balance, I fell, landing on my keister. The disenchanted part—he didn't bother to offer me his hand to help me to my feet. Instead, he hovered over me with veins in his neck standing out in livid ridges. "Can you not take a hint?" he blasted me. "If I wanted to talk to you or see you, I know exactly where to find your pampered ass."

"Yeah, I see why you haven't been returning my calls." Without delay, I shook off the embarrassment and sprang to my feet. "What are you doing with her?" I snapped, resting my hands on my hips.

Val's eyes tightened as he leaned closer. "I know what it must look like," he barely whispered. "But sometimes desperate times call for desperate measures."

"What?" I spat. "You getting laid?" The ache of betrayal struck. A pain I knew too well.

"It's not like that, Stevie," he whispered heatedly.

"What is it then? You sleeping with the enemy?"

"Not exactly." Val sighed deeply as he weaved his fingers through his hair. "Helen and I go back a long ways."

"Is she the discreet person you were hiding from me?" I hissed as I jabbed a finger in his chest.

"I didn't tell you because I knew how you'd react."

"If you can't be honest with me, how can I trust you?"

"I haven't deserted you!" His voice rose, no longer a whisper.

"Oh, really? If I hadn't thrown my knife, I think you would've taken her right there on that filthy floor!"

"If I didn't know any better," a lopsided grin stretched across his face, "I'd say you're jealous."

"Is that what you think?"

"Yes, I do." Val's eyes glistened.

"You're wrong!" I denied vehemently. "What I have a problem with is that Helen is Aidan's sister! That bitch is part of that disgusting family, the Order of the Quest, and most likely she knows where my da—"Then it hit me. Damn, how stupid could I be? I picked my hat off the ground and shook the dirt off. "I blew it!" Acidity hit me.

Val scratched his day-old stubble. "Maybe not. With her, it's hard to say." His eyes turned gentle.

"What happened to the first plan, mimicking a staff member from the hospital?" My brows knitted in confusion.

Val blew out a long sigh. "A couple of my Zops and I went to Haven. We found their files, but no sight of yours. The Order is not stupid. Do you honestly think they'd leave such salient information lying around?"

"No, of course not. I had no other recourse." I felt overwhelmed with disappointment. "I guess we're on plan B?" I attempted a forced smile.

"Yeah, it looks that way." There seemed to be something else lingering behind Val's voice that I couldn't put my finger on. Although my finding out what would have to wait. We had to go into plan B before a certain person became suspicious.

"Okay, let's make this look good." I acted before I'd given him time for-my-meaning to sink in as I hauled off and sucker-punched him in the square jaw. His face flew to the side, blood splattered from his busted lip. Then I launched curse words at him. "You dirty bastard! Don't ever call me again!" I shouted, making this feigned squabble look real.

Without hesitance, I lunged into the backseat of the cab parked by the curb. Apparently it had been waiting for me, the same driver as always, though, not surprising. This time, I paid. I watched from the rearview window as Val rubbed his jaw with stun written over his face. A tight smile lit my face. There was a part of me that took some pleasure in socking him. I guess this was becoming a bad habit, clocking men in my life. I shrugged. It could be worse. I could have to cook.

⋙ ⁂ ⋘

That night a storm blew in with sheets of steel, it seemed. From the rain pounding the rooftop and the screeching limbs of the oak tree grinding against my window, my nerves refused to settle nor would my eyes close.

Giving up on the fantasy of sleep, I high-tailed it downstairs to put on a kettle of water to heat. I figured a cup of Dom's chamomile tea might soothe my restlessness. I'd just settled down at the table, looking over one of Dom's gardening magazines on tips, when I heard light footsteps. I peeked over the rim of the mag, and in walked Dom, dressed in his night robe.

"Hey, Dom!" I smiled warmly. "You couldn't sleep either?"

"Oui." He answered in short. "Jeffery will be joining us momentarily. We want to show you something." Dom's face seemed strained.

"Okay." The magazine no longer held my interest as I tossed it aside and folded my hands. Dread had a bad habit of knocking at my door too frequent these days. I took a sip of my hot tea, trying to hold my panic in check. My fingers started strumming the table to keep myself from a full-blown breakdown.

The clock's ticking echoed through the house relentlessly. Tick-tock-tick-tock. Time seemed to stand still as I kept checking the grandfather clock. Unable to stand the wait any longer, I caterwauled, "Oh, for heaven's sake! What the hell is it?" I exhaled an irritated breath.

I'd no longer evinced my impatience when I'd heard Jeffery's bare feet padding down the stairs. My breath stopped in my throat. I wasn't sure if I felt relieved to have the suspense ending any more than hearing the disquieting news. The minute Jeffery shuffled in the kitchen, my worries ballooned. My eyes honed in on a white envelope, grasped in his hand.

"Don't get your panties in a wad!" Jeffery snipped. "I ain't break-n my damn neck!"

"What is so important that it can't wait till morning?" at that moment, I wished I was anybody but me. My stomach clenched.

"You'll see..." Jeffery buzzed. "but you need to chill! We wants to see too!" Jeffery huffed, handing the plain envelope to me. It was nothing out of the ordinary—merely a plain white envelope addressed to me. "It was left on our porch step today." Jeffery urged me to open it by swishing his hand at me. "Open it!"

"Okay!" I glared at him. I tore open the envelope and pulled out a letter. I unfolded it and began reading it silently:

Dear Stevie,

I have our daughter. I finally managed to escape the clenches of my family, but Dawn and I are still in hiding and must remain for an undisclosed time until it's safe. But we both want you with us. We are family, and she misses her mother. Go to St. Louis Cemetery tomorrow at midnight. Meet me at Marie Laveau's tomb. Wait there, darling. Don't tell anyone of our plans, and especially the Zophasemin you've been keeping company with. Trust no one. I love you, and I can't wait for you to be in my arms and meet our child for the first time.

Forever yours,

Aidan

Wide-eyed, I looked up at Jeffery and Dom. Their faces were etched in curiosity as they sat in dead quiet, staring at me. Jeffery broke the stupor between us, first. "What does the letter read?" His voice rose an octave.

I sat there for a minute, trying to decide what I should say. If I revealed the details, I might put them in danger and risk losing my daughter forever. That wasn't an option. So I squirmed for a believable lie while I feigned a smile. "Oh, this is a reminder from Val. That's all." I shrugged, nonchalantly. I wadded the letter up and stuffed it in my pocket.

I sensed that Dom and Jeffery didn't believe me by the glance they shared. Then Dom cleared his throat and added, "as I always say, *'Chacun a son gout'*" (Each to his own). However, if there is something risqué you are embarking on, you should inform us." Dom's gentle eyes glistened with concern.

"Guys," I sighed sharply, "sometimes it's best to leave well enough alone." I pulled from the table.

"Wait!" Jeffery called out. "At least leave a note for us to find. If you encounter any trouble, we need to know your whereabouts."

"That's a good idea! I'll make sure to do that." I made my way to the stairs.

"Excuse me, missy!" Jeffery's chagrin pierced the atmosphere.

I stopped in my tracts. I knew that tone all too well. "Yes." I tilted a sideways glance, not fully facing Jeffery.

"Where shall we look for this note?" he asked very innocently.

"Oh no, you don't!" I pivoted on my heels, staring at my friend. "If I tell you where the letter is, you won't wait. You'll snatch it up as quickly as my back's turned. I'll have it in a place you'll least expect, and when it's time to read the note, there will be a sign. You'll know when it happens." I grinned.

Jeffery threw his hands up in disgusted resignation. "You are too sneaky for your own damn good! Don't go off get-n yourself skinned alive, honeychile! There are tacky people out there who will cut you as to look at you." Jeffery let the anger pour."

I took a deep breath and said, "*C'est la vie,* Jeff!" (That's life) I shot back.

"You, my friend, are becoming more of a diva than even me." With that said, Jeffery pursed his lips and left the kitchen, stomping up the stairs like a jilted lover, leaving a trail of curse words in his wake.

Shortly after Jeffery's departure, Dom pulled from his chair and began with a gloomy sigh, "We knew what we were getting ourselves into when we opened our lives to you. We are well aware of how the Family operates. They are a *bete noire.*" (a black beast) Dom gave pause. "Jeffery and I have *avoir le coup de foudre* (fallen in love with you). We only want what's best for you, my dear." Dom came around the table and squeezed my shoulder and made sure I looked into his warm eyes. "Don't shut us out completely." He smiled, and without another word, he went to seek his disgruntled partner.

I swallowed the knot that lodged in my throat as I listened to Dom's footfalls fade. I never doubted Dom's and Jeffery's devotion. Still, it was nice hearing it.

Though my decision might've been right, it wasn't an easy one. Despite my better judgment, I felt guilty. They both have stuck their necks out for me. That was all the more reason why I had to protect them at all cost.

The Tomb

ONCE THE RELENTLESS rain had past, a brisk chill followed. I couldn't stop shivering. I stood in the center of St. Louis Cemetery in front of Marie Laveau's tomb. I was early, only a few minutes before midnight.

Strangely, the night appeared dead not a stir nor a soul in sight, or a black cat prowling. Flowers, beads, and Jesus candles marked the legendary Marie's grave. One candle was still burning low. The soft light gave off shadows, bouncing off the tomb. WTF! The boneyard didn't need any help with eerie, hairs pricked the back of my neck. As my eyes washed over the grave yard, I took note of row after row of weathered tombstones. The old yard had an unquiet beauty, yet, it didn't ease my tension any.

A bad feeling washed over me. I worried I might be walking into a trap. Ambush or not, I still would've come. Nothing was going to stop me from finding my child.

Apprehension rode heavily on my shoulders, if this wasn't a ruse, and I was truly meeting Aidan for the first time since that morning at the cabin, then this would change everything. Could I accept Aidan back into my life? The last time I'd seen Aidan seemed so long ago, yet the pain still stung like it was yesterday. Memories rushed through my mind. And just for a minute, I doubted my gut's warning. Despite his involvement with Sally, I couldn't erase his imprint—his passionate kisses, the warmth of his embrace. Did I still love him as Val believed? I wished I had an answer.

I released a sharp sigh. This wasn't the time to sort through my problems. I had to keep a clear head and be prepared for whatever I was about to confront.

For backup, I followed through with Jeff's suggestion in case things went south. Luckily Jeffery didn't have a clue that I knew about his *less-than-tasteful* activities a ponder, I'd rather not reminisce about.

It was the one certain venture, I could count on that Jeffery would do. Every morning like clockwork, Jeffery would steal away to his quaint little cubbyhole for a few moments of basking in his favorite magazine.

Before the tire tracks were cold, I seized my shot when Jeffery left the house for a spot of tea with a few socialites. As soon as the coast was clear, I snuck into his private nook, placing the note inside an earmarked page of his brown-paper-covered magazine. Although, I was riddled with guilt, invading his privacy, I couldn't think of a more inconspicuous spot. Still there were drawbacks— I'd forever have that unsavory vision burned into my brain. Totally gross!

If my plan panned out as I'd hoped, by the time Jeffery took his break in the morning, he'd already discovered my note, instructing him to alert Val. I felt if anyone had a chance finding me, it would be Val.

I had to admit, Val had become my rock. He deserved more from me. Unfortunately, I was a mess.

If Aidan was alive, there were unresolved issues that needed to be dealt with before I could make any decision, whether it was Val or Aidan. I wished my resolve was that simple like drawing sticks.

Of course it never works that way. Since Aidan and I shared a child, it made things much more tangled. I had to think about what was best for my child.

Whichever way I chose to look at this, I couldn't forget my mistrust for Aidan. There was too much deception that had transpired between us for me to let my guard down.

It was different with Val, despite our disparity. Perhaps, his clan might soften toward me if their leader showed mercy upon me.

Then again, I haven't been exactly great girlfriend material. Sharing my heart seemed difficult for me.

Then there was Helen. What if Val had feelings for Helen? That thought stung like a switch to bare legs.

I checked my watch again—eleven fifty-seven. What if no one showed up? What if Aidan and Dawn were captured? What if I was a sitting duck? I shook my head. I needed to stop with the what-ifs. I needed to stay alert and prepare for the unexpected.

Abruptly jarring me from my thoughts, I heard a shuffle of feet, moving over loose gravel. Swiftly I ducked behind the large grave marker, stretching my ear over my pounding heart. I glimpsed at my watch—twelve midnight. They were approaching, fast. I held my breath, listening.

Then the footfalls stopped. I peered around the tomb and gasped. A knot lodged in my gut. Then an urge of rage gushed through my veins. WTF? I came out from behind the stone, standing firm in my feet. I should've known. "Well, Helen, fancy seeing you here. I'm beginning to wonder if you've become my biggest fan? You seem to keep popping up." My eyes narrowed. Sleight of hand, I reached for my blade, tucked underneath the band of my pants right below my tramp stamp—a dagger, symbolizing strength. I grasped my fingers around the knife's hilt ready to spring.

Helen scoffed. "Don't flatter yourself. I'm here to follow through with my promise."

"Promise?" I laughed. "She keeps her promise." I mocked. My suspicions were right. I'd been set-up. Funny, though, Helen may be in for a surprise. Since last we met, I'd sharpened my skills. I kicked an empty beer bottle, feeling edgy. "And, pray tell what promise are you referring to, Aidan's-little-sister?" I hit a nerve as she grimaced.

"I warned you not to stick your nose where it didn't belong."

"I haven't a clue to what you're referring to." Could Helen have sent me the letter? Perhaps drawing me out was the only way she could get me alone.

"Don't play coy with me. Why must you keep trying to dig up something that doesn't concern you?" The blonde's lips curled with contempt.

I sighed, exasperated. "Look, we don't care for each other. I get it. So let's cut to the chase. Just tell me what I already know." *Keep calm!* I coached myself.

"Why make it easier for you?" Helen stood tall like a goddess. I wondered how someone with such beauty and grace could be as equally wicked.

"Despite popular belief, your brother had feelings for me. I think he would want you to do the right thing." My face pinched tight. "I know about my child. I gave birth during my stay at Haven Hospital. To hide my growing belly from me, the Family made sure that I had an ample amount of drugs pumped daily into my body." My voice broke. "You must...you must know your brother would never approve of such cruelty?"

Helen clapped her hands in a mock applause. "Hooray, hooray! It's a girl!" she was not congratulating me. Her tinged tone oozed with menace. "You should've moved on with your life. Forgot the child. You may be her fleshly mother, but she doesn't belong to you."

"A girl!" I mumbled to myself. Anger hit me like a bullet. I lurched forward, veins in my neck were standing out in vivid ridges. "I am her mother!" I hissed. "She is *not* a commodity. The child belongs with me!" I tightened my fingers around the dagger, white knuckled.

"Since we're being honest with each other," she suddenly deflected the subject, "your new boyfriend, Val, spoke highly of you. He laughed at how lousy of a lay you are." She cackled like a crow, lying.

I shook my head in annoyance. "Are we deviating from why we are here?"

The corner of her mouth tipped with indignation. "I think Val is very much part of this meeting." A predatory glint appeared behind her eyes. "After all, I have something you want and you have something I want."

I scoffed. "You want Val?" I laughed to myself. "Val is his own man. I have no claim on him."

"Of course you don't." She tossed a smoldering grin. "You could never hold a man of such station. You couldn't even keep your position with my brother."

I laughed back in her face. No point in arguing with her caviling insults. "Are we going to stand here the rest of the night swapping jabs? Really, I had more faith in you, Helen. It's not my fault if you can't keep a man."

Boiling steam appeared to rise from her incensed face. Damn, whata Kodak moment, I giggled to myself.

"Laugh at this, whore!" she sibilated. "I have your child!"

My laughter wedged in my throat, my body woodened. "Your bluffing!" She was baiting me. I drew in a deep, slow breath, holding my wit.

"Maybe!" she paused, smiling. "Maybe not."

"You're wasting my time." My fist tight in balls to my side, I turned to leave but stopped at her words.

"Aidan and your daughter are being contained as we speak." Her face lit with bitter triumph.

"How do I know you're not lying?"

"Because the truth hurts more than a lie." Her demeanor gave no hint of deception. I still didn't trust this bitch.

"I want proof." I waited, caution set in my stance.

Not uttering a word, Helen nodded to the left, from behind the shadows, one of her barn-side guards revealed himself with an iPad in his grasp. He halted by her side, waiting for further instructions. "Show her!" she ordered, brusque. The brawny guard stepped closer to me, almost too close, pressed play and handed me the tablet. I snatched the device abruptly from his beefy hand, my patience spent. My pulse was erratic as my eyes were glued to the screen. Everything surrounding me ceased; the only focus that mattered was that small device.

Only moments later, I heard laughter—a child giggling. My stomach clenched as my eyes watched the screen. A little girl about three years old, blowing out candles, it was her birthday. She had dark hair like Aidan and green eyes like me. In a small voice, I heard her call out, "Daddy," and that's when all my doubts vanished. Aidan appeared beside her. He looked happy, smiling, while helping her blow out the last candle. The angelic child reached up to hug her father's neck, and then the picture went blank.

My head snapped up at Helen. "Where are they now!" I demanded through snarling teeth. It took every ounce of strength I had not to throttle this evil vixen.

"Finally, I have you rattled." She dangled a wicked grin.

I didn't reply, though, the flame in my eyes gave me away—rage like no other.

Then I needed clarity. "What did I ever do to deserve such horrendous treatment from you and your iniquitous Family?" It would take me an eternity to understand such cruelty.

"You have no clue." She smirked. "This doesn't have anything to do with you. It has to do with *your* father."

"My celestial donor?" my brows furrowed, confused.

"No, not Mustafa. I'm referring to your human father."

"You're tormenting my child and me because my father defected the Family?"

"They never told you?"

"Told me what?" my fist white knuckled to my side.

"Why am I not surprised?" she smiled, not a friendly smile, one that sent chills down my spine. "I am Aidan's adopted sibling." She hesitated. "I am your blood sister."

My chin hit the floor. "You're lying!"

"I'm different from you. My blood courses strong with Druid blood. I am like my father, Jon."

"Jon Collins is *your* father?" I stood like I'd been shot, waiting to fall.

"I'm disappointed." Amusement crossed Helen's face. "I assumed my brother would've told you."

"I don't understand?" I couldn't believe my ears. How could I have not known?

"I suppose I have to enlighten you on our family's history."

"I don't need a history lesson." I hissed through clenched teeth.

"Oh, but you do." Her brow arched. "You see… before your mother came into the picture, there was someone else—my mother."

Whether I wanted to admit it or not, there was a ring of truth. "Go on." I coaxed.

"Once Jon finished law school, he was promised to wed, my mother, Lilith. The Family had arranged their union long before Jon's and my mother's birth.

"Prearranged marriages are from the dark ages. Why would anyone agree to such a burden?"

"In our family, we honor tradition. It has kept us in existence for centuries. Our magick flows strong in our blood. It is imperative we keep our bloodline pure. Which brings me back to our father."

"So what happened? Did my father marry your mother?"

"Jon and Lilith were inseparable. She loved our father. Jon, not so much."

"He hated the Family's lack of propriety. He was a good man. I'm sure it had nothing to do with your mother."

"You couldn't be more wrong." She sneered. "Our father eloped with your worthless mother. Not only did he abandoned his family, he deserted his fiancé and unborn child—a child that was fully his!" Helen shrieked, tears welled up in her eyes.

"He'd gotten *your* mother pregnant?" I'd stammered over the words. "This…this couldn't be possible?" I raked over my mind if my parents had ever mentioned an older sister. I drew a blank.

"It's true!" she wiped a stray tear. "My father, our father, had forsaken me."

"If this were true, my father must've had a reason for leaving your mother. He was an honorable man." Despite my distaste for Helen, my heart went out to her.

"Our father was a coward!" Helen spat. "Rather than living up to his obligations, he left the Family, refusing to marry my mother. Jon didn't care about her or his unborn child. He was selfish!"

I shook my head, denying this tragic tale. "You couldn't possibly be his child. My father couldn't have children."

"Are you that naïve? My mother cast a spell against him after he ditched her at the altar."

I gawked, disbelieving.

"Oh, don't look so surprised, little sister!" Helen's eyes narrowed with hatred.

"I don't believe you!" I railed. "My father wouldn't have left his own flesh and blood behind."

"Forgive me for tainting the image of perfect Daddy, but you should know who your father truly was."

I get her grief, whether it was true or not, but what did I have to do with her Daddy issues? "Let's say I give you that. I don't understand why you're dragging my family and me into this?"

"For the sins of the father, the offspring must pay the transgressions."

"Because of an act of another, you intend to punish me by taking *my* child?" My heart went out to her but holding my child hostage was playing with death.

"It's like a double-edged sword. If you will, an eye for an eye." Her lip twitched. "The child is quite amazing. She possesses great powers, much like her momma, and" she pronounced each word precisely, driving the knife further into my heart—"we intend to utilize your little girl's abilities until we drain her last breath."

"Oh hell, no!" I lurched forward in reach of the blonde. "Over my dead body, sistah!" I hissed, ready for a bloodbath.

"Careful for what you wish for. This time there will be no mercy. The Family spared you once due to my brother's pathetic pleas. This time, his begging will fall against muted ears as he sits and rots in his cell."

"Aidan *is* alive?" my heart stopped!

"After my brother escaped our clenches, that's when he sent you the letter. Personally, I feel he's wasting his time on trash."

"Tell me where they are?" I snarled like a lioness crazed for her lost cubs.

"Well, sister dear, my adopted brother, your ex-lover" she rebuffed—"is a bit under the weather. You see he received quite a beating for his disloyalty—a lesson he truly deserved. He needed his priorities set straight. Placing his loyalty to you first makes the Family very angry. After all, the Family is a very jealous god."

"God? That's a bit grandiose even for you, Helen." I was done. "Tell me where they are if want to live!"

She ignored my question. "One is never too pompous when it is true!" Her eyes shot acid at me.

"Tell me where Aidan and my child are?" I demanded with a hardline glower.

"Don't worry, little sis. You'll reunite with your lover and child soon enough." Helen's lips curled with insolence.

"If you have harmed them, I'm coming for you!" I threatened with grave intent.

"Your child is safe for now. She's having her milk and cookies." The wicked witch smirked. "We're preparing her for the celebration tonight. Since we were unable to drain you of your gifts, we'll just take the next best thing—your daughter." Her lips pursed like the kiss of death.

Alarm torpedoed my chest, nearly knocking the breath from me. "If you value your life, you'll let my child and Aidan go free, unharmed." I spoke with a steel calm. At this point, I wanted to end her pathetic life. Yet I knew that would be a grave mistake. I'd never find Aidan and my child if I took her life now. I had to be patient. She didn't meet me in this cemetery just to gloat.

"Tsk, tsk, such sisterly love."

"Let's save the love for later, dear old sister. Set them both free, and you can have me. Take what you need from me—my life, my freedom, my powers. Leave Aidan and Dawn out of it!" The way I saw it, I was a stranger to my daughter. She knew her father, and by what I saw on the video, she loved Aidan dearly as I loved my father. I refused to take the only thing she knew.

"Oh, I'd love to take you up on your offer. However, there's a slight problem." Helen sneered. "When you screwed my handsome brother, the two of you fused your powers, locking your strength together as one. You're bound to Aidan forever. One can't live without the other."

Holy mother of god! It was true. We were sealed. It wasn't a lie. The real deception wasn't between Aidan and me. Rather, the Family concealed the truth from both of us. "So I can assume since I'm standing erect, you're telling the truth about Aidan?"

"You catch on fast." Delight tipped the corner of her mouth.

"What do you want?" I met her murderous glare equally while I waited for her to make a move. She better get ready, it wouldn't be without one hell of a fight. I suspected she had brought more than one goon. Like my daddy would say, hope for the best and prepare for the worse, and tonight, I came pack-n.

"There are many things I desire, one of which is for my dead daddy's fav to suffer. I wish for my brother to look upon your once-beautiful face after it's mangled. After I'm done with you, he won't think of you as his precious princess." Then she saved the worst for last as she pierced my heart with her foreboding words. "To top it off, while you lie helpless, you'll have the pleasure of witnessing your daughter's life force stripped from her body." The frothing-out-the-mouth blonde just crossed the line.

A calm came over me as I began to speak with precision. I knew with certainty what was about to go down. "Three years ago, you and your family had the upper hand over me. Back then, I had a lot to learn about your world. Since that time, I have learned a thing or two. As a result, I've been forced to learn particular skills. So, if you don't mind me speaking candidly, let me explain exactly how this ambush is going to transpire. First, I plan to take out all your guards, one by one." Her other two escorts had stepped forward into the dim light. I expected that much. I had sensed her squires' presence lurking among the shadows.

I nodded to the man on my left. "John Doe over here has a slight vision problem that he failed to tell you. He'll be my first target. I'll take out his good eye, leaving him blind and no use to you." Helen's mouth flopped open like she was catching flies. "And when your second man, Don Juan lunges for me, I have my second knife to stop him in midair. The knife will penetrate his skull, killing him on impact before he hits the ground. Then afterward, I think you and I should have a sisterly visit. You're going to take me to my family." I stared at her with full intent of my threat.

Then suddenly an epiphany struck. At that very moment, clarity rang louder than the Liberty Bell. I understood my true purpose. The Family never intended for me to create a new world. They wanted to create an army of supernatural soldiers—for a better word, assassins—large numbers of souped-up warriors taking the world by storm, ridding the earth of innocent people, they deemed as weak. This was their abominable plan from the beginning—the New World Order—a world of perfect people just like them, vile and evil, unholy immortals with everlasting life. Wow! That was taking ambition to a whole different level, and I hated it.

I looked over at the woman claiming to be my blood. I saw pure fear in her eyes. I smiled with joy, knowing I was about to carry out my threat. Then with no thought given, I went into action. In only a matter of seconds, both guards were faced down in a puddle of blood with no sign of life from either one.

My neck snapped in the direction of my sister. Frozen, she glared at me like a frightened pig before the slaughter. As I turned to her, I felt myessence surge forth, and before I knew it, in the blink of an eye, I had my arm grasped around her throat, tight, with my dagger pressed against her jugular.

"Tell me where they are!" I hissed in a deadly whisper. The blonde tried to wiggle loose, but her efforts were futile. "I'll say this just one more time before I end your pathetic life. Where are they?" I demanded, desperate and determined. She started to speak but stopped as something hard struck the back of my head. Pain shot through my mind, and in the next breath, everything went black.

Lost and Found

WHEN I CAME to, it took a moment for me to gather my senses. Soon the harsh memory of how I'd gotten here, flooded my foggy mind. A sharp pain shot from the back of my head, confirmed I'd been shanghaied. Go figure! I sat up with difficulty, wincing. By the throbbing ache in my right side, I most likely had a few broken ribs. My left eye was swollen shut, gnawing like something fierce. I winched when I sighed. Such cowards to beat me while I was out cold. No doubt, this was the work of my lovely sister and her goons. Good thing I've had practice getting my ass kicked. I laughed, flinching.

As my one good eye adjusted to the dimness, I realized my holding cell wasn't much more than a few sprigs of hay scattered over a cold, dirty floor and iron bars. Oddly, it was as though I'd fallen through time, it was primeval in every sense, dark and musky. No bedding, no pot to piss in, not even a chair to rest my wary bones. Animals got better treatment than this.

I eased myself against the wall, drawing my knees to my chest, trying to focus on anything but my claustrophobia. Since Haven, solitary confinement became my own living hell. The staff loved tormenting me by forcing me inside a ten by ten box, with no provisions; only the confinements of a crunched up metal box. If the authorities had ever caught them, the hospital would've been shut down immediately.

I pushed up off the floor, bracing myself against the stone wall. The blow to my head must've been a humdinger, judging by my dizziness. My headache was blinding. I managed to limp over to the bars. With the one good eye, I tried to see if a guard might be on watch. Nothing, but my vision was hindered. I called out, "Hey!" I bellowed. "Anyone out there!" The echo of my voice was the sole reply. No sign of a living soul, only a faint trickle of water vibrated off the wall, down the corridor. Funny, I remembered that eerie drip from Aidan's secret chamber. It was like déjà vu, though, I shrugged it off. I had enough on my plate to worry about than some stupid flash back.

I grasped a bar in each hand and gave it a good tug. Pain shot through my entire body as I flinched. Regardless of how superhuman I might be those bars weren't budging. I slid down to the floor, leaning against the wall in a corner by the bars. I wanted to watch for anyone coming. I couldn't see much, but I still had my hearing.

I dragged in a torn breath, regretting my haste decision. How stupid could I'd been? I shouldn't have lost my temper. If I hadn't let my hardheadedness get the best of me, Aidan and Dawn would be safe, free from Helen and that vile family. Damn it!

I laid my face in my hands and began sobbing. I yearned for my child. She deserved to have her mother. "Is there something wrong with wanting to hold your own child?" I choked through the tears. The tears streamed down my cheeks and stung like hell from the cuts on my face. I didn't care. I welcomed the pain.

I wiped the tears from my face with the back of my hand. It still wasn't too late. I had to pull myself together. If I wanted to save Dawn and Aidan, I had to draw strength from my inner powers. I sensed the essence earlier. Somewhere in the depth of my core, it patiently waited.

<hr />

I must've dozed off when I heard the jingle of keys and footfalls approaching. Alerted, I pulled myself to my feet, thankful my pain had eased slightly. I privately thanked my angel genetics for that. In my world, fast healing was a welcomed thing. I leaned against the wall to balance my wobbly legs. I stilled, barely breathing, staying calm as I listened. Whoever was coming, I braced myself, expecting the worst.

Suddenly I remembered my necklace. I reached for it. It was gone! I dropped to my knees on the floor, scurrying for it, hoping it had fallen, but with no light and hindered vision, I came up empty-handed. My worst fear was that someone took it. "Shit! I'm screwed!" I murmured to myself as I rose to my feet.

When the footfalls halted, there stood my loving sister.

"I hope you are enjoying your stay?" Even through the faint light, her smug face shined like a beacon.

"I'd diffidently recommend this spot. The bed's soft as a feather." I was coy.

"We pride ourselves on our Southern hospitality." She smiled, harboring a wicked glint behind her sooty lashes.

Time was closing in. I had to reason with this woman. "Let's make a truce, Helen. Free Aidan and my daughter, and I'll do anything you want!" To beg for myself was out of the question, but to plead for my child and her father, there was nothing I wouldn't do for their safety.

"Why should I do *you* any favors?" Helen snarled.

"Don't do it for me, do it for the sake of an innocent child. For fuck's sake, do it for your brother!" I wailed.

"Tsk, tsk! Where's your inside voice?"

"I left it at the cemetery with my patience." If I could've shot fire from my eyes, I would've smacked her right between the eyes.

Helen arched a brow. It surprised me with all that Botox. "I read in the Bible once that patience is a virtue."

I snorted a laugh. "Bible school! You didn't combust?" I goaded.

"My, my, aren't we cranky when we wake up from our nap."

I didn't bother with a retort. We could do this till she grew a wart on her nose and flew off on her broomstick. Rather, I'd preferred saving my energy for things more productive, like snapping her neck.

"I hope your guest will put you in a better mood." A nefarious glitter tainted Helen's blues. I knew my sweet sister had some scheme up her sleeve. I cautioned myself.

I heard high heels approaching and getting closer. When the heavy clanking stopped as my eyes landed on the visitor, I blacked out with rage. In half a blink, I reached the bars, grabbing a fistful of hair. I intended on snapping that bitch's neck, and damn near did, until Helen shot me with some sort of souped-up TASER that knocked me off my feet, throwing me back onto the hard floor. The stun gun prevented me from killing the visitor, but it didn't stop me from taking a fistful of hair.

Simultaneously, screams belted forth. And a vindicated grin played upon my swollen lips. Despite the discomfort from my backside, I found delight in her agonized face. I called to her, "lucky for you I'm on this side of the bars." I snarled at the visitor with murder in my eyes. "No goddamn stunner will stop me from killing you, Sally!" pushing past the twinge, I pulled myself to my feet with newfound strength.

"I can't believe you ripped my hair out!" Sally bellowed, grasping the crown of her head. "I have a bloody bald spot now!" Tears gathered in her eyes.

"Come a little closer," I taunted her. "I'll gladly give you a matching one."

"You're an animal!" Sally yapped like a hyena.

"I guess I am." I spoke calmly. I could feel the rumble of my powers trying to surface. "Where have you been all these years, Sally?"

"Raising your bratty child." She shot me a smothering look. "That child's insufferable just like her mother."

"You can always give her back since you stole her from me in the first place." I felt for my knife in a hidden spot, which I shalt reveal. I had the knife's hilt in my hand, hidden behind my back. I had only one shot. There were two targets. Hard decision, I thought, until I saw the keys dangling on Helen's hip. If I take Helen down, with any luck, she'd fall close enough to the bars where I could snatch the keys from her body. If I decided to take down Sally, who's killing was, frankly, long overdue, my chances in getting the keys would be slim to none. Helen wouldn't run. She'd call the guards to punish me once more after they dispose of Sally's body. But if I took Helen out first, Sally would take flight and run. She'd be more worried about saving her ass than alerting the guards. With any luck, I'd have enough time to get the keys, free myself, and snatch up Sally before she alerted the watchmen.

So I niggled Helen. I wanted to ruffle her feathers. Once she grabbed the bars, I'd make my move. With my angelic talents, I was speedier than the average creature, even a Druid. Well, at least I hoped.

I made sure I stood back far enough. If I kept the distance between us, she might feel brave enough to step up to the bars, in my reach. Thus I began baiting her.

"Helen, rumor has it that Val dumped you. How did he put it?" I tapped my finger on my throbbing lip. "Oh, I remember— he referred to you as entertainment." I snickered. Then my eyes took on a hunted look. "You realize the only reason he spent one minute with you, it was for me? During all that time he was whispering sweet nothings into your ear, he was getting information for me." I paused, hoping my tease would kick-up some dirt. "I think he's more into younger women. You're starting to show your age. I hear Botox works well." I laughed, driving the taunt into the center of her black heart as if it was my dagger. I was quite enthralled, watching the steam roll off my sister's back.

"Careful what you say, angel! The little imp is still alive," she hissed. Right then and there, I began to seethe. I almost blew my plan. If I let her goad me, then I'd lost the fight and my daughter's life.

I smiled sweetly. "I think if you were going to kill her, you would've by now."

"What makes you think we haven't?" Helen's eyes turned icy.

"Because I'm still standing here, alive." I hit the target right on the mark. I could see it in Helen's burning eyes. "You don't have any power in this family, Helen. Both you and Sally are puppets on a string. I bet you can't wipe your ass without permission." I smiled. "I may be locked up and possibly lose my life, but at least I'm free. Bet you can't say the same."

It worked! Helen had fallen right into my hands, figuratively speaking. The next chain of events toppled like the domino effect. I went into Zop mode. Just like I'd hoped, the blonde stepped up to the bars, I heaved my dagger, piercing her heart. With a look of disbelief, the blonde collapsed to her knees. I dashed to her side before she'd hit the floor, snatching the key off her belt. Swiftly I jammed the key into the keyhole, click, the door gave, and I was out of the cell in flight for Sally as I glimpsed at her fat legs running down the corridor—just as I'd expected.

Unexpectedly, I was stopped in my tracks by the gentle grasp of a hand. Startled, my eyes fell upon Helen laying in a puddle of her own blood. It was only a matter of minutes before death took its claim. "Wait, Stevie!" the malevolence in her voice had vanished.

I knelt beside her withering body. Her face had drained of color. She spoke with difficulty. "Yes?" I whispered.

"I just want to know," she swallowed, "how do you do it?"

"How do I do what?" my eyes were drawn to a thin line of blood that trailed down her delicate chin.

"How do you get two men to fall in love with you at the same time?" her eyes were waning. "Aidan and Val are in love with you. I don't know how you have captured both their hearts when I can't hold one." In the next breath, the life in Helen's eyes smothered as her body went limp.

Suddenly I was swooned with guilt. If we had been in another life, another world, we might've been close like *real* sisters, but in this *life*, we were mortal enemies by default. Yet my heart ached for her loss. I'd have to sort this out another time. Right now I had to catch Sally. Swiftly, I grabbed the hilt of my dagger still lodged in Helen's chest. I turned my one good eye away and pulled the blade out. I cringed feeling the bloody knife slide from her limp body. She was dead, but it didn't make me feel any better. I'd never enjoyed taking the life of another.

Time was ticking away. So, I sprinted down the dark corridor, not sure which way to go. I stretched my ears for any sounds. Right away, echoes of feet tromping were in the near distance. The footfalls were heavy, and the runner's breathing appeared stressed, panting. It had to be my mistrusted friend, Sally. She weighed at least forty pounds more than her body needed. I darted up the stairs, following the dust trail. When I spotted my dear old chum, I didn't hesitate, I lunged, tackling her from behind. We both went spiraling down the flight of stairs, and with each blow, my body felt a new pain. By the time we crashed at the bottom, my agony had past, and fire had taken its place.

Dragging Sally to her feet, I seized control, holding her hostage by my knife pressed against her throat. Through clenched teeth, I demanded, "Take me to your husband, now! And don't fucking tell me you don't know where he's at!" I threatened, pressing the cold steel of my knife tighter.

"Okay, okay! Don't hurt me. It's that way." She raised her hand, pointing.

Then she started this nervous rambling. "I didn't want to betray you. They made me lie. Aidan and I were never married. He hardly knows I exist."

After all these years, I was finally getting answers to the questions that haunted me since that day I was taken. "Who put you up to framing me?" I hissed, still keeping the knife pressed against her throat.

"It was Dr. Van Dunn, Aidan's uncle and Helen. Aidan had no idea of his sister's scheming. Van forced me to join their crusade. He said since I failed the Family's expectations, I had no other choice. It was that or death." I got the feeling Sally was trying to excuse her misdeeds.

"Shut up!" I snapped. "Who helped you that day at the cottage?"

"It was Van!" she rambled, flinching from the prick of the blade. "He was the one who drugged you."

"What happened to Aidan?"

"When Aidan returned to the castle, he walked into an ambush, ordered by his uncle, Van. I lied about him taking part in your abduction. That's all I know! I swear!"

My face felt flushed with indignation. "Cough it up, Sally!" I pressed tighter. "Who killed my mother and her boyfriends?"

"All right! All right!" Sally squawked, her eyes wide with fear. "It was Helen who killed your mother. She blamed Sara for her mother's death. When Helen overheard your conversation about the angel dust with Aidan, she followed him to your house that night. When the two of you left, Helen found the angel dust on the ground by Aidan's car. He must've dropped it when he shifted. Helen took the dust, and, well, you get what happened next.

As for the boyfriends, by Van's orders, Zak, killed the owner of the grocery store. I can't remember his name."

"Charlie! Charlie was his name." I growled.

"Sorry! My mind is a bit cloudy on some details." Sally dragged in a sharp breath and continued. "It was explained to me that since Zak was dead, Nim, Zak's brother, also a man in black, finished off Francis."

"Why did the MIB take their life? They weren't a threat to the Family."

"The Family concerned themselves with Sara marrying the grocery store owner that she might skip out on the contract. I understand Charles had a nice nest egg set aside. He also planned to make Sara the beneficiary of his life insurance policy. It was well over a million. Sadly for Sara, Charles never made it to his private attorney's office that morning. He was murdered in his front yard."

Taken aback much! "Did Sara know what Charlie was doing?"

Sally paused as if she was deciding whether or not to tell me, then she spilled the beans. "To my understanding, Sara refused to marry him without the policy." Why would I be shocked? Sara was very resourceful. Of course she'd marry Charlie and take his riches. I felt like I didn't even know my own mother.

My teeth gritted, furiously. It all made sense now. "*Go* on! Finish!"

"The last one, Francis, he was a liability. He was a loose cannon and was wanted for armed robbery in Texas."

"What?" I gagged on the word.

"Francis was a small time thug, though, a bit ambitious. He knew about Sara's arrangement with the Family. After he and your mother gambled their entire fortune away, Francis set out to blackmail Van for more money. Or else he'd go public and expose the Family's dark secrets. Apparently, he was good at snooping."

I cringed inwardly. Francis was creepy and slightly deviant, but I had no idea of the level he'd stoop too.

Sally furthered her story, "Francis had to be dealt with. The Family had planned on killing Sara anyhow, so they decided to take out the boyfriend first."

"How did the Family find evidence against me?"

Sally gave way to an awkward sigh. "You should know the answer to that. They used magick on the prosecutor, the judge, your lawyer, and even the kitchen sink. Don't you know by now our family has every sort of reach there is possible?"

"They're not *my* family!" I clarified.

"Yeah, they are! Your father and mine are brothers. We're cousins."

I gasped. "You're *lying*."

"I wouldn't dare attempt that now, not with a knife pointing at my throat."

"Your father's still alive?"

"I don't know. My parents severed their ties with me. Unlike your father, mine felt the Family's beliefs were unconquerable as a god. As it seems, I'm not the only family member execrated. My father, Thaddeus, had a falling out with your dad, his brother Jon, over his marriage to Sara, an outsider. Consequently, Jon was cast out, never to return. Because of your father's status, the Family hid Lilith's pregnancy from him." Sally gave pause. I sensed her struggle, "as for Sara, she knew about Lilith's condition."

"How did my mother know?" I couldn't wrap my head around this tall tale.

"Aidan's uncle had the pleasure of confiding in Sara." Sally confessed. "Van had taken an interest to her. To encourage Sara's assistance, he offered her a generous incentive to keep the pregnancy out of earshot from Jon. Van, of course, didn't reveal the real truth of his endeavor. He had other plans for Jon and Sara.

"Let me guess—me!"

"Yes. Van is quite diabolical."

"What happened to Helen's mom?"

"As the story unfolds, Lilith had no idea of Van's involvement. She had her own selfish agenda. Lilith chose not to reveal her pregnancy to Jon. Rather, she hastily sought out a back alley abortion clinic, but the Family stepped in before she had the procedure done."

"What insidious scheme did the Family have in store for Lilith?"

"For the remaining term of her pregnancy, the Family held her as a prisoner in a small room, keeping her under lock and key. They were on a suicide watch."

All I could say was, "Wow!"

"The Family has its issues." Sally relented with a wicked grin.

I snorted, though, I didn't commit.

Sally went on with more of the story. "When she gave birth, the Family took the infant away from Lilith and gave the baby to Aidan's parents to raise. In the end, Lilith ran away with some man she'd met at a bar.

Now I understood Helen's contempt toward my parents and me. The pain of guilt really began to hit me hard. I wished I'd known. I continued to listen.

"Later Lilith was found face down, drifting in the bayou, dead. I don't know if it was by the hands of the Family or the stranger she ran away with. No one is sharing that information with me. Anyhow, Helen blamed your mom for the death of her mother, and she despised you because your dad loved you."

"Your story certainly puts a new light on things. I had no idea."

"I think things could've been different between the two of you if she had known the full story."

"Why didn't you tell her the truth? She might've been able to move past her pain. Maybe she would've had a better life." Dense much?

"The Family had forbidden anyone to tell Helen. They are masters of holding truths. Secrets amidst secrets."

"You call them family, I call them the devil. Helen may have been just as depraved, but she deserved the truth."

"I guess like all families, we have our issues too. Take me—I'm an embarrassment to the Family, a disgrace."

A part of me felt sorry for Sally and Helen. Yet I couldn't help either one. Helen was dead, and Sally needed professional help. Right now, I had my own crisis—getting Aidan and my child free from this hellhole. "Enough!" I ordered crossly. "Who has my child?"

"Dr. Van had taken her to a foster family up North." Sally rambled. "He didn't give any names—"

"Stop!" I tightened the knife. "I mean now?"

"Ouch!" Sally sputtered. "The... the child's in the... the sacred chamber. The members are having a ceremony tonight— something... something about midnight and the full moon."

"Oh mother of god!" My panic soared. Dawn in the sacred chamber meant one thing. Those monsters planned to extract her essence. Helen wasn't lying after all. With no time to lose, I had to find Aidan. I shoved Sally forward to hurry her fat legs. "We have to find Aidan!" I thrust her forward once more. "Let's go, let's go!" I rushed, hell bent on time. My daughter's life depended on me, and anyone else could meet their maker if they got in my way.

Darkness had fallen on the walls of the castle, it was a wonder we were able to find our way through the corridors. I prayed Sally didn't have guards waiting to attack. In my condition, I doubted I could fight off anyone, even a grandmother for that matter. I needed to reach Aidan fast. With any luck, he might be in better shape than me. It would take the two of us to free Dawn. His healing touch certainly would be helpful.

Around a corner and down another flight of stairs, we finally reached his cell. I noticed a torch as I snatched it off the wall. I turned to Sally. "Hand me your lighter," I pressed.

Her brows wrinkled. "What?"

"Are you that stupid? The smell of cigarettes reeks from you! Smokers have lighters. Hand the freaking thing to me!" I held out my hand, losing patience.

Sally regretfully sighed, slapping the red lighter into my palm. I flicked the lighter and a small flame popped up. I smiled into her face as if it was Christmas. Hurriedly, I lit the torch. Seconds later, a blaze ignited, shedding a generous light down the corridor.

"Take this torch," I instructed Sally, "and hold it up high where the light will shine." I paused. "If you even look like you're going to do something foolish, I will end your life. Do I make myself clear?" the promise of murder spewed from my voice.

She nodded, "I won't run." Sally's voice reminded me of a child's, small and timid. Without another word, I handed the torch to her. The flame spread its glorious light into the cell. I could see well enough now. I yanked the key out of my pocket and unlocked the iron door. The door squeaked loudly as I tugged. When my eyes landed on Aidan, my heart sank. He lay limp on the floor, unconscious. I ran to him, lifting his head into my lap, his eyes slowly opened as though he was drugged or by the looks of him, beaten silly. "Stevie?" he muttered hoarsely.

"It's me." I whispered, holding back tears. "I'm going to get you out of here." A faint smile toyed with the corners of his mouth. I smiled back, but nothing inside me felt the glee of a smile. I scanned over Aidan's pummeled body and staggered from shock. No argument, Van was a heartless bastard. He'd left his nephew rotting in this dungeon. When I thought my hatred for the Family couldn't get worse, I realized I was utterly wrong.

"How did you find me?" Aidan struggle to speak, throat parched.

"I'll explain later." I replied, curt, fumbling with the key as my hands trembled. "Hold your breath that this key works." I forced a smile at Aidan as I slipped the key into the padlock of the left cuff. I held my breath. If the key didn't match, we were as good as dead, including my child. I held my breath. The key had to work! The thin metal key slid down into the slot, fitting like a glove. "So far, so good." I breathed to Aidan. Then carefully, I turned the key. The lock clicked and the cuff opened, falling to the dirty floor with a loud clang. I glimpsed up at Aidan, he'd gave way to a sigh of relief. I joined him with a smile.

With no more time to waste, I hurried along, unlocking the other restrains. Clanging of iron echoed off the walls. The sound made me happy. It was music to my ears.

"Here! Let me help you." I slid my arm under Aidan's arm and hoisted him to his feet. This Aidan wasn't the man I remembered, strong and unstoppable. This person was weak and unsteady, his drawn face needled with pain.

When we tried to take a step, Aidan stumbled, falling back into my arms, and before I knew what had happened, he'd gathered me into his embrace, squeezing me tight. Taken off guard, I hesitated, unsure of my feelings for Aidan, or if I could trust him. Then again, he was wasting away in this dank cell, embarking upon death—I relented and returned the embrace. We stood in silence locked in each other's arms. Aidan still had that woodsy scent, and the embrace of his arms swooned my senses. Just like old times, he whispered in my ear, "I've missed you." A prick of memory lane tugged heavily at my heart. At this point, I didn't want to visit my archive of emotions. I pulled away, but lingered when I gazed into his deep blues. I lent him a tight smile, though urging him. "We have to go now. They have Dawn in that goddamn chamber. Can you walk?"

"I think so," Aidan nodded.

"Good! We have to hurry." He looked over at Sally and flashed a scornful look. "What's she doing here?"

"Sally's my prisoner. She's going to help us escape, otherwise I'm gonna slit her throat myself." I smiled up at him as if I was talking about having brunch.

Aidan half-laughed, teasing, "you're the girl of my dreams. You do me proud, babe." His eyes twinkled, reminding me of the past, and my heart skipped a beat. He still had that effect on me. I'd figure that one out later when I could think more clearly.

On the edge of spitefulness, my attention sidled to Sally. "Here, help your husband. I'll take the lead," I thought I'd let Sally sweat a bit more under Aidan's careful eye.

Aidan's brows furrowed. "Husband?"

"I'll explain later."

"Yeah! I know, later." Suspicion hid behind his glint as he glared at Sally.

"Let's go! Sally, which way is the chamber?"

Her eyes grew wide. She began fidgeting, acting strange, even for her.

"What? Spit it out!" I demanded, not hiding the asinine in my voice.

Her shoulders slumped, voice quavering. "The location of the hallowed sanctum is unknown to me! Women aren't permitted."

I dropped my arm from Aidan and stomped forward, leaning into Sally's face, sparks of fire ignited from my eyes. "Why didn't you tell me this earlier?"

"I was afraid you'd kill me." She cried.

"What the hell, Sally!" I berated her. "We could've been looking for that devil's den all this time." My voice ascended to a murderous falsetto.

"You're crazy!" Sally yammered. "I never know what's going to set you off!"

"My child is on the brink of being murdered!" I shook my white knuckled fist in her pale face. "How else do you expect me to act?" Sally had struck my last nerve, I was getting rid of a weight that was holding me down. I raised my dagger to her throat, and just when I was about to do the deed, Aidan's hand stopped me.

"Wait! I know the way." Our eyes locked, his hand remained on mine until I stepped back, dropping the dagger to my side, though, still huffed with anger. "Let's get going!" I turned a cold eye to Sally. I'd deal with her later.

Quickly we moved through the shadowy corridors, corner after corner, following Aidan to the chamber that he'd sworn on his life was the a shortcut.

I felt grateful for small favors. The torch had been a beacon, spreading its generous light down the narrow passage. Down the slippery slope and one slip, we could've fallen to our death. Once we reached ground level, my lungs expanded, opening air back through the windpipe. We were far from being out of the woods of danger; hence, our journey had just begun.

After what seemed an eternity, we came to an abrupt halt at the end of our path. Alarmed, I snatched the torch from Sally's grasp, holding it up next to the barrier. I ran my fingers across the dust and cobwebs that clung to the stone. Ready to spit nails, I spun on my heels, teeth gritting at Aidan. "I thought you said this was a short cut? Where's the freaking entrance?" I thundered.

"Wait a minute." He stepped up under the light next to me. He squatted down and brushed his hands over the wall. I watched in silence as his finger trailed up the wall. He stopped, surging to his feet, facing me, "this is a door! The chamber's just on the other side of this stone." One corner of his lip suggested a smile.

I on the other hand failed to see this as a triumph moment. "You got any brainstorm ideas how we're supposed to get past that freaking rock?" I rested my hands on my hips, ready to fire bullets.

"Hmm, dynamite?" He rubbed his stubble, seeming too calm. "Unless it's protected by a Fort Knox spell, then there's no breaking it."

I lit into him as if he was my last supper. "You mean to tell me that you didn't give that little tidbit any consideration?" WTF! I fumed. "What's wrong with you?" I wanted to shove him off his feet, instead, I did what any insane gal would do, I started pacing in a small circle, rambling like a person off Prozac. "I should've left both of you in that damn cell and did this myself!"

"No need for your cavalier babble." Acid formed off Aidan's tongue.

I stopped in my tracts, face strained. "Screw you! Move out of my way." I pushed him back. I needed space. "Since neither one of you can help, I guess it's all left up to me. Stay out of my way!" My nostrils flared.

Aidan threw his hands up in disgusted resignation, "get over yourself." He huffed, joining Sally's side. What was wrong with him? His child was in danger. He should be over here helping me, instead, he stood to the side—a bystander at best. I shot him an acid glare.

I couldn't deal with him right now. I had to set aside my irritation and focus solely on that damn door. My powers worked once before, they'd work again—I hoped.

I made my way up to the barrier. By the looks of it, it had to be more than a foot thick. I released a sharp breath and placed my hands flat against the massive rock. The stone thrummed as though it was melding to me. I instantly gasped, jerking my hands to my chest. My heart rate was soaring. Once more, I steady my feet, drawing in a deep breath and placed my hands back on the stone. This time the vibration didn't startle me. I embraced it as I closed my eyes, reaching deep to the core where my essence rested. I heaved the inner strength like a water bucket, drawing from the well. I thirst for my Essence.

Without warning, my essence surged to the surface, and fire shot forward, spewing everywhere.

When the explosion quiet, my eyes slid to Aidan and Sally. As far as I could see they were unscathed, crouched behind a boulder. As for the door—it was still intact. Pissed much? I gawked at the immovable door.

For a moment, I eyeballed the two huddled together in each other's arms. If they were an item, it meant shit to me. What got under my skin was that he wasn't offering his skills to help bust this door down. He had more Druid magick in his pinky than I had in my whole body. What was his problem?

I called to him, my eyes fixed with a level stare. "Where are your Druid abilities? I need your help here." I arched a brow.

Aidan charged to his feet, his face harsh. "I might be a Druid, but I'm not superman. My forte is of another. Not explosives." His chiseled chin tilted in defiance.

My lips pressed with suppressed fury. What crawled up his butt? "Fine! I'll move this damn rock myself." I turned my back to him, facing the door.

I took in a deep breath and exhaled, interweaving all my energy to the center of my core. I placed my hands upon the door once more and closed my eyes. Visions flashed through my mind, visions of all my pain from the past—the loss of my father, the death of my mother and her involvement in my father's death. The men in black, Helen, Sally, Van, and even Aidan, who played a large part in destroying my life. But it was not until I honed in on my child and her imminent danger that the Fifth Essence inside me began to rise. My heart started racing like a locomotive train.

I sensed the fire that consumed me might erupt to the heavens. I didn't care as long as that damn door blew off its hinges.

With no warning, the ground started to rumbled. In the next breath, things got hairy; the ground beneath us commenced shaking as though we were in an earthquake. Havoc surrounded us as huge boulders collided to the ground. Determination set as I strained, keeping my hands flat on the door. I was not letting go, even if a slab of stone toppled me.

Aidan and Sally had scurried under a small gap carved out of the wall. They hunkered down, safe from the sailing boulders.

Once the ground settled, my eyes raked over the dust-filled dungeon, and a smile traced the line of my lips, victory, a delighted taste, I thought. The gap was only a small space, but it was wide enough for us to squeeze through.

Depleted of energy, I crumpled to the ground. On my fours, I raked in the fetid air. Aidan limped to my side, gathering his arm around my waist to assist me. Instantly I felt repulsed. I jerked free of his hand. I hissed through gritted teeth, "Don't touch me!" I couldn't even look him in the eyes.

"I see some things never change." The sardonic tone in his voice felt different to me. I couldn't put my finger on it and frankly, I didn't care. I had other problems that were much more pressing.

Not without effort, I tugged on my wobbly legs and I stood erect. Still weak, I leaned against the wall for support. "That's where you're wrong, De Pont." I panted. "Everything has changed, especially me."

He glared at me as if he wanted to strangled me.

Time was running out. We had to get out of here. An argument would only delay finding Dawn. I believed in picking your battles wisely. This battle was one I'd past.

Without another word, I side stepped Aidan and made my way to the small space in the stone until I'd caught a glimpse of Sally. She'd remained frozen, wide eyed and shivering with fear. I gawked at her. "Let's go!" I urged. I suppose it wasn't enough that I had to deal with Aidan's ill manners, now Sally had gone zombie on me. WTF? My eyes narrowed. "What's wrong now?" I huffed, heatedly.

"I can't!" Her eyes welled up.

"What do you mean you can't?"

"There's no way I can fit through that tiny crack." She pointed to it. "I can stay here and stall anyone who comes my way. I won't betray you. I promise! I've done enough harm for this Family to last a lifetime."

It would be easy to think that Sally had been more of a victim than a participant. After all, the Family had a way of bringing out the worst in folks. Perhaps Sally deserved a second chance—a chance that Helen didn't have the luxury of getting because of my deadly hand. I knew my guilt would be riding on my shoulder for the rest of my life. And I guess I'd accepted my fate the moment my dagger left my hand.

"Look! I can't deny I don't harbor ill feelings toward you." I sighed. "Despite my position, I'm not leaving you to your death. If they find you, they won't spare your life."

"No! Go without me. I'll only hold you back. Save your child and then come back for me. If you can't make it back, then leave me here. I'd made my bed. I'd rather face death than live with myself." Guilt riddled her face. "I'm sure you can understand that?"

I was no stranger to self-blame. Stunned, I stared back at her. Was Sally feeling remorse? I wanted to believe her, yet, I knew far too well, her talents—cunning and manipulation. Yet considering the injustice she'd endeavored from the Family, it was not in me to turn my back on her either. I guess that was the human part of me.

"You're coming with us, cuz. We'll sort our differences out later. You're going to fit through that rock even if I have to downsize you."

Aidan stifled a laugh.

"All right! I'll try." Sally didn't sound so sure of herself. Maybe when we get back home, she and I could work on our relationship. Since our fathers were brothers that made her family, regardless of her past deeds. Dad always said family sticks together through thick and thin. That was a good enough reason for me to take Sally in.

Aidan went first and I stayed back, letting Sally go second. It didn't take a rocket scientist to understand that Sally couldn't fit through that tight space without assistance. Following the plan, Aidan took Sally's arm, and I got the wonderful pleasure of thrusting her rump.

The task was challenging. It took several tries, but we finally forced Sally through the tight opening. I reckoned after this, she'd have some serious bruises, but I had to admit, she was a trooper.

Once we were all clear of the door, not letting another minute slide the three of us hooked ass, rushing down another dark path. Aidan in the front, veered to the right, down another flight of stairs. I followed second, and Sally brought up the rear.

As we impinged upon a new passage, a faint light flickered in the distance. A familiar dripping of water bounced off the stone. Suddenly, I realized where we were. Yet how could that be possible? Aidan's castle had vanished.

I picked up the pace, joining Aidan's side. I tugged his sleeve, not wanting to alert any guards. Our voices vibrated down these dusty corridors. A mute could hear us. "De Pont," I called to him. "What is this place?" I kept my voice low.

An impish grin stretched across his face. "Don't you know?"

I tossed him an icy snarl. "Can't you just answer the question?"

"What fun is that?"

"Taunting me is fun?"

"Quite." He merely answered.

"I want to know what I'm walking into. Can you please cooperate?"

"I presume you'll find out soon enough." He haughtily replied as he pushed past me.

I didn't bother with trying to worm an answer out of him. He'd never tell me.

Sally's soft giggles wafted over my shoulder. It was more than irritating. Somehow, I managed to ignore her ridicule. Getting into a squabble with either one didn't interest me. The only thing that mattered to me was finding my child.

———— ·>✳<· ————

We seemed to have worked our way farther down into the bowl of this godforsaken place. I'd put my trust in Aidan to lead us to the sacred chamber. I hoped I hadn't made a misjudgment.

When we drew upon the soft light, we came to a shrieking halt. There in the vast chamber standing before our eyes were thirteen men in red robes, their faces obscured.

At that very minute, it was clear to me as a cloudless sky that all this time I'd been at Aidan's castle. An overwhelming sense came over me as if I'd stepped back in time. Everything had remained exactly as I remembered. The throne sat high on its platform in its grandiose stature, however, there was a different occupant this time.

Strange, I thought as if his presence held some enchantment over me. My head began to spin, my blood surged, churning and churning. Granting, I'd never met this creature, though, an introduction was not necessary. And in return, my gut assured me that he was aware of my presence as well.

Seated upon the throne in all his wicked glory, I uttered his name. "Mustafa!" we were connected. I smelt his acerbic blood, coursing through his veins.

I slipped a sideways glance at Aidan. I assumed by the starkness in his eyes, he was no stranger to this creature. I wondered how well acquainted they were.

For a second, I stared in silence, breathless of the creature's beauty. His brilliance was blinding. I squinted, cuffing my hand over my eyes to block the glare. The immortal was majestic in such a way he appeared delusive. He reminded me of the angels in the fresco paintings high above on the ceiling of Aidan's formal dining room. The similarities were staggering. I stalled, gaping at his omnipotence. The creature had massive gold wings stretched apart at least twenty feet wide. His black locks flowed to his broad shoulders. Armor draped his body in bold colors of red and glimmering gold. I wondered how a creature who possessed such magnificence could be so abominable.

Compelled, I eased out from the safety of the shadows and into the light of which may be my very death. With eerie pricking the back of my neck, the crimson cloaks parted, just like in my past dreams. I edged forward until my eyes fell upon a small table.

Suddenly my worst fear clenched my chest as my eyes landed on a toddler bound in shackles. Holy mother of god! *The sacrifice!* The young child began to whimper. "Dawn!" I cried to her. The terror in her tiny face mirrored mine.

Without thinking, I dashed to her side, but to no avail. Given no warning, my body was shoved backward into the air and violently slammed to the cold stone floor. Pain shot through my body, but rather than allowing the agony to consume me, I used it as fuel. In one sweep, I sprang to my feet ready for a fight. "I know who you are!" I bellowed at the godlike creature on the throne. I held my clenched fist to my side as I secretly tried to summon my essence. Despite my effort, I sensed nothing within my core. I didn't understand. It was as if I was empty. Absent minded, I touched my bare neck. Damn! I needed my necklace.

"Yes. Our blood is the same. We are connected, my hybrid daughter." Apart from his radiance, I knew the angel's heart reeked of decay.

I hid the urge to cringe. Instead, I stepped forward, forcing my voice out from my gut. I refused to let him see me quaking in my boots. I sure as hell wasn't going to give him that satisfaction. Shoulders straightened, I responded with renewed strength. "I might share your DNA, but I am not *your* daughter, Mustafa!" My green eyes shot daggers at the dark angel.

Suddenly his sick laughter echoed among the sea of red.

I pushed past the urge to go commando on his evil ass as I slowly inched closer to my child. With one quick glimpse, my heart sank at her sight.

The toddler had Aidan's black hair, but she had my freckles. By my calculations, Dawn couldn't have been more than three years old. Despite her condition, she was beautiful. I bit down on my lip to keep from losing it. I smiled into her sweet face. She smiled back, but her eyes were tormented. My heart was breaking in two. I had to save her! I didn't care if I lost my life doing so.

"Aw!" The dark angel reigned in my attention. I snapped my head up in his direction. I paused, remaining cautious as I kept Dawn in the corner of my eye. He spoke out, "you are more like me than you know." His voice was musical, yet cold. My finger twitched for my dagger as I kept my eyes centered on the dark angel. I crept closer to Dawn, hoping I'd go unnoticed. "She is quite lovely." The creature paused. "How wonderful you have decided to join us in our celebration."

"Yes, sorry to pop in uninvited." I tried not to sneer. Still I never was one to hide my true feelings.

"You are most welcome, my daughter," I flinched at his reference to me. I'd never claim him as my father, on second thought just maybe it might appease him.

"Since you speak of me as your blood, perhaps you will permit one request?"

"Only one?" the dark angel smiled. "You are quite bold asking such. I have yet to receive a thank-you for my help in freeing you from prison." The dark angel sat back in his throne, his eyes raked over me with disappointment.

"What are you talking about?" Narcissist much!

"Do you honestly think the human system would've let you go free with three murders against your name?"

I didn't answer.

"Of course not. It was I who set you free. And due to such, I'm afraid that you have run out of favors, dear one."

"Then let me offer something you can't refuse." I inched closer. Only a few more feet to go, and I'd be by Dawn's side. "If you accept me as your daughter, then you must accept this child as your granddaughter. Can you not take mercy upon her and allow me to take her place? My life for hers. Let my child go free, and I will stand by your side in your crusade to conquer the world!"

Yet the second I saw his bitter regard, my bargain had fallen upon muted ears.

As I stared into the depth of pure evil, I realized his part in this contrivance. He had been the anonymity who masterminded my father's death. It may have been by my mother's hand that carried out the insidious act, but it was his doings that set it into motion. It was he who brought it to the forefront. It was he who played God, destroying my life and now possibly my firstborn. For that, I had never loathed a living being more than him.

The enlightened beast eyed me with great caution as he sat with an ostentatious smirk. He was in control, and he didn't hide his obvious enjoyment either. "Yes. How righteous of you to offer yourself." One could easily fall prey to his hypnotic voice. Its strange mellow inflection was enchanting, yet it sickened me, for it was methodical. "Therefore, you must realize my answer." His eyes grew taut and deadly.

My breath caught in my throat. The dark angel had denied my plea. He wanted me gone. Perhaps my thorn in his side was a bit too much, though I didn't give a rat's ass if I inconvenienced him or not. He wouldn't get rid of me that easily.

So I went into action, letting my Zophasemin instinct take charge. I drew my dagger, aiming for the beast's cold black heart. As the knife left my palm, sailing through the air at a remarkable speed headed right for my target, I rolled on the floor in a somersault. In a fraction of a second, I'd landed by my daughter's side like a cat on all fours. Not wasting a precious moment, I began unfastening the restraints. I rushed with trembling hands, fearing I would fail. Where is Aidan! I needed goddamn backup!

Before I could gather my daughter in my arms, my body was thrust into the air, thirty feet high, dangling in suspension like a trapeze artist, only free of wires. I glimpsed below, realizing if I fell, it would be my death. Frozen, I couldn't move. I was helpless and worse, useless. Mounting fear shredded my insides. "Mustafa, please!" I cried out. Instead of his mercy, something glimmered in the corner of my eyes. I slowly lifted my eyes, and to my horror my knife hovered, pointing its deadly blade at eye level. Panic seized me and tears streamed down my cheeks. I'd whispered a prayer right before I hurled curses at the dark angel. A fool I had become for making such a hasty move, and now I may have cost my child's life. I cursed again.

Mustafa rose to his feet. "You have made a grave mistake testing me, my daughter. You cannot defeat me. I am wise, far beyond your years. That move, Essence cost your child's life!" His depraved voice sliced through my heart.

"No! Mustafa, wait! Can you not see I am terrified of you? I acted hastily. I know that now. Please forgive me. I only want to protect my child. Haven't you ever wanted to protect someone dear to you?"

"You have been with the humans far too long, my young foolish daughter. Mystical creatures like us do not waste emotions on needless things. We accept our destiny and embrace it." His voice came across as foreign and something far from natural.

"Human or not, I know you have a heart. Can you not have mercy on this innocent child and let her live?"

"There is a much-greater cause we must confront rather than saving a child's life."

"In my book, there is nothing grander than the life of an innocent child." I had to make him understand.

The dark angel gave me a sideways glance. "How so, my human daughter?"

"I may not have had the pleasure of spending time with my daughter, yet it doesn't waver my feelings. I love her with all my heart. I'd be willing to sacrifice my life, my magickal abilities, if you would let her live."

"You'd give your entire existence up for your child's life in return?"

I didn't hesitate for an instant. "Yes! A million times, *yes.* Anything. Take me! I will bow down at your feet. You will become my god, if that is what you wish. Just relinquish the child to Aidan, and I will leave with you right now. Whatever you want I will do if you spare her life. You have my loyalty!" My heart was pounding against my chest.

The dark angel pondered a moment. "For a hybrid, you do know how to appease to one's greed." He drew in a long drawl. "In spite of your offer, as grand as it may be, it is still not as grand as your daughter's life force."

"Then if not for the benefits, do the right thing and let this child go with her life still intact. You know you are wrong for doing this!" Horror seeped into my bones. It was clear to me that he'd made up his mind; and he wasn't relenting.

In a desperate attempt, I searched for Aidan, hoping he would be advancing on the dark angel. As I caught sight of him, my last hope plummeted to the ground. He had been taken down by the guardsmen. His body lay lifeless on the floor. He appeared dead as blood seeped from his forehead. Realization struck. I'd been left alone to face Mustafa.

Despair gushed through my veins.

I turned my gaze upon my child's sweet but tortured face. Even still, she managed a smile under a pool of tears. I smiled back as my spirit longed for her. This couldn't be happening! Not to this innocent child. Not my child! Is there a God who would have mercy upon me and spare my baby? Never have I asked for anything but this! "*Please...save my daughter!*" I begged of this God I didn't know.

Unexpectedly the toddler began softly singing a lullaby, one I remembered as a child that my father use to sing to me. In a soft, gentle melody, she sang.

> Star light, star bright,
> The first star I see tonight;
> I wish I may, I wish I might,
> Have the wish I wish tonight.

Through choked tears, I began singing with her. As my voice intertwined with hers, our eyes locked. I struggled to loosen the magickal grip, but it was pointless. My mind flooded with desperation, yearning to scoop her up into my arms, promising her I would love and protect her always. I wanted to whisper in her ear, reassuring her that everything was going to be all right. Yet I knew it wasn't.

My pleas fell upon muted ears. The dark angel wouldn't allow such a privilege, and my prayers went unanswered. In the next breath while forced to dangle in the air, I eyed that monster stripping my child's essence. Within seconds, Dawn's tiny body went limp, softly closing her sweet eyes as if she had fallen asleep. So peacefully, her body stilled. I knew she was gone forever, and I an all-powerful, genetically altered angel was powerless in saving my own daughter. I'd failed my baby. I lost her before I ever had a chance.

Tears blinded my vision as I cried out in raw anguish. The chamber echoed from my bloodcurdling screams.

Then an inner strength took hold. I reigned in my stricken heart and turned it into savage fury. Deadly calm fell over me as my eyes meet Mustafa's. In the pools of my menacing greens, a reflection of my threat gleamed. "Wherever you hide, I *will* find you. I will get justice for the death of my daughter. You mark my word, Dark One!"

Yet my promise didn't faze him as his body quivered. I knew what had transpired—the full moon, the gathering, the ensue of my daughter's essence.. The dark angel had stolen her life force for his own selfish gain.

Ironic, I thought. The very protection Aidan and I used to save our own lives cost the life of our firstborn. At that moment, I had a new goal in life, and as I held my blazing glare at the dark angel, I hoped he realized it too.

With no warning, I heard a familiar voice shouting in Zophasemin language. *Val!* Still jutting in the air, I twisted in the direction of his voice, and my eyes fell upon his golden glitter, and through my raspy voice, I called his name. "Val!"

He returned a look of longing, and I watched as he went into skilled action. Fighting broke out. Fireballs whizzed past me, men in armor swinging swords and violent clashing of steel ringing in my ears. My eyes followed as the Zop leader and his fighters took the red cloaks by leaps and bounds.

I turned my attention back to the dark angel. His eyes appeared glossy and his lids were droopy. For the first time, I could see his effusion illuminate. That sick son of a bitch was drunk on my daughter's life force. Worse, he took delight knowing I knew by the amusement in his face.

Then he spoke in a hurried voice. "I must leave now. It was so nice of you to drop by. We shall meet again, my daughter." A triumphant grin had spread across his hardened face right before he vanished out of sight. The murderous Zophasemin dissolved, leaving his followers to their doom.

Along with his disappearance came his release. Suddenly I began spiraling to the ground, falling to my death. I braced myself for the impact, yet to my surprise, I landed into a cushion of sturdy arms. When my gaze lifted, my eyes fell upon Val. I whispered, misty eyed, "I couldn't save her!" A deep pain struck my heart like a cold dead frost.

When our eyes locked, I threw my arms around him and hugged him tightly, weeping into his shoulder.

"You tried! You did your best!" Tenderly Val consoled me. "I got you. It's over. It's over." He repeated as he cradled me in his arms. Through the heart-wrenching tears, I pulled myself away and quickly ran to Dawn's side.

"Dawn! Oh dear god, Dawn!" I sobbed. With my trembling hands, I began tugging at the restraints, trying to rip them apart. Once she was free, I gathered her into my arms, rocking her back and forth, singing the song she and I sang before her last breath. Her body still felt warm as if she was merely sleeping. I glanced up and I saw Aidan standing behind me, silently watching.

I heard Val shout to his soldiers in his Zop tongue, giving orders. I was thankful for him taking charge. Val instructed one of his men to gather everyone up and prepare to leave. "We are getting the hell out of this fucking dungeon," he announced to his soldiers. Then he whispered in my ear. "Honey, we have to get to safety. Let me help you." He nodded over at one of his Zop soldiers, standing beside him. "Allow one of my men to take Dawn's body." Val gently placed his hand on my shoulder. The Zop stepped forward, yet I didn't yield. "I can't trust your men!" My voice was laden with blatant mistrust.

"Yes, miss, you can." The Zop spoke in a gentle voice. "I'll take care of your loved one. I promise."

"No! Get away from me!" I screeched like a mad woman. "Can't I have a moment with my daughter?" I drew Dawn closer to my chest. "Aidan," I called out. "You can heal her! You have to heal her!"

Aidan's mouth popped open and shut. His tongue appeared stuck.

Through the haze of my frenzy, I heard Val's voice of reason, "Sweetie, no one can bring her back. I'm sorry."

"I'm not letting her go! Leave me be!" I demanded, choking over tears.

Val squatted down next to me, his hand tenderly brushed my back. "We have to leave. Let me help you."

I didn't move. All I wanted to do was hold my daughter, but logic told me that I had lost my mind, and if I stayed in this dungeon, I'd lose myself completely. So I yielded, "Okay." Reluctantly, I gave Dawn's body to the soldier.

As I rose to my feet, I caught a glimpse of Aidan. He stood motionless, aloof as the Zop carried our child away. Suddenly I felt a sting of confusion and something else—envy. How blessed Aidan had been to have spent time with our child. At least one of us had been there for her.

Disrupted from my thoughts, Val nudged my arm, bringing me back to our impending situation. "We need to go!" He urged tenderly.

"Where are we?" I knew we were in the dungeon of Aidan's castle. The disappearing act, I figured it out. The castle possessed magick within its walls.

"We are in limbus," Val said.

"Limbus?"

Then Aidan interjected. "It's the fifth dimension, parallel to earth. There are twelve dimensions in the galaxy. This place is off limits to humans. Only magickal creatures are permitted to enter this realm."

I nodded as a reply. Conversation with Aidan right now would be like sandpaper skirting across raw blisters. It baffled me how cold and unattached he'd become after the death of our daughter, Dawn. There was no display of any emotion from him. For that reason, I'd prefer to keep my distance.

I turned to Val. "How do we leave this place?"

"Have you ever watched Oz?" Val smiled.

"Are we going up in an air balloon?" I didn't care if we were going on a magic carpet ride as long as we were getting the hell out of this dungeon.

Val gathered me into his arms. "Something like that." He flashed a reassuring grin.

"Wait!" I bellowed. "Where's Sally!" I scanned over the limp bodies spread about, blood veiling the cobbled-stone floor. When my eyes fell upon my cousin, I saw the fright in her face. I fretted that Sally might've been in shock. She stood half-hidden behind one of the stone pillars. Tears were streaming down her cheeks as her body heaved. I pushed off Val and made my way to her side, stepping over a sea of blood-stained bodies.

When I reached her side, I grasped my arms around her neck, drawing her into my arms, soothing her. Through all the stabbing pain of loss, I hoped she and I could become friends. I broke our embrace and looked into her tear-filled eyes. "We have to go! Come on." I reached for her hand, but her feet stayed planted. I turned, facing her.

"You're taking me with you?" She sounded surprised.

"Yeah! I'm not leaving you here."

"But I don't deserve your mercy. This is all my fault. Your child—" She struggled with the words. I understood her pain far too well. I staggered over the fact that I was still standing erect. Reckoned, I'd have my melt down when I was alone.

"Sally, we all have contributed to this. It's not just your fault. I played a part in this as well. I don't blame you no more than I blame myself. You're a victim of this family as I am." I paused. "Now come on." I grabbed her hand, and this time she followed.

When we returned to Val and the others, I climbed into Val's arms once again and nodded for us to go. Immediately, I sought out the Zop carrying Dawn, but he was absent. "Wait!" I cried. "Where is Dawn?" I panicked.

Val's eyes softened, brushing a strand of hair from my face, "the Zop carrying her went ahead. I promise he will take good care of her."

I nodded. My throat was so tight with pain, I couldn't speak.

Val took the wheel, giving directions. Aidan, due to his injuries couldn't orb on his own. Val gave orders for him to ride on the back of one of the soldiers, and another Zop had gathered Sally in his grasp.

Val had taken me into his arms. I locked my hands around his neck, and as I held tightly, I buried my face into his shoulder, bursting into tears. No one could hear me other than Val. And all awhile I was sobbing, he gently held me close, whispering consoling words and kissing me.

Regret Me Not

L IGHTNING FLASHED ACROSS the bruised sky, and thunder grumbled, announcing its presence. Then the rain came. I stared numbly out the window in the kitchen, sipping coffee. It was early morning, the day of the funeral. The house was quiet of its occupants. Since I had trouble sleeping, I decided to go ahead and get dressed for the day.

Thankfully, Jeffery and Dom took care of all the arrangements. Jeffery insisted on a jazz funeral. Aidan seemed aloof as usual, not taking an interest in our daughter. The liquor cabinet seemed to be his main concern these days. My mind was in no shape to make the simplest decision as tying a shoelace. I left the decision in the hands of my trusted friends'.

The ceremony left me speechless. Folks showed up in their best Sunday duds, ready for high-stepping to the jaunty tunes. The brass band took the lead, playing the typical jazz that New Orleans was renowned for, a tradition that went way back.

Leading the procession was the black buggy, trimmed in gold, pulled by two white stallions. The driver sat tall in his seat on top of the buggy, dressed in a tailored suit, wearing a top hat and white gloves.

Despite the constant downpour, our family followed behind the musicians, and the second line of folks soon collected, bringing up the rear from St. Charles Avenue, Canal, and even the backstreets, all marching to the lively tunes, craving a path to the grave site. It seemed the whole city had joined us on this dreary day and time of mourning.

—◆❉◇—

We stood under an umbrella, trying to shield ourselves from the storm. Against the pounding downpour, the preacher spoke loudly, giving his sermon as Dawn's small coffin lowered into the ground—a pink coffin—in her favorite color that Sally had shared with me.

My mind was riddled with shame. I didn't have a right to call myself a mother. What kind of mother didn't know her own daughter's favorite color? Me! I hated myself. Dawn's death was my fault. My stomach knotted.

—◆❉◇—

At the site, Aidan stood at my left and Jeffery on my right. Dom was on Jeff's right. With me in the middle, we all huddled as we wept over our loss. A child's death was something a parent should never have to endure—ever!

I spotted Val hanging back at the cemetery's entrance with several of his men. Sally didn't feel comfortable standing with us, so she stayed behind with Val.

I had recognized several members of Jeffery's family from Ms. Noel's funeral. The rest of the folks attending, their faces were unknown to me. I did take note neighbors from the Garden District that I had never had the pleasure of meeting had come, bearing flowers. It was nice seeing so many attending the services. I appreciated everyone's support.

This week had been one of the worst times of my life. In fact, it'd been nothing but downhill from that point on. When we first returned home from the castle, it was a bittersweet homecoming. Jeffery and Dom both couldn't tear themselves apart from Aidan. Tears were shared between the three.

Then with the announcement of Dawn's death, more tears came. I stood back and let the guys have their reuniting and time of mourning. A special bond had formed between those three, long before I came into the picture. Jeffery and Dom had been Aidan's family for many years. They needed their moment alone.

As reasonable and understanding I could be with the guys, I had never felt more alone. I was grieving over Dawn too. I yearned for comfort, someone to talk to, someone to hold me and tell me everything was going to be all right, even though I knew it wasn't.

It wasn't like I was shut-out or ignored by the guys, rather the opposite. Dom and Jeffery had been very accommodating, but it wasn't what I needed. My mind kept drifting to Val. I craved for his touch, his love. I was sure that my feelings for Aidan had changed. The intense connection we once shared was gone. It was Val that filled my heart, and the guilt burned like frostbite.

Since we'd been back, Val has been keeping his distance. I guess with Aidan alive and living with us, only temporarily, Val probably thought Aidan and I were rekindling our love. If the truth be told, it was the furthest thing from the truth. Nothing was the same.

As I stood there half listening to the preacher, I felt like I was a ticking time bomb ready to implode at any minute. Regardless of my much needed meltdown, somehow, I managed to remain silent.

Aidan squeezed my hand, the first act of kindness I'd received from him since our return. Startled, I lifted my head and glanced into his face. He responded with a thin-lined smile. His eyes were dull and bloodshot, not the vibrate blues that I remembered. Aidan had been hitting the bottle pretty hard. I reckoned he had his own way of grieving, so for now, I'd let him.

The unspoken words between Aidan and I had put both of us on edge. When we first returned, come nighttime, he'd insisted that I stay with him. I declined his offer on several occasions, and I was sure my rejection onset his cold shoulder toward me. I just couldn't make myself, and my excuses were running thin. Sooner or later, I was going to have to tell him.

Something had changed between us. Aidan seemed different—the way he moved—even his speech pattern seemed off. Then again, the death of a child could change anyone. Even though we both were suffering, I couldn't be there for him in the way he expected, especially when my heart was somewhere else. I desired Val. Yet Val wasn't here beside me, and by the distance he was keeping, I assumed he wanted it that way.

It was just as well. Right now I had unfinished business with Aidan. I had questions about his involvement with my incarceration. I especially wanted to know how he stole Dawn from the Family and managed to hide her during the period of her short life. But for now, I'd wait. I thought he needed time to heal, as I did. When we're passed our grief, Aidan and I would face these issues then. As for Val, I'd have to put him on the backburner until I had resolved my untied issues. I had to find Mustafa and end his life. Val could come with me, or he could remain behind. Either way, Mustafa *must* die.

Jarred from my thoughts, the preacher had asked everyone to bow their heads for the last prayer. I chose not to partake. At this point, if God could forsake my child and allow such cruelty to exist in this world, I figured what I had to say wouldn't be suitable at a funeral and among good Christian folks.

In the final good-byes, each person threw a white rose on the pink coffin. I found myself unable to move. The line moved forward, exiting the grave site, but I stayed still. Rain poured down in sheets, saturating me as I stood without the umbrella's protection. At this point, I didn't care. Frozen, I watched the yard keepers shovel the first dirt onto my child's tiny coffin. Soon she'd be totally entombed, and only the gravestone would be all that was left, marking her once existence.

Aidan nudged my arm, and I pulled away. "You're going to drown standing out here." He barked over the roaring rain. I didn't reply. I just looked at him blankly, then back at the increasing dirt that toppled the tiny coffin. Aidan attempted once more. "Sweetheart, come on!"

My head snapped back up at him as my eyes narrowed. I spoke as a person on the brink of insanity. "Don't call me that!"

Aidan's eyes looked confused as he asked, "What do you mean? I call you that all the time." His hand extended to me. I didn't move.

"No! Actually you haven't ever called me sweetheart." I shook my head. It didn't matter right now anyhow. "Please," I went back, watching the keepers.

"Please what?" His dark brows knitted.

I turned my eyes back to him. "Please let me have this moment alone." I dismissed Aidan and focused my gaze on the shoveling. Without looking up I said, "Let me have this time alone with our daughter? I've never had my time with her. I've never had the opportunity to sing to her or do one damn thing with her. So...do you mind leaving?" It was my last chance. "Can you give me that much?" as a tear escaped, anger tore through my spirit. It wasn't fair. Aidan had the opportunity to be with our daughter. I had only seconds, and not very pleasant ones. Every time I closed my eyes, I saw her tormented face as she lay helplessly.

I saw the confusion in Aidan's eyes. Thankfully, he backed off, appeasing my wishes. "Sure, whatever you need." He stepped away, his jaw twitched. Then I heard Jeffery say, "Sugar, do you want me to stay behind with you? I can go find a spot to sit and give you whatever time you need." His voice was soft and kind.

"No. I'm okay. Go with Aidan. He needs you...but thanks," I said as my voice sounded flat and dull to my ears. It reflected how I felt—empty inside.

My eye caught a glimpse of Val talking to Dom and Jeffery. Whatever they were discussing, it didn't last long. Val turned from them and went in another direction.

I turned my attention back to the dirt and the coffin. A rush of panic flooded my mind. I needed to be closer to Dawn. I had to see her just one last time. At this point, I'd lost my mind. I stepped up to the edge of the grave and crumbled to my knees. One of the keepers called out to me in a flash of fear. Everything after that seemed tunneled.

Water had started to collect, and I watched in horror. I screamed at the keepers, "Take her out! It's filling up with water." My face twisted with sheer fright. I couldn't abandon her again. I had to save Dawn! My flail mind reasoned. This time no one was going to permit me from saving her. As my legs went over the dugout, tears and rain blinded me. I was aware my behavior was insane, but I had snapped.

Drenched to the bone, shivering, I slipped down into the ditch. The water was freezing, but my only thoughts were, getting Dawn out of that trap. Just when my hands clasped the small coffin, I felt warm arms encircling me, lifting me out of the mud and icy water. When I looked up, it was Val bringing me back to sanity.

When our eyes locked, I touched his worried face. Right then I had no doubt of his love for me. He leaned in and kissed me softly as he held me tight in his arms. I surrendered, collapsing, nestling my rain-beaten face into the niche of his warm embrace and sobbed. I trusted him with my life. I felt—what was that strange word—*safe.*

<hr />

When I'd awaken, I sucked in a sharp breath. As the day began to seep back into my mind, I recognized the familiar scents and soft bed. Val had taken me to his pad. A relief washed over me. Going back to my house gave me a dreadful sense that I wasn't ready to face. Sooner or later I had to go back, but, for now, I wanted to be with Val, just for a little while. I heard light footsteps and glanced up. I couldn't help but smile.

"Hello, sleeping beauty!" Val grinned as he came into the dim room and sat on the edge of the bed next to me. "I thought you might like some soup or something to eat." His soft eyes glanced over me. I noticed he had put one of his T-shirts on me and rid the drenched black dress I'd worn earlier. The T-shirt felt soft against my skin, and it smelled of Val.

For a minute, we shared a glance. As if the world stood still, frozen in time, just the two of us only existed. Then Val made a move. As he rushed to my side, gently placing his weight on top of me, shifting on his elbows. I had knocked the blanket off, leaving only the thin material of his T-shirt covering me. I wanted him, and by the sensual look in his eyes, he wanted me too. Gently he kissed me, and I hungrily kissed him back. His smooth hands moved under my shirt to my bare skin. I shivered from his touch, and I began tugging at his shirt. In one sweep, he had his off, and mine followed in a puddle on the floor next to his. His pants came next, and we both relished in each other's bareness. The only frail piece of clothing left were a lacy pair of panties and his boxers.

His hands moved over my skin, and I raked his back as I pressed against him greedily. Soon we were totally immersed in each other. His hands began to explore places I had no idea existed. My mind went wild under his singeing caresses. I opened myself to this man—my desire, my heart, and, yes, my love. I should've known. It was always Val who possessed my heart.

Just when we were about to take our affections to the next level, a profound knock resonated at the door, first calm taps, but as a few moments passed, the knocking began to pound angrily. Val cursed under his breath as he started to rise from the bed. I tugged his arm, pulling him back to me. "No! They'll go away. Don't answer the door!" I practically pleaded, panting slightly.

"Don't worry. I won't be long." Val assured me in a husky voice as he kissed me on the lips before he sprang from the bed and threw on his pants.

He rushed from my sight. Quietly I lay there with the sheets drawn over my breast and listened as he threw the door wide open.

To my disappointment, alarm hit me like an iceberg. "Dammit!" I hissed under my breath. "I can't believe he followed me!" Aidan had his nerve coming here. By the sounds of it, if I didn't get in there, those two might end up in a brawl of the century. Shit! I snatched up Val's T-shirt and threw it on as I'd made a nose-dive toward the igniting commotion.

I wasn't surprised, catching both men towering over each other. I felt like an ant to their enormous size. I hesitated for a moment. WTF! I didn't know how to stop a guy fight. I ran my fingers through my hair, starting to panic. I didn't need this shit right now!

"Look! Stevie isn't your personal possession. She's free to decide for herself. If she wants to go with you, I won't stop her. But it will be a cold day in hell before I let you barge into my home and force Stevie against her will." Val stood in a war stance, facing off against Aidan. In return, Aidan sneered as he glimpsed at the small apartment. I suppose it wasn't exactly on the cover of *Homes & Gardens*. What a snob, I thought.

"She's not exactly in her right frame of mind. Contrary to her best interest, you were going to fuck her regardless?" Aidan's dark blues looked fierce.

Holy mother of god!

"Oh, that's rich! The pot's calling the kettle black?" Val fired back. By now, both men were toe-to-toe.

"What kettle is that?" Aidan stood his ground.

Oh, lord! I had to block those two before they created mass destruction. "Boys, wait!" I jumped between the two snarling men, shoving them apart. Considering their monolith frames, I could've been crushed. Thankfully, they both stepped back. "No one is fighting tonight!" I clarified, and in the same breath, I glanced up at Val. I'd already hated myself for what I was going to do next. I exhaled a sigh. "I have to go back. I'm sorry." Regret hid behind my smile—not for desiring Val, but for having to leave.

There was so much I wanted to say to him. Setting aside my breaking heart, I'd have to do this talk another time.

"You don't have to leave on his account." The inflection of Val's baritone voice was a strong clue how he felt about Aidan. As I observed the two and their heated stance, it came to mind that Val once dated Helen. I questioned whether I wasn't the only girl causing tension between the two.

Then a swirl of dread clenched my gut. I'd almost forgotten. I haven't told Aidan or Val about Helen's death. I shuttered thinking of that day when I revealed my dark secret. I sensed neither one would take her death well—a death by my hand that I was not proud to claim. I feared that once the truth came to light, both men would hate me forever. I wouldn't blame them, but for now, I'd delay my secret and deal with it later.

"I have to get back to Dom and Jeffery." I'd hoped he understood that I wasn't returning home for Aidan's sake. "Do you have my...um—clothes?" Val paused, staring back at me with a nettled face. I knew he was full of questions and ire all at the same time. I expected it. I had the same feelings too.

"Your clothes are folded up over the chair in the bedroom," he said, running his hand through his tossed hair.

"Okay, thanks!" I reached around Val's waist and gave him a tight hug. I knew he didn't want me to go. His arms were too possessive as he clung to me briefly. I wished I could've given him more reassurance. The truth be told, with everything surrounding my life, what did I have to give? I loved him, but was it enough?

On the other side of the fence, loving Val didn't help my problem with Aidan. With all things considered, my priorities had to be set in order. First on the list, I had to settle my differences with Aidan.

Then I had a debt to pay. I'd intended to hunt Mustafa down and kill him. I might be digging my own grave, but in my opinion, I didn't see another way out. Mustafa must die. I reckoned that was the human side of me.

Jaloux
(Jealously)

THE RIDE HOME resembled an eternity. We were in my Mustang, and Aidan was taking his aggression out on my car. I decided the pouty child needed to be called out, so I spoke up. "Care to share?" I was snide, but he deserved worse.

"I'm not in a talkative mood right now, if you don't mind?" He clenched his teeth as he grinded the gears.

"Suit yourself, but you're going to strip the gears if you keep jerking the stick that way." I said in a devil-may-care tone.

"If I fuck your car up, I'll buy you another."

"Whatever!" I slipped down in the seat and leaned my head back. Let him blow off some steam. If I were in his shoes, I'd feel betrayed too. Aidan and I definitely needed to talk. Considering his mood now, I'd approach him tomorrow. Not only did I have questions for him, I needed to set him straight.

Finally, we'd reached the mansion. I'd planned on ducking in my room, staying under the radar of anyone's notice. If I had to endure another guest expressing their condolences one more time, it might send me into orbit. I needed to empty my brain. I had one of Dom's sleeping pills that Jeffery slipped me earlier today. Right now all I craved was a little solitude and blissful sleep. Judging by Aidan's mood, I imagined our conversation wouldn't be a stroll in the park. So tonight, I needed rest.

Once Aidan and I entered the front door, mishmash chatter drifted from the back of the house. It sounded like the guests had congregated in the kitchen and family room.

Strange how I felt disconnected. All these good people attending my daughter's funeral, and I didn't know one. I suppose my social skills were inept.

Since everyone's attention was distracted, I thought I had a clear shot to my bedroom. Impolite or not, I wasn't in the mood for sharing my grief with strangers.

Besides Dom and Jeffery, the only family member I had was Sally, and I wasn't sure how I felt about that. Aidan had a minion of relatives, and yet no one came. What a crappy family. On the other hand, if they were like Van, Aidan's uncle, it was best they kept their distance.

I started to make a beeline for the stairs, but I was abruptly halted by a firm hand. My eyes snapped up. Two very dark blues were glaring back at me. Immediately, I tried to free myself. "You're hurting me!" I hissed, keeping my voice low. I didn't feel like putting on a sideshow for our guests.

"You're not going anywhere until you explain yourself." His voice came off hard and threatening.

I inhaled a haggard breath. "Aidan, let's not do this tonight. I'm tired."

"You can sleep later. Start explaining!" He demanded like I was his property. Strange, his behavior reminded me of Sam. Ironic, I thought.

My brow arched. "An explanation for what?"

"You can start with why you were with Valor."

My whole body stiffened. Goddammit! He had to do this with a full house of strangers? "Did I not say I'm tired?" I glared back at him as equally. Still his iron grip didn't loosen, and by the petulance in his blues, I saw he had no plans of letting this subject rest tonight. "You can't wait until morning?"

"Nope. I. Want. Answers. Now!" Aidan snarled. I took another pointed sigh. It looked like sleep for me would be stalled.

"Fire away," I demanded as he still held me captive.

"I asked you a question. I want an answer!"

Sooner or later I'd have to tell him. "Val is my friend...a very close and dear friend."

"You naked in his bed, I think pushes past the line of friendship." His eyes narrowed.

"Well, there you have it. Can I go now?" I held a bland stare.

"You're such a deceiving bitch!" Aidan growled.

"I'll take bitch, but deceiving?" WTF?

"Our bed was still warm when you jumped in that Zop's bed. Who else have you been sleeping with?" Aidan's face started to blister.

And with no more energy than I possessed, I'd wished he'd knock me out. Then I could deal with him in the morning. "I suppose if you include the men at the lovely Haven Hospital while I was drugged to oblivion, I don't know, maybe another twenty." My voice sounded hollow.

Aidan scoffed as he abruptly released his grip on my arm. "What happened to you?" his voice was acid. "You're not the same girl I fell in love with back in Tangi."

"You're right. I'm not." I looked him straight in the eyes with no apologies. It was true. The old Stevie had died the day they captured her. I lost my life and my freedom, and the worst of all, I lost my child. The old Stevie didn't exist any longer!

I spat out my last words before I turned for the stairs. "That young girl you once knew died that day at the cottage where you left her wide open to the predators of your family. Good night." I held my voice at an even tone. Then I twirled on my heels, headed to my bedroom, leaving Aidan standing alone.

Just to ease my frayed nerves, I locked my door. It wouldn't keep Aidan out, but it made me feel a little safer.

As my eyes washed over the bedroom, it suddenly felt too big for just me. I wanted to be with Val, still tucked in his bed with him. I hugged my waist trying to rein in the emptiness that threatened. Maybe when the house quiets, I'd sneak out and head back to Val's place. On second thought, I might be the last person he wanted to see right now. I did leave with Aidan.

To add to the mix of trouble, by Aidan's outburst tonight, acting like a jilted lover, Val may never believe my true feelings. The fact be told, the thought of Aidan touching me made my skin crawl. He was so different now. Or maybe I was fooled into believing Aidan was good. I shook my head, frustrated, confused and tired. I sighed and slumped my heavy shoulders.

I crossed over to my bed and flopped down, sitting. I leaned down, unbuckled the straps on my heels and kicked them off. Then I sat there for a moment, breathing in the solitude. Aidan and I had a lot to discuss. After all, we shared a child—a deceased child. There were questions concerning that day I was taken and about Dawn. It was time for Aidan and me to clear the air. I suppose I should do this in the morning, be done with it, and maybe the healing process could commence.

Too tired to undress, I just slept in my dress. Besides, it smelled of Val.

The sun popped up early, shining its stream of light right in my face. I began to stir, and before I cleared my head of sleep, all my sorrow and pain came flooding back. I stilled for a minute, dreading this day. I wanted to escape to a remote island where no one could find me. Living in bliss sounded so tempting.

I looked down, and I had forgotten I'd slept in my clothes. The black dress clung to my body, only a bit more wrinkled.

Suddenly the dress felt stifling and itchy. I had to get it off my skin. I reached to pull the zipper down, but it had jammed. With my patience depleted, I ripped it off, tearing the delicate material to shreds. As it fell to the floor in a puddle, it reminded me of last night with Val. I picked up the torn garment and buried my face into the cloth. I drew in its fragrance. Val's delicious citrus scent still lingered, along with an earthy smell, and then something else—the grave site. I dropped the dress as though it had burned my hands. Tears started to fall. I wiped the moisture from my eyes and started for the shower until I caught a glimpse of a shadow in the corner, sitting in my chair by the window. I snapped my head around, and my mouth dropped. Then it dawned on me that my body was fully exposed. Last night I'd been in such a rush I'd left behind my undergarments. I just threw on the dress and fled out the door with Aidan hot on my trail. Instantly, I tried covering myself, but I only had two hands. Flushed and vulnerable, I spoke up in a piqued voice. "How did you get in my room? I'd locked my door!"

His wolf-like eyes raked over me very slowly. By the time he reached my face, my cheeks were on fire. It reminded me of a time long ago. A pleasant time unlike this. He finally rose to his feet and stepped into the dim light. He spoke in a deep throaty voice. "My, don't you look fetching this morning." Aidan smiled, but it didn't touch his eyes.

I had no intention of dignifying that with an answer. I stood there, glowering at my intruder.

Aidan sauntered around me, slowly, circling with apparent menace in his blues. "Well, well, cat got your tongue?" His voice spewed of venom as he continued to strut, encroaching upon me as a predator. Then abruptly he halted, standing to my back. I listened over my shoulder, careful not to breath. One thing Aidan hadn't considered, since his absence, I'd had combat training. He took a strand of my hair into his hand and inhaled a deep whiff. "You cut your hair. I like it long." He scoffed against my ear. Goose bumps rolled down my neck as I turned to face him. I saw how pleased he was by the possessive glint in his eyes. I held my gaze equal to his. The sign of fear revealed weakness—I did my best to hide. "Leave my room! Now!" I demanded in his hard face.

"I'm sorry, sweetheart, but you can't get rid of me that easily." He smiled maliciously. "Don't forget, it is my money that bought you this fine house and all the exquisite accessories that come with it. Therefore, I'll leave when I'm good and fucking ready." He shoved me down to the cold floor, forcing himself on top of me. While his huge body held me trapped, he spread my legs apart. With one hand, he unfastened his pants as the other hand held me against my will. He'd been drinking. I could smell the whiskey on his breath.

"Aidan, no! Please." I begged.

"Did you say no to your boyfriend, Valor?" His eyes were bloodshot and his words were slightly slurred.

"Get off me! You're drunk!" I screamed.

Out of the blue I heard a big clang. Aidan went limp. His head was blocking my view. I strained to the side. Once my eyes landed on the obscured silhouette hovering, my heart jumped for joy. Jeffery came with a heavy cast-iron skillet to my aid. A huge relief washed over me. But then strangely, instead of assisting me from the restrain of Aidan's limp body, Jeffery leaned over, rushing his words.

"Wake up, Stevie! Wake the mofo up! Trouble is brewing!"

My brows knitted in confusion, then I sat straight up in bed, gasping. My eyes raked over the room and the corner from where Aidan sat. I exhaled. The chair was empty. Oh dear lord! Another nightmare! My forehead was beaded with cold sweat. When I threw the covers off, I realized that I was wearing the same black dress from yesterday. My instinct was to rip it off my body, but I sensed I had more urgent matters to handle, the dream, that vivid dream. I quickly jumped up, peeling the garment off. Then I threw on my sweats and rushed downstairs. Jeffery came to me in that dream. Something bad was up! I felt its chill down to the bone.

When I reached the kitchen, everyone, including Sally, was sitting at the table. Dom had made his usual breakfast.

Immediately all eyes fell upon me. I thought, how odd. Still it didn't appear any different than any other morning.

Then I glanced at Aidan. He sat there with a smirk plastered across his face. Jeffery fidgeted in his seat. Sally sat quietly. She was never silent unless she was frightened. I caught Dom fiddling with his food. Strangely, he didn't take any bites. In fact, no one was eating. Everyone's mood felt tense. Something was off. I spotted an empty bottle of bourbon on the counter then I looked back at Aidan. His eyes were heavy-lidded and red. He was shitfaced. Alcohol and bloodthirsty rage was a deadly combination.

I was dealing with a very volatile problem. Strange, it suddenly occurred to me—Aidan seemed removed from our daughter's death, but he was livid over my relationship with Val. I sensed his jealousy had nothing to do with his love for me, opposite of what I once believed. Rather, Aidan viewed me as his possession.

I had my trusted knife tucked in the back of my sweats. Although I'd gotten pretty good with my aim, Aidan was even faster. With his Druid magick, I didn't have a chance. I thought if I soothed the drunk, everyone could get away safely. I exhaled a tart breath. It would've been so much easier if Jeffery had whopped Aidan over the head with that cast-iron skillet back in my dream. Aidan would be sleeping it off or knocked out, and we'd be eating Dom's delicious breakfast.

Then I heard steps from behind. I slowly turned. I had no idea who to expect coming at this point. I braced myself. Since that day at the cottage, I was a bit jumpy of surprises.

When my eyes landed on Val, a sense of relief washed through my mind. He was standing in the kitchen door, eyeballing our situation. His body was stiff, face harsh.

I suddenly realized the profundity of our problem. Why else did Val come? As happy as I was to see the Zop leader, I still wished he'd stayed home or anywhere but here. I feared his presence might acerbate the issue.

I decided there was no time like the future to jump in. "What's going on this morning?" I kept my voice light as I glanced around at everyone. Then I saw the glint of loathing in Aidan's eyes pointed right at me.

I hoped to divert the attention on me. I'd stall Aidan while Val got everyone out before any real harm was done. I was grateful for the dream. Interesting. Old Jeff may have some of his aunt's gifts after all. Thanks to him I was alerted to a highly ignitable situation that could go bad in a split second. Quickly I needed to handle Mr. Drunk-Ass.

Val stood quiet as his eyes combed over everyone, assessing the potential problem. I avoided eye contact with him. I didn't want to make the unpredictable problem worse.

"Stevie, how nice it is that you decided to join us this gracious morning." Aidan's words were slightly slurred, just like in the dream. "Do you know the servants are quite loyal to you?

Aidan stated a rhetorical question. He wasn't searching for a reply. I held my tongue, something that didn't come easy for me.

"My servant betrayed me, calling your lover boy to come protect you from the big bad wolf." Aidan sneered at Val. The Zop remained marble-like, keeping his eyes on point.

I wasn't as controlled. Referring to a family member as a servant didn't fly with me, despite Aidan's dangerous nature. "Whoa! No one in this house is a servant. If you want something as little as toilet paper, you better learn how to fetch it yourself. No one is waiting on your pampered ass!"

"Don't tell me what I can or cannot do." Aidan sibilated. "I gifted you an exquisite lifestyle. Therefore if I dare to reference to someone as a servant or *whore*, I believe I've purchased the right." I glimpsed over at Val. His jaw was flexing. The tension was like a toxic gas, lighting a simple match and everything would blow to the heavens.

I let out a down-reaching sigh as I raked my fingers through my uncombed hair. "Aidan, let's not do this." I asked. "Why don't you get some rest. You look tired. When you wake up, I think you'll see this from a different perspective."

"A different perspective?" Aidan roared as he leaped to his feet in a fit of rage, knocking the table across the room and sending all the food and dishes crashing. I caught Val in the corner of my eye. Swiftly, he'd stepped directly in front of me, shielding me. My heart did a little pitter-patter for my hero, but still, I was a big girl. I could handle the madman and his temper tantrums.

Everyone else had scattered in different directions. By what I could tell, no one had gotten hurt except for a minor cut or two. Val remained steady, under Aidan's blaze. There was no love lost between the two men. In hindsight, I feared the outcome if they went to blows. "That's right, Zop. Step between us." Aidan reminded of a lion defending his territory.

My knees were knocking. My stomach knotted. It was me that put my family in this dangerous position, letting Aidan stay in this house. Now it was left for me to get us out of this turbulence.

So I made my move.

Distracting Val wasn't my intentions, but I had to touch him. He gave me strength in so many ways. I tugged softly on his belt loop and leaned my forehead gently against the center of his back for a brief minute before I pulled away. I had to fight my own battles. If Val got hurt in this whirlwind that I'd created, I would never forgive myself. Defusing Aidan's unpredictable temper was like treading through a mine field. Any step could cost me my life. I inhaled a deep breath, then I cautiously slid out from behind Val's protection. Now I was an open target. I caught a sideways glimpse at Val standing in his warrior stance. Alarm lodged in my throat. I needed to think fast. "Aidan, this is between you and me. Let's clear everyone out, and we can talk." I forced a smile.

"Oh, come on! It's all in the family." He threw out his arms wide as if he was embracing the city. Reasoning with a drunk was insane, but I saw no other recourse. I learned that early in life with mom. I swallowed hard. So I engaged, needles pricking my neck. "They're not part of this. Why should we bring them into our disparity?" From the corner of my eye, I caught Val ushering everyone out. A breath of relief eased into my lungs.

"Stop!" Aidan shrieked. The room stilled. He turned his icy glare on me. "Maybe they need to hear about the *whore* you have become."

His words stung more than I wanted to own, but letting Aidan anger me was what he wanted. The way I saw it, I had two choices. Either I appealed to his softer side or knock him the fuck out. While cold-cocking him was a huge stretch, but an appealing idea, I had to keep it real, so I began to negotiate.

"Look. You're right about being angry." My voice softened. "You've been very generous to me—to Jeffery and Dom too." I reasoned. "Aidan, this isn't you. Let's sit down over a cup of coffee and talk through our differences. You don't want to hurt anyone." I hoped the sober-minded Aidan would overcome the drunk, radical Aidan.

"Do I?" he mused. "Don't get self-righteous with me!" he leered. "How much pain can you be suffering when our child's body hasn't grown cold before you are in *his* bed?" Aidan cut his venomous eyes at Val.

"Aidan!" I took a step closer. "Don't do this to yourself." I choked back tears. "Please!" I begged. This hostile Aidan standing before me was a stranger to me. The swagger, the pride, the confidence had perished. Nothing made sense to me, and yet everything did. Ambivalence much?

"Please what? Please turn the other cheek while you fuck everyone, but me!" he wailed. My jaw dropped. All this time it wasn't about our daughter's death. Rather it was about me not sleeping with him. Anger, fear, regret gyrated through my mind.

Still, I had to swallow my pride. The highly expositive problem had to be contained. My heart pounded against my chest.

"I get why you're upset. Let's get everyone out. Then just you and I pop a squat and talk."

"What's there to talk about? You turned your back on me with him!"

"It's not like that, and you know it!"

"No, I don't know it! I thought we loved each other? When did you stop?" His eyes mirrored sorrow.

My heart went out to Aidan. Which prompt me to question if I still held any feelings for him? My stomach tightened. "I thought you betrayed me! When Sally came to the cottage that day, she played this elaborate scheme that the two of you were married. She was very convincing." Aidan glanced over at Sally as she quailed under his stare. "I believed her!"

"You'd believe this lying bitch over me?"

"That day at the cottage, I first thought she had lost her mind, but then—"

"Stop!" he waved his hand to shush me. "This is foolishness. Your cousin had been acting on her own accord."

"Sally wasn't alone!" my voice rose. "She was standing in front of me while my captor seized me from behind, stabbing me with some unknown drug."

"Did Sally not reveal her accomplice?"

"Yes. I suppose." Cynicism laced my voice.

"What? You don't believe her?" Aidan snapped, eyes piercing.

"No, I believe her." I lied. "She claimed it was your uncle, Van.

"Aw! There you have it. It was my uncle."

"You're right." I rolled my eyes. "How stupid of me." I forced a tight smile.

Though I held my tongue, I sensed something was off—having said that, while my captor's face remained anonymous, I caught a good look at my adductor's ringed hand—that hideous ring with the eye. Despite Sally's claims, the hand I saw belonged to a young man, a hand I was very familiar with. I might've been hazy about a lot of things that transpired that day at the cottage, but one thing I was certain—the hand of my captor looked identical to Aidan's hand. All the same, I didn't plan to share my suspicions with him, not until I'd gathered proof. Until then, my reservations about Sally, Van and Aidan continued to exist.

"You said you were drugged?" Aidan asked, drawing me back from my thoughts.

"Yes."

"I'm sorry for your misfortunes." Aidan mused as though he possessed a secret joke.

"Thank you." I eyed him dubiously.

He laughed to himself.

"Excuse me?" my brows furrowed.

"Don't you think if I wanted your family and associates dead, that you'd be dead as well? You must know, I am quite an accomplished Druid?" his arrogance beseeched him.

"I see that now." Then I shifted the subject, slightly. "Where did you go?"

"Pardon me?"

"You abandoned me at the cottage. I found that lousy newspaper!" My voice cracked.

"Come again?" he shook his head as if he'd forgotten.

"The newspaper! My mother's death! She was poisoned! Remember?" I shouted.

Val's feet shifted. Glimpsing in the corner of my eye, I saw anger rising off his shoulders. I shivered at how this scenario could pan out if I wasn't careful.

"Oh, yes. I recall." He coughed. Funny, I thought. Such a human behavior for an immortal? "I left to see if there was any truth to the story," Aidan drawled. "I was trying to prevent you unnecessary grief."

"If you didn't wanted to prevent unnecessary grief, then why didn't you take the publication with you rather than leaving it in plain sight?"

"When I realized I'd forgotten the paper, it was too late to turn back." Aidan smiled, but it wasn't the warm fuzzy kind. Everything about him seemed to clash, his demeanor, his story. Or maybe my eyes were opening up for the first time?

I walked over to where the table had been thrown, now sitting on its side. I went to lift the heavy wood, but Aidan had taken it from me and sat it upright. He placed a chair beside me and took one for himself. We both settled at the table, seated across from one another. Dom handed Aidan a cup of fresh brewed coffee and left the steaming pot on the table.

Val remained on alert, taking a stool at the island. Jeffery joined Val while Sally scurried upstairs. Dom dallied around as though he was busy cleaning the kitchen.

Apart from Sally, they all stayed. They were wary of Aidan's state of mind and leaving my side to face him alone. Obviously, I sensed the risk too. I hid my trembling hands under the table, hoping it went unnoticed.

"Why did you not return to the cottage?" I held my voice even.

"I returned, only too late. They had already taken you."

His tale had holes. Everything that Aidan did was precise, down to scratching his ass. He didn't make mistakes, and he sure as hell didn't forget. I clutched myself with great caution. "Did you try to find me?"

He shifted in his seat. "No. I didn't," he admitted too easily.

I bit back a snap. His admittance stung. "Did you not worry where I had disappeared to?"

"Yes, of course. I sought my uncle out. He informed me of your condition."

"Condition! You knew I was pregnant?"

"Yes. How could I have not known? We discussed your pregnancy that morning at the cottage."

"Of course. I'd forgotten." I rested a moment, thinking. "So, you spoke to your uncle?"

"Yes."

"What did your uncle say?"

"He explained he'd arranged for you to stay at a resort in Switzerland." It was as if Aidan was reciting a well-rehearsed play.

"So you just believed him, just like that?"

"Of course. Our child was the Family's destiny."

I leaned in closer. "While I was pregnant with your child, they discarded me like I was a bag of trash! Have you ever heard of Haven?"

"No. Matter of fact, I haven't."

"You should. The staff are such a delight." A wave of disgust welled up from my stomach.

"I presumed you were safe and happy."

"That's rich."

"How bad could it have been?" his blues raked over me. "You look pretty healthy to me."

I nearly went for his throat. But the glint in Val's eyes halted me. Instead, I bit out, "how perceptive of you, Aidan."

"Contrary to your belief, I do understand your feelings. I know our family can be harsh. Our traditions seem extreme to outsiders."

I scoffed. "More like evil."

Aidan paused, his blues sparkled. "Something you don't understand—our child, the firstborn, had to be conceived on *All Hallows' Eve* in order for her to receive the purest source of the Fifth Essence." Aidan pushed his coffee to the side. "We had been planning this for centuries." Our eyes locked. "That was the purpose of your creation."

I sat back blinking back the shock. And there I had it. It never was about us protecting ourselves against the family. "I never was in danger of losing my life was I?" my mind began spinning.

Aidan shrugged, staring at me openly. His answer remained nonverbal as I gazed into his cold blues, but I understood his truth.

273

"I see." I thrummed the table with my fingers, holding back the vile that knotted my throat. "Did I ever know the *real* you?"

"No," he simply said with no emotion in his voice. "What was the point?"

Heat from my cheeks began to surface. "I was nothing more than a duty!"

"You must understand, our moment of love making was for the greater good. I had no other choice."

I couldn't believe my own ears. "Choice!"

"Sorry to displease you." Aidan seemed stiff like a robot—remote.

"So basically the purpose was never about ridding the world of wars and disease." I choked over the words. "Rather instead, I was to produce a child so the Family could open her up like a flayed fish and take her life source?" it all seemed clear—his distance toward our child's death. He had been removed, unattached all this time. WTF?

He leaned his head to the side, as if we were having a conversation about the weather. "Unfortunately, the end did not justified the means."

"It was all a setup?"

Aidan reached to clasp my hand, but I jerked away. I shuttered over the thought of him touching me.

"Up until Dawn's death, yes." he leaned back into his chair relaxing. There were no signs of remorse.

"I remember the conversation you had with your uncle, Van. The two of you were scheming to take my essence. You mean to tell me"—I poked myself with my index finger— "that my listening to your conversation with Van and... and that discussion was staged? It was all a game to get me in your bed so you could get me pregnant."

"Precisely." He smiled like he'd butchered his first pig.

All of a sudden, I burst into laughter. I couldn't help it. "You must have no confidence in your skills?"

Aidan's eyes narrowed.

I amused. "I think an accomplished lover as yourself wouldn't need such great ploy to nail a lowly girl as me?"

His jaw flexed. "I had a mission. We were in a bit of a time crunch."

I belted out more laughter. This time it was more hysterical. "So do tell." I scoffed, testily.

He squirmed in his seat. "When one belongs to the Family, one must be aware that there are expectations for such privileges."

"Such as?"

"Such as infusing our spirits."

I folded my arms. "Did you lie about that too?"

He flashed a wicked grin. "Actually dear, that is one that not even I could fabricate."

My brow arched. "So it's true? There's some weird cosmic force between us?"

Aidan paused for a minute, locking his dark blues on me. "Yes. It's true." Then briefly he glanced over at Val, then back to me. A sardonic glare waxed his face. "You're as much a part of me as I am you. Sorry, toots. Looks like you're stuck with me."

My voice became steely calm. "That's where you are wrong. I have a choice. I will never choose you. How could I? I blame you for Dawn's death!"

"Some things are beyond our control. Even our daughter's fate."

I flinched from his words.

"How much time did you have with Dawn?" I asked.

"A year?" I stared into his empty blues.

"How did you find her?"

"Find her? I've never lost Dawn."

Jolted by his answer, I just sat there, speechless.

"The Family informed me of her caretakers."

"You knew for nearly two years where she lived, and you never bothered seeing her?"

"I did visit her once on her last birthday." The blue-eyed stranger who looked like someone I once knew, began drumming his fingers against the table as though he was becoming bored.

Suddenly I remembered the video. "I saw it. Helen showed me a brief take of you helping Dawn blowout her candles." My voice turned sour. "I'm guessing that was all for show."

"Hmm… Helen must've stolen the clip from my phone."

Funny how he had an answer for everything. I moved on to the next obvious question. "How did Mustafa get his hands on Dawn?"

"You know the answer to that."

I bit down on my lip, not to snap. "I want to hear *your* side."

Aidan sighed. "I was apprehended after I'd left you the letter. They took Dawn and hauled me to the dungeon." He confessed. "That was the last time I saw her until—" he dropped his sentence.

"Were you a participant with Mustafa?"

His eyes narrowed. "I would never agree to take the life of my own daughter."

"Is that true? I saw the look on your face when we entered the chamber. You are not a stranger to Mustafa."

"I know him."

"I don't believe Mustafa acted on his own." I paused, staring the devil in his eyes. "If you didn't help him, then tell me who did?"

"You know I can't reveal their identity."

"I deserve answers."

"Life doesn't always give us what we deserve, toots."

"No shit! Dawn is dead, and I believe you had a hand in it."

Aidan slightly rose from his seat as his face turned beet red. I spotted Val planting his feet to the floor as if he was ready to spring. "I'll tell you this once!" he snarled. "Listen carefully. I do not intend to say this again. I am not guilty of Dawn's death or throwing you in a mental hospital. End of this charade of interrogation." By his riposte, I sensed he was on the brink of exploding.

I spoke up quickly, hoping to eschew any outburst. "Okay, I believe you." My breath became notched. "My mistake."

Aidan settled back down in his seat, sneering.

Quiet wafted into the air, momentarily.

Finally Aidan counterstruck. "Your father is the blame for this mishap."

"My father?"

Suddenly a dark brow arched. "You don't know."

"Know what?" what did he mean?

"You are utterly in the dark." He mused.

A tingle began to spread over my body. I feared whatever was next.

"You don't know about your mother—" Was he stating a fact or asking a question.

"I'm not following you."

"I see that Sara kept you in the dark." He reminded me of a fat cat that just ate a rat.

"You know something about my mother that I am not aware of?"

"Sweetheart, I'm only beginning to get to the good stuff."

"Then spit it out." I drummed my fingers over the table, holding my stare.

He broke into a smile. "Mustafa and your mom had an affair. He was the one who helped provide the enchanted car for her."

It was like the bottom had fallen out, and I was falling. "My mom was messing around with... Mustafa behind my dad's back?"

"I hate to be the bearer of bad news, but yes."

"How did it happen?" I rolled my eyes by the mock in Aidan's blues. "That's not what I meant! How did my mother get involved with him?"

"If you must know." He exhaled. "In the beginning, Mustafa was assigned to watch over your parents. As the romance between Mustafa and Sara progressed into full bloom, he shirked his duties and lusted after your lovely mother. Unable to stop herself, she fell in love with him, and they ended up—"

Abruptly I interrupted. "Spare me the details. I'm not that naïve. Why are you telling me this?" *Ideeclare*, just one more knife to twist in my side.

"I'm saying you may or may *not* have any of your Druid father's DNA."

"Shut up! You never mentioned three years ago anything about conception between"—I swallowed hard—"that *monster* and my mother!"

"You seem to be missing the point!"

I glared up at him, "then freaking enlighten me."

"There is more than one way to skin a cat." He paused for his meaning to sink in… or was it to taunt me? Aidan went on to explain. "Celestial birth isn't like human birth. First of all, it's unnatural. Angels were not created to procreate. That's why the giants of old were so damn vicious."

"That's supposed to make me feel better?"

"Let me elaborate, please."

I nodded, holding my tongue any further.

"I didn't lie about the genetic alterations. The Family's scientist through alien advancement were able to create something solid unlike the giants of old. I did not lie about Sara suffering from an alien disease onset by the pregnancy." Aidan drawled. "However, I may have evaded a few details."

"Are you saying that Sara and Mustafa are—" I couldn't say it.

"Oh, they had an affair, though don't worry. You were still a test-tube baby." He grinned, he'd been jerking my leg. "You were not conceived as the Nephilim. The half angel-half human creatures were impossible to control. The Family wanted a super strength being who's manageable."

"Manageable?" I scoffed.

"Our scientist used your father's DNA in order for Sara to carry you to trimester. Once the risk of losing the fetus had waned, our scientist altered your father's DNA. They replaced those cells with a genetic DNA, enabling cell tissue to metastasize. In fact, the damage your mother suffered came from the super-cell regeneration. Coupled with the angel's DNA didn't help either." Aidan paused, dragging in a harsh breath like a longtime smoker. "There are only traces of your father's DNA. That is why you reek of human."

"I'd rather smell like my father than stink of alcohol and greed." My eyes tightened. "It sickens me to think how far your family will go to get what they want. Both my parents are dead because of your family's supreme self-preference."

"Sweetheart," his cadence in his voice spewed with arrogance. "Great achievement is usually born of great sacrifice, and is never the result of selfishness."

"That's original. You got that quote from Napoleon Hill."

"Touché! I'm impressed. You are smarter than the average hybrid."

"Thanks!" not!

"However, as irreconcilable our difference may be, it was your parents who came to my family."

I sat there appalled. Where did he and those crazy cloaks get off?

"I don't care!" I shouted. "Lives are lost because of your pernicious ambition. You and your Illuminist family has to be stopped." Aidan's brow shot up, surprised. "What? You didn't think I'd figured out your secret society?"

"Actually, I am quite surprised."

"You forget too easily. My father was one of the thirteen bloodlines."

"True, but Jon forfeited his position. The Illuminati do not take kindly to apostates."

"I remember you once carried the same beliefs and teachings as my father."

"And I remember you once shared my bed."

A short laugh escaped my lips. "I guess I saw the error of my ways."

"I can protect you."

"I'm sorry?" my brows furrowed.

"I. Can. Protect. You." He repeated, sharply.

I blinked, staring at him. Then the sting set in and I asked, "like the way you protected Dawn?"

He stilled, a vein began to throb at his temple. "Dawn's fate was out of my hands. Sad things happen, and one must move on."

"And you call this moving on?" I waved my hand at his liquor and half empty glass.

"Yes, quite frankly I do." His supremacy epitomized the true mark of the Illuminati. "We're about to be in a shit-storm."

A curt laugh escaped my lips. "I think I've been in a storm for some time now."

"You have no clue to what is coming."

"It's not exactly easy keeping up with your multiple personalities. I'm getting whiplash."

He smiled like he'd discovered the cure for cancer. "This system as we know is coming to a screeching halt. The great tribulations will devour this world." Then his eyes switched to something I couldn't describe, but it left me quaking in my shoes. "The end... is approaching, and it will destroy any living creature in its wake."

I swallowed. "Why should I believe you?"

"You don't have to trust my words. You already sense it. I see it in your eyes."

"How?" he had my attention.

"First the religions will go. Then the governments will collapse, starvation and disease will spread throughout the world." Aidan sighed. "If you don't join the Family, then I you might as well plunge a dagger through your heart. You're as good as dead. Suffering will be *boundless*." His eyes were disturbing, yet calm. There was something in his movement, his voice, that made me certain he was speaking the truth.

Then he did a one eighty flip, he flashed a lustful sneer, raking his eyes over me. I was losing my patience with all his mood swings. Dr. Jekyll and Mr. Hyde much?

He leaned in and whispered, "Join me and I'll show you what a real man does to a sweet morsel like yourself." He carefully drew back, sitting straight in his chair, watching how I'd respond.

Vile threatened as his scent of liquor and cigarettes repulsed me. *When did he start smoking?* I sat there silently, staring at the stranger who sat across from me.

I realized by Aidan's straight-line glint at Val that he had shifted his interest, riling the Zop. Yet the blue eyed stranger didn't know the Zop leader as well as I did—Val would never fall for such lame bullshit. I on the other hand didn't have that kind of moxie.

That was when I erupted. In one swift move, I grasped my knife, raising it above Aidan's head, but Val had grabbed my hand in midair, right before I thrust the steel blade through my target's stone heart. I glanced up at Val as he'd snaked one arm around my waist and held my wrist with his other hand. When our eyes locked, I calmed, nodding for him to take the knife. I glanced at Aidan, and his face gleamed with loathing.

I'd reached my limit. My lungs were closing, the air was stifling. I shared a quick glance with Val, and he took my que. In one sweep, he gathered me into his arms, and in a blink, we'd disappeared.

Considering how my presence irritated Aidan, I figured, out of sight, out of mind. The situation became too volatile for me to remain. Once I was gone, and no longer an eyesore for Aidan, he'd sleep off the booze. Although just for back up, I hoped Jeffery made good with that cast-iron skillet, just in case.

New World Order

WE LANDED IN the back alleyway a few doors down. In the background, a cat hissed, and a couple of dogs were barking.

Once my feet were planted, I'd made a run for the nearest dumpster. My dinner from last night was coming up, and I couldn't stop it. After I'd finished puking my guts up, I realized Val had been beside me, holding my hair back. Could this guy get any better? I tossed a weak smile at him as I so indelicately wiped my mouth. Then our eyes hitched. We stayed like that for a few minutes, then our moment ceased as Val asked, "Let's do something fun?" The gold specks in his eyes glistened.

I bit my bottom lip. "I don't know." I shrugged.

"I think it would do you good."

I chewed on my lip, weighing whether I should leave the guys and Sally alone. Then I caved. "Oh, why not! What do you have in mind?"

"Let's go to a good old-fashioned bayou cookout. Some human friends of mine are throwing it tonight. It'll get you out of the house and away from *him*."

"Him meaning Aidan."

"Yup!"

"Okay, but I don't have anything to wear."

Val's eyes swept over me. "I don't want to wear sweats." I tugged on my top.

"No problem. I'll take you shopping." Val offered.

"That's sweet, but I can call Jeffery and he—"

Val stopped me in midsentence. "No! I don't want to risk Aidan coming in Jeffery's place, and my pad's out." Val thought for a minute as he kicked a rock. "Aidan acts like he owns you."

"You got that too." I shook my head. "I don't know what I ever saw in him."

Val raked his fingers through his hair. "Men like that think women are a possession."

"I agree." I paused briefly. "Have you had many encounters with the pompous Aidan when you were dating his sister?"

Val released a buried sigh. "Some." He answered curt, brow arched. "I wouldn't exactly say Helen and I dated. It was more of a mutual enjoyment."

"Why do you say that?"

"She wasn't the relationship kind of gal—too unpredictable." Val leaned against the picket fence, hands stuffed in his pockets.

"How did you come to dislike Aidan so much?" Some things were better left alone, but I was more curious than nine cats.

The corner of Val's lip pinched. "Let's go somewhere a little more suited for private conversation." Val glimpsed over his shoulder.

"Lead the way, chief!"

In a single swift motion, Val had me pressed against his body, wrapping his arms around me like a warm blanket. Erratically my heart began to pound. It was obvious how he affected me. The glint in his eyes revealed he knew it too, and a faint smile painted my face. Val and I had feelings for each other. It was apparent in our gaze.

It was different with Val. Aidan and Val were as different as night and day. A relationship with Aidan had been doomed from the very start. I was so young and inexperienced. How could I have possibly known what I wanted? Setting aside all things, he was the father of my child, a child, I was denied knowing. Would I ever feel closure with Aidan? Could I walk away without looking back? These were questions I couldn't answer, and I wasn't sure I'd ever be able to.

My mind felt overloaded, like a fog in the early morning. Right now all I wanted was to be with Val. With him, everything seemed simple and easy. The dreadful memories of old seemed further in the distance when I was with him.

"You ready to fly?" Val jarred my thoughts as I looked into his smiling face.

"Ready as I'll ever be." I smiled back.

<hr />

Wow! I raked over the surroundings. We had landed somewhere in the midst of the bayou. I stood on a short dock leading up to a boathouse. In its rusty state, it was charming. Floating above water, it was nothing more than a bare, wood-framed cabin that looked like it had never been touched with paint.

In the background birds were chirping as the sound of water trickled slowly downstream, insects humming and dragonflies fluttering about, hovering on the surface of the murky water. In its rawness, it was breathtaking.

"Welcome to my humble abode." Val smiled, proudly.

"Yeah, it's pretty humble all right." Even through my climbing panic, I couldn't peel my eyes away as I peered about in every direction—Spanish moss hanging from the low branches, cypress trees, majestic, with a broad buttressed base and green foliage clinging to its massive trunk.

"It'll grow on you." Val promised.

"Are there alligators?" I felt my lips go cold.

"Silly girl, it's the bayou! Of course there are gators!"

"Holy mother of god! This is the best you can do?" My brows knitted, affright.

"Oh, come on! Where's your adventure? Don't worry! Gators aren't out."

"That's a relief." I wrapped my arms around my waist, trying to hold back my need to scream bloody hell.

"But when twilight falls, it might be best if you didn't venture too far from the cabin. They like to roam at night."

"Holy shit! Take me home! I mean it! I hate gators!" I rested my hands on my hips, glaring at Val. It didn't help ease my nerves any when he roared with laughter. Men were such difficult creatures—or should I say Zops.

I just shook my head and stalked past him, entering the dim cabin. Val followed behind me with a trail of laughter. Duct-taped much?

"I'll open up the windows. There's usually a great breeze that flows through." He turned around with a huge grin, and froze when he saw the look of terror plastered to my face. "What's wrong now?" His brows scrunched.

"Have I mentioned how much I hate snakes too?"

He cuffed his hand over his mouth. Obviously he was stifling a laugh. "No, I don't believe you have." Humor in his tone was as deep as his voice.

My face soured like a double dose of lemons. "Well, I don't like snakes either!"

Val crossed the floor in only one stride and gathered me into his arms. "Freckles, nothing is going to happen to you here. What you see is the life of the bayou, a mystical place of great wonder. That's why so many of our kind are drawn to this place."

"Just for the record, I'm not the usual Zop." Suddenly the light banter between Val and me changed as the memories flashed through my mind of the conversation with Aidan. I shivered, worrying. "Do you think Jeffery and Dom are safe? Sally too?" I chewed the inside of my cheek.

"I think they're perfectly fine. Maybe Aidan will take a liking to Sally again?"

"Aidan and Sally were a couple?"

"You didn't know?"

"I reckon not." I dragged in a fretful breath. "They both denied hooking up." In spite of their claims, I had suspicions that neither one was entirely truthful. "How long have they been messing around?"

"It's been on again and off again for years."

"Did you see them together?"

"Yeah, from time to time. I'd crossed their paths now and again when Helen and I were together."

"Really! Were they serious?"

"Not from what I could tell," Val opened a window, then made his way back to me. "Or at least Aidan wasn't committed. He had another girl stringing alone besides Sally. Why? Do you know something that I don't?" his brow arched.

I shook my head. "Probably not. It's just Aidan's and Sally's story seems off. You know, he says, she says." I tipped my shoulder, curtly. "It's not important now."

"Aidan only tells what he feels is necessary." Val's words were smothered in bitterness.

I felt unsure about the next question, but I couldn't stop myself. "Did you ever see Aidan and Sally together in Tangi?"

"No, it was here in New Orleans. They have a huge plantation on the outskirts of town." Val seemed to know more about Aidan than I did. It struck me wrong too.

"They as together?"

"Yes. As in plural, couple, pair..."

"I get it! I get it!" I held my palm out. In my next breath, I asked, "so, they have the floating castle?"

"No. This one is permanent. It's an old plantation just on the outskirt of the city."

"Plantation? On land?"

"He didn't tell you?" Val sounded as surprised as I.

"No, he didn't." Clearly I was left in the dark about a lot of things.

"Don't beat yourself up over it. Aidan is a master of deception."

I sensed something more between Val and Aidan. Funny how history repeated itself. Sam came to mind. "Why do I get the feeling that there's something you're not telling me?"

Suddenly, Val's face tensed. "Let's go sit outside on the porch and get comfortable." He touched the small of my back, ushering me to the deck.

"Sure." I smiled. While I seemed at ease on the surface, my mind was reeling on the inside. What other inconceivable trouble must I face before the sun sets today? I fretted.

I was happy to get out of the cabin and into the river air. The smell of musk and dirty socks triggered my sensitive stomach. The cabin definitely had the traits of a guy's pad.

After we both settled down in a couple of chairs in a corner of the deck, Val rested his elbows on his knees, leaning forward. When my eyes lifted, I saw uneasiness in Val's expression.

I clasped his hand. "What's wrong?" I asked, worry tingled my body.

"I've known Aidan from way back."

"Oh." I stiffened.

"I never told you this, but I have a sister."

Taken aback, "You have a sister?"

"Had, depending on how you look at it." Val's jaw twitched.

"You said had as if in the past?"

"Yes. My sister's been missing for a while now."

"Oh, my!"

"Helen and my sister were friends." A pain hit. Hearing her name whirled me back to a dark secret I'd been keeping—Helen's death. I knew eventually, I'd have to tell him. But for now, I pushed it down and focused on Val as he explained. "Aidan dated my sister, Sienna."

"I'm confused. I thought he was dating Sally?"

"He was dating both. Neither girl knew."

"Whata dog!"

"You got that right!" Val bit back a snarl. "Anyway in spite of his wondering eye, there was talk of marriage. He'd even went as far as giving my sister an engagement ring. The marriage never happened. Instead, Sienna disappeared, and Aidan ducked out of the country for months until you moved to Tangi. That's when he resurfaced."

"Do you think my coming to Tangi had anything to do with your sister's disappearance?"

"Not directly."

"I don't understand."

It seemed Val was warring with his inter-self. Then he just said it, "I think there's a triangle betwixt Aidan, you and Sienna's vanishing."

My brow perked. "You think I'm responsible?"

"No! Hell no! What I do think, is that Sienna found out about the prior arrangement between the families, the blood contract binding Aidan and you to marriage. I suspect my sister confronted Aidan and the argument went sour."

My eyes orbed, surprised. "How did you learn about the blood contract?"

"Through the grape-vine." He smiled, but it didn't match his wounded eyes.

"Rumors, huh?"

"Yeah," Val snorted a curt laugh and shrugged. "Even the angels gossip."

I smiled. "Small world, huh?"

"Yeah, very." Then the cadence in his deep voice became dour. "I never told you this," he breathed. "But, I knew you were framed. I tried finding you, but you went off the grid."

My mouth dropped. "That first night in your bar, you knew who I was?"

"Yes."

"Why are you now just telling me this?" my brows collided.

"I didn't think it was important at the time," he dropped his eyes from mine, staring out at the river.

"Why now?"

"I think you have a right to know." His brows furrowed, deeply. "I hate secrets." his eyes latched hold of mine. I looked away, feeling like the worst person ever. The secret I held was much darker and I was sure he'd hate me when I told him. I bit my lip, quickly changing the subject. "Did you hear what Aidan said about my genetic code? I don't have any trace of human."

"I heard."

"This is good news. I'm not a hybrid. I'm a full blooded Zop!"

Val rooted his fingers through his disheveled hair. "I have to be honest with you."

"Okay." I didn't breathe.

"I know about the Illuminati playing God, creating you in a lab. They used human DNA in the beginning, then they replaced it with a replica super-cell substance that they designed to boost your abilities. Making you a very powerful young lady."

"Wow!" my mouth hung open.

He tossed a lopsided grin. "I did some snooping."

"Yeah, I guess so." I paused, mulling over the enlightened facts he'd landed in my lap. Then my heart lurched. "Since I no longer have human DNA, wouldn't that make me a pure Zop?"

"Not necessarily. You are still an impure according to my kind."

I wanted to gnaw off my arm, grrr! You explained to me that I am an outcast, consequences of my human traits!

"Yes and no. There's more to it. Only those who have been blessed with divine creation are pure and natural. I'm sorry, Freckles. That's our law." Val squeezed my knee, showing empathy.

I didn't need his pity. Acceptance was what I needed. All my life, I'd been disconnected, an outsider. Now that I'd found a kinship with creatures like myself, I still was marked as an outcast. I sighed with frustration. "I hate being alone."

Val gathered my chin in his hand, drawing my eyes to his level, "you're not alone." He smiled, brightly. "I'm here with you, aren't I?"

"Yes, but for how long?" I let myself sink into his golden eyes.

"I can't answer that." Val barely whispered.

This was a battle I couldn't win. "Okay, enough about me. Tell me more about your sister. You said she disappeared?"

"Yeah," swiftly Val's face dropped as he sighed. "As it went down, Aidan wouldn't let my sister out of his sight. It was like she was his possession."

"I find it odd that Aidan never mentioned your sister." I paused, sitting straight in my chair. "Now it makes perfect sense. You didn't want to help me because of—"

"You got it!" Val interrupted.

"Why am I not surprised."

Val's upper lip twisted in vexation.

"I can't wrap my head around all this devilry. Will Aidan and the Illuminati ever stop destroying lives?"

"Good question."

"Is there anything I can do to help in your search for your sister?" My heart went out to him.

"I don't know where else to look." Pain colored his face. "I've turned every rock there is, but nothing."

Chills crept over the back of my neck as I recalled how Aidan eliminated Sam's body. Even though the death of Sam was justified, I prayed that Aidan hadn't gone to that same measure with Val's sister. Tears welled. "You can't give up!"

"I know." There was anger behind Val's glint. An anger I often saw in myself.

"Were you close?"

"Yes, very. She was my little sister, and I failed her."

"How did you fail her?"

"I tried warning her about Aidan. She wouldn't hear it. My sister idolized him. I should've forced her to listen to me."

I squeezed his hand, leaning toward him. "There was nothing you could've done. This isn't your fault."

"I should've locked her up and thrown the key away or—" Val pressed his lips tight.

"And, she would've hated you for it."

"But she'd be alive." Val's eyes filled with sorrow.

"You can't be certain she's gone now. You have to know that!"

"Yeah. I guess," Val nodded, inhaling a somber breath. "The unknowing is worse than her death."

"I know." I was familiar with that feeling far too well.

"I have to ask." His eyes, intense. "Are you still carrying a torch for him?"

Taken off guard, I paused, glimpsing over-way at the river. The buzz of night-crawlers were in harmony with the flow of the stream. I listened for a moment. As strange as it seemed, though, I wasn't a woodsy kinda girl, the strum of the bayou seemed to ease my mind. I sighed, looking Val in the face. I answered as honestly as I could, but even then, my heart acted upon its own accord. "I won't lie. I have mixed feelings. He was my first, and we did share a child together, even though there wasn't much sharing." Then I whispered. "You must know you are the one. It's you I dream about, who I desire, not Aidan."

"How can I relax knowing there is unfinished business between you two? I saw it in your eyes today." Val searched deep into my greens.

"After today, I think that business is resolved. He's not the same person." My hand lifted to his stumbled chin. His features were breathtaking, like an angel. Our eyes locked. "Let's enjoy our time together now."

"For now." Val's eyes crinkled as he leaned in and kissed me. It was sweet, yet, compared to last time, the spark seemed absent. Considering everything we'd been through today, it was no wonder. I stayed in a constant confusion. Befuddled much?

Val drew back with a possessive glint. "You can't go back to him. He's dangerous and cannot be trusted."

"I don't plan to." I inhaled. "My eyes are wide open now."

"I'm glad to hear that." he smiled, but it didn't reach his eyes. "You know, we have to stop them."

"I agree, but they're indestructible."

A mischievous grin stained Val's face. "Funny you should say that." His eyes twinkled. "We are on the brink of war."

I choked on my breath. "Oh my god! Aidan was not joking."

"As much as I hate to admit it, part of what Aidan said is true. It's the part about the Illuminati taking over that I disagree with. That's why our side is gathering forces."

Trepidation curled around my spine. "Our side! Zop?"

"Not just the Zophasemin but the entire galaxy. Spiritual forces are gathering as we speak."

"Whoa! We might be facing extermination."

"It won't come to that." Val glowered. "We plan to fight back!" The conviction in Val's tone screamed volumes.

"Oh, dear lord!"

"If the Illuminati succeeds, we are doomed. You think Hitler was bad, stick around. The Illuminati is the mother of all monstrosities."

"I'm afraid!" I was inspired looking at Val and his intensity, but in the same breath, I was utterly terrified."

"You and me both." He brushed his thumb across my cheek.

"What will come of Jeffery and Dom? Innocent people?" I sat there blinking, unable to process this nightmare. Aidan's warning of the world ending, Val speaking of war it was really happening. I snapped my head up, catching Val's eyes, "do you think we stand a chance?"

"I don't know." Wary lines etched across Val's face. "The Illuminati's enforcement is infinite, endorsed with supernatural forces far more powerful and far more advanced than we have ever went up against."

"But you're angels! You have special powers." I stared at Val with disbelief.

"Yes, we have abilities, not like the Family's."

"I can help!" I rushed. "The Illuminati created me for war. My genetic design is twofold. You said yourself I was powerful." It just hit me like a ton of bricks falling from the sky. I was a weapon.

Val raised my hand to his lips and gently kissed my palm. I blinked back.

"Absolutely, not! You are nowhere near ready for something of this magnitude."

"I might be the answer to your prayers!" I damn near screamed.

Val shook his head. "Don't you think they have created others like you?"

"If there are others like me then that's even more reason why you need me!" I countered.

"It's not only genetically altered angels in this war, Freckles."

"I already know about the fey."

"I'm not talking about the Seelie or Unseelie."

"Who, then?"

"The Illuminati has harvested the DNA of the giants. They're bringing back the Nephilim as we speak. I know you've heard of area 51?"

"I have, but I thought the Nephilim were irrepressible."

"True. They were impossible to control in the past. However the Family found a way to bypass that problem. They discovered a way to create mass armies of genetically altered giants. They are contained at area 51. It is the best unkempt secret the government has ever had. These altered giants are trained assassins, invincible and with the flip of a switch, they can eradicate an entire species. Ever heard of genocide?"

"Yes." I began to feel my skin growing pale. I thought surely I'd faint.

"If we don't fight back that's what we are facing. But the Illuminati are not the only enemies that we are dealing with." Val's jaw tightened. "Sweetie, I'm sorry to bring his name up."

My brows dipped down into a vee as my heart hammered at my chest. "No," I softly whispered.

But Val didn't listen. "Mustafa took your daughter's life force in order to preserve his own life. He no longer is an allied of the Family's. They plan to kill him. Therefore he's been gathering his own army as well. I felt you should know what you're up against."

I jumped up, knocking my chair over. "Stop, Val!" I held up my hands in protest. "I can't hear anymore." I stalked past him to the far side of the deck and held my head over to vomit. I couldn't bear thinking about that murderous angel. I was sickened with fright for my family and even Val. With my brain about to implode, I wiped my mouth with my sleeve. It wasn't long before I heard the shuffle of soft footfalls, it was Val coming up behind me. Instantaneously his arms snaked around my waist, I turned around and buried my face into his consoling chest. He towered over my small frame, and I molded easily to his body. I felt safe in his arms.

"Val," I softly spoke.

"Yeah," he replied, tenderly.

"I think I love you."

His golden eyes twinkled as he answered, "I know." Then he bent to kiss me on my forehead, and I smiled. He was being a bit funny not saying it back to me, yet I knew he had feelings too. How could he deny it? He had been by my side through everything. I trusted him with my life and even something more precious than life itself—my heart.

It seemed we stayed embraced in each other's arms for a long while. Then Val interjected, gazing into my eyes. "He can't stay with you. If he hurts you, I'll kill him." I didn't' doubt that Val would carry his threat out without hesitance or regret.

I trembled over the thought of those two brawling. "I'll handle it."

Val groaned. "I'd rather you let me take care of your rodent infestation." An impish grin stretched the corners of his lips.

"No! I rather you not." I sternly declined. "I really don't think Aidan will hurt me. Besides, if you got hurt, it'd kill me." Laughter filled my eardrums as I felt the rise and fall of Val's chest as he roared.

"Stop it!" I slugged him in the arm, then I rolled my eyes. "Of course you are more than capable of defending yourself. It's just"—I hesitated—"Aidan's diabolical, and—" I couldn't finish what I needed to say.

Val gently took my chin into his grasp. "I can take care of myself, Freckles." His eyes glittered as he smiled. His deep voice was reassuring. I loved when he spoke in his native tongue.

I needed to know the answer right then and there. Then I asked in our Zop language, "You think I'm pretty awesome, don't you?" I smiled into his bright face.

He laughed, and then he hugged me tight. "I do. I really do." I shook my head and giggled to myself. The damnedest thing— this man had me, and he knew it too. Oh, well. It could be a lot worse.

The Bayou

V AL MADE SURE the coast was clear at my house before we popped in.

It was a huge relief to discover that Aidan had clocked out from the liquor he'd ingested, sleeping most of the day. The house had settled, nothing compared to earlier today.

I had the opportunity to grab a quick bath and throw on some decent clothes for the barbecue. Even Val used my shower and changed clothing.

I found a note on the counter in the kitchen from Dom. He had taken Sally to dinner, and planned to go shopping afterward. Jeffery stayed home, spending the evening alone.

When I could no longer bear to look at his pouty face, I invited him to come along. Although before I'd finished my sentence, he'd grabbed his picnic basket full of goodies as if he'd read my mind.

Off we went, the three of us in the Mustang, Val volunteered to be the designated driver. We could've rode on his shirt-tail in a matter of seconds, but I didn't feel comfortable materializing in front of unacquainted people. Couple with Val's uncertainty of who was coming, we thought the human means of travel would be the wisest. It was a nice change. And glimpsing at Jeffery, I think he appreciated the grounded ride. I spotted him dabbing his forehead with a napkin after we'd decided on our means of transportation.

As it turned out, I think Val enjoyed the ride the most, leaving tire tracks in our wake, coiling corners, nearly tilting the car on two wheels a couple of times.

Poor Jeffery got stuck in the backseat with his long legs bunched up to his neck. I reckoned by the dire expression on his face, he didn't care much for the ride either. After a short distance down the road and the speediness of Val's playful driving, Jeffery seemed to pale. I smiled to myself. Obviously, my good friend wasn't a thrill seeker—or at least a race car thriller. I loved my Jeffery, either way.

Passed the out-shirts of the city, we ventured down an unmarked dirt-road, headed to the invite. I could hear the river only a few feet away in the distance, on the other side of the tree line. The water ebbing downstream and its strange spoor of fish and mud wafted into the air. For a second, I thought I'd seen a pair of red eyes crest the surface of the water. I shivered, drawing my knees to my chest. I slid a sideways glance at Val. "How bad are the gators in this swamp?" Dread stiffened the hairs on my neck.

A curt snicker floated over the purr of the car as Val held his laugh back. "We're at the basin, low ground. If a little old gator comes after you, you'll have plenty of time to shinny up a tree." The gold specks in his eyes sparkled with humor.

"Funny guy!" my eyes shot daggers at him.

Chile!" Jeffery chimed from the backseat. "If a gator comes for me, girrrlfriend, I'm push-n you in front!" He pursed his lips. "Ain't no gator get-n none of this!" His hands rolled over his body, fluidly.

"Jeffery, where's the love, bro?" I teased. Both Val and I laughed. Jeffery pouted.

⫸✳⫷

When we turned off the road onto a dirt drive, I presumed this must be the place. Right away, I caught sight of a lighted house nestled back amidst the mossed trees. There were telltale signs that the house once had been white. Now the paint had chipped away, giving the weather-worn house a sense of eeriness.

I picked up on a soft hum of cicadas in the background that seemed to flow with the river stream behind the house.

As I drew in my surroundings, I came to appreciate the rawness of this place. There was life here. From human to critter, they all depended on the bayou for existence.

Val parked the car in a clearing by the side of the house. Before I place my hand on the door handle, Val was opening my door and extending his hand. I thought how sweet. I smiled in his face, taking his offer.

As I eased out of the car I stopped, my smile fading. My eyes fell upon several long-haired, bandana wearing, tattooed, scruffy-looking men, chugging down long-neck beer. Though I was put off, the men appeared to be in good spirits, laughing, gathered around a home-made, cinderblock barbeque pit.

Gray smoke curled from the grill's blaze, and a sweet aroma drifted our way. Whatever they were cooking, it smelled delicious.

Mirroring my same concerns, Jeffery spoke up. "I think I might best sit in this nice car." He hugged his basket close to his chest. "Them folks ain't the sort to take kindly to me or my exquisite caviar. As lovely as I am, I gotta sneak-n suspicion, they'd prefer eat-n me rather than the fish eggs." Jeffery's lips tightened, carefully eye-balling our new acquaintances.

Val teased, "They don't bite, bro. But they might take those nasty eggs and use 'em for baiting gators." Then he winked at me.

Jeffery almost shrieked. "I say hell to the no! No ugly mofo beast is gonna touch my Beluga Caviar! It was near impossible to get these lovely black eggs. They're sorta off the market, if you get what I mean." He yammered on. "Don't think I won't hurt a bitch! Uh-hmm, I ain't play-n." He snapped his fingers and bounced his head in a rhythmic motion.

Val burst into laughter. I stifled mine, just a little. Then I had to say my worries too. "Jeff, does have a point. These folks seem a bit sketchy." They reminded me of the folks at *The Devil's Den* where I was nearly raped." I counted ten people—seven men and three women. I spotted bikes parked on the other side of the dirt drive. By the jackets that clung to their chest, it was safe to assume these locals belonged to a biker's gang, a type you didn't want to cross or meet in a dark ally. Rough folks in this neck of the bayou had a particular skill of bad. Not even a genetically altered angel wanted to cross these Louisianans.

I glared at Val, full of sarcasm. "Gee, I feel overdressed." Val's eyes combed over me from head to toe, amusement glued to his face.

I guess my raggedy jeans and scuffed-up boots might be over the top for his friends. My friend here, Jeffery, was really going to make an impression, looking like he'd just stepped out of an old black-and-white movie, starring James Cagney. Only Jeffery would wear a scarf tucked into a smoking jacket to a barbeque down by the bayou.

Val chuckled. "You and Jeff will fit in just fine. Come on. They're not so bad once you get to know them." Val smiled at me and glanced down at Jeffery coiled in the backseat. "Come on, bro! You can hold your own. Besides, I'll protect you. I give you my word." Val reached his arm out to help Jeff climb out of the tight back seat. I think Jeffery liked Val's assistance by the sparkle in his eyes. Then he had to complain. "I like tight situations, but that backseat ain't one of 'em. Uh-hmm, it sure ain't!" Jeffery pursed his lips as he held on a moment too long to Val's arm.

Val and I couldn't help laughing at that comment. Like I said, I love my Jeffery.

Soon we heard shouts coming from the circle of men. One of the bikers bellowed at Val in an offbeat French. "Qu'est-CE que tu fou la?" (What the hell you doing here)

Val yelled back. "Comme d'hab'!" (Same shit, different day.)
I just stared at him in awe. I had no idea Val spoke French.
Sometimes you think you know someone, and then you get a
surprise slapped in the face. WTF?

The tall biker stepped out from among the others and greeted
Val with a hardy bro hug. You know, the hug where men grasp
each other's hand and lean in pounding each other's back 'till it
stings like an old fashioned beating.

The biker appeared easy on the eyes in a rough, down and
dirty way. A good way, if you get my drift. His hair was coal
black, a little long, and its curls laid nicely around his ears. His
eyes gleamed of dark chocolate, matching his bronze tan. He had
defined arms with a strange tattoo starting from his biceps up to
his neck, resembling scrolls or a vine. It reminded me of ancient
scrolls or symbols like runes. It was enthralling and intimidating
at the same time. He was a big man, standing as tall and broad
as Val. Starting with his boots to his sleeveless black tee and
bandana, he fit the profile of a true biker, and that little shade
across his chiseled chin made him appear quite tantalizing.

Once I reached Val's side, the biker's deep-brown eyes hitched
with mine, though when he spoke, it wasn't directed at me. His
odd behavior threw me off a bit. Looking straight at me, he spoke
in a deep husky voice in partial French. He cursed. "Merde! (Oh,
shit!) I see you finally caught a decent fille! Non one of those
grosse puffiest? Oui?" (Skanky Sluts)

"True. Watch this one. She's a spitfire." Val winked at me. Then
Val's friend gave me his undivided attention by taking my hand
and kissing it gently. "Enchant`e!" A glint in his deep browns told
me he was trouble. Quite a ladies' man.

I replied back, "Evening!" I half smiled.

He didn't' reply back but with only a slight smirk in his
expression. Then he turned his full attention on Val and skipped
right over Jeffery. "Did you come to c'est la fete?" (Party)

"Mon un copain," (My buddy) "I sure did and brought friends too! This is my copine, (girlfriend) Stevie, and our good ami, (friend) Jeffery. Guys! Meet Nick Bourdain." Val politely introduced us.

"Bonjour, everyone! Welcome!" Then the friend leaned in to Val and whispered, "Tacopine est raiment bonne!" (Your girlfriend is hot!) The Cajun smiled as he elbowed Val in the ribs. My boyfriend just smiled, glancing over his shoulder at me. Little did they know I knew a little French myself?

Val, with a glint in his eyes, said to his tall, dark, and handsome ami, "Watch out. She doesn't play."

"What? Will elle m'a poignard`e dans le dos?" (Will she knife me in the back) The biker mocked Val's warning.

"Nope, mon ami. Copine will do it to your face. And she hits her target every time." Val smiled, proudly.

"Hmm, dat petite one?" Surprise seeped into the biker's voice, but his eyes displayed an admiration. I played along, acting as if I hadn't a clue to what they were discussing. When Francis was alive, he taught me quite a bit of Cajun French—curse words and all. I caught on pretty fast too. I smiled inwardly. This should be interesting.

"Come, let's all have a good time! Yes? C'est `a boire qu'il nous faut!" (Something to drink is what we need!) "I have a head start. Un peu saoul!" (A bit drunk!)

"Guess I better catch up, eh?" Val patted his friend on the back as we approached the small cluster of people.

Everyone stood around the warm fire as the introductions circled around with broken French and English. Jeffery started to relax after everyone welcomed him with open arms. That's what I loved about this strange place. With all its diversity and weirdness, folks here seemed to be open to everyone, no stiff shirts around the working class. Despite the bayou's constant threat, I found myself loving this extraordinary state. It felt like home.

After a while, everyone kicked back and enjoyed in the light-hearted natter. I settled down, leaning against one of the old trucks that was mostly rust and flat tires. It had to have been as old as the house. Circling the line of the vehicle, weeds had grown past the thread bared tires, and vines had taken home, creeping over the cab and bed.

Val disappeared to the bathroom, called the backwater, and I was left alone. Jeffery was handing out his expensive caviar and crackers. I never cared for the nasty stuff, myself. I hardly liked chicken eggs. Yuck!

When I looked up, the Cajun was strutting his way to me. Although the biker seemed sober by his steady feet, he must've chugged down a couple of cases of beer tonight. I watched him down one whole bottle in one gulp, and without hesitation, he opened another. Apparently, he was accustomed to drinking. There was something about a man who could hold his liquor. I watched as he approached.

"Finally, she is alone." His French accent appeared deeper than earlier. I suspect it might've had something to do with the alcohol.

"Yeah, these days that's a rarity." I tossed a slight tug of a smile at the biker.

"You are too beautiful to hang with such trash. You should get with me. I could teach you a thing or two. No?" The Cajun leaned against the truck, close in my personal space, breathing his beer breath on me. "If you like I could, chéri, take the crème de at frambroise?" (Cream off your raspberry?) "Or maybe je peux t'embrasser?" (I kiss you?)

It didn't take me speaking French to understand that this dude was coming on to me while his friend had his back turned.

"You're a pig!" I hissed.

The Cajun arched his eyebrow. "Oui, a pig you might enjoy!" He flashed a pearly smile.

"Throw in another log. I think we're not through barbequing," I replied in short.

The Cajun paused, searching deeply into my eyes. "Je suis raiment de`sole`!" (I'm truly sorry.) He flashed his dazzling teeth. "I was only having some fun with you. Nick likes to tease. Yes?"

"I see that, and Nick likes referring to himself in third person as well." I snorted.

"So are you some kind of good girl saving yourself?" His grin felt naughty.

"I don't see how that's any of your business."

"Bebè, you are wound up too tight."

"And you are an expert?" I smirked.

"I can tell. It's deep in your âme" (Soul).

I laughed. "I have no soul." My face reflected coldness.

His eyes searched deep into mine. "Qu'est-ce que tu foul`a?" (What the hell you doing here?)

I kept a straight face. "My mother moved me here." Why was he asking me all these questions?

"Smart woman, your mom. She come to the right place. Yes?"

"No," I said, irritated.

"No? Why?" His brows knitted.

"She died."

"Oh, I'm terribly sorry. You are so young to lose your mother."

"Thank you." I didn't want to share my problems with this guy. I looked away, spotting Jeffery chatting with one of the biker girls. I changed the subject quickly. "Are any of these ladies your date?"

"Maybe? The night is still young." A little arrogance flashed in his eyes.

"So what? You say 'Woman, come hither!'" I mimicked his accent, lowering my voice.

His eyes glittered. "Oui, something like that."

"You see a girl you want, you just take her even if she has a man?"

"Oui! Old Nick has his way with the ladies." He brazenly teased.

"Well, saint Nick, not this lady." I flashed a smug grin. I'd had it with his unconcealed arrogance. I pushed off from the truck and started to pass him, then he grabbed my arm, and through his throaty voice, he whispered, "If you were mine, I'd never let you out of my sight."

"So says the Cajun womanizer. You are so full of shit!" I called him out on his absurdity. When I looked into his eyes, there was laughter and something else. A challenge? Just what I needed, another man in my life. I jerked my arm free, snarled at the Cajun and without another word, I walked away.

Moments later when Val returned to my side from the call of nature, I nearly bit his head off as I lit into him, "Your friend is a horny bastard!"

Val burst into guffaws, and everyone else followed. Obviously, Nick's reputation served him well. As I stood there gawking at Val, I mumbled, "Te de vier!" (Dickhead) What else could I've said after he laughed in my face? I wasn't sure I liked Val around these friends. He was different.

———— ⟜※⟞ ————

Later after we'd eaten smoked pig, (no not the Cajun) with side dishes of roasted potatoes and corn on the cob, we all gathered around the fire. Some sat in lawn chairs, others sat on the ground. Val made a spot for himself beside Jeffery on a large tree stump. I joined them by crawling into Val's lap. There was a slight chill in the air, blowing off the river. Snuggling up to Val, embraced in his arms and sitting close to the fire, soothed my chill. I laid my head against his shoulder, resting my eyes. The day had been a tough one, and the effects of the day was starting to wear on me.

It seemed the food and drink were taking its toll as quiet began to settle over the circle of friends. Everyone seemed to drift off into their private thoughts.

When I opened my eyes, I spotted Nick eye-balling me. It took me by surprise and made me very uncomfortable. Earlier I thought his flirting was annoying but harmless. Now I was beginning to wonder if his interest was teetering on weird? I glimpsed at Val, and as we shared a familiar glance, I leaned over and kissed him for what seemed like forever. Then I heard his friend bellow out! "I didn't think ange kiss?" (angels' kiss) He taunted.

"There's lots of things a Zop can do, which I won't say in mix company." Val threw back at his friend.

"Such a gentleman. A real woman wants hot passion. Throw her down and make love to her as though it's the last. Passion, my friend, passion!"

"Don't worry, Saint Nick. I have this handled," Val called back.

"Frere! (Brother) What do you know? Il `ecoute pas personne parce qu'il est!" (He doesn't listen to anyone because he's in love)

The gang began laughing. I rolled my eyes. I glanced at Jeffery, and he had his basket of goodies clung to his chest, hugging it tightly. Maybe we should leave.

"Val, let's go!"

"Are you sure?" He looked surprised.

"Yeah. I'm feeling a bit uneasy."

"Okay." Val dragged in a deep sigh.

I slipped off him and realized, I needed to use the bathroom first. That trip back down this long bumpy road would be torture if I didn't go. "Hey, is there a bathroom I could use? And please don't you dare point to that damn swamp." I warned.

I could see the humor in Val's glint. "Yeah, go around to the back part of the house. Just go in. No one's in there."

"Okay, I'll be back." I turned to Jeff. Come with me, please."

"I'm already with you, honey. I think I need to tinkle too! And I ain't taking no risk going out by the bayou where some big alligator might think I'm dangling my thang as bait. Oh no, he can't get this!" Jeffery was up and on his way to the back of the house nearly five paces ahead of me. I think it was fair to say Jeffery hated gators worse than me. Even still, I couldn't help laughing. And at the same time, I was grossed out by the picture painted in my brain.

When we reached the back porch, the backlight was shining brightly and only the screen door closed. We stepped up to the wooden porch, our footfall thumped against the planks. I noted a couple of rocking chairs in the corner and a couple of pot plants of bright-red geranium sitting on the other side of the chairs.

Wasting no time, Jeffery made a nose dive straight for the bathroom, first. I suppose with his wiggling and holding his knees together like a five year old, he couldn't wait another minute. I stepped into the kitchen, the screen squeaking in my ear, and stood just inside, waiting. I figured by the age of the house, there was only one bathroom.

While I was picking on my nails with growing impatience for Jeffery to finish, out of nowhere, I heard a woman's voice from the back, calling, "I'm come-n! Just hold on to your knickers!" she called out in a heavy French pitch. I stiffened. I could've sworn Val said no one was here.

In my next breath, an elderly lady, small frame, limped into the kitchen. "What you need, child?" her voice was choppy like most aging.

I began to stammer. "I'm—I'm so—so sorry. We were told the house was empty. My friend and I need to borrow your bathroom, if you would be so kind, ma'am."

"Why didn't you say so? Come in!" She spread her lips into a toothless grin. I smiled back.

"The elderly lady went to the stove where a kettle was steaming. I spotted two white cups in saucers laid out on the counter. I sensed she was expecting me for tea. The lady turned the burner off and started to pour herself a hot cup of tea. She glimpsed up at me, "Would you care for some tea?" I noticed she had stunning blue eyes. They were such an odd color. I first thought she might be blind, they were so pale, but she seemed to know her way around too well to be sightless.

"Sure, thank you." I didn't know why I said yes. I wasn't in the mood for conversation. Yet I was drawn to her.

"Here, come have a seat. Your friend will be in there for a while. He's not use to spicy foods." She set a white cup and saucer full of piping tea on the table and waved for me to sit. "By the way, I'm Mable." She took her seat at the table.

"Hello, Mable. I'm Stevie." I smiled, thinking how much I dreaded using the bathroom after Jeffery. I eased out an oh-well sigh and seated myself next to the lady of the house.

For a minute I sat silent, sipping tea. The taste was a little bitter but familiar. "What kind of tea is this?" I asked, curious.

"Oolong."

"It's nice." I held my cup up, the corners of my mouth slightly tugged.

"Thank you." She placed her tea down into its saucer and cleared her throat. "The man you come with tonight, is he your boyfriend?" She inquired.

"Sorta." I tipped my shoulder upward. "We haven't made it official."

"Do you know why?" Her eyes became sober.

"Uh...we're taking it slow."

"Oh, I see."

I smiled, feeling awkward, sipping my tea.

"He is immonde?" (not of this world)

I damn near spewed my drink, choking. "Excuse me?" I coughed.

"I see him from time to time." She took a short breath as though she was a little winded, "His feet may touch dirt, but he is far from earthly. He belongs to another realm, as you are amarrer to another." (Tied) She lifted her cup to her lips and slurped the golden liquid.

"I'm sorry?" play dumb, deny, deny, I coaxed myself.

"You are locked into a bond that is unbreakable, are you not?" The elderly woman's mouth knitted tightly.

Chills began to creep down my spine. "I'm bound to many." I didn't mean to sound snide, but she caught me off guard.

Then our conversation really got weird. "The company you keep are without âme." (soul) Her eyes were too piercing. "Se prennent pour le centre da min de (Think they're the center of the universe). Those bankers," the odd lady whispered, leaning in, "maybe they are."

It was as if she was in my head. "I'm not following you." I played as if I was nescient to her meaning.

"There are consequences when you toy with black magick."

I blinked, lost for words.

"Let me see your cup," the lady soothed me into obeying.

Without a word, I slid my cup and saucer over to her. She snatched up the set, placing the saucer on top of the cup, holding it tightly together. Then she flipped the set over and separated the two dishes. She held the cup, peering inside at the wet leaves. She studied it for several minutes.

I watched, frozen.

Unannounced, the lady's face soured, lines deepened over her face. She glimpsed up at me. "There is pain. You have lost. A child?" she stared up at me, asking.

"Yes." I simply answered. I swallowed the knot rising in my throat. I didn't want to fall apart.

The lady continued. "I see trouble—a joker. This one is full of trickery. This man is wearing some sort of jewelry that marks him."

I gasped—needles pricking my neck. I sat there silent.

"He is an imposter. Beware!" She holds the cup closer. "There is going to be great change to your life and those you hold close to your heart." Her face lifted with excitement. "Aw! This is good!" I was fretful of her definition of good. "There is faire l'amour!"

(Love) You will find a lost love, your true love." She glanced up into my face and smiled.

I frowned.

"Non, non! He will be your amour ne dépendant de rien." (true love) She went on, "he is dark, but his heart will change. You like this! No?"

"I'm happy with someone now."

"I don't think so." She shook her head.

"I know my heart." I disputed.

"Maybe, maybe not. You are young."

I crossed my arms, tired of this conversation. Where is Jeffery? Did he fall in or what? I stared at the lady as she eyed me carefully through her strange colored eyes.

"I see someone from your past will emerge." She tilted the cup to the side for me to view. "See this line?"

I nodded.

"This line shows that this person from your past will become your protecteur." Her face puzzled. "Though I can't see his face." She studied the tea leaves closer, face tensed. "Something is blocking my view. He is hazy."

I rolled my eyes. I couldn't help it. "I don't need protecting."

"No?" She nodded at my boots. "Check your boots and pants too." She suggested, confidently.

I reached in both boots and found nothing. I dug in the back of my pants. Nothing! "Enculè de at mère!" (Motherf——!) I took a sharp breath. "Please excusez-moi. I need to have a word with someone," I said through clenched teeth as I leaped from my chair heading out the door.

"Oh!" the lady called out to me. "Will you give someone a message for me?"

I stopped and turned back, facing her. "Sure." I held my hand on the screen door, tapping my foot.

"Please tell my petit-fils (grandson) he needs to paint my house. I like white," the elderly lady smiled.

"CE qui est le nom de votre petit-fils?" (What is your grandson's name)

"Nicholas." She spoke one word.

"You mean Nick? Right outside here?" I pointed.

"Oui!" She nodded her head.

I went straight to the source. Peering around, I didn't see Val anywhere. It didn't matter. I had a knife to pick with his ami. (Friend) It wasn't hard finding Nick. He was the drunk in the lawn chair next to the fire. I walked straight up to him without even considering the girl he was speaking to and placed my hands on each arm of his chair. Then I leaned down low into his shit-face, "You took my knives! I want them back now. You thief!" I demanded. His eyes were heavy lidded.

"What are you talking about?" He smirked with his eyes half-closed.

"You thieving bastard! Give me my knives!" I bellowed.

"Didn't your mère (mother) teach you manners?"

Now he pissed me off. "Don't talk about my mère when ta mère elle a accouché dans une poubelle!" (your mother gave birth in a trash can)

Before I took my next breath, my feet went airborne, and I had been thrown over the Cajun's shoulder like a potato sack, and with each determined stride he brazenly took, I became angrier. He had no idea who he was messing with. Damn, where was Val? My eyes combed over the heads of folks, trying to spot the Zop.

Then abruptly, I was released on my derrière, leaving me to look up into two very heated black eyes. Before I could make my complaint known, the Cajun snatched me up on my feet. His hands were possessive, resting on my hips. Our faces were so close I could smell the liquor on his breath. "Just because you are a une belle fille (pretty girl) does not give you the right to say such defiling things about my mère!"

My hands were pressed against his chest, captive by his iron grip.

Of course, I never backed down as I fired back. "You took my knives!" I howled.

"Where did you learn Cajun French?" He appeared enamored, yet pissed.

"Does it matter?" I spat.

The Cajun paused for a second. "Val is right. You are trouble." The corner of his lip turned up.

"Yeah? You think this is bad wait till I warm up, then I'm a riot."

"Chéri, you talk too much. I'm going to kiss you. Aucun entretien." (No talk) His black eyes gleamed with determination.

"Like hell if you are!" I protested, wiggling from his grasp. Then the Frenchman made his move. Our lips locked, and I couldn't get free, or maybe I didn't try hard enough. It all was sort of fuzzy to me. The Cajun knew how to kiss, and before I realized it, I was beginning to feel a little stir. His kisses became deeper, plunging. Instead of pushing him away, I found myself grasping his hair and bringing him down to meet my height for more of his luscious kisses. His arms slipped around my waist, and lifted me off the ground. I remembered dangling my feet as he devoured my lips. I couldn't believe myself. Yet I couldn't stop either.

Then abruptly we broke apart. Both of us were heaving. I wiped the remains of his kisses off my swollen lips, and without thinking, I slapped him. "Don't ever touch me again!" I hissed. Then I remembered my promise. "Oh, I almost forgot. Your grandmother wanted me to give you a message." I paused, trying to catch my breath. "She wants her house painted white." Then I stalked past the Cajun, leaving him alone, rubbing his jaw with a dumbfounded look splattered across his face. Maybe it was the slap. I might have rattled his pea-sized brain. God! I hated that Cajun.

What's a Girl Gonna Do?

O N THE TRIP back, we all were quiet and drawn to our own thoughts. I kept telling myself, it was the combination of beer, strange food, and I'm-just-running-out-of-excuses kinda night. Man, did I feel a heavy dose of guilt, kissing that Cajun. Why did I let him do that? I didn't even like him.

Then my mind flashed to that lady and our peculiar conversation. Chills covered my body. I slipped a sideways glance at Val. I sighed, knowing that the lady, Mable, was right about Val. The thought of his origin made me feel oceans apart from him. Even still, I believed if we worked hard at it, we had a chance. Then why did I have this sinking feeling?

First things first. I needed to face Aidan. This wasn't going to be easy. I'd rather have my arms amputated than approach him and his blazing temper. Considering everything that had transpired, my imprisonment, Mom's death, the death of Dawn, feelings changing, for his sake and mine, we needed to let go of each other. We might be bound as one, but we didn't have to share the same living quarters or even the same life.

Next, Val. I wasn't sure how he'd handle it when I ask him to let me face Aidan by myself. And last but not least, I needed to tell him about the Cajun. I hoped he wouldn't be too disappointed in me. It wasn't necessary. I'd carried the weight of shame on my shoulders for the both of us.

Finally after I settled with both Aidan and Val, I intended to hunt down Mustafa and kill him. Then I might be able to get my life on the road of recovery.

When we reached home, I woke up Jeffery. It boggled me how he could fall asleep crunched up in the backseat, even snoring.

Watching Jeffery drag himself into the house, it occurred to me that we all needed a good night's rest. I couldn't wait to feel the comfort of my soft bed and the soothing purr of Snowball, my cat.

As I entered through the gate, Val softly tapped my arm and motioned for me to stay back with him. I gathered he'd sensed a shift between us by the vee in his brows. I climbed the steps leading to the front porch and flopped down on the top step, one of my favorite spots to perch. When I sat there, I felt like I was on top of the world, overlooking the neighborhood.

A cool breeze scented the air with crepe myrtle. I instinctively drew in a deep breath, flavoring the sweet perfume. I did love living in the Garden District. In my wildest dreams, I'd never imagined I would've ended up in this exquisite place. I smiled to myself, gazing down the street.

Val came and joined me. His long legs stretched out as he sighed, tiredly.

I rested my chin in my hands, elbows propped on my knees.

Val casually etched his arm around my waist, drawing me closer. "What's wrong?" he asked, weary in his voice.

I took in a piercing breath. This wasn't going to be easy. "Val, you know I love you?"

"Yeah, I know." The corner of his lips stretched.

I hid my eyes under my lashes. I couldn't look at him. I was too ashamed. "I don't know exactly how to tell you this. So I'll just say it. Your friend, Nick, kissed me."

A handful of seconds passed before he spoke. "You kissed him back?" Val's voice was even, no indication of how he was taking this.

"Not at first." I felt my pulse in my throat going off the charts.

"Not at first?" his brow shot up.

"I don't know what came over me." My eyes welled up with moisture. I still evaded his eyes.

"Did he come on to you first?" His arm fell from me as he drew away, folding his arms.

"Yes, but it's my fault." I blurted out, hastily. He'd stolen my knives! I confronted him."

"Aw hell!" Val took an irate breath. "Don't tell me you insulted his momma?" Val's face winced as if he'd eaten a spoiled lemon.

I confessed. "Yeah, I did." Quiet washed over us. So I rushed to my defense. "Neither one of us planned it. It just—happened. He was drunk and I'd had a few beers." I waited for Val to say something, but he didn't utter a word. "I'm sorry. It's been eating away at me all night." My eyes lifted to his face, pleading.

"Did it go any further?" I couldn't believe he'd ask that.

"Are you kidding me? I don't even like the guy."

"But you kissed him?"

"I know." I wanted to die. "That's what is so mind blowing!"

He sighed. "I'm glad you told me. It's okay." Val shrugged.

"It's okay?" My eyes blinked with incredulity. "If you had kissed another girl, I would've been livid."

"You're not me,"

"Are you upset with Nick?"

"Nope. He's a man. You're a beautiful woman. Nick goes after what he wants."

"And you're okay if he goes after your girlfriend?" I wanted a reaction out of him—anything but this lukewarm bullshit.

"Nick can't steal something that is not mine, Freckles."

I sat there, gaping. "Are you saying I'm not yours?"

"Do any of us actually belong to anyone?" he shrugged.

"Now you're talking crazy!" I shook my head, baffled.

"Why do you think it's crazy?"

"Because you fight for what's yours! I'd fight for you!"

"One thing you're forgetting, we are not bound like a human marriage. I have no right nor claim to you."

"What is that supposed to mean?"

"I mean, if you choose another, I will have no choice but to let you go."

"Then why are you so resolved about Aidan leaving?"

"Because he's a loose cannon, and I don't want you hurt."

"So your feelings for me plays no part in your dislike for Aidan?"

"No, actually it doesn't."

"You've got to be kidding?

"Look! I'm not saying I don't care. It's just humans are different than my kind. You're not human, but you have lived like one all your life. You are accustomed to their culture. In the Zop culture, we're not possessive. Unlike humans, my kind doesn't waste their energy on attachments and jealousy. Emotions are treacherous and will destroy a nation. We prefer to not complicate our lives." He shrugged. "We're not wired like humans."

"I'm not human, and I'm *wired* that way. I think it's called a choice."

"Your emotions stem from your upbringing. You should be happy I'm not the jealous type, kicking every man's ass for glancing at you." Val smiled while reaching for my hand.

"Sorry," I pulled away. My face pinched, "I want passion and love and possessiveness and all that crazy emotional stuff."

"Sorry, Freckles. That's not me. Don't get me wrong, I want you...a lot. However you look at it, I have to set aside my feelings and think about my kind. I'm in a high-ranking position. I have to maintain and keep my perspective in check. There's no future for us. My kind would never accept you."

"I thought we were going to work through this! Tonight you referred to me as *your* copine!" (girlfriend)

"True. I'm sorry if I mislead you. I was trying not to shame you among the others," his eyes were somber.

"Shame me!" I scoffed. "Why would I feel ashamed?"

"Humans are preoccupied with labels. I didn't want anyone to think you were—" Good thing he didn't finish that last word. My eyes were fired up.

"Most of your friends were too hammered to care." I looked away, then I turned back, facing him. "I thought we were good."

"You can't possibly think we are okay when there is unresolved dissension between us?"

"I thought we had something special." I blinked, unbelieving my ears.

"Special won't help us when the Zop society refuses to accept you."

I clenched my teeth, eyes narrowed. "I don't need acceptance from a bunch of radical angels! I thought you loved me!"

"Freckles, you know how much you mean to me. Despite my feelings, we have to take everything into consideration. And with the war brewing—"

"Don't use this war as an excuse!"

"I'm not!" Val snapped.

"Tell me this. If you don't feel jealousy then why would you not touch me as long as I had feelings for Aidan?"

"I don't want a woman whose heart belongs to another man."

"So now that my heart is free from the clenches of *the-great-white* Aidan, it's okay if your friends play grab ass with me as long as I keep my heart in check?"

"Now you're behaving ridiculous."

"Oh! Then I must be *your* entertainment?" I bit out the words like they were acid.

"You're *not* my entertainment." Val announced. "I do care about you. As for a relationship—we'd only be spinning our wheels." He shrugged.

"If we can't have a relationship, then what future do we have?"

"A future is relative." He flashed a strained smile. "Let's take this day by day. Enjoy each other while we can." Val reached to draw me into his arms, but I wasn't having it.

"Stop!" I jerked away. "If we have no future, then we have no present. According to the impure race, it's all or nothing, no settling." I'd made my decision, and I was cemented to it.

"Freckles, my hands are tied. You have to know that our antinomy breaks my heart too."

"Does it?" I raked in a wincing breath. "Do you know what I like about being human?"

"No. But I have a sneaky feeling you're going to tell me."

"I have the freedom to choose who I want to spend my life with, and no species, race, or even an angel can tell me otherwise. Good night!"

I left Val sitting there with his freaking mouth gaping.

"I'm done with men. Period!" I mumbled to myself as I shut the door behind me.

———❖———

Nearly four in the morning, and I couldn't close my eyes. After staring at the ceiling and nowhere near falling to sleep, I decided to go make myself some hot cocoa. I had just sat down at the island and took a sip when I heard footfalls. I didn't even have to look up to know who was coming. The footsteps gave it away, heavy and short. Sally peeked her head around the corner into the kitchen, and asked meekly, "Do you mind some company?" She smiled, unsure of herself.

We hadn't exactly had the best friendship. I get her hesitance, but I had softened. Setting aside my grievances, I'd began to see her in another light. She was as much a victim as I. "Sure." I smiled openly. I leaned over and pulled out the stool next to me. "Would you like some hot cocoa?"

"Oh, that does sounds good!" She started to rise.

"Have a seat. I'll get it for you." Soon I returned with a hot cup of delicious cocoa. I sat it down beside her.

"Thanks!" She lifted the cup to her lips and carefully sipped, then she exhaled. "You couldn't sleep either?"

"Yep! You too?"

"Yes." Sally nodded her head. "Are you okay?" I saw concern in her eyes. Pleasantly surprised, I might like this girl, after all.

"I will be. Thanks for asking. How about you?"

"I'm doing much better. Especially after you opened your home to me. I want to thank you for your generosity. I don't deserve—"

I stopped her. "Don't! We both were victims." I forced a painful smile. The memories were agonizing, back in that cottage. I would never forget, not even in death. Nonetheless, it helped knowing that she was remorseful. It was time to put it to rest and move on.

"Thank you. I mean that." She became a little misty eyed.

"I know you do, and you're welcome." I took another sip of my cocoa. "How's Aidan doing? Any better?"

"He's sulking." Apprehension came to mind as I watched her fidget with her hair. Then I realized why.

"You've been sleeping with him!" It was apparent, I saw it in her deep brown eyes.

Sally looked down at her cup, and she glanced back at me, embarrassment streaked her face. "He needed someone to comfort him. You were—" Her words became stifled.

Taking a weary breath, I confessed. "I sort of knew it." I leaned over and squeezed her hand. "Hey, I'm glad he has you. Really!" I smiled.

"You're not mad?" her eyes had the look of startle.

"No, not at all. Aidan and I are finished." My lips tugged at the corners, yet not quite a smile.

"Yeah. I'm not sure how long we'll last. He is a bit of a queen, always demanding."

"Well, don't let him boss you around. Stand up to him when he tries."

Silence was shared between us for a moment while we sipped our drink.

Then Sally cleared her throat. While it's been nice staying here, we can't keep accepting your hospitality. We're leaving in the morning. Aidan thinks it's best if he returns to his mansion on the outskirts of town. It once was a plantation over a hundred years ago. It's been in his family from the beginning."

"That sounds nice." I didn't tell her I'd already known about the mansion.

"He invited me to come with him. If it's okay with you, I'd like to go."

"Sally, you're an adult. If you want to be with him, then you should. In fact, you both have my blessing."

"Thanks." She paused. "I do have something to confess. You may get upset at me again?" she began fiddling with her napkin.

"Okay." My shoulders stiffened.

"Back in high school, I didn't lie about Aidan asking me to be his date at his Halloween party. He's a really good liar." She sighed. "Something else." She paused. "We were having sex too." She wrung her hands together, nervously.

I gawked at her, stunned. "Really! He lied to me!"

"Aidan has a way of making you believe anything."

I didn't know why it surprised me. "Sal, are you sure you want to stay with this guy?"

She lulled briefly, thinking. "I may not be the brightest, though, I can't help myself. I love him." She hid her eyes behind her lashes. "Unfortunately falling in love isn't necessarily a good thing." She huffed, downhearted. "His love for me is not reciprocated. He's not over you yet."

I flinched. "No, he's angry at me. Give him time. He'll come to see what a great gal you are." I rubbed her upper arm, trying to sooth her. Although, deep down, I hated to admit it to myself, I feared Sally might be right. "You'll be fine. And if you need a listening ear, I'm only a phone call away." I smiled, but underneath, I sensed trouble.

"Well," her brows furrowed, and a look of a jilted lover spurned her face. "Aidan has been making comments about you that gives me pause."

"What has he been saying?" I'd smelled mayhem.

She opened and clenched her mouth as if the words were fighting against her.

I watched under a careful eye as my suspicion spiked.

"Aidan spoke about," she swallowed hard, "some kind of supernatural infusion binding you two together." Sally fidgeted with her cup. "The alcohol was talking, you know." She glimpsed up at me, eyes sadden, forcing a smile, "he wasn't making any sense. Anyway, he was bragging about how he had no intentions of freeing you.

"Freeing me?" I froze.

"Yeah. He claimed he has the incantation that can break some spell that keeps you two in bondage together." She tipped her shoulder. "I'm not sure what that means."

The shock felt like a child on Christmas getting a pony, but then the parent for some unknown reason decided to take it away. I was mortified. "He can break the infusion!" I whispered, dazed. "Is *he* awake?"

"Yeah, he's taking a shower."

"Sally, I'm sorry, but I have to speak to him *now*." I leaped from my chair and rushed to the stairs.

"Uh, he's in the shower!" she shouted to my backside. I didn't respond, I had urgent business to settle.

Leaving Sally in my wake, I darted upstairs and coiled the corner to his bedroom. I didn't bother knocking. I marched right into his room as if I owned the place, which *I* did.

It was perfect timing. Aidan had stepped out of the bathroom as I entered. His head snapped up at me, surprise spattered his face. I reckoned he was expecting Sally. Good! Catching him off guard might work in my favor. Before he could wipe the startled look off his face, I laid into him, firing questions.

"What the hell!" I began to vociferate loudly. "You have the incantation to break our bondage, and yet, you refuse to use it?" My combative eyes narrowed at him as he didn't shy away with his nudity, all full Monty. Jackass much?

"You are correct. Nor shall I ever. It is our protection."

"Bullshit" I caterwauled. "The truth is you don't want to let me go!" Possessive much?

"Believe what you wish. There's a great deal more at stake here than a little thing such our bondage." His voice seethe of satire.

"What possibly can be lording over us that can be worse?" I countered.

A flash of humor glinted in his blues. "If we break the connection, it can put a target on your back. Do you want that?"

"The Illuminati?"

"Of course."

"Who else?"

Aidan fluidly covered himself with a towel as water dripped from his wavy black curls. A little tinge struck and the image of us together that night long ago at the cottage haunted my mind. My checks flushed.

"Otherworldly sorts." He didn't elaborate.

"I appreciate your thoughtfulness, but it's time that we cut the cord. Bottom line, I want my freedom!" I stood with my arms folded at an impasse.

"Sorry, toots. It's not going to happen."

"Aidan, don't you want to move on? You'd be free to have any woman you want!" I'd hoped reasoning with his selfish side might soften him.

"Sweetheart, I have my freedom. It's you who is held hostage."

"Hostage? If I am, so are you!"

There was a sparkle to his glint. "I am never a slave to anyone. You on the other hand will be mine for eternity."

"Why do you hate me? It's not me you want. You never have!" then I revealed his deceit. "I know about you and Sally hooking up in Tangi while you were pursuing me?"

The corner of his lip twitched. "Men will be men, Ms. Collins." His voice was as frosty as the North Pole.

"What did I ever see in you?"

"I gave you a fantasy," Aidan amused. "Just like most girls, you love make-believe."

"I never asked for a fantasy. I never asked to be sold. I never asked for *anything* from you or your family—the Illuminati. Whatever your people call yourselves." My fists white knuckled down at my sides.

He sneered, "That makes two of us. I never wanted this either. I suppose we both have suffered."

I gasped. "I'm glad you're leaving my house! The sooner, the better!" I bellowed.

"I couldn't agree more." His voice, cold, unmovable.

I spun on my heels headed for the door, my hand on the knob, I stopped and turned, facing his glare. I had one more thing I needed to clear up. I carefully pronounced each word to make sure he understood my full intentions. "I *will* find a way to break free from of this bondage. I *will* never be your prisoner!" I pivoted on my heels, leaving, but I was halted as laughter wafted over my shoulder.

The cadence in his tone chilled my bones. It came to mind a time when I once loved his laughter, but this—this was far more sinister, a stranger I did not know.

"You won't break it. A little thing you haven't considered—we both have to agree, and I will *never* in a thousand years relent."

"You're a monster!" I shouted, vehemently.

"Oh, is that all?" he mocked as if he was bursting to tell his secret. "Tell me, do you feel anything at night while alone in bed?" Aidan stomped a crossed the room. In a blink, he was in my face before I had time to react. His teeth gnashing from rage.

WTF? I thought. I held my stare equally, though, I wanted to flee. Rather instead, I planted my feet, firm. I refused to let him intimidate me.

"Say that again?"

"Can you feel me inside you?" his voice was low, deep throaty.

"What the hell are you talking about?" my heart was hammering.

"Do you feel me thrusting inside you?" His blues took on a sultry gaze, though demented. He leaned in whispering in my ear vulgarities—things he wanted to do to me. His sexual taste made my skin crawl.

"Shut-up!" I stepped back. The last thing I wanted was to be up in his crawl.

"When I'm sharing my bed with another, you should feel every inch of me." His breath became labored as if he was becoming aroused. "You will spread your legs for me while I do things to you that will make your dead father roll over in his grave."

"*You're* disgusting!"

"Am I?" His face filled with amusement as he leaned in, forcing me against the wall.

My stomach lurched, and I thought I might lose my entire insides. His crassness broke boundaries.

Then it hit me. "You knew I was with Val that day you nearly busted his door down?" I held my hand to my lips, gasping.

"You're a smart girl." His eyes glistened with loathing, but strangely, they didn't fire up.

"And Sally?"

"What about her?" His face remained cold.

Oh dear lord! "tell me you're not using her to hurt me?"

Silence hoovered. I got my answer without a single word.

"She deserves better!" I spat.

"Does she?" I perceived his voice as catty.

"Sally deserves better!"

"Sally can leave anytime." He practically cooed. "You, sweetheart, do not have that luxury."

I bit my lip, holding back the curses I wanted to hurl at him. "Do you really think holding me to this binding spell is going to make things better between us?"

"Better! I don't care about better." He chewed on that last word. "I lost that hope when you didn't wait for me."

"Don't put this blame on me! You listened to your depraved uncle rather than trying to find me." I panted, my chest heaving.

"My uncle has his flaws, but I trust his word." Frosty the Smug Man was a bit blind sighted by his uncle. He continued, "I won't apologize."

He reached to touch my face, but he stopped. With no warning, he gave way to a curt gasp. By the reflection in his orbed blues, I saw my eyes glowing. Odd, I thought. Why would he become alarmed over the exact ability I'd inherited from him? He was fully aware that our abilities would emerge as we became one.

I stared back at him, momentarily. Suddenly I realized how blessed he'd been, and here he was bellyaching over stupid crap. It struck a chord with me. Then I just said it. "You had the pleasure of spending time with Dawn. Do you know how much I hate you for that?"

"I suppose we can agree on one thing, then."

There was no question, we couldn't keep going like this. I took a sharp breath, calming myself. "Do you really want to continue torturing each other?"

He stood there smirking. "Who is doing the torturing? I have exactly what I want—your freedom." He broke out in a wide smile, but it wasn't an earnest one. It was the smile of a psychopath after a kill.

I stood there as if an ice bucket of water had been poured over me. Shock, stun, rage and pain, coursed through me like a lightning bolt. The Aidan I once knew and loved no longer existed—if he ever had.

"Yeah, we'll see about that." Leaving it as that, I twirled on my heels and left his room, slamming the door behind me.

I paused momentarily outside his door, glimpsing at my hands. They were shaking, my whole body was shaking. Suddenly my stomach began to roil. Sickness hit, and I darted for the bathroom.

The Unpainted House

A WEEK HAD past and the house had quiet. It seemed that everyone returned back to their old routines. Finally, I'd found a little peace of mind.

Since our break up, there hasn't been any word from Val. It was like he'd fallen off the face of the earth. I didn't call him or visit his bar either. We were over, and I wanted my space. Aidan stayed clear of me too.

I did hear from Sally. Things seemed well according to her. She seemed happy with Aidan. Despite my reservations, I wished her happiness.

For me, I decided to comply with an old woman's request. I had nothing better to do. I went down to the local supply store and bought ten gallons of paint and supplies. You know—paint brushes, scraper—everything one would need to paint an old house. It'd be a nice project to keep my mind from wondering. So after I loaded down my Mustang, off I went to the countryside.

I didn't get why the Cajun hadn't taken care of his grand mères' house. I assumed he stayed in a drunken stupor a tad too much. How hard would it be to paint a house?

Once I reached the house, I parked and got out. The place was quiet and felt different during the day. Its eeriness didn't seem that bad. I went to the door to let the lady of the house know what I was doing. The door was closed, and all the lights were out. I knocked several times. Still, it was quiet like as a mouse.

After no one came to the door, I assumed no one was home. Maybe she was out making groceries, as folks say around here. The locals had their unique style of lingo.

I decided to go ahead and paint. I didn't think the Cajun's grandmother would mind if I helped. I started pulling out the gallons of white paint, the best that money could buy. I laid out all my tools. Then I went to the garage and got the tall ladder. After everything was in order, I climbed to the top and started scraping. I finished one side of the house, and I started painting the cool white over the bare wood.

It was a sultry day. The heat in this neck of the woods could be brutal. Good clothes were out of the question, and heavy clothes were absolute out of the question. Instead, I found my tattered blue jean cutoffs pushed to the back of my closet. I assumed that the fashion guru, Jeffery, had a hand in hiding my favorite shorts. I slipped on a simple white T-shirt. I didn't bother with a bra, it was too hot. Anyway, what did I care? No one was going to see me. I tied my tee in a knot, hugging my boobs, and I wore a baseball cap to avoid paint in my shoulder-length hair.

I left my car radio on and sang to the hip-hop tunes as I painted, starting from the top and working my way down. This felt great. I missed labored work and helping someone out too. I was happy, the first time in a long while.

I had no idea how much time had passed. I had started early. I was enjoying the solitude, listening to the catchy tunes on my favorite radio station, Q93, when I heard a motorcycle rolling up the dirt drive. When I looked up, my heart dropped, and so did my chin. Damn! What was he doing here?

I stopped what I was doing and froze. I didn't bother coming down off the ladder. The unexpected visitor had a strange look on his face as he pulled up and got off his bike. He strutted up to the ladder and cupped his hand over his eyes and hollered, "What the hell do you think you're doing?" He spoke in his heavy Cajun voice.

"Well, I'm giving an old woman her wishes. You got a problem with that, take it up with her," I said nonchalantly. I went back to stroking the paint brush.

"You talk to me grand-mère, yes?"

"Yeah! You might not remember because you were shitfaced. She asked me to give you a message. She wanted her house painted white. I figured I didn't have anything else to do..." I kept painting.

"And you thought you'd do the old woman a favor. Yes?"

"Yes." I kept painting.

The Cajun scratched his messy hair while it gleamed almost blue in the sunlight. He was just as handsome as I'd recalled— dark tan, broad shoulders, tall, sexy accent too. Stop it! I warned myself. This guy was awful. "Hmm, do you have any more brushes? I can help," he offered.

I looked surprised. "What, no party to go to?" I smirked.

"If you are going to start with me, you will not like what I do to you, chéri!" He smiled, but it wasn't a kind one. Nice teeth though.

I stopped. "Cajun, you don't scare me. I got this, and I still want my damn knives back."

"You don't say?"

"I do very much say." I mocked his accent.

He walked over and grabbed a scraper and started below me at the bottom around the windowsill. I'd forgotten he was below me until he interrupted my humming to the catchy tune on the radio. "So what did my grandmother say to you?"

"It's personal, if you don't mind."

"Did you have a nice chat?"

"Yeah. She even fixed me tea."

"Did your friend speak to her?"

"No. Nature called him to the bathroom."

"And you didn't find this strange?" the Cajun's voice lined with suspicion.

"No, other than she said Jeffery would be in the bathroom a while." Now that I thought about it, she did seem to know things. "Your grandmother reminded me of someone I once knew."

"You don't say?"

I stopped abruptly and twisted around, looking down at the Cajun. "Why the drill? I had a conversation with a sweet little old lady. Maybe you should talk to her a little more often. She shouldn't have to ask a complete stranger to get her grandson to paint her house. You should take better care of her than getting drunk and partying all the time. Don't you have any—"

All at once I slipped from the ladder, screaming the whole way down. Just my luck, I landed in the Cajun's arms. That damn fool knocked me off the ladder! As soon as I landed in his arms, I squirmed out of his grip. I broke free and landed on my ass in the dirt which I seemed to do a lot, lately. He reached out, offering his hand, and I swatted at his lousy gesture as I gathered myself to my own damn feet.

"What the hell!" I looked at the ground on the other side of the ladder, and the paint had tumbled to the ground and splattered everywhere. "Look what you did! Now you went and spilled paint! Besides the fact that you could've broken my neck!" I yammered at him.

"I could think of other ways to break your neck, if you like for me to show you?"

"Va te faire foutre!" (Fuck off) I stormed.

"Excusez moi? You could not have possibly spoken to my grand-mère."

"Oh sweet! You think I'm lying?" I met his glare evenly.

"Non!" He smiled eerily.

"Then what?" I rolled my eyes.

"Mon grand-mère is dead."

"What?" My breath caught in my throat. "Oh my god! I'm so sorry. Where will you be holding the funeral?"

He held an odd twinkle in his eyes. "She's been gone for years now. I think you saw her ghost. You must have the gift too."

"Your grandmother! Her death wasn't recent?" I glimpsed back at the house and pointed. "She offered me tea!"

"Oui!" his eyes sparkled with amusement. "You have the gift."

"Gift? I've never heard it called that. It's more like a storm that never stops." I shook my head. "I'm sorry for overstepping my bounds. I just wanted to help." I sighed. Man, did I feel stupid. Then I remembered Ms. Noel's ghost. Maybe it's an angel thing. Come to think about it, she did mention running into Val from time to time.

"Non, non! You did good. Very sweet. Never thought you would be such a sweet..."

I shot green daggers at the Cajun. Too bad they weren't my real knives. Rather instead, I scoffed, snapping back, "Thanks for the vote of confidence." I paused. "So the lady I spoke to the other night wasn't real?" I was still shaken.

"Oh, chéri, she was real. Just not human."

"Have you ever seen her ghost?"

"Non. Only those with the gift have the privilege."

"What do you mean 'gift'?"

"Things such as speaking to the dead, healing, traiteur—those with magick."

"Oh, I get it." I averted my eyes to the dirt drive. I wasn't sure how he'd react about my true race.

"So you come today to carry out an old woman's wish? Yes?"

"Yes."

"Hmm...do you...dress this way when you paint?" The Cajun's mien pivoted into a lustful drool. "If so, I'd like to come more often. I like what you wear. Do you always look so—how do you say in English, scanty?" His wolf-like eyes crept over my body. Instinctively, I wanted to cover myself. Crap! Men are pigs! "Of course, if you were mine, I'd only want you to dress like this for my eyes only. Non for anyone else." His eyes kept roaming.

I frowned. "I wasn't expecting company. It's hot. I'm working."

"I saw that...and your ass hanging out of your shorts too. I like!" my face flushed from his wolfish smirk.

"I don't like the way you're eyeballing me. Stop it!" I demanded.

"It is a compliment. I meant no harm."

Avoiding his ogling, I quickly changed the subject. "You have my knives?"

"Those knives mean a lot to you. Yes?"

"Yeah, I keep them for souvenirs from the last three men I killed." I flashed a wicked smile. His black eyes twinkled.

"Aw, now you tease old Nick. Tsk-tsk." He wagged his finger at me.

I looked the Cajun in the face. "No, Nick, I never joke about killing. I have a nervous tic. Whenever a man gets fresh with me, he ends up with a knife thrust in his heart," I said with no glint of humor.

"Peut-être (Maybe) I shouldn't give back your knives." He threatened without any apprehension.

"So you admit you took them?"

"Non! I only admit to having possession." He smiled like a rotten thief.

"You care to wager over those knives?"

"Why are these knives so important to you?"

"They're special. And they belong to me." I placed my hands on my hips regarding him snootily. "Are we on?"

"Special, huh. I like the sound of that. What is your parié?" (wager)

"Whoever hits the target three out of four gets the knives. Deal?"

"Oh! You think you can beat Old Nick, petite-fille?" (little girl)

"I already have." I flashed a confident smile. I could see he liked a little challenge.

The tall, dark Cajun drew a small circle, making a target with the white paint on the trunk of an old cypress tree several paces away. I watched, thinking there was no way the mortal could throw a bull's-eye at that distance and hit his mark on that tiny target. I gloated to myself. He thought he had the advantage. I'd appease his ego—for a while. I smiled inwardly. This should be fun.

When he returned to my side, he said, "Ladies first. Yes!"

"Nope. I think you should go first. Show me how a real man does it." Sarcasm rolled off my tongue.

"Your petit copain (boyfriend) didn't tell me you were a séductrice." (temptress) He flashed a white wicked smile.

"Val is not my copain."

"Non?"

"Nope. Thanks to that damn kiss the other night, we are officially over." I sighed.

"Aw, chéri, I am truly sorry. I shall talk to him and tell him it was all me and my drunk ass."

"Oh! You think I meant your kiss? Sorry, I was referring to someone else's," I said very coldly. Then I heard chuckles flowing from the Cajun's mouth.

"You are one salope frigide!" (frigid bitch)

"I love it when you talk dirty." I mocked. The look he gave me might've scared most, but I wasn't the norm. "Are you going to throw, or do you need to be coddled?"

"I see why your petit copain left you standing at the altar."

"We didn't make it that far. And FYI, I left him. Sorry to disappoint." I smiled with venom.

He shook his head. "Bebè, you didn't disappoint moi! I couldn't care less."

"Then shut up and throw the knife," I ordered. Old Nick looked very irritated at me as he flipped the knife in his hand, expertly. I watched how he handled it, and I was impressed. I stood and watched him throw all four knives. Each one landed in the bull's-eye zone, but none was in the dead center.

Now it was my turn. He went and pulled the knives out of the tree and returned the knives to me with a full-on gloat. I laughed to myself as he handed them to me. I thought I might play with him a little bit first. I stepped up to the mark.

"Eh, if you need a little closer," the Cajun interrupted, "I'll allow it, since you are a fille."

I smiled. "That's so sweet of you!" Then my smile dropped, and I got real. "No chance, bucko." I firmly put my hand against his chest and shoved him out of the way. "I'm going to show you how the real pros do this." I struck a nerve as the Cajun snarled at me in silence, but there was a glint of praise in his eyes.

I started thumbing with the knife clumsily. I dropped it a couple of times. I'd switched hands as though I wasn't sure which one to use. Then I swung the knife, nearly nicking the Cajun. Luckily, he was quick on his feet. A rush of curses filled the air as I stifled a laugh. It was fun toying with this arrogant douchebag. That was what he got for laughing at me earlier, but what did he know? After all, I was a genetically altered angel. I had the upper hand. Several, in fact. I almost felt bad taking advantage of the Cajun. *Almost.*

Then within a soft breath, I barely took aim and threw the remaining three knives at the same time. My beautiful knives whizzed through the air fast and precise, hitting the tree at the same time, blade to blade clanked, dead center on the bull's-eye. Perfecto!

Suddenly silence fell as the ringing of steel plagued my ears. My non ami almost turned blue as his laughs jammed in his throat. Then I turned to him with my gloat and announced, "You have no idea what you're dealing with!" I looked him dead in the eyes. I left him gaping as I went and plucked my knives out of the tree and found the other one on the ground off to the left, only a couple of feet past the tree. I sure did miss my little shiny friends. I walked right past the Cajun without another word, got into my car, and peeled out of the drive, throwing small beads of rocks onto his Harley as I floored the gas. Bullets of curses hailed into the trail of dust that followed behind me. I laughed the whole way home.

I didn't bother taking back any of the paint and supplies. I figured he should paint his own grand-mère's house so she could rest in peace. He owed her that much. What an awful person. Funny! The ghost of the house, his grand-mère, claimed I'd meet a dark man who'd become my protector. Well, I could scratch him off the list of possible candidates. He couldn't even take care of his grandmother's house. I was done—done with men.

Babylon's Fallen

THE BOTTOM FELL out about 6:00 p.m. right after dinner. The night first started out great. After we'd finished eating dinner, I insisted on doing the dishes to give Dom and Jeffery a break. Well, mostly Dom. Jeffery usually directed more than lifted a finger, much less a dish. Rather instead, he often bragged about how a celebrity like himself should never have dishpan hands. Like I'd said often, I love my Jeffery.

As the evening unfolded, the guys had just taken a seat in the family room, sipping their wine, when Jeffery flipped on the television. Dom wanted to watch the news, and Jeffery wanted to watch the latest episode of *Housewives of Atlanta*. He was preoccupied with one of the wives' catchy tunes. Jeffery kept repeating *Fabulous* and *Gone with the Wind*. I laughed, rolling my eyes as I finished up rinsing the last dish.

Right then, I realized I belonged here with those two. They completed me. Dom kept me grounded, and Jeffery kept me in stitches. After the long journey of Dad's death, Mom's death and finally, Dawn's short life, I'd come to understand that life is precious. No one had a guarantee there would be a tomorrow. If I died tonight, I had absolute certainty that my life was complete and most of all—happy.

Then I took a bottomless breath. If I were so satisfied, why did I miss having a special man to hold me at night, to share my life with?

After leaving Val on the porch alone, he still had not bothered reaching out to me. Aidan's gone—a blessing. Of course I'd never be completely free of him unless he agreed to break the spell. Wow, a magickal divorce. How ironic? I scoffed to myself. Hell would freeze over before Aidan Bane De Pont would set me free.

Out of the blue, the doorbell rang. My head popped up. Who could that be? We weren't expecting company.

I dried my hands with the dish towel and tossed it aside. I rushed to the front door. Without checking through the peek-hole, I swung the door open, and my heart sunk. There standing on my front porch was the last person I'd expected to greet—Nicholas Bourdain. I frowned.

Disappointment painted my face red. I was hoping for Val. What a sap I was, thinking he'd changed his mind.

The Cajun interrupted my thoughts. "Don't worry! I didn't come for another kiss. I'm here on business. Val sent me. Ask me in!" he woofed. "I don't want to discuss this in front of your neighbors."

"What? No, please?" I stood there, gripping the door. The Cajun folded his arms and glared at me.

My eyes raked over him but stopped at his muddy boots. "Take your shoes off and don't sit on my furniture. Your clothes are dirty." I snarled my nose at him. "You need a bath too!"

Amusement teased his eyes.

"If you'd like to bathe me, I'd happily comply, chéri." He flashed his pearly whites.

I rolled my eyes. "Not a chance. Bye!" I went to slam the door in his face, but he quickly stepped inside the door and pushed past me. "Wait a damn minute, Frenchman!" I stormed after him.

By this time, Dom and Jeffery had come to inspect the commotion. The Cajun ignored me and started speaking to Dom in perfect French.

"Val m'a envoyé. Nous devons partir maintenant! Ils viennent après la jeune fille." (Val sent me. We have to leave now! They're coming after the girl.)

Both Dom and Jeffery shared glances.

"Holy cow! It's happening. I looked at Dom and Jeffery, fear mirrored our faces. The Illuminati are seizing the world!" Then I turned my attention to the Cajun. "Where is Val?"

"He's with his kind. They're gathering forces now."

"I want you to take me there," I demanded.

"Non! If you go anywhere near the Zop, they will kill you."

"How do you know about the Zop?" I gaped at him, perplexed.

"I know plenty. Get moving! We have to go!" The Cajun urged, barking orders. I stood there, staring at him for a brief second.

"Okay, you win!" I dropped my arms and grabbed my keys and headed out the door.

The Cajun grabbed my upper arm and jerked me around, facing him. "Those keys are no use to you!" he warned. "You have to leave your vehicles behind. They might have detectors that can trace our location."

My head was spinning, I couldn't think. "Who am I riding with?" I blurted.

The Cajun smiled. "Don't worry. I handle my bike like I handle my women." There was an intrinsic glint in his eyes.

"Disgusting pig!" I mumbled under my breath. As I stalked past him, I heard his laugh trail behind me as I slammed the door in his face.

Standing on the front porch, I paused. My mind was reeling from terror for my family; and I was angry at Val for sending that French pig in his place. How could he dismiss me at a time such as this? Then again, we were no longer together. Still I wanted to be in the mix of this battle. If anyone had reason enough, it should be me, but I was treated like a defenseless girl, even worse—an outcast. I felt betrayed by Val.

When I stepped out onto the front porch, I'd glanced down at the street spotting Nick's gang on their bikes parked against the curb. I took note of one nice-looking Harley—black and silver chrome, empty seated with the key left in its ignition. Suddenly, a spark lit under my ass, and I flew into action. I had to move fast. I took two steps at a time down the long steps, swinging the gate open and running past the bikers until I reached the Harley. Swiftly, I straddled the bike and kick-started the engine. The gentle sound and rumble of the motor between my legs gave me a little flicker of excitement. "Sweet!" I mumbled to myself. The current of daringness surged through me like a quick flash of memories before death. I eased off the throttle giving the bike more gas.

Before I knew it, I was speeding off. Quickly I hugged the corner, and as I turned, straightening the wheels, I let it rip, accelerating this sweet ride into a thundering bolt of lightning down the street. I gotta get me one of these! I smiled to myself.

I knew time wasn't on my side. I had to get to Val before any of these clowns caught up with me. I'd worry about Frenchie when he caught up. Right now, everything came second. First and foremost, I needed to speak with Val.

By the time I reached Val's place, I had figured every cop in the parish would be hot on my trail. Weaving in and out of traffic at a high speed, even I was amazed that I hadn't crashed. Although it was a delightful thought—destroying the Cajun's bike might push the guy over the ledge.

I parked directly in front of Val's bar in plain view. As much as I hated greeting an angry biker, I hated it even more if the bike ended up stolen. I clenched the key in my hand as I ran past the bar.

My next thought, I knew exactly where Val would be. The Zop race was huge. The only place that could accommodate a fraction of the Zop nation would be Val's gym. I was positive he'd be there, though I feared I might be too late and even worse, meeting an early death by a supremacist Zop. I'd darted past the stairwells and burst through the double doors.

Immediately, I was seized by two Zop-guards. They were giant size, and I fretted they might rip me in two with one jerk.

Instinct kicked in, and I screamed for my life. Through the haze of terror, I spotted Val on top of a table with his full attention on his warriors. When he heard my bellow, his head snapped up in my direction.

Silence blew in like a frigid storm, and Val's brows dipped into an angry snare. He ordered the guards, "Bring the girl here! Do not harm her." He spoke with great strength and leadership. The Zop soldiers obeyed. As they made their way, heads parted, allowing the two guards and me to pass. When we reached Val, the two guards dropped me roughly at his feet. He bent down close to my face, his expression was hard. "This better be good!" a vein in his neck was pulsing, swelling dangerously.

It threw me off momentarily, realizing that Val's anger was directed at me. Despite his vile mood, I had to push past that. I had something to say and I was determined to say it. "I might be an impure, but I can fight better than any Zop standing in this gym." I stood straight, shoulders back, eyes daring anyone to try me.

"You're over your head!" Val belted above the crowd. "Stay where you belong with the humans. Nick will protect you."

I scoffed. "You think a human can protect me?"

Val growled under his breath as he leaped down off the table. I knew this look. In five—oops, no—three seconds, my feet went airborne and the rest, well, you know.

Once we burst through the doors outside, I had to face another audience. The Cajun and his gang were all hanging directly in front of Val's bar. I noticed Jeffery and Dom were with the gang too. I felt relieved they were safe.

Val dropped me right in front of Nick. Oh, great! I thought. Deliver me to thy enemy much?

Val threw his finger in my face and bit back the strident words he wanted to say, instead he restrained himself, though, his face remained beet red.

"Look! I told Nick to help you. The Illuminati has a price on your head. This isn't a game. It's war. Do you understand?"

"Yes! I do. That's why I'm here. I want to fight too!"

"No! This war calls for heavenly creatures. You may have the making of a Zop, but you are earthbound. In order to fight this war, we have to transform into our celestial bodies, not this human body you see." Val stared at me.

"I don't understand?" My brows creased with incertitude.

Val ran his fingers through his hair and let out an exasperated sigh. "I don't have time to explain." Then he cupped my face in his hands. "You have to trust me. I'm looking out for you." Val stopped for a second as though he was getting choked up. "This war is a spiritual battle. I have to go back to my natural state. A spirit form." He hesitated. "I'm not coming back, Freckles. For the last time, allow me to gaze upon your beautiful face." Tears streamed down my face as Val gently wiped my cheeks with his thumb.

"I can't believe this is happening!"

"It's our reality."

"You're leaving me behind!" I strangled the thought of never seeing him again.

"Freckles, I do love you. The other night I want you to know that I didn't set out to hurt you. I said what I said in hopes that you might move on. I thought if you hated me, it might be easier to move on. War is at hand, and I didn't know how to explain the magnitude of what we are facing." Val's eyes filled with sorrow. "If...if not for this war, I'd give up everything for you. Unfortunately, I can't, and we can't be together, ever!"

"Why do you have to fight? Let the Illuminati have whatever it is they want," I asked earnestly.

"No. I can't do that. Don't you see? They'll come after you. I have to stop this invasion."

"You're only one Zop. You can't stop them single handedly."

"You're right. But what other choice do we have? It's more than just you and me involved here. Our whole galaxy faces annihilation. Don't you see? I can't turn away. I have a responsibility."

"I don't want to face life without you."

"Freckles, you have to move on in life. Make a new life. Fall in love. It's not destined for us to be together. Destiny has someone else for you." His golden eyes sparkled.

"No way! I'm done with you rotten men!" I crossed my arms.

Val chortled. "Somehow I think you will find some poor bastard who will love you bigger than life itself."

"It won't be you." I choked on the words. Val took my chin in his hand, and he bent down. "You'll see me in your dreams." Val's eyes searched deeply into mine. All I could do was nod. Then he kissed me gently.

When my eyes opened, he was gone, and I collapsed to the ground, blinded by tears. I knew our relationship had ended, but I guess a part of me didn't believe it until now. And it sucked!

Nick, without saying a word, gathered me into his arms and sat me on his bike. He whispered softly, "Just hang on. I won't let you fall." Strangely, his voice was comforting to me.

———— ✦ ————

Distraught and checked out, I didn't pay attention nor cared where Nick and his gang were taking me. Once we stopped, my mind was swooned over Val's last words and the horror of my whole world crumbling that I didn't bother looking up to see where we had settled.

Through my haze, I was lay across a warm bed and a soft shawl covered my body. I recalled the Cajun ordering me to drink some clear liquid. I obeyed, choking and gasping from the burn. Though, it didn't last long before the effects set in. What I believed was moonshine, did wonders, numbing my mind, my heart and my conscientiousness. Soon the darkness devoured the light. I didn't remember another thing until I woke up the next morning.

The birds seemed happy as they chirped, bouncing from limb to limb, tree to tree. It was like any other day, or at least the creatures of the bayou seemed to believe so. I kicked the shawl off and climbed out of bed, making my way throughout the house. The small rooms were dim, no lights on, just a faint light coming from the windows.

I entered the kitchen and went to the center of the room, tugging on a long chain attached to the ceiling lamp. As my eyes adjusted to light, I gasped with surprise. We were at the swamp, back at Nick's grandmother's home. The house was aged, had its original plank-board flooring. No special perks, but still cozy enough. A faint breeze blew in from the bayou. I walked to the back screen door and listened for a moment to the motion of the water and the sounds of nature.

Suddenly breakfast came to mind. I needed to feel useful. First, I checked out the fridge, I spotted a gallon of milk, butter, jam and bacon. Next I checked out the cabinet, I counted, flour, salt, baking powder and Crisco oil. Great for biscuits! I heard chickens cackling out back. I found an old basket and went for the chicken coop. It had been a while ago since I'd had the privilege of gathering eggs, but I still remembered how. Before Dad died, I had been the egg whisperer. I used to think it was the funniest thing how this big white-looking ball could pop out of a chicken's tiny rump—sort of gross when I thought about it now. I laughed to myself.

When I returned, I'd collected a brimming basket of two dozen eggs. I spotted an old apron and slipped it on and tied a bow in the back. By the small print of flowers and its tattered ends, I assumed it belonged to Nick's grandmother. Out of respect, I asked her if she didn't mind. I didn't want to offend the lady of the house.

In no time flat, I began fumbling. Fumbling through the cabinets, I spied a roller and an old cutter that came in handy. I vigorously rolled out the dough and cut each individual biscuit and placed them on a flat pan. I preheated the oven to three hundred fifty degrees Fahrenheit and stuck the pan inside to cook for twenty minutes.

Once the biscuits turned a golden brown, I snatched up a couple of potholders and pulled the piping-hot tray of bread from the oven. The sweet aroma of fresh bread spread throughout the whole house. Nick came waltzing into the kitchen. I glanced up but quickly went back to cooking.

"Oh! I didn't know you can cook. It smells good." Nick sounded surprised.

I cocked a brow and replied, "there are many things of which you do not know that I am quite capable of doing."

"I can see. You are the first rich girl I know who can make biscuits from flour." He tossed a white smile.

"I doubt you have ever been around a rich girl." I mocked.

"True. I have no use for those girls."

"I see we are going to be such great friends." I teased with spite. Little did he know I wasn't one of those girls.

"Please be respectful. This is my grand-mère's kitchen."

"I am fully aware of your grandmother. After all, I've met her. A nice lady." I went right along with preparing breakfast without looking at the annoying Cajun.

"Oui. I remember," he said right as he went out the screen door.

I just looked up and smiled. Then I went back to pulling the plates out of the cabinet.

I placed five plates on the table. We each got scrambled eggs, bacon, biscuits, and gravy. I lucked out finding blackberry jam stored in the pantry and homemade butter in the small fridge. There was enough coffee for everyone to have a large cup. Thank goodness.

When the Cajun returned, he had the strangest tint to his face. Taking his seat at the table, he glimpsed at the extra plate and back at me. A puzzled glint toyed with his deep brown eyes.

"There are only four of us. Are you expecting company?" he asked in his heavy French tone.

I didn't know how to say this to the Cajun or how he'd feel, so I replied curtly. "It's for Mable—your grandmother."

"Mon grand-mère? Are you joking?" Nick laughed, surprised.

I laid a butter-knife with the butter down on the table then I looked the Cajun in the eye, sternly. "I don't joke about the dead. If you must know, the plate is a token of appreciation to your grand-mère. Out of respect, I'm letting her know that the kitchen belongs to her."

The Cajun sat there for a minute and held my stare. His eyes were intense. I was pretty sure he'd thought I had lost my mind. Then this Cajun had a way of taking me off quard. "My grand-mère spoke about you. She saw you in a vision. She warned me of your coming and for me to be nice." He chuckled. "Obviously, I do not do everything my grand-mère asks." He waved his butter knife aimlessly. "I know she told you something. I'll find out what she confided in you. You mark my word!" He flashed an arrogant smile.

Our conversation stalled. Dom and Jeffery came into the kitchen and took their place. "Aw, Stevie, I would have gotten up and helped you with breakfast." Dom offered.

"I didn't mind. I enjoyed cooking breakfast," I took my chair. It reminded me of a time when I was a kid. "I thought you might like some extra sleep." I smiled trying to make light of our unforeseen future.

"Well, it's a lovely breakfast, if I do say," Jeffery complimented my cooking which was out of character of my dear friend. "Does anyone know when we can return home?" Jeffery bounced his glance around the table at everyone. Yet no one uttered a word.

"Jeff," I interjected. "We may never be able to go back. Time will only tell."

"What!" Jeffery squealed louder than an off-key opera singer.

"I suppose we are best to prepare for the worst and hope for the best." Dom added.

"I think the bottom is about to fall out from under us." I went on and added, "As far as we know, we are refugees running for our lives. Everything we own, our home and money is most likely gone. Though, at this point, we can only speculate."

My eyes stopped on Jeffery. Frozen, his eyes were bugged out of his head and his mouth was gaping wide enough for fly catching. "But-but," he stammered on. "I belong to the little old, fat ladies society club! How am I gonna face those old biddies with no money?"

I couldn't laugh. This poor man appeared as if he might be having a stroke. "Jeff, sweetie, those ladies' are just as poor as you are now."

"Oh lord have mercy on my ratchet soul!" He fanned himself with his hand. "Jesus come get now!" he rambled.

Forget stifling a laugh, I broke into chortles. "Jeffery," I snorted. "Bro, you might want to look the word ratchet up."

Everyone joined in laughter.

Jeffery's face twisted almost into a completely different dimension. He reminded me of a 3D movie. "I don't know what is so funny!" he fluttered. "After losing a billion lovely dollars, it makes my soul and every other part of my delicious body retch! Y'all need to get over yourselves, youse in the same poor boat as me!" Jeffery stuck his lips out snapping his fingers and bobbing his head.

I swear, someone needed to monitor that skinny man's TV viewing. He could be more dramatic than any of those housewives on Bravo.

I glimpsed over at the Cajun. He sat there quiet for a minute with a gloating face. "See, that is the very reason I am not wealthy. Take me for existence, the whole world can go to hell in a hand basket, and I will still eat and have a roof over my head. And why? Because I did not allow myself to become lazy and fat, all dependent on money. I'm smart like that." Nick tapped his temple with his butter knife as a smirk painted his face. Be that as it may, apart from his exaggerated self-opinion and uncivilized nature, the man possessed quite a come-hither charm, excluding that he needed a bath.

Before I could stop myself, the words flowed from my mouth. "Yes, Cajun, we all know what you do best. Getting shitfaced and forcing your affections upon innocent girls." I grinned right when I shoved a large bite of eggs in my mouth.

A little glint of ire played in the Cajun's dark eyes. "I've never heard any girl complain of my er, affections. Yes?" Nick took a huge bite of his eggs, mocking me. I glared at him for a moment. Then I decided, no point in slinging dirt this morning, so I turned the conversation back to earlier. "I'm hoping Mable will appear to me again. Maybe she can tell me something about the uprising."

"If our government turns on us, people are going to get desperate," the Cajun added his two cents.

"Who is Mable?" Jeff interrupted. He was always the last to know.

The Cajun answered, "she's my dead grand-mère. Her ghost appeared to Stevie the other night."

Jeffery's mouth dropped opened. "Gurrrl! Not right here in this very kitchen when I was—?"

"Yep. Right where you sit, Jeff." I smiled innocently, batting my lashes.

"Just a whole bunch of weird follows you." Jeffery's lips pursed.

I gave way to a laugh. "You can say that again. I'd take boring any day over this celte saloperie!" (peace of crap) I glared at the Cajun.

"Stevie! Not at the table, especially when we are guest." Dom scolded me. Then he turned to Nick. "Pardon! She is not herself, I'm afraid."

The Cajun slapped a couple of pieces of bacon on a dry biscuit, then he blurted out to Dom, "Il fait frais. Je l'ai vue plus mauvaise." (It is cool. I have seen her worse.)

The small kitchen filled with cackle by everyone but me. I failed to see the humor. I withdrew my napkin from my lap to my plate and scooted myself from the table and politely made my way out the screen door. I needed some swamp air.

———⟶⟶⋙❋⋘⟵———

When I came around to the front of the old house, I noticed all my tools were cleaned and placed nicely in a tool box. I spotted empty buckets in the dumpster. Then I turned my gaze toward the house. Surprise swirled around me as my eyes combed over the freshly painted house. "Well, color me stunned! The Cajun followed through with his grandmother's wishes after all."

Then it came to me why we were here and the dire predicament we were facing. I sat in one of the rockers and closed my eyes. The heat against my skin was soothing.

I think I drifted off to sleep. When I opened my eyes, the sun had climbed to mid sky. Unaware I heard crunching grass. I didn't bother looking up. With the big guy's heavy footing, I knew instantly. "Cajun, you're going to need to learn how to walk lighter. A deaf mute can hear you coming," I spoke flatly, not looking up.

"Don't worry about me, fille stupide. (stupid girl) I can handle myself when I have to. You should worry about yourself. You keep up this nasty attitude, and I might have to change it for you." The Cajun sat beside me on a turned-over bucket.

I scoffed. "You have no idea who you're dealing with, do you?" I held my face to the warm sun with my eyes shut.

"I could easily describe you"—he gave a deep grunted laugh— "but if my grandmother is listening, I'd rather she not hear the words I wish to say."

I smirked. "I didn't mean your opinion of me. I couldn't give a rat's ass what you think. I meant—what I am."

"I don't know exactly. Non! De quelque manière que. (However, you have some special gift.) Non woman can throw those daggers as far as you. Impossible!" His deep eyes sparkled with wonder.

I smiled with a wicked grin. I thought, should I warn him or show him? I pushed myself to my feet. "I think action speaks louder than words. I reached for the sheath strapped over my shoulder and grabbed my knives. The Cajun didn't waste time going stiff. "Although tempting, I'm not throwing my knives at you." I tossed a sideways smile.

"I never trust a woman with a knife who hates as you do."

I smiled brightly. "I think you're catching on! Now watch," I said. Then I summoned the voltaic magick within me. I opened my hand willing one of the knives to ascend. With ease, it lifted, hovering at eye level.

Nick's eyes orbed followed by a string of curse words, then swiftly, I released the knife straight for the tree, sailing past the Cajun, missing his ear by a fraction. I laughed to myself watching the Cajun jump. Momentarily he stood as still as a statue. Soon he returned back to life. His face turned pale then quickly blazed. I think he wanted to strangle me. At any cost, I found myself doubled over chuckling in hysterics while tears streamed down my face.

I couldn't remember the last time I'd had a good laugh. Then a noise interrupted the fun. My head snapped up as quickly as the humor vanished. Someone unexpected was approaching. Both the Cajun and I stood silently, listening to the tires rolling over gravel. The trees blocked the view, but I didn't need to see. I knew the newcomer. It was Aidan. He'd found me. That goddamn binding spell was a GPS. As long as we held that spellbound hex between us, I'd never be free of his reach. Dammit to hell!

"Do you know this intruder?" Nick asked with caution filling his voice.

"Yes," I said flatly.

"Friend or foe?"

No matter how hard I tried to pull away; my eyes stayed glued to the oncoming visitor. "Maybe both," I whispered.

"I have us protected." The Cajun lifted his shirt, showing a 44 Auto Mag pistol.

I glanced down at the steel and scoffed. "Oh, you are so out of your league here, Cajun. Put your damn gun back into your pants, and try not to blow off the parts you treasure most," I advised, hard-lined. "In fact get in the house. Keep out of sight. Let me handle him." I ordered, keeping my eyes on the approaching car.

Moments later, a bright yellow jeep cleared the stand of trees. "I have a bad feeling about this." I mumbled to Nick. "Don't do anything stupid. This guy isn't human."

"Don't worry about me. Like I said, I can handle myself."

I didn't bother to answer. I sauntered over to meet Aidan, halfway. I played it cool. "Hey! How's it going?" I smiled with my hand cupped over my eyes, blocking the sunlight.

"It's going well. I hope you didn't mind, but I took the liberty to bring some of your things. You know, clothes, toothbrush."

"Thanks!" Aidan placed the bags by my feet. "How did you get into my house?" I stayed back a few feet in case he made a move. My radar sensors were on high alert.

"Oh, I had a key." He shrugged slyly while pulling it off his key-ring. "Here!" he handed it to me. "I won't be needing it any longer." He flashed his deviled grin. Strange though, I'd seen that same grin a million times, but this one—I sensed different.

"You are very thoughtful." I kept my voice even. "How did you find me?" As if I didn't know.

He lazily kicked at the ground for a second, then he lifted his blues back at me. "The connection." Briefly he smiled. He looked away at the small white frame house for a moment then focused back on me. "I heard that Val returned to his natural state. I'm sorry about your breakup—"

"You knew this?" I stared him in the eye as suspicion oozed over me like thick-cold blood.

Aidan's attention switched to the Cajun. His eyes took on a hunted look. Strange how his eyes use to spark like fire whenever he became predatory. Nick stood back watching, a few paces behind me. Crap! I told him to keep out of sight. "Is he your new boyfriend?" Rivalry steamed off Aidan's tight shoulders. I looked back and sneered in silence at the Cajun, hoping he'd take the hint.

I turned back to Aidan and relented, "Not hardly." My snugness was apparent in my voice. Aidan laughed, but it didn't reach his eyes. I needed to stall him as long as possible. I averted the subject. Last thing I needed was a dead Cajun.

"How's Sally?"

"She's well. She wanted me to tell you, hello!"

"Tell her 'hi' for me." A moment of silence dropped between us. Then I asked, "What do you know about the uprising? Do I have anything to worry about?" My heart yammered in my ears.

"There's nothing to concern your pretty little head over. I have your back. After all, you will always be my girl. I still care about you." His voice didn't sound sincere, rather feigned.

"Aidan, if you really care, then do the ceremony. It's not fair to Sally." In a soft, soothing voice, I reasoned, "You need to be free too!" I tried to appeal to his tender side.

"Maybe." He simply answered with no sign of emotion. He kept eyeing Nick though, and just my luck, the Cajun kept growling in a low tone, taunting Aidan. Crap! That damn Cajun's head might end up on a platter yet, either by Aidan or me.

Aidan leaned in and hugged me tightly. I was taken off my feet. I didn't expect a hug, and when he kissed me, it felt unnatural and foreign. I didn't return his forwardness. It turned my stomach. When he finally released me, his eyes were smothering. Apparently, my lack of interest didn't suit his highness.

When I pulled away from his luring blues, my eyes dropped to his hand. With no warning, everything went into a tailspin. I strangled on empty words. My lips felt cold and dry. A vision wheeled in my mind to that day, to that spine-chilling day when my life ceased, and there it laid before my eyes. There was no denying it nor going back. That identical ring, the ring with that disgusting eye symbol worn on the very *same* hand, and the very *same* finger. Instantly, I wanted to vomit.

Unaware my mind had taken me back to the past. It was happening all over again—the same cologne, the same terrifying dread clawing to get out—only the face was no longer hidden. Certainty shuddered through me. With complete utter acuity, I knew that Aidan was the *faceless boy!* It was he who betrayed me, who framed me for murders I didn't commit. It was as if he locked me up himself and threw the key away. It hit me like a plane crashing into the deep blue sea, cold and bitter. Aidan had taken my mother's life. Oh dear god! His sister, Helen, didn't kill my mother. It was all a web of lies. Sally and Aidan were together in this all along. The newspaper! He left that damn paper for me to find. His plan was to arouse panic in me in order for my essence to become blocked, making me vulnerable for the taking. I'd been such a fool. Of course it was *him.* Who else could've done a more thorough job?

I glared up at him, and pure panic penetrated my blood. I turned to Nick and screamed, "Run!" Then I stretched my arm, commanding my knives, and they obeyed as the flash of steel torpedoed my target. Nick hit the ground as my knives whizzed past. The deadly blades stopped in suspension, only an inch from Aidan's throat, corralling him against a tree. My eyes flamed, and right at the moment, I was certain I was in absolute, complete control.

"It was you who framed me—you and Sally," I spoke calm yet deadly. When my eyes leveled with his, I saw the raw fear in his deep blues. This was the beginning of the end. My tribulations.

CPSIA information can be obtained
at www.ICGtesting.com
Printed in the USA
LVOW12s0006160916

504815LV00013B/82/P

9 781681 870656